CHAMPION OF THE SCARLET WOLF

BOOK ONE

GINN HALE

Blind
Eye
Books

blindeyebooks.com

Champion of the Scarlet Wolf
Book One
By Ginn Hale

Published by:
BLIND EYE BOOKS
1141 Grant Street
Bellingham, WA 98225
blindeyebooks.com

Edited by Nicole Kimberling
Cover Art by John Coulthart
Interior Art by Dawn Kimberling

This is a work of fiction. All characters places and events are fictional and
any resemblances to actual people, places or events are coincidental.

First print release October 2015
Copyright © Ginn Hale
Print ISBN:978-1-935560-32-6
Digital ISBN: 978-1-935560-33-3

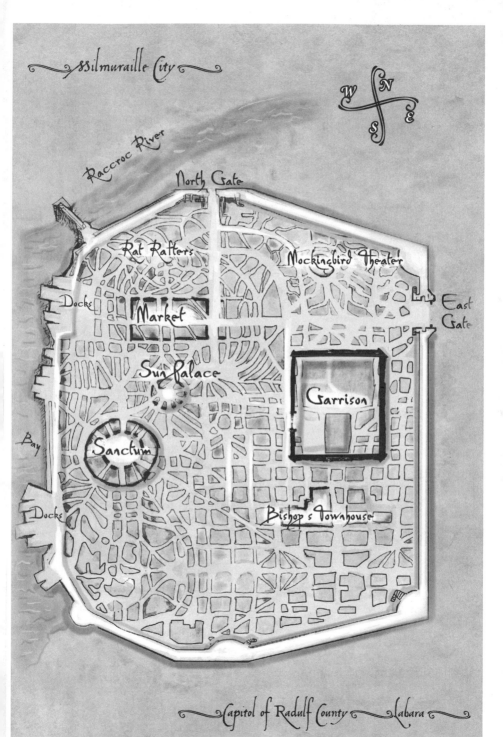

This book is dedicated to all the readers who supported the series and waited so long. Thank you!

—Ginn

CHAPTER ONE

Shadows flooded past the heavy iron bars of the cell as the light from a distant lamp guttered out. Elezar swore softly into the darkness. The enveloping black unnerved him far more than waking, half drunk, to find himself in irons again. Slowly, his eyes adjusted and the agitated rhythm of his heart steadied. The demon-haunted Sorrowlands hadn't reclaimed him yet. This was only another jail.

He drew in a deep breath and regretted it. The damp air reeked of sour sweat, moldering straw and piss. His stomach rolled with dull nausea, but then settled as if resigned. Over the past five years, he'd awakened in worse surroundings than this. He'd slept more than a few evenings in assorted jails, while local sheriffs investigated the legality of his duels, or awaited the arrival of their bribes. At least this evening he shared his prison with nothing more offensive than fetid straw rather than a herd of ergot-addled swine.

Something about the space of the cell and the feel of the stone walls made Elezar feel certain that he'd been held in this place before—though not this particular cell.

Shouts and wails of other men imprisoned in the warren of chambers both above and beyond his own cell drifted to Elezar. Most sounded drunk and furious, ranting the long strings of eastern obscenities so commonly heard in the capital.

Elezar felt certain he now resided in one of Cieloalta's three city jails. The fact that he'd merited his own cell assured him that he'd once again been deemed a murderer.

He rose and paced the confines of his cell in the slow, short steps his shackles allowed. The ache of a grazed forearm flared through him, but the wound felt neither deep nor dangerous. If he needed to, he could still put up a fight despite the torpid, sloshing sensation inside his skull.

As he moved, he caught a strong whiff of blood and another of floral cologne. The heavy odor of blood rose from his clothes but certainly that pungent perfume did not.

"Atreau?" Elezar called out to a dark form sprawled in the cell across from his own. A moan rose in response. Elezar scooped up a wet tangle of straw and hurled it across the short space.

This time the responding cry sounded far more awake and peeved.

"Are you in one piece?" Elezar demanded.

"I think so. God, my head feels like it might split of its own accord." Atreau didn't rise from where he lay, though one of his legs twitched. "What is that smell? Did you douse me in rose oil?"

"Lord Reollos hurled you through your cologne cabinet," Elezar replied.

"Ah, yes… I think I remember that… He caught me with a woman, didn't he?"

"His wife, actually." Elezar reached his cell door and tested the lock with a hard shake. The iron held. Still, it never hurt to try.

"Wife…" Atreau seemed to contemplate that—or perhaps he'd lapsed back into unconsciousness. "Yes, I remember now…the lovely, dark-eyed lady and her coy little maid. I sang for them in the morning and had them in my bed by noon."

Elezar continued to inspect the strength of each of the cell bars. It seemed that his jailors had not only paid him the compliment of shackling his ankles but had also secured him in an exceptionally sturdy cell. He hadn't put up much of a fight when they'd arrested him, but his harsh features and long, powerful build often inspired more fear than his actions merited. Of course, he'd also been the only man standing in a blood-spattered room when they'd found him, and at twenty-four he'd already earned a reputation as a frequent, merciless duelist.

Perhaps he deserved the shackles after all.

"If you're going to break the door down could you do it a little more quietly? Oh God, my head..." Atreau clambered up to a sitting position, groaning as if it were a nearly impossible feat. Straw matted his dark hair and clung to his velvet doublet. "We were the ones set upon. Reollos' pretty ass ought to be locked in this prison cell. Why exactly are we locked up, do you know?"

"Because we—I—may have killed him," Elezar replied as calmly as he could. "Reollos, that is."

In the cell across from him Atreau looked suddenly sick.

"I don't remember that," he whispered.

"You wouldn't. You were laid out limp as an eel by the time Reollos decided to skewer you."

"He tried to murder me?" Atreau didn't sound so much shocked as hurt by the thought and Elezar knew why.

"You charmed your way into his household then took his wife to bed. What did you expect him to do when he discovered you?" Elezar demanded in whisper.

Atreau went quiet, bowing his handsome head against his knees. Elezar wasn't sure if remorse or his pounding headache had inspired the forlorn slump.

The distant echo of boot heels striking hard stone filled the silence. Elezar thought he heard men whispering as well, but couldn't understand their words. For an instant he considered what hushed accusations other prisoners were exchanging and he wondered how closely the jailors might be listening.

He shouldn't have spoken so freely.

But the folly of the entire affair infuriated Elezar. He had to grind his jaw to keep silent and recapture his calm. For Atreau, the brief dalliance with Lord Reollos had been little more than a curiosity—a queer diversion he could boast of in the drunken company of his favorite whores once the thrill of forbidden flirtation dulled. But Lord Reollos hadn't shared Atreau's casual ease.

Doubtless the few teasing glances and the quick kisses that Atreau had so thoughtlessly bestowed upon the other man had touched Reollos to the very heart. Atreau with his charm and beauty had altered Reollos' whole life—promised him a paradise that he had never dared to dream of. And then, with a drunken laugh, Atreau had destroyed it all. Too clearly, Elezar recalled the raw anguish in Reollos' pale face as the man confirmed Atreau's infidelity.

"You didn't actually kill him, did you?" Atreau asked.

Elezar prayed that he had not, but Reollos had fought him with utter abandon—like a man who felt no pain, and feared no death because there was no reason left to keep living.

Elezar well understood the agony and rage of being scorned in love.

"He meant to murder you." Elezar kept his tone flat. "I couldn't have stayed my blade and kept you alive."

Again Atreau fell silent.

The sound of footsteps grew more distinct. A door nearby scraped open and golden lamplight flared through the chamber, illuminating both Atreau and himself in their narrow cells.

Through the blaze of light, Elezar picked out the dark forms of three men. From their bulky shapes he guessed that two were guards dressed in heavy byrnies. The third man stood taller than the others and offered a more refined and elegant silhouette. He took the lamp and turned to his companions.

"Leave us, will you?"

The guards bowed and withdrew. Elezar squinted into the glare. He recognized the voice as belonging to Fedeles Quemanor, the duke of Rauma and his lifelong friend. But Fedeles should have set sail for Labara hours ago. His spirits sank even lower as Elezar realized that Fedeles must be missing the tide to come search for him.

"Fedeles!" Atreau found the strength to rise to his feet.

"Indeed." Fedeles hung the lamp from an iron peg and drew near their cells. Deep shadows clung to his black hair and silken raiment, contrasting the natural fairness of his skin and lending him a ghostly pallor. Signet rings gleamed on his fingers. A gold collar proclaiming his appointment to Prince Sevanyo's cabinet hung around his neck. For all Fedeles' finery, Elezar still caught the scent of horses and saddle leather on him. Bright flecks of straw speckled the hem of his cloak. Duke or not, no one could keep Fedeles out of the stable.

Under other circumstances Elezar would have teased him for that and Fedeles would have laughed and asked after Elezar's own stallion, Cobre.

But this evening Fedeles appeared to be in no mood for any sort of humor.

"I would greet you with a good evening, but clearly it is not." Fedeles glowered at them. Despite his youth he looked every inch the condemning duke. "Are either of you sober enough to know what you've done?"

Atreau nodded, his full mouth drawn down in obvious misery.

"Is Reollos dead?" Elezar asked.

Fedeles lifted his head to meet Elezar's gaze, and his harsh expression softened. He was afraid, Elezar realized, more afraid than Elezar himself.

"Not yet," Fedeles replied. "But his physician doubts he will last another day."

Elezar didn't flinch but simply drew in a long breath, forcing himself to remain stoic despite the fate he now faced. In the five years since he'd left the Sagrada Academy he'd killed more than a dozen men. But he'd always ensured that he fought other noblemen in sanctioned duels. The bandits and highwaymen he'd slain had waylaid him as he traveled. More often than not their demises had won him rewards. But tonight he'd run Reollos through in a rented room, far from any dueling ring. He'd towered over the slim, fair-haired man, outmatching him in both reach and experience. And Elezar couldn't even claim he'd been forced to battle for his own life.

Rather, he'd been defending Atreau Vediya, a notorious libertine, from the wrath of a cuckholded husband.

No, this time he'd gone too far. He'd murdered a fellow nobleman and could be lawfully hanged.

"I thought you'd be on your way to Labara." Elezar found some pride in the fact that his voice still sounded relaxed given that he now faced the possibility of the gallows.

"And I thought you were going to join me. Your horse and trunks are stowed and waiting," Fedeles countered.

"I was delayed." For an instant Elezar wholeheartedly regretted his decision to bid Atreau a last farewell. If he hadn't gone to Atreau's cheap rooms he would never have seen Lord Reollos storming up the stairs and wouldn't have raced after the man to keep Atreau from harm.

But then Atreau certainly would have died, and Elezar couldn't wish for that either. Atreau had been a friend to him and his family for far too long.

"Elezar came to visit me, and well..." Atreau trailed off with a sheepish shrug.

"Yes, you're becoming somewhat renowned for your knack at entangling other people in your troubles." Fedeles scowled at Atreau with the expression of a disappointed father. In truth, the three of them were of an age—twenty-four this year; Fedeles simply wore his responsibilities more heavily.

"I'm the only one to blame," Elezar admitted. "Atreau was hardly conscious when Reollos and I fought."

"The man's wife was conscious enough, though," Fedeles responded. "She was overheard telling the physician that her husband went mad with jealousy and would have murdered Atreau if you hadn't interceded."

Elezar nodded but the knowledge did little to ease his guilt. He hadn't known Reollos well—and that seemed a shame now. They might have found something in each other, if they'd only had the chance. Instead he'd killed the man.

"Then she can testify before the king's court. Elezar and I both should go free. Or at worse perhaps pay a blood fine." Atreau brightened a little though his complexion still looked sickly gray.

Fedeles shook his head.

"She's the duke of Gavado's daughter and his allies are no friends of Prince Sevanyo. She isn't a foolish woman and I imagine as soon as she recovers from the shock of seeing her husband run through, she'll realize how greatly it would delight the royal bishop to do away with two of Sevanyo's loyalists—particularly two who aided Javier Tornesal in making the royal bishop look a fraud."

"Do you really think she would demand that Atreau and I both die just to better her father's standing?" Elezar had never cared for the intrigues of court and the current rivalry between the royal bishop and his brother, Crown Prince Sevanyo, struck him as more petty and vicious than usual. Five years ago machinations between the princes had resulted in his best friend Javier's exile. Elezar had lost the truest friend he'd ever known. Now he stood to lose his life.

"No. As I said, Lady Oasia Reollos isn't a fool." Fedeles spoke harshly but his expression was pensive. "I think that even now she's taking steps to keep the sordid details of this entire affair from being aired in trial before the king and his courtiers."

"There has to be a trial," Atreau objected. "Even as the fourth son of a baron I'm still a nobleman and Elezar is heir to an earldom, for God's sake!"

"Dead men don't stand for trial, regardless of title," Fedeles said. "This little jail won't offer much resistance against Lady Reollos' men-at-arms when she sends them for you."

"She wouldn't…"Atreau swayed on his feet and then bolted back into the shadows of his cell and vomited.

Fedeles frowned after him then looked back to Elezar.

"I thought you were done with your days of being Javier's Hellion," Fedeles commented under his breath. "You told me you were finished with drinking and dueling."

"Between Lady Reollos' men and the hangman's noose I definitely will be soon enough." Elezar didn't have it in him to tell Fedeles that he'd been sober as a stone these last three months. Only after he'd known there would be no escaping from his own actions—after the lady, her maid and both Reollos' pages fled, abandoning Elezar to the company of Atreau's battered, limp form and Lord Reollos' bloody dying body— had he taken up Atreau's open bottle of white ruin and drunk deeply of what respite it could offer.

"You're idiots," Fedeles ground out. "Both of you."

"But idiots you're fond of, yes?" Atreau staggered back to the bars of his cell. "You can't have come just to recriminate us and let us die, Fedeles. Five years ago we risked our lives to free you—"

"I am very aware of my debt."

"I was at sea for six months and sick the entire time and Elezar was wounded—nearly died—and suffered fines for the three men he slew in combat—"

"I'm not going to let you die." Fedeles cut him off with an annoyed flick of his hand. "But don't dream that it's because I feel I still owe you anything. My debt to you is well past paid, Atreau. I've emptied a small treasury keeping you safe, fed, and housed these past five years. If I intercede here and now, it will be you who owes me. Do you understand?"

Atreau closed his mouth and simply nodded.

Just then the door behind Fedeles swung open and the lamp flickered low, almost plunging them into darkness. Then the flame lit back up. A guard rushed in and made a quick nod of his obligatory bow to Fedeles. From the silver insignia embroidered over the breast of his cloak, Elezar guessed he was the captain of the night watch. He looked worried and somewhat young for his responsibilities.

"My lord, it is as you said," the captain told Fedeles. "A lady and her maids are at the door with a full company of men-at-arms behind them. They are too many for my own men to hold off."

"You shouldn't need to hold them off at all, my good man." Fedeles offered the guard an assured smile. "Only give me the keys to these cells and this man's shackles. I will take these two into my custody. Once that is done you only need invite the lady and a small escort in to see that she has come too late. She will see for herself that the prisoners she seeks have been taken from you."

Elezar watched as the young captain considered the proposition. He seemed to take confidence just resting his gaze on the symbols of authority engraved across Fedeles' gold collar.

"Your carriage is waiting at the rear gate, my lord." The captain took two keys from the heavy ring at his hip and placed them, with great reverence, in Fedeles' outstretched hand.

"Thank you," Fedeles said. "I will not forget the service you've rendered this evening."

The captain bowed deeply and then took his leave. The lamp's flame leapt and spat at the breeze created by the closing door. Fedeles unlocked Elezar's cell and removed his shackles. Then he freed Atreau. Though Elezar's left forearm still bled and his bruises ached, he was in far better condition than Atreau. Up close Elezar saw the long, deep gash where his scalp had split open almost to the bone. Blood and straw matted his black hair and dark bruises colored the swollen skin around his split lip.

"Where will we go?" Atreau managed a few steps toward the door but then lurched as his balance failed him. Elezar caught him and easily took his weight.

"The ship bound for the north of Labara?" Elezar guessed. He all but carried Atreau, while Fedeles took the lamp and led their way through the dank stone corridors of the jail.

"Yes, the capital city, Milmuraille." Fedeles spared a quick glance over his shoulder at them and then continued, "There you will remain until I send word that it is safe for you to return home."

"You won't come as well?" Elezar asked.

"I think I'll have my work cut out for me here."

They passed through a set of doors and then ascended a staircase. Elezar caught the shrill timbre of a woman shouting, but not so close that he could distinguish her words. Fedeles quickened his pace and Elezar abandoned the pretense of Atreau's dignity. He hefted his friend's slack body over his shoulder like a felled hind and raced after Fedeles.

"Bloody beast," Atreau muttered but he offered no resistance.

Someone in a dark cell begged for water and another prisoner spat insults intended for his jailors. A weathered older guard waved them through another door and then they were out in the fresh, cool air of the late autumn night.

When they reached Fedeles' glossy black carriage, Elezar lay Atreau down on one green padded-leather seat then took his place beside Fedeles on the opposite side. The driver reined his horses ahead even before the footman had fully closed the carriage door.

"Ostensibly, I was visiting Milmuraille to pay court to Bishop Palo's young niece." Fedeles' gaze settled on Atreau for a worried moment.

Atreau flopped with the rhythm of the carriage then finally seemed to rouse himself enough to ask, "Attractive young niece?"

"Pleasant enough, if you believe the portrait her uncle sent," Fedeles replied. "The bishop expects me, my pages and a companion to stay with him at his townhouse while his niece also visits."

"And now?" Elezar asked.

"Now I obviously won't be arriving… However, no one in his household—or the city as far as I know—has ever laid eyes on me in person and the portraits I've sent were not well made." Fedeles looked a little embarrassed, as if Elezar had caught him purposely misrepresenting himself as a homely hunchback. "I never have the patience to sit still long enough for the painter to capture more than my coloring. They could be pictures of any man with black hair and pale skin."

Elezar considered this as they raced over rough cobbles. The smell of the air took on the slight tang of the river docks. "Do you mean for Atreau to pass himself off as you?"

"It would serve to hide him well enough and my pages are quite loyal." Fedeles raked Atreau's sprawled form with a disapproving gaze. "Though I find it difficult to imagine a worse man to send in my place to meet a prospective bride."

Elezar couldn't either, even after mentally running through a list of several well-known scoundrels.

"I'll keep him in hand," Elezar assured Fedeles.

Fedeles looked unconvinced. "You'll have to for both your sakes."

"Does the bishop know that I'm the companion you were bringing?" Elezar asked.

"No, I wasn't certain you'd agree to come when last I wrote to him."

"Just as well that I don't reveal my title to the bishop then," Elezar said. "I'll go as a varlet in the service of the duke of Rauma. No one will pay me any heed after that."

"My thought exactly," Fedeles said.

The carriage turned sharply and the clatter of horseshoes against stone cobbles muted. They'd reached the wooden planks of the pier.

"There was to be another purpose to my visit to Labara." Fedeles lowered his voice, though Elezar felt certain that Atreau had lapsed into unconsciousness once again. His mouth hung open in a lolling gape.

"Prince Sevanyo hoped you could parlay with Drigfan, the Sumar witch queen?" Elezar guessed. "He wants you to find some way to stop her from razing any more Cadeleonian monasteries."

"Yes." Fedeles didn't disguise the surprise in his voice. "How did you know?"

"I've listened to talk in taverns and managed to pick up this and that from the royal couriers visiting your stables," Elezar said, with a shrug. "It's common enough knowledge that the Sumar witch queen has made a show of murdering Cadeleonians who enter her lands—priests in particular, but traders as well. There are only two ways to stop something like that, and knowing Sevanyo he'd rather it be through diplomacy than battle."

"He's not the only one. The Sumar forest is not a place I would choose to wage a war—particularly not a war against Mirogoth witches. But it will come to that soon if these atrocities against our holy men are not stopped." Fedeles scowled down at his hands but then lifted his gaze to meet Elezar's. "If you can make peace with the Sumar witch queen in my stead, then both Sevanyo and the royal bishop will have to welcome you back to Cadeleon as a friend."

Elezar nodded numbly. All he knew about the four Mirogoth tribes, their warlords and witch queens, he'd learned from a pompous ass called Scholar Habalan years ago at the Sagrada Academy. If Habalan's knowledge of the Mirogoths was on par with the rest of his teaching, it was likely to be riddled with patriotic inaccuracy and convenient omission as well as being decades out of date. Still Elezar wracked his mind for every detail he could recollect.

Of the four Mirogoth tribes, the Sumar people were the most powerful. Their territories bordered Labara directly to the north.

Nearly a hundred years ago a coalition of Mirogoth tribes had swept through the Labaran peninsula to penetrate deep into Cadeleon. Elezar's own ancestors had been among those who had driven them back through Labara into their forest holdings. In the processes of being twice overrun, Labara had lost her king and broken into several counties, which had all fallen under Cadeleonian protection.

To this day, the four counts of Labara still tithed to the Cadeleonian king, who used the taxes to fund the garrisons and troops he maintained in major cities. Throughout the land Cadeleonian bishops consecrated churches and monasteries alongside native Labaran temples.

It was said that a Cadeleonian man could visit any of the three smaller southern counties of Labara and never know he'd strayed from his homeland. But the northernmost county of Radulf, whence Elezar was bound, was infamous for its street witches and its ruling count, who was reputed to be descended directly from a Mirogoth lineage of warlords and shapechangers.

A witch queen even resided in the capital city of Milmuraille where, in return for defending the Labaran border, she was indulged and supported by the count.

How Fedeles expected him to wrangle a cessation of hostilities in this environment that he knew nothing about, Elezar could not even hazard a guess. Particularly not from any sort of witch queen. He only kept regular company with two women and one of them was his mother.

"I'm not sure I'm fit for this," Elezar confessed. "I'm no man of manners or letters. We both know I've spent more time in dueling rings than attending court."

"You certainly aren't a typical diplomat," Fedeles conceded and Elezar saw the flash of his white teeth. "But you might be better suited than you'd first think. Mirogoths aren't a courtly people, not even their grimma—"

"Who?"

"Grimma," Fedeles repeated. "That's what the Mirogoths call their four witch queens."

"Is the title plural as well as singular?" Elezar asked reflexively. Coming from the trade city of Anacleto, he spoke

a smattering of several languages, and at least enough Mirogothic to know that they rarely designated a plural form of
nouns. A man had to be very specific about numbers when
he traded with Mirogoths or the shoal of fish he thought he'd
bought for a pittance could all too easily turn out to be a single
costly fry.

"Ah, a good question. It's both. One or many." Fedeles
sounded pleased. "And you say you aren't made for this. You're
just the man, Elezar. The truth is that both Prince Sevanyo and
the royal bishop have already sent cultured envoys and clever
monks to parlay with the Sumar grimma. None of those men
even managed to locate her stronghold—her sanctum as it's
called. Two returned half mad from fevers and babbling about
walking mountains and stone giants. Another crawled back
after eight months lost in the Mirogoth wilderness and immediately died of the flux. The other men in his party had all
either succumbed to the elements or been torn apart by wild
animals."

"That's encouraging." Elezar glanced to Atreau's limp form,
watching the way his loose limbs jostled with the motions of
the carriage. Atreau's mother heralded from southern Labara
and had taught her son her language but as far as Elezar knew
that was the full extent of Atreau's knowledge of the land. He'd
been born in Cadeleon and spent most of his life being passed
between the households of Cadeleonian lords whom his father
desired as allies. Most recently he'd been taken in by Fedeles.

He wasn't made for the hardship of a wilderness.

"Apparently even in this modern age," Fedeles went on,
"Mirogoths still live among beasts in rocky palaces, hidden by
dark forests and witchcraft."

"So no one has even a guess as to where this Sumar grimma keeps her court?"

"Glimmerings, but precious little more," Fedeles admitted.
"According to Mirogoth lore her sanctum lies at the heart of an
enchanted forest where it is forever summer and all the beasts

are hers to command. The road there is paved in moonlight and no man can find her unless she wishes it."

"Must make it hell to get her market deliveries to her," Elezar responded.

Fedeles laughed lightly at that.

Elezar gazed at him through the darkness. "You meant me to do this even before this trouble with Reollos, didn't you?"

Fedeles looked a little sheepish. "I'd planned to explain it all once we were under sail and—"

"It was too late for me to turn back?" Elezar finished.

Fedeles nodded.

"Well, I'm certainly past turning back now, have no fear," Elezar assured him.

Despite the ominous failures of previous envoys, Elezar took a kind of comfort in the knowledge that Fedeles had wanted him to do this and that the work ahead would require more than good manners and a glib smile. God knew, he'd solved enough problems with his fists and sword. He was, as Atreau had called him, a bloody beast. He felt sick with the knowledge but he couldn't deny it. Perhaps this once he could do more than leave a trail of weeping relatives in his wake.

"I'll show you the books I've packed as well as a few maps previous envoys cobbled together. It's all already aboard our ship… I hope I don't have to mention that this task isn't something Prince Sevanyo particularly wants any Labarans finding out about, particularly not Oesir, the current Labaran grimma."

Elezar considered this and then nodded.

"The grimma or even Count Radulf might take inspiration from the Sumar grimma's actions and demand their own negotiations for greater power, yes?" Elezar asked.

"Quite," Fedeles responded.

The carriage drew to a halt and Fedeles opened the door. Atreau roused himself and wiped his mouth. Something about the clumsy motion made Elezar think suddenly of his artless younger brothers. He hoped they would be well in his absence.

"Have we arrived already?" Atreau asked and from his voice Elezar guessed that he'd been awake for more than a little of the conversation.

"Yes. Can you walk on your own yet?" Elezar asked.

"I think so," Atreau replied.

Elezar ducked out of the cramped confines. Through the evening darkness he made out the black silhouette of a tall ship. Before him deep waters and a foreign land awaited.

CHAPTER TWO

The black wall rose above Skellan, flashing long spikes from behind pretty scrolls of corbelling like some immense beast drawing back its heavy stone lips to display iron teeth.

Skellan grinned back and climbed higher.

Oh yes, this deeply carved stone troll knew he was no harmless scamp clambering up. The troll sensed the fire in Skellan's bones just as charms and wards hidden throughout the vast city recognized Skellan's presence when he laid his bare hands against them. But this petrified and spellbound troll could not easily break the enchantment that had stilled him a century before—and in any case Skellan knew the huge granite creature who stood guard over the east wall of the sanctum very well.

He scampered up the ornate façade that some ass had carved across the troll's towering body long ago. Winter cold made his hands clumsy and slicked the stone with frost, but Skellan didn't slow until he reached a rolling ledge that sheltered a deep black niche. The hole was wider than Skellan's arm and clotted with cobwebs, moss and a decade of decayed pine needles. He scraped and scratched, digging out an abandoned wasp's nest along with the desiccated remains of a few rock mice until at last he reached hard granite. Then he caressed the exposed stone as he once had stroked the silky ears of tame rabbits.

"It's been too long since you've been attended, Master Bone-crusher," Skellan whispered into the dark hollow. "Oesir doesn't give you the honor you deserve for standing guard against all the cold and curses the winds carry from the river and sea."

Despite the winter frost and twilight chill, Skellan felt the rough stone warm beneath his fingers. He tickled the curve of what he knew was once an immense ear, and the stone flushed further, warming Skellan's body far better than his patched clothes or tattered dogskin cloak could.

"I've missed you, Bone-crusher," Skellan whispered. It served him to say as much but it was also true. He clung to the stone, embracing what small warmth and comfort the dark rock offered his gaunt body.

Then he heard the low voice—an echo of winter wind through granite hollows.

You mean to challenge Oesir in his own sanctum?

"That I do."

It seems too soon, Little Thorn. You still feel so small. Bone-crusher's low words vibrated up Skellan's body, making the hair on his arms stand up. He'd almost forgotten how those resonant, low murmurs could thrill through him. No creature as ancient, mythical or proud as Bone-crusher inhabited the dueling alleys, cockerel taverns and playhouses of Milmuraille.

Briefly Skellan turned his dark-adapted eyes back to the twilight world where he'd eluded Grimma Oesir's hunters and kept himself alive these past ten years.

From the height of Bone-crusher's shoulder he took in the vastness of the surrounding city. Mazes of timber-framed buildings crowded cobbled roads and hunched over the south bank of the wide Raccroc River. To the west lay the vast harbor, where the river spilled into the bay and hundreds of trading ships bobbed like autumn leaves.

There, along the shore, warehouses mixed with torch-lit taverns and boarding houses. The market squares, where fish-mongers, fur traders, tinkers and butter maids sold their wares and did what they could to evade tax collectors, still bustled with closing business despite the falling darkness. Not far east of the markets, Skellan picked out the brilliant flares of lamps and torches igniting for the real trade of the night: theaters, bawdy houses, taverns and gaming halls all across the tangled streets came to life and wouldn't close until well after the sun came up. These streets were all the world that Skellan had known for the past ten years. It looked so small and distant from the height of Oesir's sanctum.

Directly surrounding the sanctum where Skellan now stood were the wealthiest of guildhouses and the most costly of the city's hundreds of bell towers. Ring roads circled the most stately of residences like ripples. At the center of them all, Count Radulf's resplendent gold and scarlet Sun Palace rose like the very embodiment of the count himself. Stately residences of courtiers and ministers bowed in the shadows. Only the sanctum rose higher, but even so it did not hold the center of the entire city as did the palace.

To the southeast another great structure arose, far more vast than either the palace or the sanctum, but built from dull gray slabs of stone and topped with a crown of black cannons. The Cadeleonian garrison looked like the graceless invader it was. Beyond it an entire city of square Cadeleonian houses and businesses spread along streets as straight as teeth.

From this vantage point Skellan felt a kind of wonder that such a huge and diverse population could all be held together in one city. And yet the thin red line of Milmuraille's city wall embraced them all. Its two gates, oaken timbers and rust-red sandstone supports encircled thousands and thousands of folk, sheltering them from a deep, wild darkness.

Beyond the wall lay the boundary of the river and beyond that rose the dense forest and forbidding mountains of the Mirogoth lands where the Sumar grimma ruled. A shiver of excitement and fear wriggled up Skellan's spine, but he drew his gaze back to the black walls of the sanctum and to Master Bone-crusher.

"Ten years, I've been gone," Skellan whispered into the troll's ear. "I've made the stones of this city mine."

Hardly an instant in a life measured by the ages of stone, but more than long enough for Skellan. He'd grown tall and quick outside the sanctum's shelter, but became lean and tattered as well. He'd worn rags and darkened his bright red hair into a filthy coil of oily soot for so long that he hardly remembered what it felt like to be clean. He'd kept company with plenty of folk in the crowds of the city but none that he loved so much as Bone-crusher.

Skellan pressed his face close to the black granite, drinking in the thick musky scent of the living body lying just beneath the stone. Old memories of summer afternoons spent sprawled across this warm rock, licking honey from his fingers and laughing as Bone-crusher's deep voice shook his whole body flickered through the cold hunger of his mind. For an instant he felt a chasm of raw sorrow open in him—he would never know that life again.

But he caught himself. He wasn't a child anymore and he'd have his revenge soon enough. Then he'd eat pork and cherries in winter, and he'd wear mink-lined gloves. He'd possess sweet beeswax tapers, burn butter in his lamps if he wanted, and at night he'd sleep on silk and goose down. But he'd get none of that by scrubbing his face raw against a rough stone while mourning the ruin of his boyhood.

Oesir's treachery had taught him one thing very well: Fortune favored those with the daring and drive to seize what they wanted.

"Tonight I'll break Oesir and take the sanctum," Skellan whispered. "And I will keep my promise to you, Bone-crusher."

A warm sigh passed through the stone and gently rocked Skellan's body.

Then go and do him all the harm you will, Little Thorn. You will find him walking near the water gardens.

"Thank you." Skellan bounded up. He climbed quick as a rat—edging up crevices then leaping out to silently catch the overhang of decorative columns and shimmy farther up. Sweat beaded his arms and trickled down his spine as he forced himself to move faster still, to keep ahead of the guard pacing the top of the wall. He threw himself into reckless momentum with defiant exhilaration. Then at last he dug his long, calloused fingers into a crevice of dark granite and pulled his limber body up between the turrets topping the wall.

And then he was back within the sanctum, staring at the gleaming black stone of the grimma's palace where a halo of green flame shone over the highest spire—Oesir's witchflame—proclaiming him grimma over this sanctum and all Labara by extension. Before Oesir, the spire had blazed with Lundag's gold flame. Soon, Skellan told himself, it would shine as red as cinnabar, lit by the ferocity of Skellan's soul—his witchflame.

The bare trees of the surrounding orchards and gardens cast long, shivering shadows as Oesir's soul flickered and spat from its height. Something agitated the usurper's mind enough to set his witchflame roiling. Watching it, Skellan felt uneasy as well. Oesir couldn't know he was coming. Yet it seemed a very strange coincidence that the grimma should stroll along the very water garden where he'd committed his treachery, just when Skellan chose to avenge those murders.

Skellan studied the grounds, watching the brawny blond Mirogoth mercenaries Oesir had hired after the slaughter of Lundag's guardian wolves. They wore wolfskin cloaks over their leather armor and they paced the walls and grounds of the grimma's palace holding their short spears like walking sticks. They and the young, silk-garbed torchbearers standing at the palace doors looked cold and bored. One guard lingered outside the scullery stroking his braided beard and teasing a young maid as she chased a sow into its pen. At the foregates, the archers lounged together like gossips in a tavern. One set his longbow aside to warm his hands in his heavy coat. Most tellingly, the portcullis still hung high and open. As Skellan watched, a gilded carriage drawn by four sleek Cadeleonian horses swept from the stables and out through the gates.

No, Skellan reassured himself, none of them even suspected his return, much less planned to take him.

Still, his heart quickened as he dropped to the oak planks of the walkway and raced between shadows to the narrow stone steps that lead down to the palace grounds. Despite his need for stealth and speed, Skellan stopped several times both on the stairs and as he raced beneath the cover of the walnut grove. Where he found old stones that knew him, he traced their surfaces and whispered their names, and in return they warmed his cold hands, sheltered him with their shadows and silenced his passage.

He skirted the open cobblestone courtyard where the light of Oesir's witchflame burned every shadow to the luminous green of a willow grove. From a distance Skellan caught a taste of the churning air; it felt warm and smelled sweet as spring—like Oesir himself. Despite himself, Skellan felt awed by the intensity of the other man's spirit. No other witch in all of Milmuraille possessed the willpower or audacity to tear his very soul from his body and set it shining overhead like a star.

Even if Bone-crusher had not told him where to look, Skellan could have found Oesir just by following the heat and scent of him on the frigid air.

Oesir stood completely alone beneath the bare branches of beech trees, beside the long stone pool of the water garden. A faint verdant glow radiated from him and lit him like the light of a full moon. He struck Skellan as smaller than he remembered and he appeared surprisingly young, with his slim body enveloped by the great white mass of a bearskin cloak. His flaxen hair hung in short curls. His hands and feet, like Skellan's own, were bare to touch the earth and stone beneath them.

All around him the green light of his witchflame gleamed off thin sheets of frost. Overhanging tree branches sparkled as if studded with emeralds, and the broken crusts of ice drifting on the surface of the pool shone like jade. An aged water bucket lay beside the pool and Skellan wondered why Oesir contemplated it so very intently. But as he crept closer, Skellan realized that Oesir's attention was directed at a small golden coffer in his hands. He gazed down at it as if transfixed.

Even when Skellan stepped out from the cover of the trees and reached down to the ground to trace a ward ring around himself, Oesir seemed to take no notice of him. Skellan's entire body trembled with tension. Before him, Oesir ran a hand slowly over the lid of the coffer, studying it as if nothing else in the world existed.

For all his earlier fear—the sweat-soaked, sleepless nights spent fighting for the courage to risk death, and knowing that no betting man would put even an acorn on him walking out of Oesir's sanctum alive—Skellan flushed with anger. He'd eluded Oesir's hunters for ten years, surviving in a city of cutthroats, whoremongers, brigands and press gangs just to reach his majority so that he could challenge Oesir in the heart of his sanctum. The least the arrogant bastard could do was look up and notice that he faced a witch's challenge to mortal combat.

Skellan almost regretted his decision to fight the man honorably. By now he could have slipped up behind Oesir, shoved a knife in his back, and had it done with.

But if he did that then dominion over the sanctum would not pass to Skellan. The witchflame burning so brilliantly over the spire would simply die and the Mirogoth grimma would all feel that absence. In a matter of days they would raise armies to march against Milmuraille and seize the sanctum for their own. No, he had to take Oesir's life and the sanctum in fair combat for the sake of everyone.

"For fuck's sake, Oesir," Skellan snapped, "I stand before you with my ward raised and all you can do is ogle some box?"

His words seemed to break the spell. Oesir's head came up fast and the coffer slipped from his hands as his face lit with shocked recognition. Perhaps it was only a trick of the flickering shadows but it seemed that Oesir smiled at him.

"Thorn—" Oesir began and at the same instant the gold coffer crashed open at Oesir's feet. A geyser of violet flame shot up from the depths of the coffer to engulf Oesir. His words contorted into a scream of pain and he fell to his knees.

Horrified reflex moved Skellan. He bounded from the protection of his ward circle and grabbed the water bucket. He swept up ice and water from the pool and hurled it over

Oesir. The flame fell back for only an instant, revealing Oesir's charred and blistered body. Smoke and the smell of seared hair and flesh choked the air. Then the flame surged up again from the open coffer like a serpent preparing to strike. Its violet light and sweltering heat rose up over Skellan. But Oesir reached out a black, smoking hand and caught the flame, pulling it to him.

"Flee!" Oesir gasped before the violet fire fell on him. Then only choked howls of agony escaped Oesir.

Skellan ran, terrified and confused but sure of the need to escape. He pelted for the open maw of the portcullis, while all across the grounds and on the wall guards called out in alarm.

"Look there!" a man shouted from above him. Arrows whistled past Skellan, one grazing his ear. Behind him he heard the pounding thunder of guards racing after him. They shouted for other men and a din of voices rose from all across the grounds. As he ran, the cover of the trees thinned. He tore away the rags of his clothes and hurled them up to take the distracting forms of doves and swifts—anything to draw the eyes of the archers from him. He threw himself ahead, calling on every shred of strength he possessed to lend him speed. His heart hammered in his chest and his muscles burned as he tore across the orchard. Another arrow whipped past his face. He felt the wet heat of blood trickling down his neck.

He refused to die like this, shot full of arrows like some gamecock.

Fear and fury surged through him and he felt the witch-flame within him blaze to life. A man couldn't cross open cobblestone and reach the foregates faster than archers could loose their arrows but a beast might.

As Skellan sprinted he called up the fierce heat of his own soul and the scarlet fire of his witchflame rolled over him and his tattered cloak. His body stretched, arms reaching to the ground, legs swinging forward and then hurling him ahead in a huge leap. His battered dogskin cloak flexed and closed against his body, growing hot and alive around him. His toes tore into the stones beneath him, clawing traction from even the sheen of ice encasing them.

Transformed, he raced lower and faster, his lungs drinking in the frigid night air and tasting everything—sweat, smoke, leaves rotting beneath the frost. His ears rang with the noise of men and beasts, the beating wings of a hunting nighthawk and the squeal of terrified mice. And far away the river slapped and hissed against the hulls of moored boats. He took it all in and kept running, just as he'd run from the grimma's palace ten years before, cloaked in the flesh and muscle of a wild-eyed mongrel.

He became that filthy dog again.

He burst from the cover of the trees, reached the gates in a heartbeat and crossed through without a pause. Mounted men armed with spears followed him, swearing and shouting from high up in their saddles. Instinct more than intellect warned him not to lead them to the nest he called his home. Instead he fled into the crowded chaos of the Theater District where traveler's taverns, playhouses, brothels and gambling dens kept crowds carousing and wagering all through the night.

Skellan dodged between carriages and darted past clusters of startled drunks.

The grimma's guards thundered after him, bellowing, "Clear the way in the name of Grimma Oesir! Clear the way or be cut down!"

Men in heavy furs and women wrapped in bright silks cowered back into painted doorways, abandoning the walkways to the charging guards.

Skellan snarled in frustration then bounded into the street, dashing through the noisy traffic of mounted travelers, horse-drawn carriages and ox wagons. Horses stamped and kicked as he yapped at their hind legs and round bellies. Carriage drivers shouted and more than one rider laid open a bloody weal across Skellan's back with a whip. But with his barred teeth and wild snarls he startled men and beasts alike, leaving pandemonium in his wake. He needed the men angry and the animals ready to bite and rear as the grimma's guards pursued him into their midst.

The grimma's guards bellowed threats, but they hardly carried over the cacophony of lowing oxen, indignant traders and unsettled horses. From some wagon, a flock of geese hissed and honked. When Skellan stole a glance over his shoulder he saw only two the grimma's guards still in chase.

Still too many.

His whole body ached and his strength flagged but he didn't dare slow. He bounded down a maze of narrow alleys, hoping to lose the guards in the dark, but they kept after him, steadily closing the distance. Their horses' hooves hammered the cobblestone streets like thunder, and Skellan smelled the sweat lathering their hides and heard the fast rhythm of their breath as if they were already on top of him. On either side of him the wood and stone backs of taverns and alehouses formed high walls and offered him nowhere to hide.

Then ahead, he glimpsed the wide wooden beams of some kind of corral—the pungent scents of horseshit, leather and sweet hay rolled over him. Skellan dived beneath the corral wall, plowing his chest through muck and mud to get under. Then he raced for the shelter of the dark stables ahead of him. A thin shaft of lamplight shone through the narrow gap in the doors. At his back he heard a horse whinny and stamp in refusal but the other cleared the corral and charged after him.

Skellan sprinted into the stables—warmth and light flooded over him—and then he slammed into a tower of hard flesh and bone. The big man stumbled back only a step, but the collision sent Skellan skittering off his feet and into a heap of damp wood shavings and straw. He lay stunned and gasping as the big man strode to where he lay. He loomed over Skellan like a winter oak, huge, dark and all hard angles. And Skellan deliriously remembered that the Irabiim always said that those oaks were omens of death.

A heavy, black traveler's cloak hid most of the man's clothes, but not the sword at his hip, nor the way his hand rested upon the hilt. His thick, dark hair looked unruly even cropped so very short, and his features were sharp and harsh as those of the stone saints who glowered down from the walls of Cadeleonian churches.

Skellan tried to lift his head, but he didn't possess the vigor to even bare his teeth. He'd burned through all his strength when he'd assumed this emaciated dog's body. Only the animal drive of panic had kept him running after that. And now even that dissipated before his exhaustion and wounds. His head fell back into the filthy shavings. He'd known he might die tonight, but he hadn't thought it would be like this.

The shadow of the man's hand stretched over him, but he didn't strike Skellan. Instead he knelt and held his broad, bare palm out, allowing Skellan to take his scent. Sea salt, sweat, fresh hay and a deep earthy aroma filled Skellan's mouth. He remembered the comfort of Bone-crusher then and weakly pressed his face against the man's warm, callused hand. Overhead, the stable lamps flickered at the evening shadows.

"I won't hurt you." The man's voice sounded deep and soft, and though he spoke Labaran his strong Cadeleonian accent made his words sound as strange as the intonations of a spell. He stroked Skellan's muzzle very gently. Skellan winced when the Cadeleonian's fingers brushed the open gashes that arrows and whips had torn across his skull and neck. The Cadeleonian drew his hand back, frowning at the traces of oily soot and blood on his fingers. "What kind of bastard did this to you?"

As if in answer to his question the stable door swung open. One of the grimma's guards stepped in from the evening darkness. Mud flecked his yellow beard and the front of his leather armor. He held his short spear up and at the ready. Just behind him a second guard sat atop his stallion holding the reins of the first man's horse.

The Cadeleonian straightened and once again his hand

slid to his sword hilt.

"Move back from that beast!" The guard hefted his spear. Skellan tried to regain his feet. His muscles shuddered with pain and he collapsed back down to his side.

The Cadeleonian stepped between him and the guard.

"Move, you ugly bear!" the guard shouted. "That cur is a witch's familiar. It has trespassed into the grimma's sanctum and by his law must be put to death."

To Skellan's surprise the big Cadeleonian didn't budge.

"You're going to die for the sake of a filthy mongrel," the guard sneered.

"No." The Cadeleonian sounded calm—almost amused. "But you certainly will if you try to harm him further."

The guard stared at the Cadeleonian in total incredulity, as if he'd somehow misunderstood the Cadeleonian's words. No one disregarded an order from one of the grimma's guards—not directly to their faces. In that instant of confusion, the Cadeleonian lunged forward with alarming speed, grasped the guard's spear and slammed the shaft up into the man's face with cracking force. The guard fell to the ground and the Cadeleonian deftly drew his sword and brought the tip down to the stunned guard's throat. He kicked the fallen spear aside as if the motion were a reflex.

Skellan stared at the Cadeleonian's massive dark form. He'd moved too well and fast to be a man of any peaceable trade. No, Skellan decided, his easy insolence and practiced violence were much more likely the traits of a criminal—a highwayman perhaps.

"Shall we discuss your options?" The Cadeleonian's hard gaze shifted to the mounted guard at the stable doors. Even through the darkness Skellan saw the young guard blanch.

Skellan's own heart hammered in his chest. It would only be a matter of time before more of the guards found them. If the grimma's guards took them they'd die, but not quickly.

"It's a filthy cur," the mounted guard quavered. "You can't mean to kill a man for a creature like that."

"I happen to like dogs," the Cadeleonian replied. Again Skellan caught that tone of amusement in the man's voice.

A weak bark of laughter escaped Skellan and he was glad, despite his pain and fear, that he had lived to see two of the grimma's arrogant, extorting guards looking so cowed in the hands of this rough Cadeleonian brigand.

"I beg you—" the guard on the ground moaned, but the Cadeleonian cut him off with a shake of his head.

"In your place, I wouldn't rely on my pity."

"What then?" the mounted guard demanded. "You can't believe that you could kill us both."

"That would require some effort," the Cadeleonian admitted. "But whether I have to go to the trouble is entirely up to the two of you." He slipped his free hand into the folds of his cloak and brought out a velvet coin purse with an ornate silver clasp. It looked like a small treasure itself and Skellan wondered who the Cadeleonian had robbed for it.

"I'm looking to buy a dog," the Cadeleonian stated. "And the two of you could profit well enough by selling this one to me, don't you think?"

The guards were quiet, and Skellan watched the way they stared at the bulging coin purse in the Cadeleonian's hand.

"All right," the mounted guard agreed. "If you want to take in some witch's familiar, then let that be on your own head. The beast doesn't look like it will survive the night in any case."

"It may not," the Cadeleonian conceded.

"The grimma must not know." The other guard spoke in a hushed tone, as if miles away the grimma might still overhear them.

"When next he invites me to dine with him in his fine palace, I promise you that I won't say a thing about it," the Cadeleonian responded. The absurdity of this ruffian at the grimma's opulent table seemed to amuse at least one of the guards. A flicker of a smile broke across the mounted man's face.

"Do we have a bargain?" the Cadeleonian asked.

Both the guards agreed that they did. The Cadeleonian ordered the mounted guard out and back across the corral. Then he handed the coin purse over to the man he'd knocked flat on his back and sent him running after his companion. He collected the man's fallen spear and turned back to Skellan.

"Well, dog," he said, as he knelt beside Skellan, "I think we'd be wise to move along before they decide to return with their friends to sell me a noose."

Skellan tried to rise but couldn't. He could hardly keep his eyes open. The man didn't seem to expect him to get up. Instead he reached out and gathered Skellan very carefully in his arms. As the man lifted him, Skellan glimpsed the small golden star hanging from a chain around the man's neck. The same symbol had decorated Oesir's golden coffer.

CHAPTER THREE

The gaunt, bleeding hound hung across Elezar's legs and saddle, looking like the corpse of a mauled fawn. Yet Elezar felt the slow steady beat of the dog's heart and took assurance that he hadn't courted death at the hands of the Grimma Oesir's guards for nothing. He could still save the animal. A shudder passed through the unconscious beast and Elezar pulled more of his traveling cloak over its body.

In truth, he wasn't certain why the survival of this one dog mattered to him so much or why he'd acted so rashly in defense of the animal. Except that he could still feel the warmth on his hand where the beaten creature had laid its head. He'd been moved that the dog had trusted him—of all men—despite the abuse it had obviously endured.

As a low groan escaped the dog Elezar slowed his stallion's gait to keep from jostling the hound's wounds open.

His horse, Cobre, snorted at being reined back, but obeyed. The slower pace offered Elezar more opportunity to take in the street through the gloom. Even at this hour the city of Milmuraille bustled with people from a multitude of nations. Northern Labarans—the men sporting neat mustaches and the women wearing their hair braided in ornate crowns and loops—made up the majority of the populace. But lanky blond Mirogoths and dark-skinned Irabiim also plied the streets. They often hawked skins and furs, though a few traded in fortune-telling or simply slouched in the alcoves or doorways waiting to be solicited for services Elezar could only guess at.

Two dark-haired Labaran women pulled a small cart past Elezar. Their cargo of firewood and patties of dried dung added a ripe scent to air already pungent of open sewers, fish oil lamps and spilled beer. Elezar made room to allow them past. A group of four drunk Cadeleonian soldiers dressed in the royal blue followed the women, hooting and slurring propositions. One of the men staggered toward Elezar but meeting Elezar's condemning gaze, he seemed to briefly come to his senses and veered quickly back into the arms of his fellow soldiers. He and his companions soon tired of their pursuit of the Labaran women and lurched into a tavern.

After three months in Milmuraille Elezar didn't have it in him to feel more than a tired disgust at the way so many of the Cadeleonian soldiers disgraced their king's colors. Now he simply turned Cobre ahead and continued his ride toward the walled courtyards and costly townhouses that made up the newer Cadeleonian district of the city.

Then, through the crowds of wagons and carriages he made out another four of Grimma Oesir's guards. Their golden spears caught in the light of the lamps hanging outside one of the many Labaran taverns. Another two rode up beside them and saluted.

Elezar glanced down at the dog stretched across his legs and saddle. Were they all out for this pathetic animal's blood?

Elezar decided not to find out. He turned Cobre down a crowded, noisy side avenue. Overhanging balconies blotted out most of the darkening sky but cast pools of light from hanging lamps and torches. Elezar stole a glance behind him but didn't see any of the grimma's guards following.

Gaudily painted Labaran signs hung beneath the lamps, promising tankards of beer as well as busty barmaids and inexplicably—at least to Elezar—plates of frogs and snails. The drone of Labaran pipes and choruses of jaunty drinking songs drifted around Elezar. From the shadows of alley openings groups of rangy men eyed him, but seemed to quickly assess that he wouldn't make for an easy mugging. Elezar wasn't certain but he thought he glimpsed a few Cadeleonian soldiers among these opportunists.

As a rule he preferred to travel the wider main roads in the twilight hours but this particular avenue seemed more bustling in the evening than most were during daylight hours. Many establishments retained brawny men of Mirogoth descent to ensure the safety of their patrons and their fat purses, at least until they got inside. The taverns and gambling houses—often indicated by signs displaying a grinning, three-legged piglet—thinned, and steadily carved signs for theaters and brothels began to appear. A variety of women called sweetly from the overhanging balconies. Some sang and many danced, backlit by lamps to expose the curves of their figures through their white shifts.

And this being Milmuraille, Elezar found himself passing under one balcony where several young men lounged dressed in flimsy clothing utterly unsuited to the biting chill of the evening wind. Just passing them Elezar's heart began to hammer in his chest and sweat rose at the back of his neck.

He couldn't keep from lifting his gaze to take two of the men in. Both looked to be Labarans but of mixed heritage, one running pale and broad boned, the other darker and more delicate, like a Haldiim. They draped their arms around each other and passed a pipe between them. Despite himself, Elezar stilled Cobre, unable to pull his gaze from the way the two men's hands touched and caressed each other's shoulders. Then the fairer of the two cocked his head in Elezar's direction and Elezar jerked his gaze away.

"Disgusting harlots! You will burn on spits in the flames of all three hells!" a distinctly Cadeleonian voice shouted from across the street.

Elezar felt a guilty flush color his face but the men on the balcony just laughed. Elezar nudged Cobre ahead, but looked back to see the darker of the two men bare his buttocks at the paunchy Cadeleonian merchant who shouted at them from the steps of a brothel across the way. The Labaran women dancing on the balcony above the merchant giggled and several people on the street laughed at the scene, but it horrified Elezar. The Cadeleonian merchant skulked into a tavern and the young man on the balcony pulled his breeches back up.

Elezar kept riding and didn't look back again.

The last twilight rays of sun fell into the gloaming long before Elezar even reached the Cadeleonian district. Fortunately little Labaran temples abounded through out the city, most sitting at the foot of some ornate bell tower. All of them maintained blazes of lamps and often boys and girls stood at hand to be hired as torchbearers, lighting the way for travelers traversing the city in the dark. Elezar rarely procured their services. It seemed cruel to make children attempt to keep pace alongside him or his horse. However, the sheer number of temples and torchbearers ensured that little fires flickered up and down nearly every street and avenue.

Two sweating teenaged torchbearers pelted past Elezar, racing hard alongside a glossy carriage. Golden light swept up illuminating a new example of the strange carven creatures that seemed to lurk in odd corners throughout the city. These looked to Elezar like large-eyed bats except that instead of legs long trails of curling squid-like tentacles swirled out behind them. At the entryway of an alley a carving of a slender, long-limbed woman burdened with a frog-like face and shaggy breasts crouched as if ready to snap up a passing fly.

"Clear the way!" a man shouted in Labaran. "By authority of Grimma Oesir, move or be cut down!" Three of the grimma's guards urged their horses down the street in the opposite direction. Elezar watched them disappear into the shadows, though their shouts continued to carry back to him.

"A fire at the sanctum, that's what I heard," a woman seated in a goat cart a few feet ahead of Elezar murmured to the old man walking alongside her. "Why they don't sound the Columbe Tower Bell and summon the fireguard I can't figure."

"True, our Sheriff Hirbe would have that fire doused in no time," the old man opined, bobbing his head in a loose nod.

"Unless it were unnatural," the woman whispered.

Again the man nodded, instinctually concurring with his wife's suspicions.

Elezar wondered if somehow the sad animal hanging

across his lap had taken the blame for starting a fire. Perhaps it had knocked over an oil lamp and for that had been deemed the familiar of an enemy witch. Elezar had heard of stranger things in these northern lands.

Supposedly the Labaran grimma, Oesir, had a dread of other witches and had convinced Count Radulf to outlaw all other schools of witchcraft but his own.

Absently, Elezar stroked the dog's chest and felt a sigh pass through its lean body.

Then the old couple's conversation turned to a gripe against the butter tax, which helped to fund the Cadeleonian garrison and the soldiers tasked with protecting the city—the same soldiers whom Elezar had seen staggering drunk in the street. Though harboring drunken belligerents was far from the worst of the garrison's offenses.

Elezar rode passed the old couple and their goats hoping that his beard and weathered cloak would let him pass for a Labaran fur trader. From the way the couple went suddenly silent he guessed that his broad build and the fine horse he rode gave him away.

Despite the boisterous noise rolling from the theaters and taverns surrounding them he still picked up the woman's whisper.

"Bound for the Cradle, you reckon?"

A shameful feeling, far worse than what he'd experienced looking at the men on the balcony, swept through Elezar. His ears burned and revulsion clenched the pit of his stomach. He wanted to turn back and protest that he had nothing to do with the Cradle but he suspected such a response would only make him appear all the more guilty.

Elezar let Cobre quicken his pace, carrying him farther ahead of the couple.

He wasn't used to feeling anything but proud of his Cadeleonian heritage but Commander Zangre Lecha and his Cradle had tainted that. Elezar almost wished that he could have remained ignorant of the existence of the place, but it had been inevitable that within the first week of their arrival to the city, Atreau found friends to guide him on a tour of all the bawdyhouses in the city. He'd returned early one evening looking incensed and sporting a split lip. Elezar remembered fearing that Atreau had been recognized and that they would need to flee before they could complete Fedeles' mission. But after downing half a bottle of wine Atreau explained that he'd been shown to the massive Cadeleonian garrison where, after handing over a few coins to a surly guard he was offered the opportunity to bed any one of a dozen children. Not a single one of the girls paraded before him had been more than eleven years of age.

Atreau had stormed out and nearly gotten himself run through when he accosted the commander of the garrison on the open street. Only the fact that he wore Fedeles' signet and had been accompanied by a group of quick-thinking Labaran courtiers had gotten him home in one piece. Making a scene and blackening one of the commander's eyes hadn't been wise but the fact that Atreau had taken a stand only made Elezar think the better of his friend.

Soon after that Elezar discovered that the Cradle was infamous throughout the city. The upright Cadeleonians in residence adamantly refused to acknowledge the existence of the place but nearly every Labaran knew the name and given the opportunity in a tavern or common inn most would rant furiously about it. The fact that it operated within the Cadeleonian garrison meant that the Labaran sheriff had no right to enter or lay charges despite the fact that the girls kept within were well below the age of legal consent in Labara. That would have been offensive enough but the outrageous insult was the fact that gold from a butter tax levied on all Labarans went directly to Commander Zangre Lecha's coffers to fund the upkeep of that same garrison.

Rumor had it that Count Radulf had sworn off butter and refused to prosecute those who sold it illegally in the markets in protest. Cadeleonian soldiers stationed at the garrison commonly found themselves ordered to hunt down and demand payment from common folk working churns. Little wonder that so many of them either turned to drink or deserted their duties to turn mercenary.

Neither Elezar nor Atreau were in positions to do more than write to Fedeles about the matter and turn a blind eye whenever they noticed one of the Labaran maids stealing untaxed Cadeleonian butter from their host's table.

For the time being Elezar had enough challenges before him, attempting to find a guide to lead him through the vast forest that fell under the dominion of the Sumar grimma. He'd spent weeks traveling between taverns and inns, making the acquaintances of fur traders and secretive Mirogoth trappers. Only this evening he'd found a guide willing to allow him to join a party into the forest to acquire and trade in winter pelts.

Elezar's contemplation of all he would need to pack to make ready was interrupted suddenly by wild shouts and the sound of dozens of horses pounded down upon him. Torches flared from a street ahead of him as two full ranks of the grimma's guards swung around the corner and charged.

Cobre tensed and Elezar's hand went reflexively to his sword hilt.

"Out of the way!" one of the big blond guards bellowed. "Clear the road in the name of Grimma Oesir! Make way!"

Elezar turned Cobre aside, urging him up onto the boardwalk just as the first of a dozen horses and riders barreled past. The dog shuddered against Elezar but made no motion otherwise.

Road dust swirled through the air, casting a haze over the lamps dangling from nearby balconies. All around men and women rushed to windows, doorway and balconies to witness the commotion. A few feet from Elezar, three pretty young women clothed in the scarlet robes of sister-physicians peered out from the door of their temple. They stared as the last of the grimma's guards thundered past, then the tallest of them stepped out only to startle back as the light of her lamp fell across Elezar and his stallion standing on the boardwalk.

"Forgive the intrusion," Elezar said, "but the road was a little too occupied."

The tall young woman gave a nervous laugh. Her companions joined her, looking serious and severe with their dark hair bound back in snoods and their hands resting on the thick leather of their knife belts.

"It's all right," the taller woman assured the others, though how she knew that Elezar couldn't guess. "You aren't a garrison soldier, are you?" She phrased the assertion like a question but her expression and tone were certain.

"I serve the duke of Rauma as a varlet," Elezar replied.

"Oh yes, we've heard about the duke." She offered Elezar a knowing smile and the younger woman standing next to her seemed to light up with excitement.

"I swear by the Columbe Bell, your duke's visits to our Theater District have sold more lamb-gut condoms for me than anything for months! Apparently, mine are his favorite." The young sister-physician's grin displayed an impressive set of large, white teeth. "He must be taking them by the two and threes!"

That was no revelation to Elezar and still he felt slightly shocked hearing such a thing from a holy woman. All three women laughed.

Even after months in Milmuraille, northern women still often surprised him. Most resembled Cadeleonian ladies with their dark hair and fair skin, and some even presented themselves in a decorous and modest manner. But others—sister-physicians in particular—seemed bold as men and twice as likely to tease a stranger.

Several innkeepers had advised Elezar not to confuse the sister-physicians of Radulf County for the meek nuns of southern Labara and Cadeleon. The Radulf women were well learned and could as easily kill a man as heal him with their potions and scalpels. Taking in the gruesome medical procedures painted like advertisements across the walls of the temple, Elezar could well believe that the women living within were no strangers to bloodshed and gore.

As overhead lamps flickered and flared, Elezar's eyes fell across the illustration of several amputations. The depictions of severed limbs and digits seemed somewhat at odds with the inscription over the door, which proclaimed in three languages that this was house of holy mercy.

The shortest and eldest of the three women cocked her head and stared at Elezar's lap. Then she stepped forward.

"Is that your pet or your supper hanging there?"

"An injured dog I found," Elezar replied. Then he added, "From the stringy look of him, he'll likely make a better pet than meal."

"Wait here, I've a poultice," she informed him. Without further explanation she whisked away back inside the temple. Elezar waited and the other two women stared past him, watching the grimma's guards race into the distance.

"They're going to the Sun Palace, don't you think?" the young sister-physician asked her companion.

The other woman nodded and both looked concerned.

"Something's gone very wrong if Grimma Oesir is summoning the count at this hour."

Elezar, too, watched the swirling torchlight fade from sight. The sound of alarm dulled, leaving crowds of curious onlookers blinking at each other through the dust and darkness. Certainly this represented much more than the little trouble caused by an errant dog.

"It could be good news," someone commented from the balcony overhead—another woman but Elezar couldn't make out her face through the flare of lamplight. She sounded very young. Likely a novice, just beginning her studies at the temple. "Maybe Oesir's found the count's stolen son at long last."

"The count's son is just a smoke dream. The boy's long dead," the tall sister-physician commented. "You shouldn't speak of him."

The girl overhead murmured something in response but Elezar missed it as the elder sister-physician reappeared and hurried to him. She handed him a rank-smelling flask, but didn't let go when he took hold of it.

"A silver lady, if you will," the sister-physician insisted while smiling warmly at him.

Elezar fished out the Labaran coin, stamped with the handsome profile of Count Radulf's daughter, and tossed it to the sister-physician. She released the flask to catch the coin and Elezar quickly tucked the flask away into an inner pocket of his cloak.

"You move fast enough, don't you?" the sister-physician commented with a broad grin. "Clean the poor beast with water that you've boiled hard and cooled, then treat those wounds with the poultice once a day. It stinks but it'll keep fever and rot away."

Elezar nodded and then took his leave before the woman could demand a further payment for the instruction.

The rest of his ride to the Cadeleonian District passed uneventfully. The wild variety of Labaran temples, massive bell towers and tiny wooden shrines dedicated to obscure, mythic figures thinned. It their place, stately shops and gated, stone townhouses rose up. The convoluted street straightened, falling into place on a neat grid of wide roads. Every effort had gone into recreating a replica of Cadeleon, albeit a Cadeleon designed some hundred years past and built to endure the long, dark, cold of northern winters. Still, a man would be hard pressed to find any trace of Labaran culture or language here. The Cadeleonian residents even maintained their own printing press, which turned out a broadsheet that published distinctly Cadeleonian perspectives on local events.

At last Elezar reached the heavy iron gates surrounding the rolling grounds of Bishop Palo's townhouse and vast garden. From the gate Elezar could just make out the sprawling two-story stone house and the spire of the decrepit chapel beyond. According to the wizened bishop, the grounds had once witnessed the defeat of a demon lord at the hands of a holy warrior and the crumbling Cadeleonian chapel was one of the oldest in all the northlands.

Thankfully, the construction taking place in the chapel made it impossible for the bishop to take his guests on a tour of the dank crypt or decayed alcoves within. The bishop had promised that once the work was completed he would personally guide them through and explain the significance of every stone. Elezar could only hope that he'd be on his way back home or even lost in the depth of a Mirogoth forest before the opportunity arose to enjoy Bishop Palo's enlightening lecture.

One of the multitude of priests employed by the bishop opened the gate to admit Elezar. The young man wrinkled his nose as he caught sight of the bloody dog but made no comment. Clearly a mere varlet, like Elezar, didn't merit conversation. Elezar made his way to the stables where the grooms were busy wiping road dust from one of the bishop's gilded carriages.

From far across the city a bell began to ring and then suddenly went silent.

The grooms all looked up from their work and Elezar, too, stilled, waiting to hear the bell ring again, but silence stretched on until Elezar felt a fool for expecting anything else. He turned his attention back to gently lifting the dog down.

Whatever troubles lurked in the city beyond they were none of his concern.

CHAPTER FOUR

Skellan woke, kicking free from the grip of a terrible dream. A violet flame arched over him in the form of a giant serpent, its mouth gaping like a roaring forge.

But it had only been a dream, Skellan assured himself.

Beech wood logs snapped and popped as they burned bright and hot in the stone hearth before him. Beneath him, he felt soft, plush fabric. He remembered waking like this a number of times before. He thought that a week might have passed since the night his big Cadeleonian had carried him to this comfortable chamber to wash and feed him. As always, a warm hand stroked his head and when he cracked his eyes open he saw the man sitting beside him on the red wool carpet. Afternoon light poured in from a narrow window and lit the long lines of his Cadeleonian's leather jerkin.

The light of day did nothing to soften the man's daunting appearance. Though he seemed younger than Skellan had first thought, not weathered enough to be past thirty but still built like a towering oak and endowed with the hard, angular features of ragged marble. His heavy, dark brows and thick beard hid any trace of delicacy that his mouth or eyes could have betrayed.

"Hungry?" The Cadeleonian's voice drifted over him in a low rumble.

Skellan instinctively nuzzled the man's tan, callused hand and a smile broke across the Cadeleonian's harsh face. "You're always hungry, aren't you?"

The man rose and strode to an iron-studded door, then slipped out beyond the line of Skellan's sight. The door fell shut behind him and Skellan's attention returned to the fire. Bright yellow flames sparked and danced and for an instant he remembered Oesir burning and screaming—his flesh blistered, cracked, bled and blackened before Skellan's eyes.

Skellan hated the man but even he would never have wished such agony upon anyone. The witch who'd created that golden coffer must have meant the thing within to kill cruelly and not just Oesir.

Skellan couldn't help but remember how those consuming violet flames had arched over him. Then Oesir had reached out and pulled them to his own flesh, instead of allowing them to engulf Skellan. It made no sense that Oesir, the man who'd destroyed Skellan's home and hunted him for years, should choose to save him and at such a cost to himself.

Skellan wished he had familiar stones beneath his feet so that they might carry him news from beyond the walls of the grimma's sanctum. But the wood and rock of this great, sprawling house were dead things—inert as common dirt. Still, if he closed his eyes and lay very still, Skellan could just feel Oesir's viridian witchflame. No longer the majestic blaze that oppressed the awareness of any other witch within miles of his sanctum, now it shivered like a candle flame drowning in wax. He was cocooned inwards, dying, slowly and in immense pain.

Skellan shuddered and turned his face from the fire. He didn't yet possess the strength to return to his own form, much less discover just what had happened in the sanctum, but he would. In the meantime he knew he ought to pay a little more attention to where he was right now.

His Cadeleonian wore a pendant of the same four-pointed star that had gleamed across Oesir's golden coffer. The symbol also stood out on the door, beaten into the oak timbers with iron studs. It decorated the headboard of the bed, standing across the room and glinted from the floor tiles. Skellan knew the star was a Cadeleonian holy symbol, a sign of protection and had seen it in chapels, bars and even in brothels—but never adorning such a terrifying thing as that golden coffer.

Skellan grumbled in annoyance. He had to get that damn thing out of his mind. Think about something else, until he had the strength to actually find anything out. He scratched his ear with his back leg and briefly marveled at the flexibility of his animal body.

Then something caught his eye.

A book lay open on the rug and Skellan peered at the ornately illustrated pages. The script appeared to be Cadeleonian, but the style of the illuminations looked Mirogoth. The crests of the four Mirogoth grimma's sanctums twisted the forms of wild beasts into decorative knots. As a boy in the Labaran grimma's sanctum Skellan had learned to read and converse in a diversity of languages. Outside the sanctum, the profusion of wealthy foreign traders in the city ensured that he'd kept in practice. Some weeks he thought he heard more Cadeleonian and Mirogothic than Labaran.

Skellan inched closer to the book. The wounds across his neck ached but not so badly now. The pages lay open to an account of the battles fought between the Mirogoth grimma and their Cadeleonian adversaries over the lands and people of Labara. The Cadeleonian warriors wielded flame-forged steel and their champion opened the blazing mouth of their white hell while the grimma called ancient beasts from the stones and pulled murderous spirits from the skies. The people of Labara died or fled and the war raged on, until at last the young witch Lundag betrayed the grimma who had trained her and took the side of the holy Cadeleonian armies. She raised a sanctum, named herself the Labaran grimma, and at last the Mirogoths were forced to forge a truce.

They gave Labara over to the protection of the Cadeleonians and swore to uphold the peace so long as a witchflame burned over the Labaran sanctum here in Milmuraille.

Such was the power and glory of our true God and his Kingdom Everlasting that the witches lay down their arms and fled from the land like shadows withering before His Most Holy Light. And in His Wisdom, He allowed the unclean sanctum at Milmuraille to stand, as reminder and monument of the heathen witches' defeat.

Skellan snorted at the prose.

The so-called unclean sanctum in Milmuraille had been the only thing that had kept the Cadeleonians from being crushed by the ancient, wild power of the grimma and also the only force that held back the Mirogoths from invading all of Labara and returning it to the savage wilderness that they worshiped. Peace held only so long as a witchflame burned over the sanctum here in Milmuraille.

Everyone knew that.

Skellan pawed at the pages and they fell back to an even older tale: the summoning of the Old Gods. When the first witches found their magical dabblings attracted the hungry attention of hordes of demons they called powerful spirits from the sky, sea and earth, and captured them in the flesh of creatures mighty enough to battle entire armies of demons. *And so the Old Gods came into being and made war against the demons. But after destroying the demons the monstrous Old Gods wandered the world untamed, crushing cities, sinking fleets of ships and laying waste to entire kingdoms.*

Along the side of the page an illustration depicted four jewel-toned dragons as they breathed huge plumes of fire over a tiny, walled city. Skellan remembered Bone-crusher telling him about the four daughters of the sky, the immense dragons born from the winds of the four directions. For an instant Skellan felt a thrill gazing upon the image and imagining the wild magnificence that had once filled the world. Then he shook his head. That age had passed. Even the daughters of the sky had eventually been bound and buried away to make all the realms of the world safe for mortal men and women.

Now only the deepest sea and perhaps the darkest corners of the Mirogoth forest still sheltered those beings, too strange and powerful for humanity to tolerate in anything but stories. Or stones, like Bone-crusher.

Skellan found nothing new in these dull, dead words written across yellow pages. Stories such as these were far better if they could be embodied and witnessed in the wild plays Rafale staged at his Mockingbird Playhouse. Even when he knew the tales already, Skellan always loved watching Rafale's acrobats in their bright-plumed costumes as they tumbled and clowned between acts. And of course there was Rafale himself, ever easy on the eyes and in the bed. But that, Skellan reminded himself, made for a hurtful pleasure and one he'd sworn off.

Best not to think on that either.

He wondered what his Cadeleonian found of interest in this tome. He hadn't impressed Skellan as a scholarly man… Maybe he enjoyed the pictures. The delicate touches of gold leaf gleamed in the firelight. Pretty enough, but hardly gripping.

Skellan's ears pricked up as he recognized the tread of steps outside the door and smelled hot meat on the air. He slid back from the book, dismissing it. His thoughts suddenly swirled with the excited senses of a young, ravenous hound. The strong meaty aroma floated nearer and Skellan's mouth began to water in spite of his will. A moment later his Cadeleonian stepped through the door, carrying a fine porcelain bowl brimming with beef stew. Skellan's nose brought his head up and a hungry keening escaped him.

"Fear not, my boy." His Cadeleonian sounded amused. "It's all just for you."

He placed the bowl down before Skellan and then sat back down at his side, taking his book up again. Skellan lapped the hot stew eagerly.

"You're eating well enough now, aren't you? There's a good boy." The Cadeleonian encouraged and praised him. And though Skellan wanted to find the kind words laughable, the animal flesh he wore responded to them with a sense of comfort and safety. His long, skinny tail wagged wildly each time his Cadeleonian absently patted his head. After he'd eaten his fill, Skellan took an absurd pleasure in laying his head on the Cadeleonian's leg and drinking in the earthy scents of him.

He felt so warm and full. Blissful. He didn't think he'd

known such comfort since he'd been ten years old. Then he hadn't appreciated what luxuries a good meal, a warm hearth and a kind touch could be to him.

Skellan napped and his Cadeleonian read. Slowly the fire burned low.

When Skellan woke again only embers glowed in the hearth and a pale predawn light cast faint blue shadows across the white plaster walls. His Cadeleonian wore his heavy traveling clothes again and stood at his writing desk, with a crude map in one gloved hand.

Another dark-haired man lounged in one of the two carved chairs near the hearth. The man smelled a little of roses and a great deal of women's bodies. His fine green and gold silk clothes looked rumpled, as if he'd slept in them. He'd visited this room before and Skellan remembered that he was a Cadeleonian duke called Fedeles Quemanor. Skellan had imagined such a powerful lord would be older and carry himself less like a rent-boy. Not that Skellan minded. The musical quality of the duke's voice reminded him just a little of Rafale when he was at his kindest. And more than once Skellan amused himself by imaging the cardsharps and sailors mistaking the duke for a costly tart: all those brutish, bearded toughs jostling to impress the rose-perfumed duke with displays of their meager coin purses and padded crotches. Knowing the Cadeleonian horror of such couplings it was all too easy to imagine the duke swooning in a heap of silk and velvet. Skellan snickered into the wooly rug.

"Your dog is twitching again," the duke announced. "He does that often, doesn't he?"

"He has nightmares, I think," Skellan's Cadeleonian replied. He folded the map and tucked it away inside his cloak. "I can't imagine that he wouldn't, considering everything that was done to him."

"It's hard to credit that he's the same animal that you first brought back. He looked dead and so filthy that I would have sworn he was black. He smelled like he was rotting..." The duke cocked his handsome head to the side and gave Skellan a long look. "You know it's not impossible that those men were right. He's a striking animal, so big and red. He could be a witch's familiar."

Skellan's heart lurched at the duke's words, but his Cadeleonian just laughed.

"It's not so funny as all that," the duke protested. "The Labaran grimma may have abolished all competing schools of witchcraft but there are still plenty of witches who practice secretly out in the countryside and alleys."

"Milkmaids and goose girls stuffing sachets with wild savory and calling them love charms, you mean?"

"I'm serious, Elezar."

Skellan's attention caught on the last word. Then he realized why he didn't know its meaning; it was a name: his Cadeleonian's name.

And not for the first time he wondered at the nature of the relationship between these two men. They seemed too at ease with each other's given names and too relaxed in one another's company for a master and servant. Though they looked nothing like brothers, something in the parity of their exchanges reminded Skellan of the way siblings conversed.

"I can see why you'd be worried." Elezar flashed the duke a hard smile. "What would become of you if some homely peasant girl brought you to your knees with a love spell? The horror."

"Very amusing." The duke didn't look amused. "What if he's the familiar to some Mirogoth witch? Every single Mirogoth woman and half the boys practice witchcraft, you know. And the old districts of the city are populated with dozens of covens. Even the count's astrologer is said to cast spells. In fact there are rumors that old Count Radulf himself—"

"All of them out to ensnare you in love spells as well?" Elezar teased.

The duke rolled his eyes. "You're hopeless. You of all people know that there is sorcery out there. How dangerous it can be!"

"I do know," Elezar responded. His expression turned grim. "But I'm not going to see a defenseless animal beaten and drowned just because someone thinks he looks like he could belong to a witch."

"But he does have a certain look in his eyes," the duke said.

"That's intelligence," Elezar replied. "By that measure we'd have to put down half the scholars in the city and all of the moneylenders."

The duke appeared ready to protest but Elezar went on, "Allay your fears. Even if he were a witch's familiar, he won't be making any mischief. Last night I gave him a collar strung with charms that both Bishop Palo and a fair number of crafty milkmaids have assured me will keep any witch from taking possession of him."

Skellan almost jumped in alarm, but stopped himself, realizing how very suspicious that would look. Instead he pretended to scratch at his ear and managed to run his paw over the braided leather collar that now circled his neck. It hung loose and light. More than a dozen metal pendants and glass baubles dangled from it; they jingled like bells as his toes batted them. If they housed charms of any real power Skellan couldn't sense it. Certainly they wouldn't keep him from freeing himself from this animal flesh.

He calmed and lay his head back down on his front paw. The duke contemplated him while Elezar packed his saddlebags.

"If we're going to nurse him back to health and give him a collar we ought name him." The duke stared intently at Skellan. Then he said, "Windsrunner."

Skellan just blinked at him then glanced to where Elezar stood.

"I don't think he's impressed," Elezar commented.

"Sunfire," the duke suggested. Skellan didn't roll his eyes

but it required an effort. What had he done to deserve having to share a name with a tarty little sprite from a ribald poem? Then with a sly expression the duke called out sweetly, "Randy-boy! I'm right, aren't I? You're a Randy-boy, aren't you?"

It was a fairly good joke, and not too far off the mark. Still, Skellan considered showing his teeth to the duke.

"Not really a name I want to be shouting across the grounds of Bishop Palo's residence," Elezar remarked. He hefted up his packed saddlebags from the bedside. "Once he's healthy we'll see who he really is. Dog is good enough for just now. I'm more concerned that he's well fed and cared for while I'm away. He'll want exercise—short walks at first, though he looks bred for the speed of chasing game and I imagine he'll want to run, sooner than he ought to be allowed."

"You could just stay and take care of him yourself," the duke replied.

"I've already delayed my trip by a week to look after him." Elezar drew near and gently patted Skellan. Then he looked to the duke. "If I wait any longer I'll miss the fur traders and I'll have a prayer's chance in hell of getting into Mirogoth territory unnoticed."

The duke scowled. Skellan would have scowled as well if he could have. The Sumar grimma's lands were no place for a Cadeleonian.

"You don't really think you have to risk your life out in that dark forest, do you? I'm almost certain that once Fede—" The duke suddenly caught himself and cast a quick look to the door as if he feared that someone could have been lurking there. Skellan pricked his ears and drew in a deep breath, tasting for anyone beyond the door. Nothing but the scrabble of a tiny rock mouse and still air. The nearest activity sounded as if it came from a kitchen far away.

"Elezar, listen." The duke bent forward in his chair, leaning in toward Elezar and speaking low. "I don't think that our friend who kindly sent us here would want you taking these risks. The Mirogoth forest isn't just wild. It's infested by un-natural creatures. Trolls, shapechangers, leeches the size of a man's arm. That huge skin in the bishop's study came from a bear that devoured five men before it was brought down by the bishop's hunters. And Ulli in the kitchen told me that covens of exiled witches hunt those woods enchanting and torturing Cadeleonian travelers as their revenge against the Labaran grimma."

Skellan had heard as much himself in cockerel taverns and at card tables. And he'd seen the scars and curse burns that disfigured the men telling those tales.

"The Labaran grimma isn't Cadeleonian," Elezar replied.

"Of course not, but you know just as well as I do that Cadeleonian conquest made it possible for her sanctum to take dominion over every other coven in Labara—"

"His sanctum," Elezar put in and Skellan thought he might have been smiling behind his beard. "The current grimma here is a man named Oesir."

"Really?" The duke raised his plucked brows. "A man? But the grimma are witch queens. Queen—that's what the word means, doesn't it?"

"No, as it turns out, the word itself is feminine, in the Miro-goth tongue, but the title can be held men or women. Though apparently only one man has ever managed it. And that's the current grimma here in Labara. Oesir." Elezar shrugged.

The duke opened his mouth and then scowled at Elezar. "You only brought that up to throw me off my subject."

"You were scaring my dog." Elezar patted Skellan again. "He already has nightmares, you know."

"Very funny."

"Look, someone has to go." Elezar rose to his feet. "And I'm the one he asked."

Skellan wished he could know just who or what was so important that it drove his Cadeleonian to trespass into Sumar lands. Drigfan, the statuesque Sumar grimma whose green

witchflame held dominion there, was infamous for her loath-
ing of Cadeleonians. She made very public knowledge of her
practice of capturing Cadeleonian missionaries who ventured
into her lands and allowing her bears to sport with them for
hours on end. Skellan had seen the wagons heaped with the
mauled remains that Drigfan sent each year to the Cadeleonian cathedral in Milmuraille.

Instinctively he placed his paw over Elezar's booted foot,
and that strange keening sound escaped him before he could
stop it.

"God's teeth!" Elezar gave the duke a hard look. "You really
have frightened the dog." Then he knelt, stroked Skellan's head
and then very gently moved Skellan off his foot. "It's all right.
I'll be back in no time. Don't worry. You'll be fed. And you'll
have my bed to sleep on while I'm gone. There, there, you'll be
fine..."

"It's not my fault," the duke said. "Obviously he's just noticed
you're dressed to travel and he's probably worried you're going
to make him get up off his beloved rug. Not that he need be.
He's got your whole room to himself when he rightly should be
sleeping in a kennel. Lucky mongrel."

Skellan buried his nose in wool rug ashamed of how
quickly his natural detachment failed him in this pathetic, animal body. He hardly knew this Elezar and yet he felt genuinely
frightened for him. The duke reached out and patted Skellan
with a hand that smelled of flowers and wine.

"He's heartless to abandon us like this, isn't he?" The duke
pretended to address Skellan but then looked up at Elezar.
"You know, I'm going to get bored with nothing but your dog
for company the whole time you're gone."

"Think how the poor dog feels about it," Elezar answered.
Then he swung his saddlebags over his shoulder and left Skellan
and the duke alone in the quiet of his rooms.

CHAPTER FIVE

Only three hours beyond Milmuraille's city gates, the road north began to diminish. Elezar coaxed his stallion, Cobre, over the exposed stones that studded a half-frozen brook. The dense beech and fir forest surrounding them grew taller and darker than the lush southern woodlands where Elezar had grown up hunting boar and stag. Colder too. Despite the vibrant green color of the spruce branches and mounding mosses, ice sheeted the muddy ground and frost covered the exposed patches of earth. Thin, white shafts of noonday sun hardly pierced the deep shadows and where they did, an icy mist rose to veil the narrow dirt road.

Perhaps "road" was something of an overstatement. Little more than a rutted path remained of the wide lane their party had followed north across the Raccroc River. Beyond the cobbled streets and farmland of Labara they entered the forest. Now, a mere hour into the woods, all signs of civilization diminished or disappeared completely. The tang of spruce replaced the smoky scents of hearth fires, stillness filled the air where it had once resounded with the bustling noise of traffic and trade. Steadily creeping willows and wild brambles transformed the wide stone road into a wandering goat trail, studded here and there with mossy rocks.

Studying the rough, icy trail ahead and the bulky wagon of the elegant Labaran fur traders riding behind him, Elezar guessed that this was a fledgling expedition for these dapper merchants' sons. He certainly wouldn't have dressed in fine velvet and kid leather shoes for this journey. Nor would he have bothered to shave, trim and wax his mustache to the shape of a sweet pea's tendril. Though Elezar rather liked the look of the young man who had—he possessed a good height for a Labaran and the kind of joyous smile that distracted Elezar a little—he clearly did not belong in this dark, wild place. He and his four companions teased each other and speculated upon the upcoming summer ball, and whether Count Radulf's daughter might attend.

Six blond, bearded mercenary guards trailed the traders' wagon—the path being too narrow to allow them alongside—looking obvious and ill at ease beneath the walls of looming dark trees.

Their three guides, on the other hand, were barefoot, pale-eyed Mirogoths whose big lanky limbs and ratted white-blond hair faded readily into the pale lichen-studded stones, wild grass and gnarled branches of the forest. Standing still in their weathered leather clothes they looked more like thin trunks of silver birches than women. When they spoke it was in low whispers of Mirogothic and sharp birdcalls.

While the two elder guides ran ahead of the party, the third, a very young-looking woman, dropped back to walk beside Elezar's mount. She studied Elezar brazenly, as no Cadeleonian and few Labaran women would dare to do. Then she tossed an easy glance back at the traders, with their glossy wagon and blond guards.

"How will you carry back your furs?" The guide spoke in a mix of Mirogothic and more familiar Labaran.

"My master wants only the finest pelt from a scarlet wolf, which he will present it to his betrothed as a cloak," Elezar replied in heavily accented Mirogothic. He needed to practice the tongue as much as he could, and it always seemed to amuse the Mirogoths to hear him try.

The guide gave a very unlady-like snort. "There are no scarlet wolves anymore. Will your master also gift his betrothed with hen's teeth and toad wings?"

"Yes, as soon as I find those for him as well," Elezar replied. "So, I've brought my invisible wagon to cart his treasures back to him."

The guide laughed out loud and the sound echoed through trees.

"I'm called Eski," the guide told him.

"Elezar," he supplied.

"You're Cadeleonian," she said. "That can be very danger-ous here."

"If it weren't, then my master could easily come himself," Elezar responded. "And how would I have my pay?"

Overhead, a flock of birds flushed from green branches and though he recognized them as crows, their cries sounded foreign. He watched them rise, flashing glossy wings as they broke through shafts of sunlight and then settled in the dark cover of a towering blue fir.

Bahiim kept crows and a few of the most powerful trav-eled in the form of the birds, it was said. Though Elezar doubt-ed that many of them would venture into theses cold northern reaches. Most of the Bahiim he'd met weren't the demon-fight-ing ascetics of their lore. They struck him more as sociable hucksters and storytellers, very much at home amidst the cherry trees and festival feasts of Anacleto city life. But there were exceptions. Elezar had known two in his life.

"Do you know of any Bahiim traveling near here?" Elezar asked.

"One passed through six months ago, though he wasn't what I would have expected. A little like you…" Eski's light green eyes narrowed. Her white brows looked like a scattering of frost on her pale brow. "How is it that you carry a spear marked with the blessings of a witch?"

"How do most men end up with things that aren't theirs?" Elezar replied, but then added, "I took the spear from a man I bested in a fight."

"That's the right of a champion," Eski said easily. "And the charm you wear around your neck? Did you defeat a Bahiim, as well?"

"No, my younger brother gave it to me." Elezar touched the gold pendant very lightly. Before he'd left Milmuraille he'd reversed the Cadeleonian star on the face of the pendant to display the curling form of the sacred Bahiim tree that normally lay hidden against his skin. In Prince Sevanyo's court at Cieloalta he could have been scourged if the wrong person had seen the pretty little tree and now he might be killed if the wrong person saw the star.

He shouldn't have worn either symbol, but the pendant meant more to him than any religion. Nestor had given it to him along with his trust that Elezar—of all their sprawling family—would accept his decision to secretly convert to the Bahiim religion. In this distant land it was the only memento of his brother that he still retained; he wouldn't give it up.

"Most Cadeleonians wear a crossed star," Eski commented.

"You mean the ones who end up as bear bait?" Elezar returned.

Eski's knowing grin displayed long white teeth and assured Elezar that she felt no sympathy for the priests murdered in her homelands.

Elezar didn't particularly hold with a crusade to convert the Mirogoths, himself. It struck him as a waste of good money and brave men. He'd learned quickly that Mirogoths were proud of their ways. They might be savages but they did each other no more harm than devout noblemen when they quarreled. The Mirogoths' talismans, witchcraft and blood oaths suited the hard lives they led in these cold, dark lands. They had no need of a distant, disdainful God, a martyred savior, confessionals or calendars of fasts.

Still, having another brother in the priesthood, Elezar couldn't even feign amusement at the brutal deaths of so many devout men. He took consolation in knowing that Timoteo preached his sermons far from here.

"I'm glad you aren't like those Cadeleonians," Eski said. "My auntie was afraid that you might be and then the grimma's champions would come for you in the night and probably scare off our other customers, as well."

As Elezar understood it, the Sumar grimma's so called champions were six great white snow bears—standing taller than a mounted man and with teeth like ivory daggers. Elezar had no doubt that having one of their party dragged away by such beasts would more than scare away the young Labaran merchants, mercenary guards or not.

Reflexively, Elezar gazed out into the walls of trees and underbrush rising on either side of the path. A huge pale form caught his attention. Then he realized that it was only an outcropping of stone. However as he rode on, Eski trotting alongside, he noticed more of the free-standing stones. Some lay half buried beneath moss and fallen leaves, while others stood free of debris, their exposed surfaces lustrous as polished marble. As his gaze adjusted to searching the deep shadows, he picked out details carved into the massive stones—hunched haunches, long lowered muzzles and beastly jaws. Huge bears and winged horses to the west of the road. Giant serpents and lions with the heads and wings of eagles lined the east. Their numbers grew the further he traveled into Mirogoth lands and more and more, Elezar noted how very life-like the statues seemed; the way the forest shadows played across one winged mare made it look as if its ribs rose and fell; cold mist drifted off it like breath.

"What is his name?" Eski's question interrupted Elezar's growing uneasiness. He glanced down at her and saw that her eyes were on his handsome black stallion.

"Cobre. Be careful of touching him," Elezar warned her. "He's a warhorse and he doesn't give his trust too easily."

"Not even if I found a root to feed him?"

"Just walk beside him. He may grow accustomed to you if he sees that you're no threat."

Eski sighed heavily at the suggestion but continued strolling alongside Elezar's stallion, giving the glossy animal the kind of longing glances that most young women reserved for men like Atreau, or the handsome Labaran merchant riding behind them. Elezar decided that he might as well find out what he could from the girl. Though he didn't think a direct question would get him too far.

"Tell me something, will you?" Elezar asked.

Eski responded with a Mirogoth gesture, somewhere between a nod and a shrug. Elezar had encountered it enough in taverns and markets to understand it as an offhanded affirmative, one that promised nothing.

"How is it that you can stroll barefoot across this ice and frozen mud in a only a thin cloak while those big Mirogoth guards behind us are shivering in their fur coats and riding boots?"

Eski opened her mouth but paused as a sly look came over her.

"Perhaps it's because I am not alive at all but a ghoul wakened from her grave!" Eski looked gleeful and something in her tone reminded Elezar very much of his brother Nestor when he'd been ten years old and prone to lurking behind doors giggling to himself before he leapt out in hopes of startling someone.

"You're no ghoul," Elezar responded.

"How do you know?" Eski demanded, but with a playful expression.

"Because we who've been raised from the dead know our own kind," Elezar replied dryly. Eski looked momentarily startled but then she laughed. Elezar smiled; she had no idea how honest he'd been with her.

"You truly aren't like the other Cadeleonians." She smiled and then said, "I can walk barefoot because I'm known to these stones like you are known to your horse."

She offered her hand experimentally to Cobre, but he snorted at her and she tucked her fingers back into her cloak. "In the summer when I run along the road I sing their names and the stones draw the heat off me and in the winter they give it back to me."

"You're a witch, then?" Elezar asked. Atreau had warned him that every Mirogoth woman was but he wasn't inclined to put too much stock in Atreau's knowledge of Mirogoths, since most of it stemmed from a collection of erotic novels.

Eski answered with that Mirogoth shrug.

"I know some roadcraft. Not so much as my aunt. But we're none of us true witches. We couldn't change men into beasts or command armies of mordwolves and bears as the grimma can. I couldn't turn a giant into stone or awaken it again." She nodded to a stand of hazel trees where another of the giant carved wolves lay curled as if it were sleeping. "The only stones that know me are pebbles and cobblestones and that's only because my mother and her mother's mother for nine generations have traveled these same trails over and over... It's boring, actually."

"You'd rather be elsewhere?"

"I want to see other forests and maybe even a city." Eski didn't look at Elezar but his horse. "More than anything I want to ride a wethra-steed!"

"A wethra-steed? That's aiming high," Elezar said. A man couldn't spend any time on the road, at markets and in taverns making conversation about Mirogoth witch queens without hearing a multitude of wild fantasies concerning all the mythic beasts supposedly under the dominion of the various grimma.

If stories were to be believed, wethra-steeds were born of split lightning and only came to earth to take up a rider whose soul carried the other half of the lightning strike that had birthed them. They ate flesh, pissed mead, and could outdistance the wind. Elezar guessed that if the animals existed at all, they were a hearty northern breed of gray horses much like those that Irabiim traded.

He'd only seen one as a drawing in a book, but he knew that they were bred for a single purpose. "You want to become an emissary for one of the grimma? A witch's herald?"

Eski's entire countenance brightened, but only briefly. Then she scowled and kicked a stone out of her way.

"I should already be one. I've felt my steed calling to me

for two years now and I was going to join my uncle in service to a grimma last fall," Eski told him. "But neither mother nor auntie will allow me to go. They're afraid that we'll soon see another war. They think I'll be killed."

Elezar thought that Eski's mother and aunt were wise women to keep the child from service. The grimma could call upon all the myths they liked, but they would be facing an arsenal of black-barreled cannons forged and refined by Prince Sevanyo's mechanists.

Aloud he said, "Perhaps your family is right to make you wait for more peaceable times."

"How could I die if I were carried by a wethra-steed? The ones serving the Sumar grimma are such powerful, ancient creatures. My heart aches just thinking of them," Eski went on wistfully. "And when my uncle last visited he allowed me to help him tend his beautiful Vakri. Vakri knew right away that I should be riding among the heralds instead of trudging along on the dirt roads. He said that I bore the mark within me and that I'd been chosen."

"Your uncle serves the Sumar grimma?" Elezar had heard that Mirogoth guides traditionally sent their children to serve each of the grimma whose territories they traveled through. But he hadn't hoped to come across ones tied directly to the Sumar grimma so quickly or easily. Still, he didn't hold out much hope of learning the secret to safe passage into the Sumar grimma's sanctum in just one week.

"Yes, my uncle, Jarn, and his beautiful Vakri are Grimma Drigfan's envoy." Eski nodded to the north. "But of course, now my uncle doesn't want me to serve either. He told my aunt to send me south with the next caravan of Irabiim. He and Vakri argued over that half the night and my uncle refused to bed with Vakri and slept up in the tree branches with mother and me."

Elezar frowned. He wasn't certain if it was his grasp of Mirogothic or Eski's youthful telling of the events, but he couldn't quite work out if Vakri was a man or a horse.

"They departed early the next morning and left me behind." Eski heaved another sigh, her expression disheartened. Again she cast a longing glace at Cobre. Elezar couldn't remember a time in his life when he hadn't known and ridden horses. But then that was the privilege of a Cadeleonian nobleman. Sword and saddle from infancy to the grave. He doubted he could truly understand what it meant to a Mirogoth to be carried on the back of one of their mythic gray chargers, but he did know what it was to want something with all his soul and be denied.

Despite his better sense, he felt a kind of sympathy for this gangly, wild girl and her frustrated longing.

"If there's time and light after we make camp this evening," Elezar offered. "I'll introduce you properly to Cobre and see if he won't allow you on his back for a bit."

"You'd do that?" Eski stopped in her tracks, looking as stunned as if Elezar had just proposed marriage.

"Well, it couldn't hurt to learn to ride a common horse before you lay your claim to your wethra-steed, could it?" Elezar replied as if it were nothing but common sense.

Joy lit Eski's pale face and she let out cry of delight and bounded forward like she'd been lifted from the mud, ice and darkness of their path and transported into a glorious ballroom.

"Thank you, thank you, thank you!" She beamed at Elezar as she twirled and skipped alongside him.

"You're welcome," Elezar replied. He wondered briefly what the men behind made of all this. "But I don't think your mother or your aunt would be quite so happy if they knew, so let's keep this between us, shall we?"

"Of course!" Eski agreed. Her radiant, guileless grin assured Elezar that within the week everyone traveling with them—as well as any random passersby—would know.

Three nights later, Elezar lay wrapped in his heavy cloak beneath the moonless night sky in the shadows of dark trees. The Labaran merchants and their Mirogoth guards sheltered in a nearby cave. Just watching the light of their fire flicker over the carvings in the stone walls and drawing in a breath of the stale air, he'd known he would never find sleep in that moldering, rocky hollow. So despite the biting cold and wind he took himself outside and made his bed beneath a great gnarled oak, near the horses.

Yet the dank, dead smell followed him, rolling into his dreams and enclosing him between decaying stone walls, where the red flames of torches flicked and spat over his brother's bloodied body.

Even dreaming, Elezar knew these images to be figments of memory dredged up from his past. It was all done and gone. The men were dead. He'd seen to that with his own hands and blade. And still the terror he'd felt as a boy of eleven churned through him.

And at the same time, in his dream, he rode proudly at his eldest brother's side, beaming with satisfaction that this day their hunting party would go where he pleased in recognition of his eleventh birthday. His brother's school companions played at making him the leader of the hunt, and Elezar knew they teased him, but he still enjoyed being brought into the company of men so much older and more worldly.

His tall, muscular brother, Isandro, wanted to take a boar, but one of his more handsome friends had put it in Elezar's mind that they should all climb up into the crumbling ruins of an ancient barrow and test their courage against the ghost stories told by the city priests. Easygoing and indulgent, Isandro relented to Elezar's demand.

And so he and his brother rode deep into the forest and fought their way to the dark heart of the barrow, where they were easily trapped and cut down by the men Isandro had called his friends.

Beyond acting as bait to help lure Isandro, Elezar had meant nothing to them. They laid him open and left him to bleed to death in a heap of rotting leaves and decayed animal nests. It was Isandro who had defied Cadeleonian holy law and then made the fatal mistake of confiding in a friend. Now claiming to put him to trial by ordeal, the group of six young men beat, bled and tortured Isandro, castrating and disemboweling him before at last severing his head. All the while Elezar looked on from the shadows—his thigh slashed open from knee to hip—screaming without producing a sound.

Elezar bolted upright, gasping and clutching his scarred right thigh. He thought he would be sick. He fought the urge, calmed himself and yet could not keep the tears from spilling down his face. He wiped at them furiously.

What was the point of weeping now? His regret changed nothing.

He'd let his brother's murderers ride away that day and had kept their crimes to himself in a child's attempt to shield his brother's shame. He couldn't have stood for their mother to have discovered the real horror of it—or to have endured the king judging her best beloved son rightly slain for his crimes. Though if she'd known the truth she might have understood why Elezar trained so hard after that and why years later he challenged and killed six of his brother's old companions one by one in dueling rings.

Though just as likely, knowing would only have broken her heart.

Elezar shook his head. It was done now: all six noblemen dead by his hand and the truth buried with them. He couldn't regret their deaths, only the loss that had made each of those brutal killings necessary and inevitable.

He leaned back against the rough trunk of the oak, taking in the cold white stars that shone between the bare black branches. The eerie call of an owl echoed through the stands of trees and a fox cried as if in answer.

Elezar closed his eyes. He wondered if those wild creatures ever dreamed of the deaths of their prey or if the cruelty of hunters ever troubled their sleep?

Fourteen days later, as Elezar packed away the map he'd been painstakingly filling in, Eski's broad-boned aunt, Elrath, approached him through the twilight gloom. She waited silently while Elezar rubbed Cobre down and offered him oat seeds as a reward for his patience in carrying Eski most of the day. The stallion greedily devoured the extra handfuls of oat seeds Elezar offered him then he gently nuzzled Elezar, warming his cheeks with his breath. At last Elezar turned him out to join the other horses grazing in their makeshift corral.

Across the glade, Elezar could see the rest of their company already gathered around a fire in the shelter of an immense stone bear. Eski flirted with the handsome Labaran, while two of the Mirogoth guards displayed their little treasures of bone hilt knives and embossed leather gauntlets to the other merchants. Another guard attended a small cook pot.

They were all of them filthy from travel and exertion. Chalky gray mud spattered Elezar's clothes, hands, face and hair. He reeked of sweat and the wool horse blanket that he slept in every night. His arms and back ached from two full days of clearing fallen trees from the road and then helping to push the Labarans' heavy wagon through deep, muddy bogs.

Now the wagon stood half full of mink, sable, fox, hind and even seal skins and it required guarding.

"Do you want me to take first watch tonight?" Elezar asked Elrath.

"The mercenaries will see to that. It's what they are paid for." She drew closer, though Elezar had noticed that both Eski's mother and Elrath, always kept just out of easy reach. They moved with the wary watchfulness of feral creatures. He suspected that if it hadn't been for himself and the Labaran merchants neither woman would have built a fire, or bothered to cook the clutch of birds they'd netted for supper.

"Will you walk with me?" Elrath asked. "There is something I think you would like to see but the light will not last long."

"Of course," Elezar replied despite his uneasiness. Total darkness fell fast in this forest and a stranger could all too easily stumble off a cliff or into a sinkhole.

Still, he followed Elrath away from the warm light of the fire and out into the shadows of fragrant spruce. She moved quickly and Elezar just barely kept abreast of her without missing his footing. He'd grown more accustomed to navigating the ice-slick rocks and deceptively solid expanses of moss. They climbed steadily up a steep hill to a cliff where the trees thinned to frail shoots and the dusk blue sky spread overhead in an open expanse of waking stars. The land below looked flat as if it had been cut from black velvet.

Elezar halted well short of the cliff's edge but Elrath stepped out to the very brink of the precipice. She turned back to Elezar. Her round pale gaze and the muted motions of her body beneath her ragged cloak reminded Elezar of the white owls he'd heard calling through the forest. He almost expected her to leap from the cliff and take flight.

Instead she pointed out at the dark silhouettes of the land below them.

"That shining little ribbon is the Raccroc River, winding its way down to Milmuraille and the sea and all this darkness beyond it is our land. Mirogoth lands."

Elezar didn't know what he was meant to take from this but he nodded.

"It's a vast country," he said at last because Elrath seemed to expect a response.

"Yes, an immense, unconquerable wilderness but not populous. Our children are few and each is precious to us." Elrath eyed Elezar intensely then. "We are not so many as you Cadeleonians. We do not clear the trees or tear up the earth so that we can fill slums with our breeding. We do not happily throw our children before warhorses and cannons."

"No, of course not," Elezar replied. Now he thought he knew where this conversation was leading. "I didn't intend any offense in teaching Eski to ride. Certainly, I wouldn't suggest she be sent into battle."

"Send her, no. You're not such a man as that." Elrath tilted her head slightly. She looked younger in the twilight and very much like Eski. "I've watched you with her and with the Labarans as well. You would not do them harm. But you Cadeleonians bring danger with you when you walk among us. You carry war into our midst and you do not even know it."

Elezar studied Elrath, trying to understand just what it was that she wanted to convey to him and what assurance she wanted in return.

"I haven't come here to start a war."

"You haven't come to buy furs," Elrath snapped.

"No, I haven't," Elezar admitted. He was tired, hungry and sore and lying seemed like a waste of time. "I've come to try and parlay with the Sumar grimma. I'm sent to discover what can be done to keep the peace between her and my own people."

"Keep your priests from her lands," Elrath responded. That struck Elezar as an obvious solution as well, but not one he could carry back to Prince Sevanyo, much less the royal bishop.

"Perhaps," Elezar said. "But why now? Why after a decade of allowing priests to wander where they will through the wilds does the Sumar grimma suddenly order them to be dragged from their meager chapels and wantonly murdered? What has changed in the last few years that has made her lash out so violently against the Cadeleonian church?"

"Drigfan is a grimma. She doesn't have to answer to you or your church," Elrath said, as if they were discussing the whims of a creature far beyond mortal understanding.

"All right, she isn't answerable to me." Elezar peered past Elrath at the dark forest that seemed to stretch to the horizon. Somewhere out there lay the Sumar grimma's sanctum, but he would never find it on his own. "But perhaps she should make an account to you and yours, since her actions threaten to bring the full force of the Cadeleonian armies into your forest and against your children. Do you even know why she's decided to go out of her way to provoke the Cadeleonian crown and church?"

"No." An expression like sharp pain flickered across Elrath's face. "My brother has told me that she has good reason."

"Has he told you that it's worth his life? Your sister's? Or yours and Eski's?"

Elrath glared into Elezar's face for a long, silent moment and he thought she might try to strike him. Then she turned her attention to the view beyond the precipice. Elezar followed her gaze. Before them the sky dimmed, slowly swallowing up the silhouettes of the land below. Only the stars remained visible, shivering in the halos of their own cold light.

"You can send me back to Milmuraille. You could even have a go at shoving me off this cliff," Elezar said at last. "But after you've sent me home or to the three hells, I can promise you that the next Cadeleonians who arrive here won't be alone and they won't be concerned with keeping the peace."

Elrath sighed heavily and out in the darkness a fox cried out.

"You're traveling with us hoping that we will betray the path to the Sumar grimma's sanctum to you." Elrath sounded not only frustrated, but tired as well.

"I'm not asking you to betray anything," Elezar answered. "Just help me however you can. Even if that only means leaving me to my own methods."

"I could leave you," Elrath said. "By morning we would be gone and you would be alone and lost or more likely laying at the bottom of a cliff with a broken neck—"

"And other Cadeleonians would still come with their cannons and warhorses," Elezar said. "You have a chance to stop them, but only if you help me."

Elrath said nothing, but Elezar heard her sigh and then kick a stone off the cliff. It clattered to the ground below after a long fall.

"Eski's right. You don't seem like the other Cadeleonians," she muttered.

Then she reached out and gripped Elezar's hand. Her fingers felt nearly as tough as a falcon's claw, but her skin was warm. She led him away from the precipice and back down the cliff toward the campfire. When she spoke again her voice sounded amused.

"You're much more annoying than the others... But you may well be the first in nearly a hundred years to walk into the Sumar grimma's sanctum of your own free will."

"You'll take me there?" Elezar asked.

He felt Elrath offer him that ubiquitous Mirogoth shrug.

They wound their way through the fir trees, skirting the campfire where their companions waited. Elezar glimpsed both Eski and the handsome Labaran scanning the darkness and he wondered if they searched for him. He felt tired and hungry and longed to join them beside the fire. Instead he followed Elrath to the corral where Cobre stood as if waiting for him.

"I will tell you a way in," Elrath said at last. "But you will have to find your own way out."

CHAPTER
SIX

Gathering tiny white pebbles from a frigid streamed in the dead of night struck Elezar as a quick way for a fool to freeze his hands off or, worse, slip and drown himself. However, he'd already committed a good hour to the endeavor and wasn't about to give up now. He felt blindly through the glacial waters, dragging a single smooth stone over the worn river rocks at his feet. A stone of passage, Elrath had called it as she'd traced a rough finger over the sinuous lines carved into its polished surface.

Careful of his footing, he waded deeper into the stream. The freezing current lapped over his bare calves and forearms. His submerged hands ached and his naked feet felt like blocks of ice. He moved as quickly as he could, sweeping his hands over the river rocks, grazing the white stone of passage across countless others pebbles and rocks that made up the streamed.

Nothing happened. There was no result but continuing darkness and the gurgle of cold waters lapping the living warmth from him. He tried again. Still nothing. Tremors of cold shuddered up his muscles, but those at least assured him that he could still feel something.

Then he took another step and scraped the stone of passage along a string of river rocks at his feet. A swath of pebbles sparked like flint struck with steel and then ignited. White light flared through the water, illuminating Elezar's pale, hairy legs as well as the rocky streamed, green rivergrass and a school of startled frost carp. A burst of warmth rushed from the rocks up over Elezar's bare skin. His fingers tingled and his toes burned in the sudden heat. In the brief time that the flash lasted Elezar quickly snatched up the shining pebbles, just as he'd gathered dozens of others. Then the night closed in again, leaving Elezar to peer through the murky dark to the bank of the stream.

"Are you certain there isn't any easier way to do this?" Elezar inquired as he slogged back to the bank and dropped the smooth rocks at Elrath's feet.

"There could be," Elrath allowed. "But I don't know it."

Elezar peered through the gloom at the heap of stones he'd fished from the creek. Either his eyes were at last adjusting to the darkness or the sky had grown lighter, because he could much more readily make out the mound of small, smooth rocks—something in the order of fifty, but none much larger than the tip of his little finger—as well as Elrath's thoughtful expression.

"Enough pebbles, you think?" Elezar asked.

"Probably," Elrath replied.

Elezar smiled into his beard. Mirogoths certainly weren't a people likely to overcommit themselves in a conversation. Just beyond Elrath, Cobre lay sleeping beneath a waxcone pine tree. The big warhorse's soft snores drifted through the still of the night. Well, at least one of them had gotten his supper and some rest.

"You should be on your way before the sun rises. Otherwise Eski will be up and running right after you," Elrath told him.

Elezar clambered quickly up the rocky bank, relieved to get out of the water and dry his wet numb limbs in the folds of his cloak. Once his hands stopped shaking he gathered up the small stones and filled his pockets with them. Then he reached for his wool socks and heavy leather boots.

"Leave them. You will need to feel the path under your feet as much as see it." Elrath crouched down beside him. He wasn't certain how he'd won her trust, but where hours earlier she'd kept out of arm's reach she now hunched so near him that he could see the tiny bone beads woven through her white braids. He smelled juniper and mushrooms on her body.

"Mirogoth stones don't know you," Elrath said. "But the pebbles you've gathered are sisters to those that guard the grimma's road. When they touch their sisters they flash with recognition, but only briefly. They remain hot much longer. You will need to feel their warmth under your feet if you are to make their vei your own."

"Vei? I don't know that word," Elezar admitted. This didn't seem the time to be guessing at meanings. He already felt far enough out of his depth.

"It's a course taken. A path that always leads you where you must go..." Elrath paused as if searching for better words.

Only once had Elezar traveled a road that led anywhere the traveler wished to go. But that route had crossed an unearthly realm of devils and required Javier to ignite the furious light of the white hell to guide them through. The pile of weakly glowing pebbles filling his pockets seemed a poor substitute if he had to pass through that darkness again.

"Do you mean I should take the Old Road of the Bahiim?" Elezar asked, though the thought of ever traveling that way again chilled him far worse than the frigid stream had.

"No!" Elrath's pale lips curled in revulsion and she pulled her cloak closer around her shoulders. "Bahiim hunt demons and travel through realms of darkness. They stir monsters that are better left at rest and they invade the paths of the dead to go where they wish, not where they should. There is no light in the heart of a Bahiim. No open place for their vei to awaken and lead them to their true fates. But you will travel the forest as you should and your vei will awaken."

"I'm not so sure there's a place for a vei in me either."

"Of course there is," Elrath replied as if he'd made an absurd claim.

But the truth was that as Elezar had traveled the Old Road and looked into the darkness of the Sorrowlands, he'd seen Isandro's tortured remains there and ridden on without a word.

Elezar knew he'd done terrible, cruel things: killed honest men along with the wicked and even raised his blade against friends. Jealous passion had blazed through him like madness, distorting and destroying his idea of himself as a man of sanctity, loyalty and honesty. And in the end he'd felt both desolate and relieved when his friends Javier and Kiram had fled Cadeleon leaving him behind. The torment in his heart had died giving way to a dull darkness. After five years Elezar couldn't imagine it ever leaving him. He wasn't even certain that he wanted it to.

"I've watched you," Elrath stated firmly and Elezar remembered that she had told him as much before. "You're a Cadeleonian but not a liar, nor a coward. In your heart you are searching for something. In that, you remind me of my younger brother. And if Jarn could win Vakri and become a grimma's herald then you can certainly find your way to her door."

"Or die trying, as my mother would say," Elezar replied.

Elrath flashed her crooked teeth in a quick smile then rose to her feet. Elezar stood as well.

"Throw the stones and follow their flash and fire to the Sumar grimma's sanctum. Once you step onto the path your vei will guide you. Stay true to your cause—true to your heart," Elrath told him. "And once you are there remember what I've told you. Stay on your path and the grimma will have to hear you out."

"I will. Thank you for your help." Elezar bowed to her out of Cadeleonian courtesy and the gesture brought another softer smile to Elrath's weathered face.

"Keep your war from coming and that will be thanks enough for me." Then she turned and in only a few steps melted into the shadows and brambles of the forest.

Elezar stuffed his socks into his boots and slung them over his shoulder. His feet tingled as if they were already going numb from the chill of the damp, frost-laden ground. Nothing for it now but to get moving, Elezar thought. In his left hand he gripped Elrath's polished white stone—a stone of passage, she had called it. With his right hand he plucked several pebbles from his pocket and then threw them before him.

He expected to see only the small flares that had lit the stream, little more than the flickering of fireflies in summer. Instead an immense stone blazed to life, throwing light up into the overhanging branches of the black yew trees. Beyond it a dozen more stones lit up in a straight line. Birds startled from the trees and a pair of foxes bounded away.

Elezar moved quickly, racing over the moss and mud chasing the light and feeling amazed at how deeply the heat of the stones radiated through him. The light faded almost as quickly as it had blazed up but the warmth guided Elezar's steps. He tossed out two more pebbles and they skipped across the ground, lighting his path further ahead of him.

At his back Elezar heard a concerned whinny and the clatter of Cobre's hooves as the stallion roused himself to follow. Elezar wasn't surprised. Cobre hated to be left behind even when it might be for his own good. Elezar guessed it had been too much to expect that the stallion would stay where Elezar left him in Elrath's care.

He'd been Elezar's one constant companion through the chaos of battle, across the desolation of the Sorrowlands and during the reckless years that followed. The big black stallion reached Elezar's side and gave a nervous toss of his head. Elezar soothed him, scratching his neck and jaw.

"Sure you're up for another of my terrible adventures?" Elezar asked. His words didn't matter, but Cobre always relaxed hearing a calm voice. The stallion exhaled softly against Elezar's cheek, sharing his breath as if it were a pledge of loyalty. Elezar stroked the stallion's velvety nose and Cobre calmed.

"Come along then."

Elezar sent another small rock skipping across the forest floor, throwing off light like ripples on the surface of a lake. He chased the light and Cobre trotted alongside him. Summer warmth enfolded him. Light glowed around him, illuminating the tall trees, mossy rocks and the winding trail like sunlight breaking through banks of clouds. A scent like fallow fields filled Elezar's lungs as he ran.

Sprinting faster than the light faded, Elezar didn't look too long or hard at the strange angles of the surrounding shadows or the gleaming strings of icicles adorning the bare branches overhead. He simply ran, accepting the path offered to him. Perhaps exhaustion had worn him to delirium or maybe Elrath had been right about traveling some magical path—his vei— but as he dashed along the glowing trail he felt as carefree as a child, skipping stones and racing alongside his horse.

Bounding over fallen branches and leaping across narrow creeks of meltwater, he remembered the delight of running, sloshing and jumping his way across the countryside. His heart hammered in exhilaration and his muscles hummed with the pleasure of exertion. Pure happiness came as a relief and he threw himself into the simple joy that he'd thought long lost to him.

Next to him Cobre cantered and kicked like a playful foal.

Inexorably the gleaming trail grew brighter and led Elezar farther down from a landscape of rocky cliffs and ice into rolling eastern valleys. Hardy pine and fir trees left behind, Elezar descended past stands of beech, walnut and oak and then at last broke into an open meadow.

He flung four pebbles ahead of him and a wide avenue of blazing light burst up, illuminating his surroundings like a morning sun. A vast green field of wild grass and flowers rolled out on either side of him and standing in scattered groups, hundreds of dun reindeer grazed among them. All of their heads came up at once, many displaying fierce antlers. Their dark eyes fixed upon Elezar. But it wasn't the watchful stares of the deer that made Elezar's heart lurch in his chest or caused Cobre to snort and stamp nervously at the ground. The bears did that. At least twelve of them, golden-red and standing on their hind legs among the reindeer like shaggy shepherds.

Elezar had encountered bears in the wilds of Cadeleon— he'd tracked and killed two after they mauled farmers outside of Anacleto—but those dark rangy creatures behaved nothing like the beasts surrounding him now. No Cadeleonian bear would have stood among this sea of fawns, does and stags in such placid silence. For that matter, he couldn't imagine any breed of Cadeleonian deer grazing serenely while towering predators watched over their young.

Cobre gave another agitated whinny and Elezar caught his bridle. He shared Cobre's fear. His heart hammered in his chest but he kept his voice soft and even as he calmed Cobre. The stallion drew close beside him, ready for him to mount and for the two of them to fight their way through these beasts. Elezar slid his hand down to where the spear hung from Cobre's saddle.

But he didn't pull it free nor did he draw his sword. He watched the way the bears seemed to study his actions. They regarded Elezar in a curious, almost human manner. One cocked its head and another peered at him as if expecting to recognize his face. Were they all witches' familiars? Were they men and women whom the grimma had enthralled turned into animals? Elrath had told him he would encounter such creatures but somehow he'd imagined something more in the way of a little black cat or a fox. Not bears—certainly not a dozen huge red bears.

"I'm sent as an emissary to the grimma of Sumar." Elezar raised the stone of passage. "I mean you and yours no harm."

One of the bears blew out a snort of white breath. Another made a low clacking noise with its teeth. Elezar strained to make out the reactions of the others, standing farther away but the light of the path around him was fading fast to darkness. Then one of the bears dropped to all fours and started for him. Elezar knew he had enough time to either scatter more pebbles or pull his spear free. He doubted the spear would do him or Cobre any good in the dark, so he hurled another handful of pebbles out and was answered with a flood of light.

Elezar swore and narrowed his eyes against the sudden glare. As it faded to the glow of a summer afternoon, Elezar found that the charging bear had stopped just short of him. It slowly extended its big head to Elezar's hand, snuffling at the stone of passage. Then it rose again onto its hind legs and regarded Elezar's face. Up close the earthy musk of the animal's body filled Elezar's lungs and its hot breath rolled over his face in plumes of salmon and anise. Elezar fought the reflex to draw for his sword or better yet get the distance of a spear between himself and the creature.

He returned the bear's gaze, meeting those pale green eyes as if he were staring down a common guard. For all that it looked like a wild animal, he reassured himself, there was a human mind controlling it. Arguing with a human being seemed far less dangerous than fighting a bear.

"My business is with Grimma Drigfan." Elezar felt anxious sweat beading the back of his neck but he kept his voice even. "If you are loyal to her you will either move aside and let me pass or better yet run ahead and announce my coming so that she can prepare to meet with me."

The bear blew out a steaming breath and Elezar reflexively dropped his free hand to the hilt of his sword. When the bear leaned in toward him, Elezar held his ground. The bear looked to have a solid forty stone of weight on him, and its powerful jaws and long ivory claws could easily tear through the leather protecting his body; still, Elezar's stance wasn't all bluff. He'd killed armed men with a very fast thrust through the neck and a twist that severed the head. At such close range he might manage the strike before the bear could react... Though he felt loathe to gamble his life on that.

His muscles trembled with the racing drive of his pulse. His breath came fast and deep, the air feeling icy in his lungs.

"Well?" Elezar demanded.

The bear held his gaze for just an instant longer then turned its head aside and dropped back down to all fours. It let out a very low rumble that seemed to vibrate through Elezar's chest then it charged ahead along the fading path of light.

Rushing to announce Elezar's approach to Grimma Drigfan, he guessed.

Amazed relief washed over Elezar and if it hadn't been for the audience of unnatural creatures still watching him he would have dropped to his knees and laughed for joy at the sudden reprieve. Instead he patted Cobre, praising the stallion for his courage, then he mounted and rode after the bear before he lost it in the fading light. He was done with tripping along on foot; he wanted his spear at hand and Cobre beneath him.

The animals in the surrounding fields took little note of his passage now. A few reindeer flicked their ears as he cantered past but most ignored him and returned to grazing. Though more than once Elezar thought he glimpsed a slim rider atop some huge mount following him. But every time he turned to look all he saw were fluttering shadows dancing beneath stands of silver birch and willow trees.

He turned his attention quickly back to the glowing path before him as he and Cobre left the open meadow behind and plunged into a wood of willow and birch. The rush of flowing water sounded through the still of the night and twice they crossed narrow stone bridges where bears watched them pass from the banks of the river below. The air felt warmer and the sky grew faintly lighter.

Through the few breaks in the trees, Elezar made out a faint golden glow lighting the jagged line of the eastern horizon. Light crept in through the pale green leaves and white birch tree trunks. The overgrown path of moss and gleaming white cobbles ahead seemed dim in comparison. But Elezar no longer needed the light of the stones to direct him.

Not only could he clearly follow the tracks of the bear running far ahead of him, but between the trees he caught glimpses of pale angular towers and white stone walls.

Gold rays of morning sun perfectly outlined the Sumar grimma's sanctum where it rose, white and imperious as a mountaintop dominating the green earth at its foot. As Elezar drew near he noted how unlike any Cadeleonian palace or fortress this sanctum appeared. The walls betrayed no hint of masonry or brick work, looking instead like slabs of solid stone ripped from some distant quarry and hurled into the lush, green meadowland. The towers rose like spires of raw rock, unrefined and ragged as if they'd been dropped into place by passing giants. But utterly at odds with the craggy, unfinished surfaces of the walls hunched four immense statues, each nearly as tall as the walls themselves and all carved in exquisite, if grotesque, detail.

At first glance they reminded Elezar of a party of leering, gash-mouthed men slouching over the sanctum's iron gates like drunks lingering outside a closed tavern. Despite their satirical features, some unnervingly life-like aspect haunted the statues. The stone wolves and bears he'd seen while traveling through the Mirogoth forest had possessed the same quality. Countless natural details of flesh and muscle, expression and stance lent them a distinct individuality, making it seem as if these four giants had been standing there before the grimma's gates then been unexpectedly turned stone.

As Elezar drew nearer he realized that these four giants were not quite as human as he'd first thought. Their fingers and toes elongated and curled like knotted roots clutching the stone walls of the sanctum and sinking into the ground. Stone saplings and grasses sprouted from their backs like a forest of body hair. Branches of beautifully chiseled flowers and leaves curled around the jagged horns crowning their skulls, and each of them sported a stumpy tail that looked like nothing so much as a huge, gnarled carrot root. Their dangling genitals appeared nearly the same, though Elezar quickly surmised that either two of the statues had suffered significant losses since they'd been carved or they represented brawny, hard-faced females.

Trolls, he guessed. Mirogoth lore abounded with stories of grimma binding the giant creatures to their wills and trapping them in stone. Labaran books were filled with funny little illustrations of the awkward creatures, but seeing them represented at such a grand scale produced a much different effect. The thought that these four could actually have been alive sent a shudder down Elezar's spine as he rode alongside one's massive foot. The thing could have crushed him and Cobre with a tap of its heel.

Beneath the statues, the sanctum gates stood open, the portcullis raised like a gaping mouth full of jagged iron spikes. A warm breeze rolled over Elezar like a fragrant breath. Past the portcullis two reddish bears stood in the shadows, as if awaiting him. Perhaps they were—their fellow bear must have passed through several minutes before. However, the silhouettes of these two struck Elezar as wrong.

Were the bears holding spears?

Why that should have struck Elezar as strange, after the dream-like quality of the entire night, he didn't know, but he slowed Cobre. He squinted at the figures beyond the portcullis. Not bears, he decided, but stout guardsmen dressed in bearskins with the dead animals' faces drawn over their own like hoods. They neither called out a warning nor greeting to Elezar but stood still and silent as he rode past them.

He passed through the portcullis and crossed the threshold of the immense courtyard then drew Cobre to a halt.

A sea of white cobblestones and wildflowers spilled out before him and arches of jade-green stone rose over him like immense trees. Flowering vines cascaded down from the arches' heights while brambles of blooming thimbleberry and mountain grape clambered up. A fragrant, warm breeze rolled over Elezar and the air hummed with the flights of bees and butterflies. The Sumar sanctum seemed both outside the land Elezar knew and beyond the season as well. Here a perfume of summer fruit and flowers filled Elezar's lungs. Morning dew beaded leaves and cobwebs that should have shone white with frost.

When Elezar blinked he felt radiant light shining through his closed eyelids. Heat of a summer sun beat down on his bare skin. But when he opened his eyes he found himself gazing up at highest spire of a distant white tower. For just an instant he thought something brilliant green flashed from the white stone filial. It could be nothing but the fabled viridian witchflame of the Sumar grimma.

Then it was gone and Elezar lowered his gaze from the witchflame that he couldn't see but felt blazing over him.

In the shadow of cascading violet wisteria, beneath an archway, a shaggy golden bear waited for Elezar. It raised a big paw and beckoned once before turning to run farther into the maze of archways and overgrown vines.

Elezar followed the beast, and did his best not to feel unnerved when he caught sight of other wild animals darting through the archways, trailing his passage into the heart of the sanctum. Stags, foxes, a lynx, wolves and even a great cat of some northern breed stalked him. From the heights of the archways, gray hawks and gold eagles took flight and circled him as if he were a rabbit flushed from a briar.

He remembered Fedeles informing him that other envoys had been torn apart by wild animals and realized these must be the very creatures who had dispatched them. Then he wished that he hadn't made the connection.

He felt Cobre's tension shuddering through his body and stroked the stallion's neck reassuringly. "We have a stone of passage. We'll be fine," he murmured just to let Cobre hear his voice. "After this it'll all be pastures and mares."

Soon they reached the clearing where the white tower shot up like a splintered mountain and the cobblestones below lay pale and exposed as bone. The stones formed a perfect ring around the tower and not a single moss or flower grew there.

A tall woman with hair the color of polished copper stood atop the steps before the carven tower doors. She wore a white fur cloak and so many strings of cascading, polished stones that they fell over the curves of her large breasts and full hips like a gown. Her feet were bare and only a hunting knife hung from the braided leather belt wound around her waist.

Between her and Elezar stood six white bears. Each was twice the size of the ones Elezar had seen on the road, but all standing so still that for an instant he'd mistaken them for statues. Elezar reined Cobre to a halt at the edge of the cobblestones. Behind him and on either side he noted that the beasts stalking him had stilled as well. Even the birds circled the stone perimeter of the tower but did not fly over it.

From the corner of his eye Elezar caught the motion of a figure moving though the lush foliage on his left. Elezar felt almost startled to recognize a man among all these animals. He moved like a youth, quick and slim, and something about his round eyes and blonde braids reminded Elezar a little of Eski, though the man's expression made him think more of Elrath. Little more than a leather cloak, a loincloth and a knife belt protected his pale, naked body, though around his neck hung a string of polished stones, each one very like the stone of passage Elrath had given Elezar.

As if noting the same thing, the man's gaze lingered on the stone in Elezar's left hand. When he looked up at Elezar's face it was with curiosity.

"You do not come to us by chance." The man spoke softly in Mirogothic.

"No," Elezar replied. He didn't intend to betray Elrath, not even to a man whom he suspected was her brother. "Someone wiser than me showed me how to find my vei. That has led me here."

"So the stone you hold…?"

"Came to me fairly," Elezar assured him.

The man gave an easy nod and his hand fell away from the knife at his hip. He turned his attention to Cobre, smiling at the stallion almost as happily as Eski might have.

"He is a beautiful mount—and so brave. It makes my spirit

lift just to look upon him. His willingness to carry you even to this place does you credit. But Grimma Drigfan will allow only one emissary to stand before her in the circle of her wards."

Elezar nodded and swung down from Cobre's back. He retrieved his saddlebag. Then briefly he allowed Cobre to nuzzle his hair and face. At last he forced himself to proffer Cobre's reins to the man. Whatever fate awaited him across these white cobblestones he didn't want Cobre to suffer it as well.

"If I'm… gone too long, would you see to it that he's fed and watered?" Elezar asked.

"Vakri and I will look after him." The man accepted the reins and laid his hand easily on Cobre's neck. Normally the stallion wouldn't have allowed such presumption, but he relaxed under this Mirogoth's touch as if the man were one of his favorite grooms.

"Thank you." Elezar knew he couldn't ask for more. He turned to the sea of cobblestones before him and felt his heartbeat quicken as he met the warning gazes of the six white bears awaiting him. Instinctively his free right hand dropped to his sword hilt, but he stopped himself. An envoy did not approach with a naked blade. In Cadeleonian court they were not permitted to carry weapons at all, but Elezar wasn't prepared to go quite that far here. He let his hand drop to the pocket of his coat suddenly remembered the pebbles remaining there.

Elrath had told him that they would lead him to the Sumar grimma, and she hadn't misled him so far. He tossed a pebble out before him. Not only did five stones light to a shining gold blaze, but Elezar heard faint notes rise from them like the ringing of delicate bells. He stepped out onto the stones. His bare feet felt raw from running over rocks all night, but the warmth of the stones soothed them a little. He threw another pebble and continued. As he walked the white bears closed in around him and Grimma Drigfan watched him with a narrow, displeased gaze. Elezar could feel the hot breath of one of the bears at the nape of his neck but he kept walking on the path of illuminated stones, and all around him the musical notes seemed to build to an eerie fanfare.

A yard from the grimma, Elezar misstepped, allowing his left foot to fall on a cold, dull cobble. Instantly one of the bears lashed out. Elezar jerked back but not quickly enough. Ivory claws raked across his calf and shin, ripping deep furrows open. Elezar choked on an enraged howl of pain. In fury, he tore his sword from its scabbard and spun on the bear.

"Come and I'll end you, beast!" Elezar roared.

But the bear didn't charge him. None of them did. They waited at the edge of the shining cobbles, just beyond the reach of his sword. And they watched Elezar with something like anticipation in their green eyes. One of them lifted a paw and, gazing straight into Elezar's face, licked his vivid red blood from its long claws. Another bear pulled back its lips in a surly grin.

They were baiting him, Elezar realized, exploiting his rage to lure him off his path. And suddenly he understood why Elrath had been so intent that he not leave his path—his vei as she'd called it. It wasn't just a means to find the grimma. It and the stone of passage offered him protection—the only protection he could rely upon.

With that thought, Elezar's anger cooled, though the pain in his leg seemed to only grow greater. He sheathed his sword. Then he threw down another pebble. There were only a few left to him now and he had to stop himself from wondering how he would make his way out of the grimma's sanctum.

Hot blood poured down his calf, and he didn't dare to look to see how badly he'd been injured. His leg hurt like hell but it held him. That was all that mattered now as he closed the distance between himself and the Sumar grimma.

He stopped at the steps of the jagged white tower and knelt on his right knee as if he were in the presence of a civilized queen and not a half -naked, glowering witch queen.

"My respect to you, Grimma Drigfan, ruler of all the Sumar lands." Elezar met the woman's cold gaze. She wasn't beautiful, but strikingly fierce and imperious. Her wide-set green eyes tilted upward at an almost unnerving angle, and her long scarlet mouth looked like it hid far too many teeth. Elezar lowered his eyes respectfully. His gaze fell on Grimma Drigfan's bare, callused feet. Her skin looked tough as leather and her long, arching nails seemed nearly as thick as horns.

"I come to you as an emissary of peace and goodwill from Prince Sevanyo Sagrada of Cadeleon," Elezar said.

"The goodwill of a Cadeleonian prince?" Grimma Drigfan stated with a cold smile. "Will you scatter hen's teeth before my feet as well?"

"No, Grimma," Elezar replied. "Prince Sevanyo is heir to our kingdom. His word can raise armies and destroy citadels. But his goodwill is true as gold." He drew the saddlebag down from his shoulder and withdrew the silver coffer that Fedeles had entrusted into his care.

Careful not to leave the safety of the cobbles where he knelt, Elezar stretched forward, laying the coffer at the grimma's feet. Intense pain flared through his left calf as he moved, but he suppressed any sign of the hurt. He wouldn't give the grimma or her companions that satisfaction. Still, a chill filled his gut as he bowed his head and glimpsed the wide scarlet wash of his own blood pooling across the white cobblestone. He was bleeding badly.

Grimma Drigfan took the coffer but didn't open it immediately. Elezar watched her, clenching his jaw against the growing pain shooting through his calf. She lifted a string of glittering blue stones from her breast and held them over the coffer. The stones caught the morning light, flashing a cerulean blue as brilliant as a damselfly.

Grimma Drigfan dropped the stones back to her chest and opened the silver coffer. She tossed the strings of pearls to the ground as if they were rat droppings but obviously found the jewel-studded gold necklace beautiful. Even to Elezar's eyes it looked to be a treasure. The lustrous gold beads were each nearly as large as his palm; diamonds and rubies glittered across their surfaces, forming the constellations of a summer night. Grimma Drigfan caressed the gleaming necklace and lifted it to her lips as if she were kissing a pet stoat. Then she wrapped it around her left wrist and tossed the silver coffer to the waiting grasp of one of her great white bears.

"These ancient stones do please me," she said at last. "But they are far less than your priest has robbed from me."

"Robbed?" Elezar asked. Why hadn't he been told about this—unless Fedeles hadn't known either? "Forgive my ignorance, but what has been taken?"

"You do not know?" Grimma Drigfan stared down at him and then let out a sharp laugh. "No wonder you walk into the circle of my wards so bravely, Emissary. No doubt you expect to escape my sanctum with your life."

Elezar didn't respond to the taunt—didn't allow himself to be cowed, not even here bleeding and surrounded by her beasts. He still possessed that much pride.

"As you say, I did not know of the wrong done you. I do not think that it is known to my master, either. If you would enlighten me, Grimma, perhaps I can arrange for Prince Sevanyo to compensate your loss."

Grimma Drigfan's expression went suddenly very hard and she glowered at the diamonds glittering around her wrist. "Your prince could command all the treasures of the earth and sea and he still could not give me recompense for what was taken, Emissary. He could not even understand my loss because you Cadeleonians do not treasure your children. You breed like lice and send your young to war the way you drive your pigs to market for slaughter."

Elezar understood at once and felt a dawning dread. Her child.

"What Cadeleonian priest took your child from you?" Elezar asked.

"Your holy priest, Palo." Grimma Drigfan ground the bishop's name between her teeth. "Once he seemed a man to be trusted as much as any of your race can be trusted. I allowed his varlets to build their ugly chapels and walk upon Sumar soil as a bear indulges her fleas. But seventeen years ago he conspired with the Labaran bitch. They stole my little Hilthorn from the escort sent to make him known to his father."

Elezar couldn't easily imagine the benign, absent-minded bishop in such a role. Still, he'd learned well enough that even the vilest of men often passed for innocuous. The bishop's fatherly smile and delicate build no more ensured a gentle character than Elezar's own towering height and harsh features proved his cruel nature.

"For years, I stilled my rage while Hilthorn's father negotiated and paid endless ransoms to that bitch in her Labaran sanctum. But my son—my one and only precious abomination—never returned. And now I am done with promises and waiting." Grimma Drigfan's fingers dug into the diamonds and gold entwining her wrist. Then the necklace snapped, sending jewel-studded gold beads flying over the cobblestones like terrified finches. With an expression of disgust, Grimma Drigfan tossed the remains of the necklace to the ground. "I will cost you Cadeleonians so many lives that even in your millions you will feel the loss. We will have vengeance in blood."

Doubtless she meant Elezar's blood as well as that of every other Cadeleonian she could lay her hands upon. And yet Elezar couldn't believe that she would have bothered to tell him this much if she didn't in some corner of her heart still pray to have her child delivered to her. Her eyes shining with unshed tears, she glared at him and growled of vengeance, but Elezar recognized the desperate hope beneath her rage.

He'd seen the same longing burning behind a mask of fury on his own mother's face long ago. How she had howled and wept over the remains of his eldest brother. She had even stormed through the splendor of their private chapel, screaming to God and all his saints for the return of her child.

Elezar still remembered hearing her from his sickbed and wanting to somehow console her. But he'd only been eleven and the savagery of genuine grief had been as new to him as to his mother. Later he'd realized that nothing he could do would return his mother's most beloved son to her. The greatest kindness he could offer her was to protect her memory of Isandro's perfection—to let him shine in her ideal of heaven like a sainted martyr.

But for Grimma Drigfan, perhaps there was still a chance. And if so, then a chance for peace between their nations existed as well.

And perhaps, very secretly Grimma Drigfan hoped for the same. Why else answer his question with such meaningful details? She had admitted that her child was in Labaran lands in the grasp of the Labaran grimma—a territory that she could not enter herself so long as the witchflame burned in the Labaran grimma's sanctum. But Elezar could easily cross the border, enter the city of Milmuraille and, given enough time and bribes, find a way into the Labaran grimma's sanctum. Why shouldn't he do what he could to reunite mother and son? The idea of such a decent task appealed to him deeply.

"If by some chance I do leave your sanctum alive, Grimma, I am willing to search for your child for you." He didn't delude himself that after so many years the child was likely to be easily found, much less found alive, but he also saw no point in allowing improbability to defeat him before he even made the suggestion.

"Do you offer your services just to save your miserable life, Cadeleonian?" Grimma Drigfan smirked at him. "Or is it that even you Cadeleonians have felt the Labaran grimma's witchflame dying? Soon the forces of Sumar could arise and seize Milmuraille. You would be wise to curry my favor then, would you not? You think perhaps I can shelter you from the others of my kind?"

Elezar didn't take offense at the accusations, though he did wonder about the suggestion that the Labaran grimma's witchflame was dying. A dim recollection Grimma Oesir's guards racing through the streets of Milmuraille in alarm stirred from his memory, but now wasn't the time or place to ponder that.

"I'm not so cunning a man as you seem to take me for, Grimma," Elezar replied. "If I were, certainly I would have arranged for some hapless proxy to be kneeling before you in my place right now."

Grimma Drigfan snorted at that—almost laughing, in spite of herself.

Then something in her expression altered just slightly. She still glowered at Elezar but for the first time he sensed that she studied him not just as any Cadeleonian but as an individual, as a man.

"What are you called, Emissary?" Grimma Drigfan asked.

"Elezar."

"Elezar." Grimma Drigfan's accent lent his name an odd lilt. "You are the first Cadeleonian to enter my sanctum since red wolves ran wild through these lands, so perhaps there is something more to your vei. Perhaps we shall see…"

She glanced down to the broken necklace and scattered beads at her feet. Her expression grew a little distant and the lines of sorrow returned to her face.

"You Cadeleonians lie so easily." Almost absently Grimma Drigfan lifted a string of dark red stones from her chest and studied Elezar through them. "Tell me true, why would you wish to return my son to me?"

"I have been charged to do all I can to make peace between our two nations," Elezar answered but then further words seemed to be drawn from him. "It would be a noble act, a just cause and I want—I need to find a purpose beyond the vengeance that has ruled my life. I want to be worthy of—" Elezar clenched his mouth shut against any further confession. He half choked on the words fighting to escape him but forced them back. He wouldn't be toyed with like one of her beasts.

Grimma Drigfan frowned at him. She released the string of stones and they clattered back down against the countless other bright baubles draped down her naked breasts.

"My reason is neither malicious nor deceitful," Elezar snapped, "but it is my own."

"So you say, but Cadeleonians before you have promised me much the same thing—even sworn on their most holy books and still they lied. I will not be deceived again," Grimma Drigfan said. "If you will not submit to candor stones then perhaps you should prove your conviction to me by martial trial."

Out of the corner of his eye, Elezar saw one of the huge white bears stretch and display its long teeth in a yawn. He considered that brutal gape, hulking body and display of long claws. For his part, he was exhausted and already bleeding, but he would not—could not—simply submit himself to this witch's thrall. Too many secrets lay unspoken and unspeakable in his heart. Some he was not yet ready to hear himself, much less give up to a stranger.

"With all respect, Grimma, I have already answered your question. If you require me to kill one of your servants as well, so be it. But after his death you will still have the same answer I've already given you." Elezar looked directly into her face, meeting her hard glare with his own defiance. He had nothing to lose; she'd intended to kill him from the first moment he'd entered her sanctum. She'd made that clear enough, and the longer he knelt here in respectful subservience the more likely he'd simply bleed to death on her cobblestones.

In the morning quiet Elezar thought he could hear girls laughing somewhere beyond the surrounding walls of cascading vines and wildflowers. Grimma Drigfan turned her head in the direction of the noise and for just an instant Elezar saw her expression soften, turning almost kind. Then she returned her attention to Elezar.

"Go," she told him at last. "I will not break faith with a stone of passage, not even one held by a Cadeleonian—but take care where you step. Stray from the path and no creature in all the Sumar lands will show you a moment's mercy."

"As you wish," Elezar replied. He rose to his feet but not easily. He felt the blood draining from his face. The numb of his left leg flared to agony as he retraced his steps over the warm, blood-stained cobbles he'd first crossed. Grimma Drigfan's white bears shadowed his unsteady progress. Elezar concentrated on the heat of the stones under his bare feet. Beneath the vines and brambles ahead of him he glimpsed a shadowy motion. To his immense relief he recognized Cobre. The stallion greeted him with an excited nicker, and Elezar's heart lifted despite the pain.

He'd nearly reached the perimeter when Grimma Drigfan suddenly called his name. He turned back. She tore a brilliant red bauble from the cascade of stones gleaming across her breast and hurled it to him. Elezar caught it and recognized it as a kind of signet ring, a bloodred stone set in gold. It felt warm in his hand.

"Hilthorn's ring will know him even if all that remains are his bones." Sorrow trembled beneath the anger in Grimma Drigfan's voice. "Try not to bleed to death before you can use it."

Elezar smiled at the grim sentiment and offered her a brief salute.

CHAPTER
SEVEN

Skellan slept often and ate well. Three times daily, the duke or a servant walked him through the sprawling winter-barren gardens of the bishop's vast townhouse on a silk leash. When the duke took him out, two lanky adolescent page boys dressed in fox fur cloaks always trailed their wandering procession past the beds of violet crocus and white snowdrops. But when he was turned over to a groom, the young Labaran man raced him alongside hunting horses and set him loose after game rabbits. Then Skellan tore across the grounds, running nearly to exhaustion. Afterwards the groom allowed him to nap in the straw-scented stables.

Skellan lazily watched dozens of carriages come and go. Some reminded him of the one he'd glimpsed leaving Oesir's sanctum. He tried not to think too much about that. He still hadn't recovered enough strength to leave the dog's body that hid his witchflame and protected him from that terrible violet fire. He needed more time to regain his strength before he could turn his thoughts to working out just what it was that Oesir had unleashed and how to secure the sanctum before Oesir's witchflame died.

He wasn't naturally patient, but his canine flesh was at least prone to distractions. So he amused himself sniffing out mice and taking a quiet inventory of the bishop's wealth. The largest, most ornate carriages belonged to Bishop Palo while his servants and guests tended to employ swift, simple two-seaters. The bishop's sacrist, an angular, tanned priest called Bois, seemed particularly fond of such quick vehicles and often drove himself all across Milmuraille while conducting the bishop's business. His elegant black and violet robes often looked dull from road dust and smelled of distant places.

Once after returning from the grand cathedral Bois caught Skellan watching him and to Skellan's surprise he bounded down from his carriage and walked closer to where Skellan lay atop a bale of yellow hay. The sacrist's fit, tan body created the impression of youth but studying his face Skellan suspected Bois' age to be well past forty. The years seemed to have added character to what must have been a rather bland countenance in youth. Hard lines of intense concentration crossed his brow and etched the corners of his thin lips. His eyes narrowed as he took Skellan in more closely.

"Whose animal is this, then?" Bois demanded of the nearest groom—a stout, bearded Labaran.

"He belongs to the duke of Rauma's varlet, sir. Elezar, he's called—the varlet, not the dog." The groom seemed flustered to have even been addressed by a priest of Bois' standing. Though Bois' interested expression must have encouraged him, because he went on. "The dog don't have a proper name, I think, though the duke tries to call him all kinds of things. He's a good hound though, sir. Big, but he don't bite."

"Big indeed. And red as a scarlet wolf." Bois cautiously extended an elegant hand to Skellan. His skin smelled of incense, and holy talismans adorned his many rings. Playing the part of the obedient dog, Skellan lowered his head to allow Bois to pet him. Instead, Bois caught his collar and inspected the charms hanging from it. Copper stars, tin doves and several dozen cheap glassy beads promising protection from a multitude of evils: everything from fleas to possession. Bois raised his dark brows then released the collar of trinkets.

"It would seem that the duke isn't taking any chances, is he?" Bois commented.

"That's a fact. But considering the duke's history..." The groom trailed off seeming to realize that it was not his place to speak so frankly to Bois about a nobleman—not even a Cadeleonian nobleman.

"Quite," Bois said, and with that he continued on his way. Though Bois betrayed no suspicion, Skellan took a little trouble to avoid him from then on. He seemed like a man who looked at everything too closely.

Fortunately the rest of Bishop Palo's household didn't seem to share that trait. Skellan grew steadily more familiar with them all and they with him. In two weeks' time he knew the names and faces of all seven priests whom the frail old bishop housed and employed to restore and repair his archaic chapel. The Labaran footmen, cooks, groundskeepers and grooms who ate and often gossiped in their own austere hall were all friendly with him to some degree. Several of them fed him treats from time to time.

On one occasion he even took tidbits of duck from the bishop himself. The old man rhapsodized to his supper guests about the ancient history of Milmuraille and all the ruins of lost civilizations upon which the city now stood, while under the table he indulged Skellan with scraps of gamey gristle.

"It isn't inconceivable that the Holy Martyr himself once walked upon these grounds, when he came to challenge the demon king to combat." The bishop stroked Skellan's ear and Skellan licked duck fat from his frail, warm fingers.

"Here?" the duke asked from across the table. "You really think the battle took place in the north?"

"I do, indeed!"

Skellan could tell the man was grinning just from the bright tone of his voice. He was prone to excitement even at his advanced age, and Skellan imagined he must have been a wildly energetic youth. Certainly the wrinkles that lined his pale face demonstrated a lifetime of laughter as well as contemplation.

"I've read the scriptures very closely and made lists of both the landscapes described and the plant and animal life mentioned." Bishop Palo paused to drink more wine then went on. "Others may not agree with me, but I am certain that our Holy Martyr's bones will be found here and not in some god-forsaken corner of Yuan."

"Under your very chapel, perhaps?" The duke's tone teased, but gently. Even when he was very drunk the duke remained surprisingly cordial and perceptive. "Is that the secret behind all the restoration work being done?"

"It's nothing more than restoration, I swear!" The bishop laughed like a little boy caught in a rude prank. "But can you imagine how their mouths would fall open in awe if I did uncover our Savior's bones here? Can you imagine how sacred that would make all these northern lands to our Cadeleonian church?"

"Most holy," the duke replied. "We'd have to move the capital city and the royal cathedral. But can you imagine the rent these Labarans would charge us?"

The bishop and his Cadeleonian guests laughed. The two Labaran noblemen in attendance had the good grace not to remark upon the suggestion of further Cadeleonian occupation. Soon enough the subject changed to the upcoming ball being held in honor of Count Radulf's daughter's debut. Lady Hylanya Radulf was only fourteen but already men discussed the likelihood of the count choosing her husband as his heir. Skellan found it a dull subject and a little sad. He knew two lively girls nearly the same age as the count's daughter and couldn't imagine either of them being happy with any of these ambitious, dough-faced courtiers.

As the evening stretched on and more wine flowed, the bishop slowly drifted off to sleep in his seat, leaving Skellan free to devour the duck leg that had slipped from his grip.

The bishop might entertain fantasies about the ruins beneath his chapel but they inspired a sensation more akin to dread in Skellan. If he concentrated and lay very still against the ground he could feel the eight great and ancient foundation stones pulling at him like a cold undertow. He didn't know what coven of witches had laid those stones or why they supported the crumbling remains of a Cadeleonian chapel, but he very much doubted the wisdom of disturbing the secrets they guarded.

By comparison the rest of the grounds seemed to radiate warmth. Beneath his feet, he felt the brittle chill of winter receding before spring's slow heat. Pale green buds dotted once bare branches and gold catkins burst like streamers from the hazel trees. Soon he smelled cedar pollen and sweet flowing sap scenting the very air.

The duke in his sable coat, his attendant page boys, and the violet-robed priests complained of the cold, bemoaning the long dreary Milmuraille winter, but Skellan felt life coursing back into the land. And just as flights of migratory birds reappeared in the clear skies and new shoots crowned the dark branches of pines, his own strength returned.

And still his Cadeleonian, Elezar, remained absent. Alone in the man's room every night, Skellan grew more anxious and restless. He paced the floor and gnawed at the leather bindings of his Cadeleonian's traveling trunk. Once he'd gotten into the trunk he found almost nothing within it: a few letters, old history books and a handsome enameled ring depicting a scarlet bull against a blue field. Skellan guessed that Elezar had stolen the ring as well as the few other small treasures he seemed to possess.

The letters confirmed that suspicion, albeit in euphemistic prose and quite a refined script. It only required a few passages for Skellan to realize that his Elezar was not just a criminal but a fugitive as well, and that Cadeleonian noblemen meant to hunt him down and have their justice. The correspondent, who closed with only the initial F, warned Elezar against returning or even using his full name in mixed company. Only twice did he mention the duke, and then only to remind Elezar to do what he could to keep him in hand.

The comments made Skellan consider what he knew of the duke of Rauma. Between the scullery and stables he'd overheard a great deal of gossip concerning the very wealthy, and possibly mad, Fedeles Quemanor. According to everyone, the duke had been betrayed by a scholar, possessed and tortured for years. His cousin and a few friends managed to free him but the duke was said to be forever changed, distrustful of his fellow men and haunted by the unholy creature that had lived within him. Rumors abounded of a curse that still followed him like his shadow.

Yet, having now spent weeks with the man, Skellan couldn't credit any of it.

The duke he knew drank and flirted more readily and indiscriminately than most Cadeleonians, but he hardly seemed haunted. He complained to Skellan and the walls about Elezar's absence and once, staggering drunk, he'd exposed himself lewdly before an icon of the Cadeleonian Savior, but that seemed more rebellion than any demonic possession. The only curses Skellan could imagine afflicting the duke's careless disposition were hangovers and venereal disease.

Elezar's correspondent seemed too discreet to mention either directly, but Skellan noted that the man obviously knew the duke's habits well enough to voice a concern about what vices he might communicate to his young pages.

The remaining letters were missives forwarded by F from a relative of Elezar's named Nestor.

Nestor wrote rather excitedly and illustrated nearly every inch of empty space in his exuberant wandering narratives. The inky images captured packs of hunting dogs and children, teams of horses, exotic Irabiim merchants and the bustling, rich streets of a distant southern port city. By the time Skellan read through everything he found he'd grown fond of Nestor though he'd learned little more of Elezar than the fact that he was now twice an uncle, hailed from a beautiful city and that his brothers worried at his extended absence.

Skellan shared the feeling.

His uneasiness seeped into even his days, making him long to do more than merely exert himself, running through the familiar paths of Bishop Palo's gardens. He wanted to investigate the fragrant kitchen and smokehouse. He wanted to throw off his animal hide and pick open all the locked doors and treasure boxes hidden in the bishop's house. Most particularly he wanted into the gold-steepled chapel, because he could have sworn that two days ago he'd seen one of the dark-haired, violet-robed priests carry an ornate gold coffer into the building. He glimpsed it only for an instant and yet it had seemed so like the coffer that had nearly consumed Oesir that now the need to be certain nagged at him like a biting flea.

But he still was not strong enough to leave the animal body sheltering him. He could only vent his frustrations as a dog.

Skellan jerked against his lead each time he was walked past the chapel. But he was not free to wander where he would, and neither the stable grooms nor the duke crossed the threshold of the chapel since it was still under repairs.

The duke seemed quite content to stroll the grounds leisurely, flirting with a variety of pretty scullery maids and washerwomen. When coy servant girls weren't trailing them, the duke flattered and entertained Labaran noblemen and Cadeleonian priests with clever banter. When only his two pale-faced page boys and Skellan accompanied him, he dictated a memoir, which he apparently planned to have published as *Anonymous Confessions: The Education of a Degenerate Sensualist.*

The duke's young Cadeleonian pages seemed both scandalized and delighted with their duty. Aroused, embarrassed blushes regularly colored their wan faces as they studiously recorded every detail of the duke's varied sexual exploits. When Bois and the bishop greeted the duke in passing the flustered page boys hid their small copybooks in the folds of their soft fur cloaks.

Skellan's own thoughts dashed from curiosity about what lay inside the chapel to a surging animal fascination with the pungent aroma of the squirrels frolicking across the grounds. He felt so bored with playing docile and toothless.

This bright morning they strolled along a path that wound behind the house and chapel down to Bishop Palo's stables. The duke paused beside a bare rose trellis, overlooking the paddocks to reminisce upon his school days. Skellan watched the nearby expanse of lawn, only half aware to the duke's recollections. Though when the duke mentioned Elezar's name Skellan almost tripped over his own paws, turning back to hear him.

"Even in our academy days he possessed an immense height and strength. His nakedness beside the stream in the heat of summer revealed a proud manhood of proportions yet beyond most of us. He, being from a brood of eleven brothers, accepted our gawking and prodding in good humor. It was only Javier whom he would not suffer to tease him. The two of them often wasted afternoons wrestling and taunting each other in the water, sensual and careless as boys can only be before they know themselves as men…"

The image of his grim Cadeleonian frolicking naked in a stream struck Skellan as both strange and fascinating, nearly as unimaginable as the thought of him schooling alongside a duke, though perhaps Elezar had been the duke's varlet even then.

The duke offered no explanation of their relationship nor did he make even a passing mention of his own period of demonic possession. Instead he went on to ponder the loss of childhood attachments before returning to what Skellan had come to realize was the duke's favorite subject: orgiastic sex.

"…an abundance of whores displayed themselves before us, some hiding their cunts behind coarse red hands but all so very proud of their pretty tits. They boasted such sweet varieties: maidenly rosebuds, full bosoms soft as pillows, perfumed breasts fragrant as peaches, breasts still glistening with the pearls of other men's spent lust. Joy arose in me, and at once I remembered those fat breasts I suckled so ecstatically as a babe." The duke paused, gazing across the grounds to where a group of stable hands stood laughing together.

"And in truth I found beauty, too, in the hard, scarred breasts of those battle-tested men among our company. Both Javier and Elezar, champions among us. My whole naked body delighted at the thought of sharing in their conquests, if not in the dueling circles then there in those red velvet chambers..."

The duke rhapsodized on while his red-faced pages scribbled furiously in their copybooks, and Skellan tried not to appear too disturbed by words he shouldn't have understood at all. But the images, scents and sensations the duke conjured affected him nearly as much as they did the page boys. He could too easily remember the heat and earthy scent of Elezar as he'd held him in his arms. Tense frustration pulsed through his body and he scanned the grounds for any form of distraction.

An enormously fat squirrel scuttled across the lawn to dig beneath a bare walnut tree. It found an aged nut and sat eating not six feet away. And on another path, just beyond the walnut tree Bois and two other priests strolled with Bishop Palo. Bois held something before the frail, white-haired bishop. When a sudden spring breeze caught the violet silk obscuring the object, Skellan briefly glimpsed a flash of brilliant gold stars studding a darker gold surface. Then a stand of hazel trees blocked Skellan's view and the entire party disappeared into the chapel.

Skellan strained against his leash, longing to give chase but only managing to choke himself on his collar. He shouted his frustration, producing a string of frantic barks. The plump squirrel heaved its rotund body up the tree and out of his sight.

"Hush." The duke flicked his nose lightly and Skellan yelped at the indignity as much as the pain. Then he pinned the duke with a look of recrimination. How could the man be so completely disinterested in the activities of those priests? Couldn't he feel that dark power that seemed to seep from the ancient stones of the chapel? Didn't he wonder why he was invited to this household where they fed and fattened him like a sacrificial calf?

The duke merely offered him a handsome bemused smile.

"You're as restless in a domestic setting as our Elezar, aren't you?" the duke commented. "Or were you objecting to my degenerate adventures? No, I doubt that. You've probably bedded far worse bitches than I."

Skellan grumbled and the duke and his pages laughed.

The next days progressed much the same. Skellan's frustration at being still trapped in dogflesh, and restrained by the whims of a pampered nobleman, only intensified. Until, in exasperation, he chewed through his leash and then led the duke and half the bishop's staff on a wild chase across the grounds. First he made straight for the chapel but found the stones surrounding the entrance too much like the powerful wards of a sanctum for him to carelessly cross—particularly not while his own witchflame lay locked up in dogflesh.

His human curiosity stymied, he gave himself over to bestial desire and raced into an out-building where the glorious perfumes of cured hams and duck sausages at last brought him to a stop. He mauled a side of pork and downed nearly a dozen links of duck sausage before the duke collared him and dragged him out, calling him a variety of unlovely Cadeleonian names.

He wasn't sorry for it—not even when the duke hurled him into a kennel cage reeking of puppies, sickness and piss. At least he'd done away with that damn leash and run free as he pleased. And he'd do it again soon enough.

Or so he thought.

But as morning passed into afternoon and then evening gave way to a new day Skellan realized that the duke might well leave him to rot here until Elezar returned—if Elezar returned. And in the hard dawn light Skellan allowed himself to consider just how very long Elezar had been gone. A month now, he felt certain. He didn't want to his Cadeleonian have died in the wilds of the Sumar lands, but in all likelihood that had been his fate. What point in waiting for a dead man to return?

And why had he been waiting for him at all?

The bitch in the cage across from him growled as he paced the small confines of his prison. Skellan ignored her and she returned her attention to nursing her three fat newborn pups. In another cage an injured hound lay curled, whimpering piteously to himself.

Was this really what he'd allowed his life to come to?

He didn't even know why he'd though he should wait or why it pained him so to accept that fact that he would never see his Cadeleonian again. Skellan could only blame the flesh he inhabited for this pathetic loyalty and stupid longing to belong beside someone like Elezar. But that was just the instinct of an ignorant animal. Skellan wasn't the dog he pretended to be. He needed to face the fact that it no longer suited nor served him to play the faithful hound awaiting the return of his master.

He'd sheltered long enough in the comfort of Bishop Palo's house. He'd recovered his health and if he possessed the restless vigor to snoop around the ruins of some ancient Cadeleonian chapel then he was well enough to take himself back out to the streets of Milmuraille and find his way to win Oesir's sanctum before the witchflame there failed.

Skellan's ears pricked up at the sound of grooms tromping into the stables. The scent of fresh hay drifted through the air, mingling with the sharp odor of horseshit. Soon Miche would arrive to tend the kennels as well. Most of the high-strung bird hounds already circled each other and whined in anticipation of their morning feeding. All at once Skellan felt disgusted at the idea of slobbering up offal deemed unworthy of the bishop's table.

In a day or so he'd probably manage to call back his human form. But not here. No, it was well past time he set himself free.

So before the groom reached the kennels, he nudged up the bolt that kept his cage closed and slunk back into the long shadows and winding, witch-cobbled streets of Milmuraille.

CHAPTER EIGHT

A cool mist drifted from the river, diffusing the first rays of sun and tantalizing Skellan with the perfumes of cargo from distant lands. He recalled the pretty drawings that Elezar's brother had made of the wealthy warmth of Anacleto. His mind filled with boughs of cherry and almond blossoms drooping like bowers over the streets perfumed by strange spices and candied fish. He wondered what the warm ocean-washed stones there felt like. Did they coil underfoot like sleeping sea serpents? Would they taste of salt or whisper like crashing surf?

Then Skellan scowled at the direction of his own thoughts.

It wasn't like him to daydream of exotic, far-away lands. As long as he could remember, his place and all his purpose had been in Milmuraille. He didn't even need to cast stones to know his vei lay in the city that towered over him. He'd known as much since he'd been homeless and hunted at eleven, and he'd sworn to one day reclaim the grimma's sanctum from Oesir. While he'd swallowed garbage and insults to survive on the streets, he'd fed his spirit with the vision of his scarlet witchflame blazing over the courtiers and guildmasters of Milmuraille. He'd sneered back at the merchants who laughed at his dirty, ragged body, knowing that one day they would bow down before him.

For ten years that had been the unwavering course of his vei. All he possessed—hurt, rage, hunger and muscle—he'd honed with street craft to seize the Labaran sanctum. He'd become a witch of his own schooling, quicker than Oesir's mercenaries and relentless as winter wind. He'd walked ice-slick roads with his bare feet, sinking his will into bricks and cobbles, forcing his way into the very structures of the city.

And yet today he did not feel the reassuring warmth in the cobbles beneath his feet. A cold uncertainty crept through him, as if he'd walked miles only to realize that he'd long ago lost his intended path, as if all he'd done had melted away in a month along with the winter snow.

As he moved deeper into the winding old sections of Milmuraille, the unctuous odor of river eels and fish oil lamps enveloped the chill air. It tasted odd and almost alien this morning. He tried to reassure himself that nothing had changed but his own senses. His hound's nose drank in shit and decay too keenly. Once he returned to his own flesh he'd shake off this uneasy feeling.

A bell in a tower dedicated to the piglet patron of gamblers rang out the first hour of day, though it would still be some time before the greater populace of Labarans agreed and rose from the comfort of their beds. In these earliest hours of morning only a few fishmongers and sad-faced herb sellers plied their wares through the streets. Though today even they seemed scarce. The infamous gangs of beggars and cutpurses who normally sheltered under the Fardee Bridge seemed to have vanished. Skellan wondered if they'd found some other haven to keep them warm until the sun climbed high enough to lure the wealthier inhabitants outdoors.

Skellan made his way easily through the empty, misty streets and though he walked old familiars ways, everything felt wrong. Even Bone-crusher's huge body smelled dull and dead this morning as if something had drained the life from him and left only hollow stone. Skellan knew he had to go to him.

He padded swiftly through the shadows of the ornately decorated Brewers' Guildhouse. But his gaze remained fixed upon the closed portcullis and the dark walls of the Oesir's sanctum. At the pinnacle of the tower a spiking corona of violet flames roiled over Oesir's viridian witchflame like a mass of writhing parasites. Even at this distance the violet fire slithered across Skellan's senses, filling him with queasy vertigo.

A month ago Oesir's witchflame had blazed from the black tower with the imperious vibrance of a summer sun.

All witches within the city had felt Oesir's presence like a star shining over them. Skellan had always despised that warm green light but until now he hadn't realized how gently it had fallen upon him.

Now as he took a single step nearer the sanctum, blinding blows of violet fire struck against his skull and back. His vision blurred and he staggered, feeling as nauseated and clumsy as a dying drunk. The charms dangling from his collar grew hot against his hide, and he heard alarm ringing through them. Had his own witchflame not been buried deep within the flesh of a dog, he felt certain that the violet flames would have engulfed him at once.

Skellan stumbled back from the sanctum another six feet before his vision cleared. He rolled against the ground, smothering and crushing the tiny violet sparks that clung to his coat like grasping worms. They hissed like furious asps as they died. Even after that Skellan remained, belly to the cobbles, fighting down dry heaves as if he'd taken houndbane.

Oblivious to him, a young woman swathed in several patched wool cloaks and selling winter herbs and dried rosehips approached the side door of the Brewers' Guildhouse. A plump Labaran cook sporting a thick mustache answered her knock. After a few minutes of friendly conversation they exchanged goose eggs and loaves of steaming bread for sprigs of silver thyme and pungent licorice roots.

Skellan hung his head over the scrape of a gutter and wretched up what little remained in his belly.

"Sick as a dog," the cook commented and the herb seller made a sympathetic sound but she walked well clear of him as she continued on her way toward the grimma's sanctum. Perhaps she traded goods with the cooks there as well.

The harmless charms dangling from her bracelets chimed like bells in Skellan's ears, but the herb seller strolled past unaware of their warnings. She called out the virtues of her fragrant wares and the surrounding mist seemed to swallow her small voice. Three careless steps past Skellan and her voice twisted into a shriek as violet flames slithered up over her arms, consuming the tiny charms completely and burning her wrists to red welts and fat blisters.

The stench of burned hair and metal plumed through the air. The woman fell to the ground with another scream, as a thick violet ribbon lashed at the blessings tattooed around her ankles. She swore with tears pouring down her contorted face as she slapped uselessly at the flames she could not see while they continued to burn into her legs.

Skellan had witnessed Oesir burn in the grip of those flames and he couldn't bear to see it happen to another. He closed his mind to his own nausea and silently drew his witchflame into the hollow of his mouth. He whispered a blessing into the saliva behind his lips and then hacked it out across the stones of the street.

Presented with the work of a true witch—even if it only suffused a pool of mongrel spit—the violet flames abandoned the herb seller's tiny charms and engulfed the wet cobblestones.

The herb seller scrambled to her feet in a panic, and bleeding, she raced to the side door of the Brewers' Guildhouse, leaving a trail of winter savory, sage and silver mint behind her. The same plump cook answered her frantic pounding and took her inside immediately.

Steam rose from the cobblestones as the violet flames consumed Skellan's blessing. They seemed to grow brighter and larger before Skellan's eyes. Unlike the creation of any witch he knew, these flames did not appear to unravel the fine weave of his spell but devoured it completely. Almost nothing remained of Skellan's blessing now. If the flames recognized him beneath the animal guise that masked his power Skellan didn't know how he would drive them off. Skellan turned then and fled, a feeling of dread growing behind him like a shadow.

He didn't know how to fight this infecting violet fire. What circle of wards could he draw up against a force that fed on magic itself? If he'd spent all his life learning witchcraft in the sanctum, he might have at least known what this violet flame was, but he'd lost all connection to mentors and peers when Oesir had murdered Lundag and purged the Labaran sanctum of her followers. Skellan had fled with only a rudimentary understanding of the raw power he possessed and that only gleaned by eavesdropping as a curious child.

None of the street witches he'd crossed paths with since then had been inclined to share their hard-won tricks or knowledge. Only Cire, who'd taken pity on him and rented him a room, had admitted that most of them had no learning to share, only instinct and intuition and that could not be taught.

The wild, scarlet spells Skellan commanded were of his own devising—the results of ten years of back alley audacity and experiments. But now his instincts only told him to run, hard and fast as he could. So, he raced through familiar, narrow streets hoping that distance would provide some protection.

He passed the Cockerel Gambling Den and Two Toads Alehouse, where he'd often sold grass charms and lucky dice in the past. He didn't slow now. He could still feel a hungry presence at his back. He raced deeper into the confusion of the old city. Here traces of magic forged by witches now long dead still lingered on the buildings and cobblestones like the stench of cat piss. Foreign travelers, native tramps, gamblers and cutpurses inhabited the winding lanes, all carrying tiny charms to bring luck, health, wealth or love. He hoped the chaos of so much small, strange power would mask his own presence for the time being at least.

Outside the slouching, two-story edifice of the Rat Rafters he slowed to an exhausted walk. Overhead the first rays of hard sun began to break through veils of mist. The street still seemed strangely empty. An actress caked with stage paint staggered past Skellan, her arms wrapped around an aged Labaran cardcounter who mumbled to her about better luck and other games in the south counties. They disappeared into the shadows of the Rat Rafters' warren of rented rooms.

Skellan almost went himself, but it wasn't as if Cire would recognize him or let him pass. She hated dogs in anything but stew. If she caught sight of him in her establishment, she'd beat him like a rug and chase him back out onto the street. Still Skellan stood there, longing for the familiarity of his few possessions. He suspected that he was recovered enough now to leave behind his disguise, but the threat of the violet flame made him wary. The dog's flesh he wore had hidden him once before, and he felt deeply loathe to leave it and reveal the full blaze of his witchflame.

The actress emerged from the Rat Rafters carrying two bags of her possessions and wearing all of her costume jewelry. Her lover followed with a pack slung across his back and a bedroll under one arm. They had lived below Skellan for nearly two years, and their sudden departure struck him as ominous.

Skellan pushed down his own fear to take in the city and the folk surrounding him. Up the lane a few dung mongers gathered leavings from the open gutters, and a tinker called out the price of his many services in a thin voice. But where were the crowds of rag traders, needle sharps, sham cripples and illicit butter maids who normally would have filled the narrow lane with so much warmth and noise? Two rats scurried past Skellan and skittered up the wall of the Rat Rafters, assuring Skellan that at least Cire still remained in residence with her plague of familiars. And the street wasn't abandoned, only strangely sedate.

Skellan hung his head low. His guts ached, his skull buzzed, his home had somehow grown strange to him and he didn't know what to do. The uncertainty that invaded him wasn't just indecision but the desolating sensation that for the first time in a decade he'd utterly lost his vei.

He knew every stone and timber surrounding him and yet felt completely lost.

For an instant he even stared blankly at the wild curling blond hair and mahogany skin of a lone Irabiim fortune-teller. She sang out promises and enticements while the tame crow perched on her slim shoulder shifted and flicked its wings. She was so small and delicately built that she reminded Skellan of a child dressed up in colorful rags, her eyes blackened with heavy circles of kohl.

"The cards know all," the Irabiim woman called to a passing pickle seller. He slowed with his cart of brine barrels.

Skellan scratched violently at an itch in his ear. A pack of painted cards wasn't going to tell him, the pickle seller, or anyone else anything they didn't already know. Then Skellan stilled, struck by the idea. He should have thought of it sooner. He probably would have if he hadn't been so long in this dog body; it was beginning to dull his mind to that of an animal. There was a reason that none but the most desperate witches ever took an animal form for themselves. More often than not they never found their way back to human flesh.

The knowledge troubled Skellan but no more than a tick might. He scratched at his ear with his hind leg again. Then he forced himself to concentrate on the collection of granite and quartz pebbles laying in the rutted gutter. He nosed them up onto the open street and placed his paws atop their rough little surfaces. What seemed distant memories came back to him more clearly as he reacquainted himself with the minerals.

They did not sing to his senses as they might have two months ago, but he tasted something strong and welcoming rising to him like a faint scent drifting on the wind. Once these small broken rocks had been part of a fiery sea and then risen with great mountains. Pride and power still clung to them and there Skellan found himself reflected in them. He poured the scarlet light of his witchflame into that connection, until the pebbles seemed pulse with the beat of Skellan's heart and shine with his longing.

The thin crowds moving past him could have been phantoms. He hardly noticed wagons rolling past or the pounding hooves of heavy carthorses. He wrapped himself into these small rocks and then sent them flying with a kick of his paw. The pebbles skittered and ricocheted and with each impact Skellan saw red sparks escape into the ground. The pebbles stilled but the scarlet light shot onward, illuminating Skellan's vei to his eyes alone.

He raced after it, exhilarated and nervous at the same time.

He didn't know where it would lead but he had to find out. He didn't like its direction but he couldn't deny its sure course. He dashed between tin merchants, teams of oxen and travelers following the road to the city's northern gates. His vei lead on and Skellan followed though he'd never left Milmuraille and suddenly feared that would be his fate. He nearly faltered as he glimpsed the wide-open road leading out between spring fields and on into the dark shadows of the Mirogoth forests.

That couldn't be his vei. He couldn't simply abandon the pain and aspiration of his past to make his way out into a wilderness that meant nothing to him.

Carts loaded with casks and redolent of goat cheese rolled through the wide gates. A potter exchanged pleasantries with the brightly dressed Labaran guards as three women herded their flock of fat geese past.

No one noticed Skellan staring straight ahead. Nor were they aware of the shining ruby road that rolled out before him. He took a step forward, feeling sick and at the same time sure that this was his vei. Never before had his true path blazed so brilliantly for him. Yet his whole being rebelled at the thought of leaving Milmuraille behind. It was his city; he felt that to the depth of his soul. He took another uneasy step, striding nearly beyond the iron and heavy timbers of the city gates. Three more paces and he was through. The crowd of travelers thinned here on the open road and the scarlet light of his vei rose like a wildfire encircling a single mounted figure.

Elezar gazed back at Skellan from atop his huge dark horse. He looked exhausted and gaunt. Even at a distance, Skellan could smell the sweat, blood and dirt on him. The fading light of Skellan's witchflame lent his pale skin and dark eyes a hint of warmth.

Skellan stared at him with his mouth half open in shock. Alive—his Cadeleonian was alive and returned to him! More than that, he seemed to be the key to Skellan's own destiny.

"It is you, isn't it? I'll be damned." Elezar swung down from his dusty stallion and, still watching Skellan intently, extended his hand. "Won't you come and greet me?" Suddenly Skellan's heart pounded with a rush of wild relief and animal delight. He raced to Elezar, tail wagging and barks of happiness escaping him. Elezar hugged him with weary, fevered affection. He stroked Skellan's face gently and straightened the tangle that his collar had become. Then with an almost reluctant sigh he rose to his feet.

"Well, boy, we have an entire city before us. Shall we take it on together, then?"

CHAPTER NINE

Only after they'd crossed through the city gates and abandoned the busy main thoroughfare for the winding narrow shadows of Joie Lane—Elezar riding and Skellan trotting alongside his stallion—did Skellan find himself growing disconcerted.

A strange satisfaction sang through his animal body as if simply joining his companion was all he could desire of life. At long last he'd found a place and the company seemed so comforting. That sea of aimless, ambitionless happiness rolling through him horrified Skellan.

He was the street witch who plotted to seize the city of Milmuraille—and the whole county by extension. Trolls answered his call and ancient stones recognized his dominion. Most importantly, he might be one of the only folk in all of Milmuraille who could kindle a new witchflame over the Labaran sanctum before the Mirogoth grimma arrived with their beasts and armies to conquer the country.

He was not merely a "good boy," as Elezar called him. And it incensed him that his tail wagged so wildly each time Elezar said so.

He couldn't deny that in following his vei he'd found Elezar, but he very much doubted that his entire future was meant to be spent ambling alongside the servant of a dissolute nobleman as a dog. There had to be something greater in their meeting, some role Elezar was meant to play in Skellan's ascent to grimma.

He peered up at Elezar.

The big man hunched in his saddle with his reins wound around his hands like ship's lashing. His head hung low. His dark eyes hardly opened and still he directed his stallion with just the slightest nudges and a few murmured words. He looked like he could be dead and still have kept riding.

He smelled like he was dead already, or at least his left calf did. The fetid stench of infection and rotting blood drifted from his flesh. Looking more closely, Skellan realized that the leather of Elezar's boot was swollen and soaked through with blood. Fresh droplets spattered the ground, leaving a fine, dark trail.

"We're nearly there," Elezar whispered. Skellan didn't know if he was talking to himself or his exhausted horse.

They turned into the busy courtyard of a modest two-story travelers' inn. The wood sign over the door depicted a pig roasting on a spit. Beneath the carved image were painted the words "Good Rest." That pig was certainly going to be resting a good long time, Skellan thought and snickered to himself.

"Master Elezar!" A plump Labaran youth who sported the uneven beginnings of a mustache darted between two parties of departing merchant-sailors. He came to a halt before Elezar's horse. The youth beamed at Elezar as if he were a rum cake that had somehow fallen into his hands.

"It's so good to see you again! After an entire month of your absence we'd feared our Elezar had returned to Cadeleon."

"Well met, Doue," Elezar responded and Skellan noticed that he made the effort of straightening in his saddle and smiling. "Have you quarters free for me, you think?"

"Three rooms emptied today." Doue eyed Skellan then turned his attention back to Elezar. "Mum and Sis was just talking about you."

"Weren't saying anything too good, I hope?"

Doue grinned at that and something in his expression made Skellan think that the youth would be echoing Elezar's reply as his own later.

"A room on the ground level if one's available, the nearer the stable the better. If your sister would be so kind I could use a basin of wash water and an extra sheet." Elezar reached into his cloak and tossed Doue a shining silver coin. "And I'd be very much obliged to you if a jug from your father's still found its way into my room."

"I'll have it for you 'fore you're done in the stable." Doue pocketed the coin and then pelted into the inn as if he were on Count Radulf's private business.

An almost fond expression played over Elezar's harsh features as he watched the boy go, then he turned his stallion to the stable. As they drew close Skellan realized that they'd been here before. The night he'd fled Oesir's sanctum this had been where he'd collapsed and Elezar had saved him. The long wooden building, with its bales of gold hay, paddocks of horses and mules, and rafter of nesting swallows seemed so unremarkable now in the light of day.

Elezar dismounted and this time Skellan noticed how he favored his left leg and how he fought to suppress the expression of pain that flickered across his stern face. Despite the drizzle of blood seeping from his boot, Elezar took time to see to his mount, brushing him down, supplying him with fresh water and a generous heap of feed. After he finished, Elezar slumped against a paddock wall looking utterly drained.

Skellan started toward him and the black stallion bowed its big head into Elezar, offering the support of its powerful neck. As Skellan drew closer the horse barred its teeth at him as if he were guarding Elezar.

"All is well, Cobre," Elezar murmured. "He doesn't mean any harm."

Elezar gently scratched his horse's brow and nose and the stallion relaxed, at last allowing Skellan to approach. When Elezar petted Skellan's head the big horse nervously lowered its velvety nose and drew in a deep breath of Skellan's body. He watched Skellan with his huge black eye, as if assessing his quality. At last, with a snort, the stallion turned his attention back to his feed.

Most of what Skellan knew of horses he'd learned in the last month while roving through Bishop Palo's stables. The big animals had struck him as dumb and easily frightened. But this beast brought to mind the old stories Bone-crusher used to tell him of wethra-steeds who descended from thunder-clouds, accepted only one rider and defended their chosen one with their lives. Cadeleonian warhorses, too, were said to fight to the death to protect their masters.

This was the first time that Skellan thought there might be a grain of truth behind such tales. If he'd been in a body that had allowed it—perhaps in another place and time—Skellan would have liked to ask Elezar how he inspired a naturally fearful animal to loyalty verging on valor. Skellan envied him such a devoted companion. But as it was, Skellan remained quiet and found a sense of well-being spread through him as Elezar stroked his ears.

"If only peace were so easily achieved beyond this paddock," Elezar murmured. Then with an effort he gathered his gear and led Skellan to the quarters he'd rented at the inn.

A shapely Labaran girl, wearing her lustrous brown braids in draping loops and balancing a basin of wash water against her hip greeted Elezar with a wide smile. She resembled the boy Doue so closely that Skellan felt certain that she was the sister Doue had previously mentioned.

"Well met, Fluer." Elezar returned her greeting. "Any hope that basin is meant for me?"

She assured Elezar that it was and that his extra sheet and the liquor waited for him in his room. Like her brother, Fluer seemed quite taken with Elezar though her glances were more coy than worshipful. For his part Elezar treated her like a little sister. Skellan could see that Elezar's demeanor vexed the girl. Skellan, however, found Elezar's polite disinterest in Fluer reassuring, though he didn't dare to make too much of it.

Cadeleonian men—even the few who wouldn't bed an innkeeper's daughter the moment she offered—were infamous for their hatred of male lovers. In their homeland they were said to treat both men and women who loved their own kind as criminals. Thankfully, in Labara, Cadeleonian authority didn't extend quite so far—not yet at least. The Cadeleonian priests might rail against what they called "heathen vices" but powerful Labarans like Count Radulf had always refused to codify Cadeleonian prudery. Skellan sank to the flagstones of the floor feeling suddenly uneasy with the direction of his own thoughts.

Fluer giggled and pranced into Elezar's simple room and then set the washbasin on a bedside table. She lingered at the bedside, going suddenly quiet and looking nervous. Elezar said nothing, only cast her a questioning glance.

"Mother says that a man, like yourself—coming from the house of a rich Cadeleonian master... Well, you could afford to take a girl on to see to your needs... and to help you with other things as well... your bath..." The girl's voice faltered and her face flushed. "Mother says a good man like you would reward a woman handsomely for her... services..."

Skellan glimpsed a strange tension in Elezar's face but he couldn't give a name to it, only he thought that something like pity showed in the man's eyes as he looked down at Fluer's bowed head. It was common enough for poor Labaran parents to sell their daughters into service to wealthy Cadeleonians and call the money exchanged a virgin price. Some virgins had been sold a good dozen times over and most had borne at least one whelp to carry his father's blood if not his name.

"You're kind to offer, Fluer. But I—it wouldn't be right." Elezar stepped back so that the sturdy little bedside table stood between them. "Besides, it's my dog that I'm intending to wash."

"Your dog..." Fluer's wide brown eyes fell on Skellan, who shared her skepticism. Between himself and Elezar there was no question as to who needed washing more badly.

Elezar gripped the white basin with his dirty, scratched hands and placed it on the flagstone floor. Skellan thought he could see the strain kneeling caused Elezar. His face went taut as he suppressed all expression but his voice betrayed nothing.

"Just smell him," Elezar suggested. Fluer took a breath then wrinkled her delicate nose and shot Skellan a repulsed look.

"I think he rolled in something dead." Elezar gave Skellan a wry smile as if he were his cohort in a prank. "You know how dogs are."

Skellan almost felt offended—as if his dignity as a hound could have been wounded. After all, it was Elezar who stank from an open wound.

But then he realized that it was also Elezar who stood there filmed in road dust affecting a careless demeanor while a pool of his own blood slowly seeped from his left leg to form a dark shadow at the heel of his boot. And he did it just to ease a green trollop's embarrassment. At the same time he said nothing of his own injury and nor did he ask the girl to summon one of the red-robed sister-physicians from the nearest temple.

"I'd best see to him myself," Elezar told the girl and he handed her a coin as large as the one he'd bestowed upon her brother. "But thank you for the offer. It was kind of you."

Fluer nodded and then, bereft of anything else to add, took her leave.

Elezar locked the door behind her then dropped onto the edge of the bed. The smile fell from his face instantly. He threw off his riding cloak and it hit the floor as if it weighed two stone. Dark circles of sweat soaked through the front of his shirt. For a moment he simply sat there with his eyes closed. Then he took in a deep breath as if he were stealing himself for a plunge into ice water.

He drew his long hunting knife and quickly sliced through the engorged laces of his left boot. As he peeled the boot leather back from his calf black scabs and rafts of putrid skin tore away. Fresh blood poured from the newly opened gashes in his leg. Skellan almost choked on the smell but he couldn't turn away. Horror riveted him. Whole strips of Elezar's muscle lay open nearly to the bone. Something dark and festering jutted out just above his ankle.

How he'd walked, much less knelt and made easy conversation earlier, Skellan couldn't imagine.

Skellan's stomach lurched as he watched Elezar reach down and dig his fingers into the gore of his mutilated leg. Elezar's face contorted with pain but he didn't make a sound. The tendons of his hand stood out as he strained for a grasp and then with a choking groan he wrenched something free from his calf. He hurled the bloody fragment to the floor, sending it skittering to where Skellan crouched. It was the long, curving tip of a bear claw.

Elezar sank his left foot into the basin. He washed his leg quickly and with shaking hands. Soon the water was red with blood, but when Elezar lifted his calf out, Skellan noted that the festering and putrid seams of exposed muscle had been rinsed clean. Elezar's face looked white as chalk. Sweat drenched his whole body.

He took the liquor from the bedside table and gulped back a swig. Then he slowly poured the rest over the deep gashes in his calf.

"God," Elezar whispered to himself and his eyes shone dark and glassy with pain. Skellan thought Elezar might faint—he felt certain he would have passed out much sooner if it had been him. But Elezar kept himself moving long enough to bandage his calf with the sheet he'd requested. Then he collapsed back onto his bed.

As Skellan crept closer he heard Elezar's ragged breathing. He sounded like he'd just sprinted across the whole city. One of his hands dangled off the edge of the bed, but it didn't hang limp, as Skellan expected. His blood-streaked fingers trembled like the wings of a dove dying on an arrow shaft.

As Skellan drew near the bedside Elezar cracked one red-rimmed eye open.

"It's all right, boy. You don't need to be afraid," Elezar whispered. Then he reached out just a little—Skellan didn't know if it was to give assurance or receive it—and stroked

Skellan's muzzle. His hand was hot and damp with growing fever. He patted Skellan a few more times but his eye fluttered closed and his hand slipped from Skellan's neck.

He lay like a fallen statue beneath a summer sun—arms flung out, legs planted and face chiseled with lines of determination even in the still silence. Skellan circled the bed and then bounded up onto the straw-stuffed mattress. He crouched beside Elezar and very carefully placed his front paw against Elezar's brow. Tender, burning skin met the rough calluses of his pads.

As Elezar slept his fever only grew more intense. Soon it eroded his rest, making him shudder as though the balmy afternoon air fell like sleet against his skin. He didn't wake when Skellan nudged him with his nose and then with his paws. Instead, fever dreams consumed him. He whispered names Skellan didn't know and groaned in pain.

Skellan's fear for him grew as the fever stretched on into the dusky evening.

He hadn't found his Cadeleonian just to watch the man burn up before his eyes. And yet he could command little more than a few stones and his own spit, while his power remained buried in this dog flesh. Skellan gazed down at his clumsy, rough paws. This animal guise was all he possessed to hide himself from the grasping violet flame that had engulfed Oesir.

Elezar groaned an inarticulate name. His hand closed as if grasping his sword hilt and he clenched his jaw, grimacing as he fought to suppress any further words even in his delirium.

"Please, don't die…" Elezar whispered.

He could have been voicing Skellan's own fear. Skellan owed Elezar his life but it wasn't the debt that moved him as much as the memory of Elezar sitting beside him, nursing his ugly body and comforting him with sweet words and a gentle touch. Few people had ever shown Skellan such kindness, fewer still without asking something of him in return.

Looking down at Elezar's pale, fevered brow and the locks of sweat-damp dark hair hanging in his face, Skellan wanted only to brush them aside.

He reached, calling on that dark scarlet flame that smoldered like an ember buried deep in his bones. The spark of power sputtered and smoldered, feeling raw. Skellan gritted his teeth against the discomfort and pushed his will against the pain. Fire flared through his motion, tracing the length of his spine and limbs. His fingers uncurled and pushed through the dog skin as if they were sliding out of a coat sleeve. He extended his feet, splitting invisible seams of animal hide and rich red fur. Then his naked legs, hips and belly came free. Every exposed inch of skin added to the dull ache of the flesh still trapped in hide. The sensation flared like the pang of a loose milk tooth already giving way to the sharp canines beneath. Skellan rolled his shoulders and flexed his back, slipping free of the skin that had only minutes before sheltered him.

Last, Skellan closed his eyes and with a quick motion peeled his heavy muzzle back from his face as if he were pushing aside a heavy hood. The hide tugged at the tender skin of his lips and eyelids but then gave way and fell from Skellan's body entirely. He sat, pale and naked, his red hair damp and hanging down his shoulders. The collar Elezar had given him hung loose, its charms felt cool against his exposed collarbones.

While his sense of smell dulled and his hearing dimmed, all around him a world of magics, immense and minute, burst into vibrant resounding life. The charms hanging from his collar gleamed with the palest yellow loops of little spells and sang well wishes against his bare skin. Shimmering scarlet patterns glowed up from some love charm or good-luck token hidden deep in the folds of Elezar's traveling cloak. Even buried, the spell struck Skellan as beautiful and its light seemed to pulse with the beat of his heart. He doubted he could have ever crafted such a pretty spell and could only imaging one reason another witch would entrust something so precious into the hands of a common man. Suddenly he found its warm light and longing song painful to consider and turned his attention across the room.

On the door, the remnants of some Bahiim traveler's ward still smoldered where, months ago, its maker willed a watchful white eye deep into the wood. And as Skellan looked closely he noticed here and there flagstones all across the floor glinted gold with the broken flecks of what once must have been the long veins blazing with the raw power of a great mountain. They still flashed like the bodies of fireflies despite the ages long past since Labaran quarrymen had broken them to rubble.

The shafts of fading sun filtering in through the two small windows sparkled with the emerald tones of Oesir's witch-flame, but it felt ever so faint now, like the wing of a moth brushing his cheek.

Far more powerful and frightening came the flare of violet light. Where it struck the flagstones it seared into the golden flecks of magic. Skellan went perfectly still though his heart pounded wildly in his chest. Then in an instant the light fled leaving the flagstones pockmarked and barren to Skellan's senses.

Instinctively Skellan reached behind him and drew his cloak back up over his bare shoulders. Its closeness comforted him and he dug his long fingers into the thick soft hair.

Weeks of rich food and easy living had transformed the once ragged, dull cloak into a cascade of glossy red. Even the leather felt stronger and more supple—almost as Skellan remembered it feeling in those few, fragmented memories of his earliest childhood. He'd imagined himself the descendant of the scarlet wolf warlord then, but only Bone-crusher had indulged that flight of fantasy. Lundag had soon taught him his rightful place as her faithful dog.

Still, seeing his cloak shining and vibrant, Skellan felt a flush of that fantastic pride and assurance. As he gazed down at Elezar he felt certain he could save the man. Belatedly he realized that Elezar had cracked open one eye and was gazing back at him with bleary suspicion.

"Who the hell are you?" Elezar rasped. He tensed as if to rise and Skellan reached out to place his hand against Elezar's fevered chest. But contact that had been easy when Skellan had worn another body now brought Elezar's hand up fast. He caught Skellan in a strong and brutal grip.

"Who are you?" Elezar demanded a second time. His powerful fingers nearly crushed Skellan's hand.

"I'm called Skellan—"

"You're naked…" Elezar's dark eyes briefly raked the planes of Skellan's body. Then he lifted his narrow gaze back to Skellan's face. His grip on Skellan's hand remained tight as a trap. "A Mirogoth witch?"

"A witch, yes," Skellan allowed. "But no Mirogoth tribe can claim my allegiance. Milmuraille is my home."

Elezar's crushing grasp relented a little. He considered Skellan. "Milmuraille may be your home, but my room isn't. Why are you here? What do you want?"

"You brought me here."

"I brought my dog." Elezar glanced around the room as if to locate the hound.

"Yes." Skellan jingled the collar around his neck.

The expression of angry confusion on Elezar's face gave way to angry realization.

Elezar said, "You were the dog all along."

"And when I was your dog you protected me so now I'm going to save you."

"What?"

"It's my vei, perhaps yours as well," Skellan replied. From Elezar's expression he knew that his answer meant almost nothing to Elezar, though now that Skellan had said the words aloud he felt sure they must be true. Elezar's vei must be with him. Why else would Skellan have been drawn to him with such certain accuracy?

"You're going to save me..." Elezar gave a rough, raw laugh and shook his head. "The naked man in my bed thinks he can save me."

"I know I can," Skellan snapped. "The wounds in your leg are going rotten and your fever is burning you hollow. You need help."

Elezar's mouth tightened into a hard line but he didn't deny Skellan's words.

"Let me heal you."

"Because it's your vei?" Elezar's dark brows rose skeptically, as though Skellan had claimed to be the West Wind, come to carry him to her cloud kingdom.

"Yes, but also because you—I..." Words of gratitude didn't come easily or naturally to Skellan. Rarely had he been given the occasion to offer thanks. "I repay my debts. Witches must, you know. You came to my aid when I needed it. So, now I'm offering you recompense."

A glazed look of fatigue moved over Elezar's rugged features. He frowned down at Skellan's hand, trapped in his grasp. Then he opened his fingers, releasing Skellan, who drew his hand back to his lap.

Elezar asked, "Why were Grimma Oesir's guards pursuing you the night we met?"

"You didn't care when you rescued me. Why ask now?"

"Because I put more faith in the intentions of dogs than men," Elezar told him. "What crime did you commit against the Labaran grimma?"

"No crime." Skellan met Elezar's gaze directly. "I went to the sanctum that night to fairly challenge Oesir for the title of grimma. Someone else attacked him and I was blamed." Skellan could have mentioned the violet flame, the golden coffer, or the malevolent hunger lying beneath Bishop Palo's chapel but thought better of it. Elezar was a Cadeleonian after all and unlikely to view his own holy man—and his master's host—with a witch's suspicion. And they had not come to that yet.

Now he just needed to convince Elezar to let him heal his injuries. Later he would worry about bringing Elezar into his service.

"So you haplessly stumbled into an assassination attempt and Oesir mistakenly sent his men after you."

"Oesir sent no one. He and I were both attacked. I escaped and he…" Skellan flinched from the memory of Oesir shrieking and burning before him.

"He what?" Elezar prompted.

"Didn't escape." Skellan remembered the violet flame rising over him. Again, he saw Oesir reach out and pull the ravaging fire to his own flesh. Skellan couldn't imagine what had motivated Oesir's action but he understood what price Oesir had paid and was still paying. "I don't think he will live much longer."

Oddly a look like sudden recollection came over Elezar. "She said Oesir's witchflame was dying…"

Skellan almost asked whom he meant then he remembered the token in Elezar's cloak. He scowled at the idea of some rival witch enchanting his Cadeleonian out in the Mirogoth wilds.

Elezar's gaze locked onto his face. "Does a witchflame still shine over the Labaran sanctum? Can you tell?"

"Oesir still holds the sanctum, but his flame is a guttering candle where it once blazed like a summer sun."

Under other circumstances Skellan suspected that he, as well as every fortune-teller, herbalist and street witch in the city would be pounding down the sanctum doors demanding the right to challenge Oesir if only to place a new witchflame over the sanctum before Mirogoth armies arose to seize the entire country. But Skellan couldn't imagine any of them braving the violet flame that ensconced Oesir's sanctum, much less overcoming it.

"Can you say how much time before it's gone completely?" Elezar asked.

"I don't know how he's held out this long. He's in agony, I know that." Skellan felt ashamed of the sympathy in his own voice. He pushed the memory of Oesir away and focused his attention on Elezar's intent face. "Maybe a month, at most."

"A month." Elezar fell back into his pillow with a weary expression. "A month is too soon..."

For a while both of them remained silent. The sinking sun cast long shadows through the latticework of the windows and belatedly Skellan realized that there would be no fire to warm them in the cold of the night. Elezar gazed up at the dark ceiling, his expression drawn.

"We aren't out of time yet," Skellan stated as much to himself as Elezar.

Elezar shot him a dubious glance. "We?"

"I know, I know," Skellan responded glibly. "You look bad at the moment but I think I'll be able to make something of you."

Elezar gave another of his dry laughs at that then shook his head. Just the hint of a smile seemed to linger on his lips. Again they both quieted. Skellan watched Elezar out of the corner of his eye. Then Elezar pushed himself up to his elbows to study the blood that had bloomed up through the makeshift bandage that engulfed his calf.

"What do you need to treat my leg?" Elezar asked at last.

"Your consent should be enough," Skellan responded, though in truth, he could have forced his will upon the other man, but that wasn't how Bone-crusher had brought him up.

"All right, do what you will," Elezar conceded. He let his head fall back on the pillow. He wore the same hard expression he'd worn while preparing to clean his wounds.

Skellan nodded. He didn't intend to hurt Elezar but with the violet flame hunting the city streets for any spark of magic he might need to build his spell in ways he normally wouldn't have. Better they both suffer a little than be consumed by flames.

Skellan reached out and very gently rested his hand against the heat of Elezar's muscular left thigh. Elezar glanced to him.

"You've done this before, I hope?" Elezar asked.

"Don't disturb me. My spirit must abandon my body to search for the means," Skellan responded. His own words and flesh felt distant already. His senses drifted like an exhalation of breath. Only the finest red thread anchored him to the body crouching at Elezar's side far, far below him.

Skellan focused intently, reaching out across the twilight streets of the city to those hidden recesses where fragments of derelict and forgotten spells lingered. Disused wards lay like splintered sapphires within the gray stones of doorsteps and windowsills, tattered pink love knots wriggled in house timbers like hungry beetle grubs. Cracked candor stones glinted like bright pebbles from the mortar of garden walls, and the names of strength and valor faintly sang out from the heap of tinder that had once been a ship hull.

Skellan held the neglected spells in his mind like scattered bells collected from a dozen shattered chimes. Notes clashed, others reverberated as he sounded them out. He felt their purposes burn like embers against his fingers as he turned and twisted them to his own use. Before his glazed eyes geometric forms in luminous colors blazed and flickered, slowly taking on a harmony of light and sound, as he aligned them to reflect and resonate one another.

At last one odd, but complete spell hung before him, restrung from the abandoned endeavors of dozens of other witches. Not a shred of it arose from the forge of Skellan's own scarlet witchflame, but still the whole form bore the stamp of his creation.

Oesir would have crafted a more lovely spell—hammering perfect symmetry into the fusion of looping blue wards and tangled orange love knots—while Lundag wouldn't have bothered with so much discarded trash in the first place. But Skellan was more practical than either grimma and took a kind of pride in the thrift and ingenuity of this spell. It hung together like happenstance, could be mistaken for chance.

A long ray of setting sunlight fell across a single cracked cobblestone, the entire spell blazed to life, illuminating a molten gold spiral and throwing off a deep resounding note.

Skellan felt the violet flame rise from Oesir's sanctum like a frigid shadow.

He didn't waste time with words, but immediately drew the brilliant golden spell into his hands and then plunged all its power into the ruined flesh of Elezar's leg. To his credit Elezar jerked once violently but neither cried out nor attempted to escape Skellan's hard grip.

Skellan's senses sank into Elezar's flesh and he shared the agony of Elezar's bleeding, open wounds. Then the hot shock of the spell flooded his nerves like lightning coursing through him. An instant later the blaze and power of the spell dissipated into a tapestry of new muscle, blood, sinew and skin. Relief washed over Skellan, but he wasn't certain if it was his own or Elezar's.

He didn't have the luxury to ponder the question. He felt the icy hunger of the violet flame searching through the streets. Skellan quickly pulled his cloak close around his body and hunched over Elezar's leg, hiding the fading traces of magic with his own body. The violet flame's shadow fell across him, engulfing him in a repulsive sensation like that of snails crawling over his naked body. It took all of Skellan's will not to lash out and drive the shadow back. He knew that would draw the violet flame directly to him. He shuddered and clenched his eyes closed, waiting for the slimy dead sickness to pass.

Slowly the violet flame turned east where Labaran temples and Cadeleonian churches stood and where Skellan had found several of the wards he used. It lingered there, grasping and prying at fragments. Skellan watched it flicker with frustration as it found only crumbs of magic. At last, lashing like a furious cat's tail, the violet flame withdrew back behind the walls of Oesir's sanctum.

Skellan remained hunched beneath the protection of his cloak.

Not only did the violet flame seem to be growing more powerful, but it also seemed more alive. When it had first burst from the golden coffer it had moved with the direct quality of a mindless spell, but now it lurked and hunted like it possessed thoughts of its own.

"Are you all right?" Elezar's low voice broke into Skellan's fear. He realized that to Elezar, who couldn't see or sense the violet flame, he must have seemed to collapse without cause. Skellan straightened and flashed a wide smile. He wasn't about to betray fear to a man he wanted to follow him.

"Fine!" Beneath Skellan's hands, Elezar's bandage lay in tatters, torn through by the impact of the healing spell. Three wide, white scars ran the length of Elezar' muscular calf but otherwise all traces of his wounds were gone. Tentatively, Elezar rolled his left ankle then flexed his calf. Muscles bulged under Skellan's hand and Skellan proudly ran his fingers over the warm, healthy skin and fine dark hairs.

"What are you doing?" Elezar asked.

"Admiring my work," Skellan replied. "Sometimes I even amaze myself."

Elezar gave a short snort and Skellan looked up at him.

"Are you implying that you've seen better?" Skellan demanded. He'd expected Elezar to show a little more amazement or at least thank him.

"You don't want to know what I've seen," Elezar replied.

"You sound like a country boy boasting about attending a town fair," Skellan informed him. What could a common man know of the splendor of true magics? "Did an Irabiim fortune-teller reveal your fate in a six-card hand?"

Elezar met his gaze and something in the hard lines of his face warned Skellan that he was making a mistake. Then he recalled the token hidden in Elezar's cloak and how quickly

Elezar accepted his transformation. He hadn't gaped like a yokel or called Skellan a demon. He'd demanded his name and surmised that he was a witch immediately.

"All right, that was uncalled for and rude of me," Skellan admitted. He was better at making apologies than offering his thanks but it still came out stilted. "I forget my manners when I'm hungry."

"You have manners to forget?" Elezar asked. Skellan almost responded with an obscenity but then he noticed Elezar's slight smile. Was he teasing him?

Elezar sat up and quickly stripped his boot from his right foot and after a moment of obvious hesitation, unbuckled and laid aside his sword. Then he took a cautious step away from the bed. Only after two more strides did he seem to trust his left leg. He knelt and a last shaft of setting sunlight fell across his broad back as he dug through his saddlebags.

"At least I have the grace to thank someone for a kindness done me," Skellan muttered under his breath. Elezar turned back to the bed. He held a gray clay jar with a braided grass clasp in his hand.

"Ah yes, that. You're welcome." Elezar tossed Skellan the jar and then sat back on the mattress.

"I meant that you should thank me for healing you," Skellan snapped. Absently, he turned the heavy clay jar in his hands. The braids of grass and rough clay reminded him of the salt pots Mirogoths often carried.

"Weren't you doing that to thank me for saving you earlier?" Elezar raised his dark brows. "So, you're welcome."

Skellan glowered at him. How could he be so charming to a wretched dog and so annoying to a fellow man?

"Salted venison." Elezar indicated the jar. "Help yourself." Then he lay back against his pillow and closed his eyes.

At a loss for a response, Skellan studied the homely jar then loosened the braided clasp and opened it. A perfume of cinnamon, yellow pepper and sweet balsam rose over him, almost masking the sharp tang of raw meat. Inside he found cured strips of red-black venison packed in sea salt and dry spices. Leather tough, the dry meat tasted of iron and the ocean and filled Skellan's mouth with the fragrance as powerful as incense. Skellan devoured nearly everything before he remembered himself.

"Don't you want any?" Skellan asked Elezar. Despite his still form and closed eyes, Skellan didn't think he slept yet.

"Later," Elezar replied.

"Thank you," Skellan added belatedly. He thought a smile tugged at Elezar's lips but he couldn't be sure in the twilight gloom of the room. Soon the first night bells would sound and city guards would close the gates against the wild nocturnal creatures that crept from the forests under cover of darkness. Within the walls of the inn, straggling travelers claimed the last rooms; Skellan heard three of them speaking in heavy Cadeleonian accents to Fleur.

Skellan ate more venison and listened as Elezar's breathing deepened. One of his hands slid from his chest and fell across the hem of Skellan's cloak. His fingers curled in the soft fur, reflexively stroking it, as he'd previously patted Skellan.

Skellan sealed the jar and set it aside. Then he curled up under his cloak with his back to Elezar and wondered what tomorrow would bring.

CHAPTER
TEN

Elezar drifted, no longer asleep but still unwilling to leave the languid respite of rest. For the first time in years, he hadn't dreamed of the Sorrowlands or woken aching from some galling injury. Instead he lazed beneath soft blankets feeling so well and warm that he couldn't quite credit that he'd awoken at all.

He considered opening his eyes, but resisted. He wanted just a few more moments of this peace. Neither human voices nor songbirds broke the quiet. And if chapel bells rang they sounded far from where he now lay. Though he knew a multitude of duties awaited him, he yearned to linger in this half dream for a little longer.

He drew in a deep breath, tasting as much as smelling the familiar, musky aroma of another man's body. He realized that the warm weight nestled against his chest was a man's bare back. An alarming excitement thrilled through his body and his pulse suddenly kicked into a wild rhythm. A low voice rumbled soft and inarticulate with sleep and a long leg brushed up against Elezar's thigh.

All at once Elezar was wide awake.

He stared at his bedmate. Surprisingly little covered the young man's sprawled, naked form. Faintly Elezar recalled him from the fever haze of the previous night. The witch. In the darkness of dusk, he'd seemed strange and feral: the brazen nudity of his body only emphasized by the cloak of animal hide that he peered out from with his eerie, pale eyes.

Now as the first rays of morning light crept in past the latticed shutters, his unconscious, exposed form struck Elezar as much more human and vulnerable than he'd first thought, though he remained a striking sight even in the light of day. His red hair blazed like cinnabar, and something in the set of his curved lips and the sharp angle of his red brows imbued his sleeping countenance with an almost mischievous expression. The angular planes of his long, lean body lent him a hungry appearance, sinewy muscle stretched taut over big bones. Elezar noted that his long hands curled into the fur cloak he'd rolled up to serve as his pillow.

Elezar couldn't quite tell if he found the young man beautiful or vulgar with his careless sprawl of long legs and unconscious erection. He shifted and Elezar guiltily tore his gaze away from the witch's body.

It wasn't that he had lived a life protected from the sight of other men—quite the opposite. Between his pack of younger brothers and the wild rebellions of the Hellions at the Sagrada Academy he'd bathed, wrestled, fought and even shared whores while in various states of undress with other men. But that had been before he'd understood how different he really was from those others—before he'd discovered the kind of murderous creature he could become in the throes of lust and jealousy. Once he'd been at ease among them. Now he no longer trusted himself.

If this mongrel witch had possessed any genuine mystical intuition he would have fled in the night while Elezar slept. Instead he moved closer to settle his cold shoulder blades against Elezar's chest.

"You're tempting fate, witch," Elezar murmured. The witch only heaved a contented, almost animal, sigh. He was like a fox kit mistaking a wolf for his mother. Elezar's whole body hummed with a predatory hunger while this naïve fool laid himself out before him like a harvest feast.

Elezar struggled against the urge to touch and take what he wanted. He cursed himself silently. Had he descended so far from his own ideals that he couldn't keep himself from assaulting a sleeping youth? Could he even call himself a man if he allowed himself to act like a rabid, raping beast?

No, he'd cut his own throat before he allowed mere loneliness to make that much of a monster of him.

He slid back from the witch and rose from bed. The young man offered a vexed groan at his absence. Elezar quickly caught the corner of the blanket and pulled it over the witch, protecting him from the early chill and himself from so much blatant temptation.

After brief consideration, Elezar dressed and crept barefoot from his rented room to steal out to the well near the stables. He doused himself in frigid water, washing as best he could with the contents of the ice-crusted bucket. His teeth chattered with cold but the worst of the mud and blood rinsed away. His clothes still reeked, but Elezar wasn't willing to either walk around in soaking clothes or go naked waiting for his breeches and shirt to dry.

He caught the sound of voices rising from the inn. Columns of thick smoke chuffed from the kitchen chimney and the scent of baking bread began to pervade the air. Soon either Fluer or her mother would come to fetch water. Elezar didn't feel particularly suited to morning conversation just yet.

He retreated to the stables and looked in on Cobre. The stallion greeted him happily enough but soon returned to sleep. He'd endured a hard month of constant travel and deprivation and deserved his rest. Elezar brought him fresh feed for when he next woke and then let him be.

Outside the stable the bright sunlight fell across Elezar's face and warmed him despite his damp hair. As he crossed the courtyard the first loud morning bell rang out. Soon the entire city would be awake and alive with people going about their business. Elezar felt suddenly self-conscious of his bare feet and restless early morning rambling. He slunk quickly and quietly through the side door that Doue had shown him months before and slipped back into his rented room.

Little had changed in his absence. Gold light fell through the latticed shutters, throwing a shining pattern across the floor and far wall. The witch still slept, arms curled around his fur cloak and long legs jutting out from under the blankets.

Elezar took up his sword belt and as he returned its comforting weight to his hips he contemplated his boots—the bloodstained, filthy left boot with its slit laces, in particular.

He smirked at his own first impulse. Only a brat born and bred to great privilege would even considered discarding a pair of solid boots for merely being unsightly and smelling of blood. No doubt the penniless naked witch lying in his bed right now would have thought himself blessed to even possess a pair of boots—not to mention pants—regardless of their condition. But the truth was that at home in Anacleto, Elezar had owned dozens of fine boots as well as handsomely embroidered shoes intended only for ballroom floors. Even while he'd recklessly brawled with highwaymen, dueled nobles and drunk himself blind in the capital of Cieloalta, he'd possessed the wealth and resources to discard or dress in any garment that pleased him.

He'd never been as poor and certainly never as deprived as the witch, who appeared to own only a cloak and the collar Elezar had put on him.

Despite himself Elezar glanced to where the young man lay. Even in full morning light he looked unaccountably smug, as if a smile were carved into his face.

He'd given Elezar his name last night. Yes, he remembered it now: Skellan. Named for the famous scarlet wolf warlord, no doubt. Despite himself Elezar laughed at the idea of this starved beggar passing for the mythical Mirogoth warlord who was said to have slain lions and sired the Radulf bloodline. What illusions had the witch's parents entertained at his birth? Elezar's laugh was quiet enough but still Skellan's eerie green eyes opened to stare at him.

A truly pleased smile lit his face, and he sat up at once.

"You look better, my Cadeleonian," Skellan proclaimed. He threw back the blankets and bounded out of the bed as if utterly unaware that he remained naked. Elezar quickly averted his gaze back to his boots.

"I need a piss so badly my eyes are about to turn yellow," Skellan announced.

"There's a chamber pot beneath the bed," Elezar informed him.

"I'd never get it in a pot with my dick sticking straight up at the sky like this." Skellan padded past Elezar and to his shock pushed open one of the shutters and proceeded to piss out the window into the bed of rose tulips below. He sighed contentedly as the golden stream arched high into the air and pattered across the delicate pink blossom in an obscene rain.

"Were you raised in a barn?" Elezar demanded. He could clearly remember his mother clouting for such behavior when he'd been a child.

"No," Skellan replied easily as he continued to drench the flowers. "I spent most of my childhood in a walnut orchard, though now I have a room at the Rat Rafters. Why?"

"Because no civilized man greets the woman working in the courtyard by waving his cock out the window and pissing on her sachet flowers. He uses a chamber pot, don't you think?"

"When he's stiff as a stick?" Skellan laughed. "Your civilized man would douse himself and the floor before he'd get soft enough to shoot into the pot. Anyway, that scrawny matron and her daughter are far too interested in those three men milling around the stable to even notice me."

"Not being caught doesn't make you less unseemly." Elezar picked up his right boot and pulled it on. He hesitated before taking up the left boot. "In the future, make use of the privy just out the door and down at the end of the hall."

"Hmmm," Skellan replied. But he didn't seem to be paying Elezar the least attention and Elezar himself wondered why he was bothering with the conversation at all.

In the future? What future was he imagining? It wasn't as if he was going to keep this mongrel witch around like the dog he'd played at being and teach him table manners.

"There's something I don't like about the look of them…" Skellan murmured as he continued to peer past the shutters.

"I'm sure there are several things most people wouldn't like about the look of you right now too." Elezar stripped the severed laces from his left boot, knotted them into a couple strings and used them to secure his footwear. It smelled off and looked awkward but held together.

When he glanced over his shoulder to Skellan he found the witch still gazing out the window, though he'd long since finished passing water. Sunlight played over his body and lit his hair to the color of molten iron. The trinkets dangling from the collar he wore glinted cheaply as counterfeit coins.

"Don't you have any clothes?" Elezar asked.

"Of course. My cloak and the collar you gave me," Skellan replied. The way he narrowed his eyes and hunched forward as he continued to watch the courtyard reminded Elezar more than a little of a hunting hound catching scent of some quarry. "They're paying the old woman too much and her daughter looks miserable about it."

Elezar could guess what the men in the courtyard were buying. He felt a stab of sympathy for Fluer, but being neither her father nor brother, there was nothing he could do for her other than treat her as honorably as if he didn't know that her parents sold her into their guests' beds.

"Come away from the window and leave that be," Elezar commanded.

Skellan looked to him, seeming to find something amusing in Elezar's tone, but then with a smile he closed the shutter. He sauntered a few steps closer to where Elezar stood.

"You need some kind of clothing—more than a cloak," Elezar told him. He only briefly met Skellan's gaze then scowled down at his saddlebags. He'd purchased a hide of smoked buckskin while traveling with Eski and her family and had intended to gift the supple amber leather to Fedeles.

"Great witches need wear only the elements. It's a sign of our prowess," Skellan informed him.

Remembering the Sumar grimma, Elezar suspected there was some truth to Skellan's claim but even among Mirogoths, the witches adorned themselves with fine leather, beautifully crafted belts, rich furs and cascades of polished stones. And among the men of Milmuraille he'd only seen beggars wearing less than hose, breeches, shirts and coats. How poor and proud did this witch have to be to parade naked and attempt to call it prowess?

"Even the greatest witches I met wore more than you have on now. A knife belt and loincloth at the least," Elezar argued. Then thinking of a new tactic he added, "And in any case, didn't you say last night that you were in hiding?"

Skellan seemed to consider him quite seriously before responding.

"Yes, you're right. The way things are now, I'd be stupid not to remain disguised. I have some common rags back in my rooms at the Rat Rafters. I suppose I can throw those on. And what I'm lacking I'll get out of Rafale." Then Skellan grinned at Elezar as if they were in league. "I've saved his skin so many times he owes me a full wardrobe worth of his hide... But what about you?"

"Me?"

With a smile that struck Elezar as both handsome and wicked, Skellan closed the distance between them. Despite himself Elezar felt painfully aware of the heat of Skellan's naked body and the stench of his own filthy clothes.

"You reek like the king of vultures," Skellan told him as if Elezar could have failed to notice.

"I intend to have these laundered once I've returned to Bishop Palo's townhouse."

"We would be wiser not to return there straight away," Skellan replied. "As I see it, we first need to consider—"

"We?" Elezar growled though he knew the comment alone

hadn't merited such rancor. Being compared to a fetid vulture had stung his pride, and moreover annoyance gave him relief from his unnerving feeling of attraction. "There is no *we* to consider. I have my own business to return to and you... You can slink back to whatever rat hole you crawled out of."

"Rat Rafters," Skellan corrected. "And why are you snapping at me like baited bear? I'm trying to protect you."

That brought Elezar up short in confusion. Protect him? How deluded was this lithe, naked youth that he thought a man like Elezar would need his protection? What was he going to do, distract bandits and assassins by flashing his milky white ass at them? As absurd as the thought was, it was also obvious from Skellan's expression that he actually believed what he was saying.

"Do you think you can really continue to be my dog?" Elezar demanded. To his surprise, Skellan flushed slightly then narrowed his gaze at Elezar.

"I told you." Skellan drew himself up straight, nearly reaching Elezar's height. "You are my vei, part of my destiny. We shall take on the city together just as you said. You have a greater purpose than to serve a spoiled, pretty duke or rut with a Mirogoth wood witch."

"Mirogoth wood witch?" Elezar had no idea how the conversation had come to this point but the younger man certainly looked vexed at the notion of him interacting with other witches.

"You carry her charm in your traveling cloak. I can feel it even now," Skellan informed him as if he'd been caught with a card up his sleeve. "For all you know, she's placed a spell on it to enthrall you. You should give the charm to me and let me destroy it."

"Charm..." The ring Grimma Drigfan had entrusted to him, Elezar realized. "That is none of your concern," Elezar told him flatly. "And what the hell are you going on about with your vei and destiny? I don't know anything about you except that you've made an enemy of the Labaran grimma, pawned yourself off on me as a dog and you feel no shame for urinating out open windows—"

"You really are sensitive as a virgin countess about a little piss—" Skellan began with an amused tone but Elezar cut him off.

"Which brings me to the more important point in this conversation." Elezar glared hard at the faint smile on Skellan's face. "You don't know the first thing about me. You act as though having me in your destiny is something to celebrate. But let me tell you, I've been other men's destinies already. I was the end of them, you understand? I cut them down in cold blood. How's that for your vei?"

Skellan stepped back from him just a little and somehow Elezar felt both triumphant and disappointed. Doubtless another man would have found a gentler way to brush the witch off, but Elezar was in no position to be coddling. Both he and Atreau's safety depended upon secrecy and discretion. This naked witch seemed anything but discreet.

"I wasn't true in my name or form when you took me in, but I did you no wrong. I even cast off the protection of my dog skin to look after you," Skellan stated. "Why would you harm me?"

"Because I'm not a particularly decent fellow. Just trust me, you don't want me to play any part in your destiny." The temptations he'd fought this morning made Elezar certain that he and Skellan would not make for easy company. "Honestly, I cannot take you in, especially not if what you told me about Oesir's witchflame is true."

"It's true," Skellan assured him though his tone was dull. He turned from Elezar and gathered his cloak from where it lay on the bed.

"If you need a little money…" Elezar didn't know why he was offering except that he felt like he'd just punted a puppy, and he'd done it after Skellan had helped him. It was easy to forget in the mess of his fevered memories, but the witch had healed him and he suspected that it hadn't been an easy thing for Skellan to do.

Skellan shook his head before Elezar could complete the offer. He drew his cloak over his shoulders.

"At least take this for your troubles." Elezar dug into his saddlebags and drew out the soft roll of smoked buckskin. Skellan looked back at him, eyed the costly leather, and then laughed.

"You're not going to win your argument that you're a bad man, are you?"

"I'm a terrible man, but I'm normally a little better mannered about it." Elezar studied the fine, golden leather in his hands then held it out. "Will you accept this in parting?"

"I'd be more cheaply bought off with some of that bread I can smell baking." Skellan closed his eyes and lifted his face to draw in a deep breath. "Cured ham as well."

"Really?" Elezar didn't quite know what to make of having such a valuable offering refused for nothing more than a little meat and bread.

"Of course." Skellan flashed him a quick smile. "Don't you know that's the other reason witches are always barefoot? We get so hungry we eat our own shoe leather."

Elezar laughed and felt better for it. "All right, a meal and then I have to be on my way. Agreed?"

Skellan shrugged and Elezar decided to take it as concurrence. After that it took him only a few minutes to find Doue and bribe him into fetching him a platter loaded with steaming bread, smoked meat and cheese from his mother's kitchen. The boy returned to him in the narrow hall and proudly confessed to snatching the fresh woodberries and two smoked eels for Elezar as well.

"To think, you've turned robber and risked hanging on my behalf. I'm touched." Elezar took the heavy wooden platter from the Doue. The boy's plump face, glossy brown hair and feathery mustache reminded him a little of his brother Nestor when he'd still been impressionable enough to stumble around Elezar's heels like a hungry pup.

"Was that really a scarlet wolf you brought in with you yesterday?" Doue inquired and his eyes were wide with excitement. The question caught Elezar a little off guard but then he remembered that Doue seen Skellan yesterday.

"He'd like to be, no doubt," Elezar replied. Then with Skellan in his thoughts he asked, "You have three other Cadeleonians staying here, do you? My mutt noticed them."

Doue made a sour face. "Them horse traders, you mean? Did they wake you when they swaggered in last night?"

"Not a chance. Last night I was dead to the world." Though he said it with a smile Elezar knew he wasn't far from telling the truth.

"They ogled your handsome Cobre some but I told 'em flat out there's no hope of buying him off you. Mother said I shouldn't even bother telling you about them."

Elezar simply nodded. Having settled several bills with Doue's mother, he'd found her tight-lipped, hard-eyed and more than a little calculating. Patrons of the tavern next door often argued whether her husband's heavy drinking explained her flinty demeanor or caused it.

"You ain't setting off again soon, are you?" Doue asked when they'd reached the door to Elezar's room.

"Directly after I've eaten. Why?"

"Mother wanted to know," Doue replied absently. His gaze lingered on the small dish of woodberries on Elezar's platter.

"Go on." Elezar lowered the platter. "Take them."

Doue grinned, swiped a few of the bright red berries, and then darted down the hall and disappeared out the narrow side door that led out to the courtyard.

Elezar let himself into his room to find Skellan crouched in his red cloak tracing lines on the stones of the floor. As he looked up the hood fell back from his face. The yearning in his expression as he stared at the full platter wasn't any more subtle than Doue's had been. Despite himself, Elezar laughed.

"What?" Skellan cocked his head slightly.

"You looked less eager when you were a dog." Elezar rested the heavy platter on the bedside table. "Come. Help yourself."

Skellan appeared torn but then shook his head.

"I need to work something out…" He turned his attention back to the flagstones.

Elezar cut himself a serving of smoked eel and folded it in a thick slice of hot bread. Unctuous fish and dark northern bread were not normally to his taste, but this morning they seemed to melt across his hungry tongue.

As he ate he watched Skellan trace his long fingers over the pitted stonework of the floor as if he was manipulating invisible cogs in some intricate device. His pale gaze searched empty spaces and his hands darted out, grasping and twisting nothing that Elezar could see.

Elezar had witnessed great magic enacted both by his friend Javier and the Bahiim mystics of Anacleto. He'd seen an entire grove set ablaze with golden blessings. He'd felt punishing agony in the grasp of the black shadow of a living curse. By comparison, Skellan's small, weird gestures appeared insignificant.

"What are you doing?" Elezar asked.

"Testing our—my enemy," Skellan replied, but his voice was distant. His attention remained on the floor. His fingers flew with a musical quickness, reminding Elezar of a frantic minstrel working at a harp with far too many strings. Then without warning Skellan leapt back and hurled a charm from his collar onto the floor. The leaf-stamped medallion clattered against the flagstones and lay there.

Skellan stared at it intently and Elezar too watched the little charm, waiting.

"Is nothing supposed to happen—" Elezar began but then was cut short when the charm gave out a piercing tone and then in an instant blackened and crumpled like kindling before a flame. Skellan jerked his cloak close around his body and Elezar reflexively sprang to his feet, gripping his sword hilt.

"Did you do that?" Elezar demanded.

Skellan shook his head from beneath the hood of his cloak. His attention remained intent upon the flagstone. Elezar followed his gaze. He thought he glimpsed tiny violet sparks skipping, like hungry fleas, over every spot where Skellan had earlier laid his fingers. A pattern of charred specks darkened the pale gray stone and an odor like singed hair drifted on the air.

Elezar waited for something more. His whole body tensed with memories of wings and talons erupting from writhing shadows. But the floor remained the same and the acrid scent quickly dissipated.

Skellan sighed and straightened. He said nothing but joined Elezar at the bedside, helping himself to a thick hunk of the dark rye bread.

"Was that Oesir's work, then?" Elezar asked. He released his sword, feeling a little foolish for grasping it in the first place. He knew better than most what little protection a blade offered against conjury.

Mouth stuffed full of bread, Skellan simply rolled his eyes at the suggestion.

"Who then?" Elezar asked.

Skellan wolfed down another hunk of bread then answered, "That's what I'm trying to learn. Who or what it is." He reached for one of the eels but then paused. "You couldn't see it, I suppose."

"Just a few purplish sparks but even those I wouldn't have noticed if I hadn't been watching closely," Elezar admitted as much readily. He wasn't one to pretend at mystical sensitivity.

"If you were a witch you'd have seen an immense tongue of violet fire surge in through the shutters. Remember when I told you that Oesir and I were attacked before we could battle?"

"I remember. Oesir was nearly killed, you said, and now his witchflame is dying." He'd been fevered but that hadn't been something he was likely to forget. If Oesir's witchflame failed it freed all four Mirogoth grimma to invade Labara and that would result in a greater war than the one Elezar had been sent to prevent. Before he could even consider searching for the Sumar grimma's missing son he needed to find who among Count Radulf's court and the city's priests already knew of the dying witchflame and what was being done.

"Was it that"—Elezar didn't know what to call the invisible force—"that thing you just summoned that nearly killed Oesir?"

"Yes, that violet flame attacked and engulfed him. It's consuming him even now. If it can't be stopped it will devour his witchflame." Skellan scowled at the eel in his hand and then bit the head off. "But it isn't feeding from just Oesir. It's hunting the city and devouring even little magics like that charm just now."

"But it didn't attack you." Elezar wondered if Skellan possessed too little power to attract the violet flame. Oddly, Skellan offered him a smile that would have suited a fox slinking into a henhouse.

"I know how to hide myself," Skellan replied. "And just now, the charms I used to lure the violet flame weren't forged by my witchflame, but strung together from abandoned and broken spells. When the violet flame fell upon them, they couldn't lead it back to anyone. And I strung the charms so that they turned it full circle and sent it crashing back to the sanctum."

Elezar thought he understood a little of what Skellan described but wasn't certain if it held a greater importance in the context of stopping a war. Though he had to admit that if it came to destroying this violet flame, then having a witch who could at least see the thing working for him would be wise. That Skellan was the best choice of witches, Elezar very much doubted.

Next to him, Skellan tore a hunk of pork free with his bare hands and gulped it down. He reached for another.

"You have the table manners of a jackal." Elezar handed him his knife. "At least cut the meat from the bone cleanly."

Skellan looked almost startled, but then took Elezar's knife and carefully cut free another piece of pork. "Thank you," he added belatedly.

Elezar simply nodded, his thoughts already returned to their conversation. "So, could your trick with the broken spells be used to free Oesir?"

"I doubt a mere distraction would lure it completely away from him and the power it can now command from within the sanctum. More than that, I'd need to find a way to trap the violet flame once it did release Oesir, otherwise it would simply take hold of him again once it had fed." Skellan cut a slice of bread with self-conscious care, then took another thick serving of pork and heaped it with cheese. He ate the whole thing in two bites. "What I did just now was to test for the kinds of magics that the violet flame wouldn't devour. I created eight different forms of charms."

"And?" Elezar asked.

"It destroyed all of them, broke through them and fed on the magic that shaped them." Even as Skellan spoke a wily smile curved his lips. "But I noticed that it didn't devour several fragments of ancient blessings that I'd used to rig up the charms. It didn't touch those."

From Skellan's expression Elezar guessed that this information was extremely suggestive. Again he noted that having a witch or priest to advise him could be key to averting war with the Mirogoths. He needed to report this—along with his meeting with the Sumar grimma—to Fedeles. Hopefully Fedeles could recommend a local witch or send a trustworthy priest whom Elezar could confide in without fear of himself or Atreau being exposed.

But for now his only resource appeared to be Skellan, sitting on the bed beside him wearing only a cloak. As impoverished as he was, he'd probably turn his own mother in for a reward, or even a hearty meal. This close Elezar noticed how the sunlight played over the fine hairs of Skellan's legs, lighting then like copper thread. Pale freckles dappled his thighs.

"So, what do those ancient blessings tell you exactly?" Elezar pulled his gaze back to the pitted flagstone.

"That the violet flame is something very old." Skellan absently stretched, allowing his cloak to slip off one angular shoulder. Elezar suppressed the urge to pull it back up for him.

"I think it's something that was banished from this world so long ago that no witch, priest or mystic has needed to raise a ward against it in ages. The spells that were forged to fight it have been forgotten by the living." Skellan seemed utterly at ease beside Elezar, and the lure of that made Elezar all the more uneasy. "Though maybe, far back in history, there might be a record of them."

"How far back? A hundred years? Two hundred?" Elezar wondered suddenly if this violet flame could be another resurrected Bahiim curse, like the Shadow Curse. It had required immense magic and mechanical genius to defeat that thing. No such resources were available to him here and now.

"How would I know its age? Am I a historian? It's just very, very old." Skellan stuffed the last of the bread and cheese in his mouth and chewed with a troubled expression. He swallowed. "Definitely older than the Cadeleonian occupation and the Labaran sanctum, because none of the sanctum's wards protected Oesir from the violet flame. The blessings that did withstand it all came from those worn fragments of carved topaz that you find from time to time in the old section of the city."

"Topaz?" Elezar hadn't noticed the muddy streets of Milmuraille glittering with semi-precious stones.

"Yes, dull blue and brown ones and most aren't even as big as the top of my thumb. It's only the blessings carved into their surfaces that make them stand out from pebbles." Skellan wiped the blade of Elezar's knife clean but didn't hand it back. "Bone-crusher told me that they're remains of the cairns built by an ancient sect who lived even before witches learned to raise sanctums."

"When was that supposed to have happened?" Elezar had familiarized himself with some Labaran and Mirogoth history but certainly not all. If he was to hunt down some ancient blessings—either in texts or among ruins—he'd need something resembling a date.

"Days of yore." Skellan shrugged. "You know, when demon lords hunted the land and the Old Gods still walked the earth. Fable times of great battles when dragons arose and battled demons and the first witches fought both."

There were similar mythic histories among Cadeleonians as well. The Savior and his four warrior disciples were said to have founded the first Cadeleonian church on ruins where they'd driven a demon king back to his hell. The Haldiim's sacred Bahiim, too, claimed to have forged their mystic order in the heat of combat against demonic monstrosities.

"It can't have all just been fables," Elezar said. "As you said, the blessings from the cairns affecting this violet flame must mean it harkens from the far past. It could be something from legend, itself…"

This talk of old evil hidden among the ruins of cairns stirred uneasy thoughts in Elezar. Memories skipped through his mind before he could stop them and in an instant he slipped from considering the shadowy, ancient magics like the Old Road to recalling the damp scent of a crumbling stone barrow lost deep in a dark wood.

Elezar stopped himself from thinking any further of that place. Reflexively, he touched the pendant hanging from his neck. His fingers brushed both the Cadeleonian star on the face and the Bahiim tree at its back. The two faiths shared little in their modern practice, but Elezar took a kind of comfort in knowing that both had arisen from the ideals of courage and valor. Both promised salvation beyond death.

"Most legends grow from something true and very rarely are they forgotten completely," Elezar said quickly and he stood. "Perhaps there's a mention of some violet flame in Bishop Palo's collection of relics or in Count Radulf's library. I'll have to go to both places and make inquiries of the scholars there."

Skellan eyed him from the bed, where he sat with Elezar's knife resting across his bare thigh.

"You should be very careful in the bishop's household."

"I know," Elezar replied. "You're the second witch to have warned me against him. You think he had some part in this violet flame?"

Skellan nodded. There was something in his open expression that made it difficult for Elezar to break from his gaze. He forced himself to turn and gather his riding cloak and then his saddlebags. He felt Skellan's gaze on him, even glimpsed his concerned face out of the corner of his eye, but feigned preoccupation. He secured the buckles of his saddlebags and brushed road dust and pine needles from his cloak.

"Do you know what it means among Labarans when you give a witch your knife?" Skellan called from the bed.

"No." Elezar turned to meet Skellan's curious expression.

"I didn't think that you did." Skellan glanced down at the knife and something like melancholy passed over his expression but then he looked up at Elezar and brightened again. "Let me keep it anyway, will you?"

It was a good hunting knife, long bladed and slightly curved in the Irabiim style. He'd received it as a gift from the handsome young man who later won the first love of his life from him. Not a fair trade, that, but still Elezar had carried the knife with him for five years now.

He almost refused Skellan's request but then, looking at Skellan, he wondered if perhaps five years had been long enough to hold onto something that pained him. He could buy himself any number of hunting knives, but for Skellan this one was probably a small treasure.

"All right, keep it," Elezar told him. Seeing Skellan's face light up with pleasure, Elezar felt oddly touched and then embarrassed by his own sentimentality. Had a month in the Mirogoth forest turned him into a misty-eyed idiot? Elezar hardened his expression. "You're not holding me to any witch's promise with it, you understand?"

Skellan laughed in response. "You are not beholden to me, never fear. But it is a good blade and I'll do right by it, I can promise you that."

Elezar tossed him his knife sheath, hoping Skellan really did own a belt to put it on back at whatever slum passed for his lodgings.

"We should be on our way," Elezar announced. He expected something of a fight, particularly after all the earlier talk of them sharing a destiny but Skellan only nodded.

"You go first," Skellan told him. "I'll slip out the window once the courtyard is empty. It would be best if we weren't seen leaving together, wouldn't it?"

"Indeed," Elezar agreed. Then he wished Skellan luck and left the room.

He spied Fluer in the hall and greeted her politely but she didn't meet his gaze. He only vaguely recollected conversing with her the night before. Had he said something terrible in his fevered state, he wondered. Had he given himself away as a man who'd bed her brother before her?

No, Elezar decided as he studied her face. It wasn't recrimination he read in her countenance but something nearer guilt.

"Something amiss, Fluer?" Elezar asked though he didn't expect any real response.

But Fluer looked up at him almost like a startled doe and then glanced quickly across the empty hall.

"Is it true that you killed a nobleman in Cadeleon?" she asked in a whisper. "Was it over his wife?"

A cold alarm shot through Elezar. Fluer wouldn't have been asking if someone hadn't told her as much. Fedeles had warned him that Lady Reollos might send men after him. He recalled the Cadeleonian horse traders that Skellan hadn't liked the look of and who'd paid the innkeeper's wife too well.

"Where are they waiting for me?" Elezar demanded.

"I don't—" Fluer looked like she might burst into tears as she met Elezar's glare. "In the stable."

Of course. They had to know he wouldn't abandon Cobre, not even if an ambush lay in wait for him.

"Keep Doue inside with you," Elezar told Fluer. He started for the door.

"You aren't going to fight them?" Fluer caught at his arm. "There are three of them and they know you're ill. I told them that your left leg looked hurt and you were fevered—I'm so sorry—"

It was almost amusing to realize now that what he'd mistaken for Fluer's mother whoring her to merchants had in fact been Fluer and her mother selling him out to assassins. To think, he'd felt such pity for her. Elezar pulled free of her small hand easily. Fluer didn't attempt to stop him again.

Elezar reached the door quickly. He stepped outside into the bright, sunlit courtyard and laid his saddlebags aside. Then he drew his sword and strode toward the stable.

The sun burned in the clear blue sky, flashing across the slick flagstones where water from Elezar's bath by the well still stood in pools. Elezar noted the shining path of reflected light leading to the watering trough beside the tall wooden stable. The footing just there could turn tricky.

A forgotten-looking cord of wood leaned against the near wall of the smokehouse. Stripped bark littered the ground and the heavy splitting maul had been left jutting from a stump. Two lines of abandoned laundry hung out, drying in the morning sun. Pale yellow sheets billowed in the breeze as if beckoning Elezar. Just beyond the courtyard walls he heard goose girls chattering over the honks of the flocks they drove to market. Their voices sounded sharp and distinct as they carried through the quiet emptiness of the courtyard.

Elezar studied the heavy stable doors then gave a long, loud whistle. Cobre called back to him from behind the wooden walls. Neither pain nor fear sounded in his whinny, so the men waiting in ambush hadn't harmed him. Whether that was because they hadn't yet considered it or because they planned to sell the stallion once they'd killed his master, Elezar didn't care. Just so long as he was alive and there.

"No doubt you've sailed through rough weather and spent some hard weeks searching for me," Elezar called out. "After so much effort it seems unworthy of you to cower in a stable now that I stand before you."

No response came from the stable, but Elezar felt certain that the men inside were peering after him through the cracks in the doors. Men of the law would have announced themselves. Their skulking silence reassured Elezar that neither Prince Sevanyo nor Count Radulf had proclaimed him a criminal or issued a warrant for his execution—at least not yet. So, if these men served anyone, they were most likely Lady

Reollos' assassins. That gave Elezar the legal right to defend himself.

He strode to the smokehouse and jerked the splitting maul free. He swung the wooden handle with his left hand, testing the weight and balance of the maul. It arced through the air as heavy as a war hammer, but much more blunt. The naked blade of his sword flashed white razor edges, while the maul's angles looked dull as granite. Still, Elezar liked its weight in his hand.

"Come now, gentlemen," Elezar shouted as he strode back to the center of the courtyard. "After pursuing me so far how can you have turned so timid? I'd hate to have to burn that stable down just to see your faces!"

That brought them out promptly enough: two brawny Cadeleonian men wearing neither livery colors nor badges of law but dressed in thick fighting leathers. Cold, professional expressions showed on their tanned faces. Mercenaries, Elezar thought, and well armed. One carried a pike and the other drew a sword. They charged fast and in close formation.

No sign of the third member of their group, but then Elezar hadn't expected them to make a clean showing. More likely these two planned to jab and drive him round till his back was turned to the stable door. Then the third mercenary would take him from behind.

Elezar's heartbeat quickened with a brutal anticipation.

The pikeman thrust for Elezar's gut and Elezar darted left, using the wall of the well to cover his exposed left side. The pikeman bounded after Elezar while the swordsman edged to Elezar's right to pin him down. Elezar fought a surging reflex to force the swordsman back. His pulse raced, but he waited, drawing them both closer.

The pikeman looked to be the older of the two and the more assured. The younger, leaner swordsman kept close to the perimeter of the pike's long reach. The pikeman jabbed in again, swiftly, nearly spearing Elezar's shoulder. But Elezar bounded back another step and the pikeman followed him just a little too eagerly. Then the pikeman's foot slid in one of the standing pools of water.

A furious exhilaration flooded Elezar and he exploded forward. He knocked the off-balance pikeman's weapon aside with the flat of his sword, lunging past the man's defense. A roar tore free from him as he brought the maul down across the pikeman's head with all his might. He felt flesh and bone crumpling as the maul split the man's helmet and tore through his face. The pikeman made a thick choking noise and fell. Elezar left the maul jutting from his crushed skull and spun back on the swordsman.

The swordsman reflexively thrust for Elezar's right flank but flinched as Elezar parried his blow and came after him with another roar. Their blades rang with the force of their clashing bodies. Elezar felt the other man's strength and weight like a reverberation trembling through the hilt of his sword into the palm of his hand. He thrust and sent the slimmer man stumbling back. Twice more he tested the swordsman's reach and reflexes. He met Elezar with speed and well-balanced parries. Strong and long limbed, a fine Cadeleonian swordsman, he blocked and pivoted almost swiftly enough to shield his entire body with just a narrow blade.

He lunged to Elezar's left and Elezar allowed him to nearly land the blow. The sword tip punched into Elezar's cloak, inches from his hip. Sweat streamed down Elezar's back. His whole body blazed like a furnace, and his nerves sang as if only in this moment was he fully alive. Elezar twisted and plunged his sword into the other man's exposed flank, piercing him above the hip, driving deep into his bowels, and punching through his back.

Elezar jerked his sword free from the tight grip of the other man's clenched body immediately. Dark arterial blood spilled down the man's groin, but the swordsman still held his own blade ready. Even so, Elezar knew only minutes remained now.

He quickly parried the gored swordsman's slashing blade, tearing a gash open across the man's drooping forearm. His opponent looked suddenly small and very pale. As Elezar came at him again, he retreated quickly back to the shadow of the stable. He moved clumsily, his feet catching on the flagstones. Then he fell against the water trough.

Elezar almost followed to finish him; worthy swordsmen deserved the mercy of swift deaths. Then he glimpsed a flicker of reflected color in the surface of the water trough. He leapt back from the direct line of the stable doors as an arrow shot from the open crack. The gray fletching slashed Elezar's cheek. The arrow flashed past and cracked across the flagstones. Elezar bounded to the cover of the well wall and crouched low.

His right ear throbbed as if stung by a furious bee. A hot trickle of blood dribbled down his neck. A second arrow arched high overhead and then whistled down to crack against the flagstones only a foot from Elezar's thigh.

"Damn archers," Elezar muttered. He didn't dare to peer over the edge of the well. At this range a good archer could pierce his skull as easily as a muskmelon. Instead he studied what few reflections the scattered pools of water offered him. He could see the dead pikeman's outstretched leg and beyond that the fallen swordsman slumped across the trough. His seeping blood slowly darkened the water.

Then Elezar glimpsed a thick hand reach out and nudge the swordsman—the archer's ring on the thumb told Elezar just whose hand it was. If the swordsman gave a response to his comrade it was too slight for Elezar to see. Then the archer pushed the swordsman's wide eyes closed. From what Elezar knew of the dead he doubted that it was managed too gently.

An instant later another arrow shrieked through air and narrowly missed Elezar's shoulder. The archer might be shooting blind but Elezar was too large of a man to shelter behind so little cover for much longer. Soon enough the archer would strike him.

"You've nowhere to go," the archer called as if reading Elezar's thoughts.

"Well, that all depends on how many arrows are left in your quiver," Elezar replied. He caught the distinct sound of a light footstep and realized that the archer was closing the distance between them.

"Plenty of arrows," the archer replied. His voice sounded much nearer. Elezar guessed that he was working his way around the well to get a clear shot.

The fallen pike lay beyond Elezar's reach but only by a few feet, not that it would offer him an arrow's reach. But if the archer came much closer it might give Elezar a chance of striking the man down before he could loose a shaft into Elezar's skull—if he didn't kill Elezar the instant he broke from the cover of the well.

Hell of a gamble, either way.

"Too bad your friend isn't here to have your back," the archer called out. His voice definitely sounded off to the right now, nearer to where the sheets rustled in the breeze. "You know, we might be able to come to terms—you and me—if you would tell me where you and the duke have hidden Atreau Vediya."

So, they didn't know that it was Atreau impersonating Fedeles. That was good.

"What sort of terms?" Elezar asked. He listened intently for the archer's voice. Was he still closing in or creeping farther to Elezar's right?

"Maybe I could lose track of you in the Mirogoth forest," the archer suggested from closer still. Elezar couldn't imagine any man who took the time to close a fallen comrade's eyes simply allowing his killer to walk away. He guessed that he and the archer were both playing at the same game, talking not because they believed anything the other said but to work out just where the other lurked.

Elezar edged a little left while straining to hear the tread of footsteps. The pike still lay out of reach, inches from the dead pikeman's right arm, far too exposed for comfort.

"Thinking about it?" the archer inquired. He was too near now, Elezar realized. Another foot or so and he'd be able to shoot Elezar as easily as he might spear a big fish in a small barrel.

Heart hammering, Elezar burst from the cover of the well and snatched the long pike from the pikeman's lifeless grip. He caught his first clear sight of the archer as he spun on the man. Stout, grizzled and clothed in a heavy pale gray wool and leather, he stood close enough that Elezar could clearly see the taut string of his short bow as well as the black bars marking the gray fletching of his arrow.

Elezar hurled the pike but the archer had already released his arrow. Though strangely his arm jerked as he did so and the arrow flew wide. Elezar's pike missed as well, by a hand's breadth. Still the archer lurched and then suddenly collapsed like a slack sail.

And then Elezar saw Skellan, wrapped in his dark red cloak and holding Elezar's hunting knife, as he stood over the archer. A froth of blood bubbled up from the archer's back as his ruptured lung blew his last breath out the gaping wound. Skellan stared down at the man's prone form with a strained expression; but as the archer raised his arm just slightly, Skellan dropped down over him and with a very quick motion slit the struggling man's throat wide. Blood darker than even Skellan's cloak spilled across the flagstones.

"Where did you come from?" Elezar's heart still pounded in his chest. He'd been certain that he was going to die when the archer had loosed his arrow.

"Out from the window. I hid behind the hanging sheets." Skellan only briefly looked up from the dead archer to Elezar. "He meant to murder you."

"You noticed that, did you?" Elezar laughed, though it came out shaky.

"He was lying about letting you go." Skellan's scowled at the archer. "I could see he meant to kill you no matter what. There wasn't time to call a challenge to him."

And suddenly Elezar realized that Skellan was offering up this explanation to himself, rationalizing the bloody act he'd just committed, because unlike Elezar he wasn't a murderer, wasn't a beast—not even after he'd taken the shape of one. Killing another human being in cold blood came as a shock to him. He wiped the blade of the hunting knife clean on the archer's sleeve, but with such a care that Elezar wondered if the action carried a Labaran symbolism. Putting the archer's spilled blood on his own hands, perhaps.

"You saved my life. Thank you." Elezar closed the space between them and lowered his voice to a whisper. "There may be others already on their way after these three. We can't tarry here."

Skellan nodded and stood. He looked embarrassed at being so shaken after slitting another man's throat.

"Who are—were they?" Skellan asked.

"Mercenaries sent as assassins." Elezar only spared the dead men a glance. He'd learned long ago not to indulge in curiosity about the qualities and characters of the men he killed.

"Why were they set on you?" Skellan asked.

"I'm not the only one they were after, just the easiest to find." Elezar wiped the blade of his sword clean with the cloth he carried for just that purpose. The fact that he always kept such a cloth at hand struck him as speaking volumes about the life he'd made for himself as opposed to the one this witch led. "It's too long of a story to tell here and now, but the short of it is that I killed a lord and his widow wants me dead before the matter goes to court."

"Nothing to do with you being sent to the Sumar grimma's lands?"

"Nothing," Elezar replied flatly. Just how much did Skellan know about that? But this wasn't the time or place to ask.

"But they know you serve the duke of Rauma and everyone knows he's a guest at Bishop Palo's townhouse," Skellan said. "They'll expect you to go there, won't they?"

Elezar nodded, considering what Skellan said.

Much of the city knew him as the duke of Rauma's varlet, and they would expect him to flee to Bishop Palo's house. If another ambush was waiting for him, it would be on the road there, which was reason enough not to go. On top of that Elezar didn't want anyone looking too closely at the supposed duke. It would be better if he were known to have fled the duke's service. Though where he would go, Elezar didn't know, only that he couldn't be seen in Atreau's company again without endangering them both.

He frowned back at the walls of the inn and thought he glimpsed Fluer peering out from a window, or it could have been her mother. In either case the shutter closed right away.

"God, what a mess," Elezar muttered. As if stopping a war by finding some witch's lost brat wasn't enough trouble, now Lady Reollos sent assassins for him to contend with as well. He'd be lucky if he lived to see the next month—luckier still if he didn't get anyone else killed while doing so. And all because he'd been too stupid to save Atreau without killing Lord Reollos. A better man would have found a way to protect them both.

"Can you leave your horse?" Skellan asked. Such a pragmatic question from a man wearing nothing but a fur cloak, Elezar thought.

"If I could have abandoned Cobre, I wouldn't have had to fight these men in the first place."

Skellan nodded like he'd known as much.

"Fetch him then," Skellan said. "It will take some doing, but I should be able to hide the both of you."

"You still want to get involved in my business after this?" Elezar gestured from the archer's dead body to the pikeman and then across the courtyard where the slain swordsman lay slumped over the trough. Flies already buzzed over the ruin of the pikeman's face. Soon the bright sun would turn the faint tang of spilled blood thick and rank as spoiling meat.

"I'm already involved," Skellan replied. "We both are, you just don't understand that yet. And I'm offering to take you in, not the other way around."

Elezar scowled at Skellan. Here he stood, naked and still shaking from the shock of stabbing a man in the back, but convinced that this was his destiny. And by what? Mere happenstance and faith. Elezar had seen too much of where unquestioning belief led to just let it go.

"Just because you think something is your fate—your vei—that doesn't mean you have to give up and accept it, you know. You always have a choice."

"Of course I have a choice," Skellan replied. "My vei has been forged by every choice I've made in my life. That's what makes it mine and mine alone." He frowned at Elezar. "Honestly, I don't see why you're even trying to argue with me about it. You need my help and I'm offering it. Have you been fighting so long that you just don't know how to recognize an ally any longer?"

The question took Elezar off guard and he would have refuted it but he knew he'd just be wasting time by arguing any further.

As uneasy as he felt about embroiling Skellan in his affairs, he had no one else to trust and no more time to waste. Three men were dead and Count Radulf's appointed sheriff would soon arrive. While Elezar had acted within the law, word that a wealthy Cadeleonian lady was offering gold for his head would soon spread through Milmuraille, if it hadn't already. Sheriff's men were as likely as most others to be tempted by the prospect of a reward—particularly if Elezar was already in their grasp.

He retrieved his saddlebags and then hurried to fetch Cobre. He bridled and saddled the stallion quickly while barn swallows flitted between the rafters overhead. Shafts of morning sun fell between the open doors and lit the fragrant bales of hay like gold. A plump little mare called flirtatiously to Cobre as Elezar led him from his stall. They just reached the stable doors when Skellan stepped inside.

His feet were still bare but beneath his red cloak he now wore a leather jerkin and gray breaches. Elezar's sheathed hunting knife and a bulging coin purse hung from the black calfskin belt slung across Skellan's hips. The witch might have qualms with killing a man but he certainly wasn't timid about stripping a corpse.

That's the right of a champion, wasn't that what Eski had said? He'd been told that the same held true for Labaran law—in the north at least. In the southern counties, where Cadeleonian influence was stronger, the goods would have belonged to the dead men's families.

"Will your mount allow me to lay my hands on him?" Skellan asked.

"If I'm at his side, Cobre will even let you ride him. Why?"

"I was just thinking that a man—even one as striking as you—might hide himself about anywhere or as nearly anyone in a city the size of Milmuraille. But a big black charger like your Cobre will stand out among even a hundred other horses." Skellan drew close and Cobre took in a deep breath of the witch and nickered softly as if he already knew him. When Skellan held out his hand Cobre allowed himself to be scratched. "If I were an assassin looking for you, I'd search for your horse."

Elezar nodded. Plainly that was how he'd been located last night.

Skellan brushed his fingers over his own red cloak and then lifted his cupped hand to his mouth. He whispered a Mirogoth word that Elezar didn't know and then leaned into Cobre, pressing his hands and face against the stallion's powerful neck. Skellan's fingers curled and trembled as if struggling to grip a force too powerful for him. His brow furrowed with strained concentration. Cobre went very still, looking at ease, almost sleepy. Then before Elezar's eyes, long chestnut hair began to sprout through Cobre's glossy coat while Skellan's cloak steadily darkened to gleaming jet black. In a heartbeat Cobre became nearly unrecognizable, his hide shaggy and red, his ears slightly tattered. Even his brand had disappeared under the long red hair.

Skellan released Cobre and staggered back. Elezar caught his shoulder, fearing he might collapse. He felt deathly cold in Elezar's grip and a scent like singed hair hung over him. He shook as if he'd just been pulled from icy waters and his skin looked damp. But then he steadied himself and pulled a grimace of a smile.

"It's like walking on knife blades, working spells with that violet flame in the sanctum... Dyeing him would have been better but we haven't the time and your horse would have hated it." A deep shudder passed through his body. "We need to go before we're discovered here."

"We do," Elezar agreed but he didn't release his hold on Skellan. "You ride. I'll walk alongside."

He helped Skellan up into his saddle. He clearly hadn't been brought up riding, but he had instinct enough to keep his seat. Elezar led Cobre out of the stable, through the courtyard and onto the street. The stallion snorted as if he found the entire charade amusing. Carts loaded with spring crops of black kale, winter peas and cabbages as small and bright as limes rolled past, while shepherds and goose girls drove their flocks up the street to the Auguiday market. Elezar thought he glimpsed Doue pelting up the street, doubtlessly bound to fetch the sheriff.

"So." Elezar glanced to Skellan. A little color had returned to his face. "Where does this vei of yours lead now?"

"Ahead," Skellan replied. "Always ahead."

CHAPTER TWELVE

Elezar shadowed Skellan through the crowded avenues of Milmuraille, feeling as if he were visiting an entirely different city than the one he'd come to know these past months. The voices of street hawkers, arguing couples, gossips and boisterous children rolled through the din of dogs, pigs, geese and hens. Laundry fluttered overhead like tattered flags and second-story balconies jutted so far out over the narrow avenues that they blocked all but the narrowest seam of the bright blue sky.

Previously he'd kept to the well-traveled thoroughfares, frequenting the tidy timber-framed taverns and inns that lined them. Only rarely and with caution had he ventured into the dank dueling alleys where street gangs gathered like packs of feral dogs. He never allowed himself to become lost in the spiderweb of narrow paths, looped roads and dark stairwells that riddled the noisy old section of the city. But Skellan navigated the infamous catacombs and maze-like arcades with the ease of a true native.

On either side of them, clouds of smoke plumed from open fires where fishwives smoked eels on long wooden spits and children bundled in rabbit furs tossed balls of fragrant tree sap into the flames. Blue haze rolled over Elezar, the scent of it reminding him of a fire at sea.

"Look there." Skellan pointed to a gray cracked stone that might have once been the base of some monument. Now it squatted in the shadows beneath the bay window of a bakery. Despite the lichen and weathering Elezar could still make a string of spiraling symbols carved into the stone. Charred craters broke the ring of symbols in several places, reminding Elezar of the pitted pockmarks that had remained of Skellan's spells this morning.

"Did the violet flame do that to it?" Elezar wanted to whisper but the din of the street forced him to nearly shout. No one took any notice.

Skellan nodded.

"Do you recognize the symbols that survived?" They looked decorative to Elezar but he knew very little of how a spell might be written. It had to mean something that the violet flame hadn't destroyed these markings.

"Nothing. The null sign." Skellan leaned from Cobre's saddle and frowned at the stone. "They're like the naught in your Cadeleonian number system, an indication of an empty place. They are the absence of magic... of anything, really. In a spoken spell they represent the pause of a drawn breath."

Elezar considered that, but then his attention was caught by a horde of brilliant green frogs that bounded from a nearby alley and flooded the street. They sang like larks as they leapt over his boots and threw themselves into rain puddles at the side of the road. A moment later a skinny Mirogoth girl with a woven basket on her back came racing after them. Skellan and she exchanged a brief wave of hands in passing. Then he and Elezar moved on.

"There are other relics like the one behind us, hidden throughout the city," Skellan called down from Cobre's back. "Bone-crusher said that they once supported statues of Old Gods and forest spirits, but they were all torn down by Cadeleonian priests after the war. If the violet flame hadn't burned it away you would have been able to read a prayer to Irnan, the first wethra-steed to take up a rider. There was a statue of a river wyrm as well. It was chiseled there when this whole city was still a wild, holy place where the Old Gods gathered at the river's edge."

Elezar knew the tales of the Old Gods, but largely from the Cadeleonian sermons intended to reminded all young men that only the valor and sacrifice of the Savior had banished those ancient monstrosities from their homeland and driven them into the north.

Skellan pointed west toward the curve of the river where it spilled into the bay. "The stone of Dammri, the chief of the frogwives, stands guard just down Warf Road."

"You know your city well," Elezar commented. Skellan shrugged as if it were nothing, but after that he went out of his way to inform Elezar of other eccentricities and interests hidden all around them. For the first time Elezar noticed the stone trolls glowering from beneath the bridges built across their backs as well as beautifully carved wethra-steeds that lay nearly buried beneath the collapsed remains of an abandoned Mirogoth temple. Skellan knew the names of all the ruined deities just as he seemed to know all the populace they passed on the street.

And much of the old city knew Skellan as well Elezar surmised from the number of herb girls, dung mongers, tinkers and shiftless roughs who greeted him as they passed. Skellan offered most a smile and the wave of his hand. Though when one comely, half-dressed woman shouted his name and leaned out from the orange sill of a gaudy bay window, Skellan paused. Her loose red hair floated around her face in the breeze. Skellan assured her that tonight he'd be home.

Elezar tried not to think too much about the familiarity in her voice as she berated Skellan for his long absence. Their relationship—even her name—was none of his concern. Though Skellan readily informed him that she was called Cire and was widely rumored to have enchanted Count Radulf's secretary briefly some twenty years ago. By Skellan's threadbare standards, she was a prosperous fortune-teller, possessing both a property and two coops of big mountain hens. She had apparently taught Skellan what etiquette he knew and rented a room to him.

Soon after that, Skellan stopped at a well-kept courier stable were they could lodge Cobre. The two gray-haired ruddy-faced Labaran women running the place were built as solid as Cadeleonian soldiers, and the rose-red rag skirts they wore did little to soften their rugged appearances. Skellan called them by their names—Merle and Navet—and despite their hard features they greeted Skellan in return with wide smiles and teased him like a pair of maiden aunts.

"Bless me, but it's come back so fat and washed I hardly knew it was my own Skellan!" Merle, the taller of the two women, ruffled Skellan's hair. "Here we were gone all grim thinking you'd got yourself killed by the grimma."

"No such luck," Skellan replied.

"And what's this then?" Navet asked, jutting her thumb at Elezar. "Not a man you're taking on, is it? Finally scraped off that rascal Rafale?"

"Elezar." Skellan gave his name casually enough but both women scrutinized him like he might be passing counterfeit coins.

Their stable, called the Fairwind, was small but very well tended and seemed in far better repair than the little house at the other end of the grassy yard.

"We're keeping company," Skellan stated while Elezar brushed Cobre down. "He's the one that fed me and all."

"Really?" Navet looked Elezar up and down. "He don't rightly look like he's fed himself in a month."

"You ain't been eating everything out this poor tough's mouth, have you, Skellan?" Merle asked. She hefted a thick flake of summer grass down for Cobre. Better fodder and more than Elezar had expected even at the good price he'd paid for Cobre's board.

"I'll have you know I ate like a gentleman when we shared a plate," Skellan replied, and Elezar had to cover his laugh with a rough cough. Merle leaned a little closer to Elezar. The pleasant scent of hay and horse leathers drifted off her.

"You take care, big 'un; that boy can cost more to feed than a stable full of stallions."

"He did say something like that earlier," Elezar replied. "Something about not having shoes because he'd eaten the laces and leather alike."

"Well, that's how it is with witches, ain't it?" Merle grinned, displaying a surprisingly white set of teeth.

Elezar could think of nothing to add. He wasn't used to speaking so freely of witches or magic. In Cadeleon such matters were most often shouted as accusations at trials. In the capital, and many duchies, witches were still hanged as heretics. His own mother had undergone a crisis of faith upon discovering that Elezar's best friend, Javier, whom she'd doted on like one of her own sons, had been decried by the Holy Cadeleonian church for practicing Bahiim sorcery.

"We suppose you heard about the nastiness that's slithered out of the sanctum?" Navet asked Skellan.

"More than heard. It nearly got me in a scrape just this morning." Skellan's face went grim. "It hasn't given you any trouble, has it?"

"Burned up the doorframe some, but nothing much worse than that for us. Though there's talk that the real witches around town are going up in smoke. Some of them you know—"

"Vieve's missing and there are others as well," Merle called. "Witches all along Charm Row gone. Nothing but ash left in their beds and chairs. And even Count Radulf's astrologer fell down writhing like he was burning alive and then died in the count's garden. The count's men are denying it, of course, but it's out all across the city. Most of them, what are still alive, have packed up and fled south. The rest of us are meeting up at the Rat Rafters tomorrow night."

"You can't know how relieved we are to see you alive after hearing about that." Navet hugged Skellan to her chest. He looked embarrassed but accepted the embrace. "You shouldn't stay here, our boy. Not with that thing hunting witches and no one here who can make you safe. The Sumar grimma could well use a witch as handsome as you, and that nastiness wouldn't dare cross her, I don't think."

"I'm not going to run whimpering to the Sumar grimma, and I won't abandon Milmuraille. This city is mine."

"I told you he wouldn't be swayed," Merle called back. She glanced to Elezar and said much more quietly, "You know he's a half wild and willful thing, he is. Don't go thinking you can put a collar on him and take him with you to church."

"The idea never even crossed my mind," Elezar replied, though he couldn't help but note that he'd collared the witch rather easily.

Skellan smiled at the two women, and Elezar noticed how very young the expression made him look.

"Now, are we feeding you?" Navet inquired.

"I already ate. For now, I'm only taking Elezar to the Mockingbird Playhouse to collect on a few debts."

"We're going to a theater?" Elezar asked. That could be useful to him; after all, Atreau loved the bawdy Labaran playhouses and Elezar needed to contact him outside of the bishop's house. If he could arrange for Atreau to come to the playhouse, perhaps he could convince Skellan to take a report to him. Then there would be no chance of anyone seeing him in Atreau's company.

"Not just any theater," Skellan informed him with an arched brow. "The Mockingbird is a blazing palace of trap doors and floating sets and so much bare flesh on view that it puts the bawdyhouses all around it to shame. The master and playwright, Rafale, is the bastard of one of Count Radulf's favorite barons and gets away with worse than scandal on and off the boards."

"One of your Cadeleonian clergy accused Rafale of corrupting the morals of the city with his performances—the entire city, can you imagine!" Navet laughed. Both she and Merle looked just as delighted as Skellan.

Doubtless Atreau would be overjoyed at the prospect of patronizing such an infamous establishment. In fact Elezar felt certain he'd heard Atreau mention a fellow by the name of Rafale previously. As Elezar vaguely recalled there had been some rumor of the playwright serving as a spy when he'd run a traveling theater troupe in his youth. Though that hardly mattered to Elezar.

In the dim light of a crowded theater chances were good that no one would notice if Atreau received a bundle of notes along with the inevitable flurry of perfumed invitations from available courtesans and actresses. All that need to be done was to get a missive to Atreau.

"It sounds interesting," Elezar responded. "But before we go, I'd like to hire one of your messengers to take a note for me. As discreetly as possible."

"Ah, well since you're keeping our Skellan company I can personally carry any regrets to debt collectors or abandoned wives. We'll keep the matter just between the four of us here." Merle winked at Elezar. "So, what fine establishment will you have me ride my dusty ass out to?"

Elezar told her, allowing himself a little satisfaction at the look of shock on both the stablewomen's faces when he gave Bishop Palo's address and the duke of Rauma's name.

Less than an hour later Elezar took in the Mockingbird Playhouse. It rose like a small palace over a sea of brothels and smaller, open-air theaters. Its plastered walls shone like pearl in the sharp noonday sun, and the dome crowning its three floors gleamed like burnished gold. Gilded knot work encircled the round windows that lined the third floor and the double doors of the front entry flashed with brightly painted motifs of naked human bodies entangled with those of wild beasts. Elezar wasn't certain if the men and women were being ravaged or ravished.

He didn't have the opportunity to find out. Instead of entering via the main door he followed Skellan as he skirted around the building to a shadowed alley where he drew open a plain white door that Elezar suspected he, himself, would have mistaken for nothing more than a few cracks in the plastered walls.

Inside, the noonday heat hung between the intricately carved and painted walls. Shafts of sunlight pierced the high, circular windows to illuminate the ornately gilded box seats and the nearly empty stage beyond. Over the mysteries of the backstage was the rail of the musician's balcony. A handsome, dark-haired man leaned there, brooding as he studied eaves far above his head. On the stage below him two mahogany-skinned Yuanese men, dressed in the matching halves of a lion costume, gawked up at him. The tawny head and mane of the costume engulfed most of the smaller man's upper body. Elezar caught only a glimpse of his round face and the tight curls of his short black hair poking out from between the lion's gaping jaws.

"It would be exciting if we climbed down this pillar from the balcony to the stage and then mauled the concubine," the smaller actor called out to the man on the balcony.

"It would be at that." The man sounded distracted. "Though not as exciting as the entire city going up in flames."

The actors on the stage didn't seem to know quite what to make of that but then the smaller simply plowed on to discuss how the scene could be best blocked.

Elezar trailed Skellan from the side door down through rows of low-backed wooden benches. Three levels of much more opulent box seats towered over him. He noticed several men napping in one of the boxes. Long-necked lutes and a brassy horn leaned against the arms of their seats.

Elezar pointed to them and Skellan nodded.

"Rafale often keeps the troupe rehearsing so late that about half of them just sleep here."

The way the voices of the men on stage boomed across the theater, it amazed Elezar that anyone could remain asleep, but none of the musicians stirred. And only when Skellan and he had reached the steps to the stage did anyone take note of their approach.

The man on the balcony, Rafale, suddenly looked up and narrowed his gaze at Skellan. An instant later he swung over the balcony railing, slithered down the wooden pillar and bounded past the actors.

"Skellan!" Rafale called as if the sight of the street witch were a revelation. "Mother's Blood, it is you. We'd thought you died! But your hair looks so... red. What have you done to it?"

"Washed," Skellan replied as if it were a shame of some kind. He took the steps up the stage two at a time and accepted Rafale's embrace. Elezar followed him feeling like a long, black shadow.

"This is Elezar." Skellan withdrew from Rafale's arms to indicate Elezar with a motion of his hand. "Elezar, this is Rafale. He's the playwright and owner of the Mockingbird Playhouse."

"Pleased to meet you." Elezar offered his right hand in Labaran fashion and Rafale lightly touched his own open palm against Elezar's. His fingers felt soft as a child's and though gray streaked his long black hair, his skin looked neither as tanned nor as weathered as Elezar's. His glossy mustache curled like a smirk above his full mouth. A white linen shirt showed through the slashed sleeves of his deep blue doublet and pretty green stones decorated the hilt of the delicate knife that hung from his belt. Elezar guessed that he wielded the blade against pen quills and little else.

"Likewise, I'm sure," Rafale replied but his light gaze returned to Skellan immediately. "Where have you been? Nearly every witch in the city has come here at one point or another this last month looking for you. And, listen, there's a man as well—a well-appointed man who wishes very much to make your acquaintance—"

"I'm not looking for work just now," Skellan replied.

"But this fellow is from the count's court—"

"So send Cire to him. There's nothing she'd like better—"

"This isn't something Cire could do."

"You haven't become the count's pimp have you, Rafale?" Skellan smirked at the handsome playwright. "Even if you have, the answer would still be no. I haven't the time now."

Rafale looked like he might offer an argument but Skellan turned from him to exchange warm greetings with the Yuanese actors standing back stage.

Elezar found himself and this Rafale standing together with nothing to say to each other. The playwright studied Elezar with haughty expression that struck Elezar as quite familiar. He guessed that Rafale wasn't just a lordling's bastard but that he'd kept courtly company long enough to perfectly absorb more of a nobleman's demeanor than Elezar often managed.

"Cadeleonian mercenary?" Rafale asked.

Elezar simply offered his own version of the Mirogoth shrug, which worked perfectly. Rafale appeared to abandon all interest in further conversation.

Then Skellan bounded back to them and Rafale's attention fell on him like a grasping hand. Elezar had seen desire in men's gazes before, but rarely had it shown so intensely and openly.

"You wouldn't believe how worried about you I've been, Skellan," Rafale told him.

"True, I wouldn't." Skellan laughed and offered Rafale an amused smile. "But it's kind of you to say."

"How callous he is to us, isn't he?" This Rafale addressed to Elezar, though in a bright, theatrical tone.

"And it only gets worse, my good fellow," Skellan responded in Elezar's silence. "Because I've come to call up debts owed me."

The smile remained plastered to Rafale's lips but Elezar recognized how his eyes went suddenly wary. Elezar didn't trust that amicable insincerity, particularly not after this morning's ambush. Hardly aware of his own motion, Elezar felt his fingers curling around the hilt of his sword, just in case there was a little venom in that decorative knife after all.

"Haven't I always said, anything for my own, Skellan? I'm

glad to give you all I have." Rafale draped his arm over Skellan's shoulder. "But, my dear, the truth is you'd be wisest to go to this fellow I was talking about. This latest production has nearly bankrupted me but I'm certain that he—"

Skellan brushed the handsome playwright's arm off him.

"You pen sad tales much more naturally than you live them. This new velvet doublet and the gold lover's locket pinned to your sleeve call you the most charming liar in five leagues."

Rafale looked like he might protest when a sharp laugh sounded from behind them. The Yuanese actors grinned from where they both lounged against the wooden pillar. The younger of the two held a pipe but hadn't lit it yet.

"You missed last month's performance, Skellan. Guild Master Houblon's wife got the whole show to herself," the elder Yuanese actor called out with glee. "Exhausted, dressed in rags and only a turnip to hang from his rope belt, our poor Rafale was such a sight!"

"Moved the lady to tears, seeing him so near ruin just for the sake of his art. She handed over two gold rings and her pearls right on the spot." The younger Yuanese actor snickered. Seeing them both with the same expression of their faces, Elezar thought they must be father and son.

"There's a waste," Skellan called back to the two of them. "As I remember, our Rafale has gone off pearls all together, ever since Master Ivette's wife nearly buried him in them last summer."

"You know him like your own," the elder Yuanese actor replied. "He did complain about them directly after the good mistress departed!"

Rafale's face flushed with anger and despite all the surrounding laughter, Elezar kept close watch on him. He didn't like how near Skellan the man stood. If Rafale went for his knife, Elezar would need to shoulder Skellan to the side to keep him out of Rafale's reach.

Fortunately, when Rafale did lash out, it was only to gesture obscenely at the Yuanese actors.

"Enough from you two," Rafale shouted. "If you've got time to gossip then you have time to rehearse your plan of slithering down that pillar!"

The actors went quiet, making a little show of studying the pillar before each shimmied up it to the balcony above. Rafale watched them briefly then, with a sigh, returned his attention to Skellan and Elezar.

"All right, fine. You've caught me out." Rafale sounded almost amused now. "So, I'm still a lying ass, as you well know. But I do keep my word when cornered. Tell me what you need and I'll supply what I can."

Elezar relaxed a little. So, Rafale was the sort whose temper flared like lit liquor only to burn away in an instant. He clearly possessed none of Elezar's own murderous reflexes, not even when he was red faced with fury.

"Hot bath and fresh clothes for my Elezar," Skellan replied. "A bit of comfort is all, really."

"That's all?" Rafale's blue eyes darted between Skellan and Elezar as if suspecting some kind of snare.

Skellan laughed at his disbelieving expression and said, "I wouldn't say no to table beer and stew as well, if it wouldn't overtax your strained finances."

To Elezar's surprise Rafale chuckled and then threw his arm around Skellan's shoulder again, hugging him to his side. Skellan allowed it with the amiable ease of an old friend well accustomed to his comrade's flawed character. The exchange seemed friendly enough though Elezar didn't particularly like seeing Rafale's hands linger on Skellan. The way Rafale caressed Skellan's shoulder filled Elezar with a terrible uneasiness. He looked away.

"He's a grim one, this man of yours, particularly for your free company," Rafale commented to Skellan. He studied Elezar as if trying to place his face from some distant memory.

Elezar, too, felt that he might have seen Rafale before. Perhaps in passing at the bishop's townhouse, he thought vaguely, but he felt far from certain.

"You must tell me how the two of you met," Rafale purred to Skellan. "And where you will be staying."

"Not before a bath and beer," Skellan replied. "Oh, and Elezar will need paper and pen as well."

"My little kingdom is at your disposal," Rafale replied. He led them across the stage and through a door, which turned out to be little more than a piece of set dressing that opened to long black velvet curtains. Stepping through those Elezar found himself in a cluttered, bare wood chamber that seemed halfway between a warehouse of gaudy, gold furnishings and the antechamber of a derelict whorehouse.

Stuffed parrots, stage knives and glittering strings of costume jewelry lay across a table like a strange buffet. Gold feather gowns fluttered from iron hooks, beside a series of false beards and several bloody paper-mache heads. Three live doves cooed from a cage balanced atop a stack of wooden chairs. Four beer barrels supported a spindly, bauble-encrusted armory of toy swords and spears.

Another door brought them into a surprisingly clean common washroom. Sunlight filtered down from the windows high above and shone across the surface of the large washtub. White tiles stamped with a floral motif covered the floor and two smaller washbasins stood on the dressing table. It could have been a washroom from Elezar's schoolboy days. In that context, the most shocking sight to catch Elezar's eye was his own savage face staring back at him from the dressing mirror.

Haggard, filthy and drawn, Elezar more closely resembled a forest brigand than a wealthy nobleman. He'd lost so much weight in the last month that his clothes looked like booty he'd scavenged from a body, rather than tailored finery.

He and Skellan must seem quite the pair of mongrels. Small wonder that Rafale, who spent much time among the

GINN HALE

Labaran nobility, should fail to recognize any cultured qualities in him.

It was just as well for it certainly served as a disguise.

Briefly Elezar considered keeping his worn, filthy attire but the reek of his garments seemed so overwhelming as to attract attention on their own. He needed to pass as best he could without remark of one kind or another. He shed the vile garments and got down to scrubbing their lingering stench from his body. It felt relieving to rinse the stink of sickness and pain from his skin.

Glancing over his shoulder he caught Skellan watching him with what seemed like worried fascination; Elezar felt a flush begin to creep over his naked body.

"Are you going to stand there gawking or are you going to bathe?" Elezar demanded.

"I'm done already. I've washed my face and both hands full well." Skellan held up both palms as if to give evidence.

"What about the rest of you?"

"My whole body in winter? I'm not mad," Skellan replied. Then, shaking his head slightly, he continued, "I'll go find some togs big enough for you."

Skellan returned after his bath, allowing Elezar to trade his filthy, worn clothes for the far more flamboyant attire worn by a villainous stormgiant from a previous season's play. Mirogoth patterns of tangled gray clouds and red lightning flashed across the breast of the black doublet, and the full sleeves of the gray shirt hid a cheat's pocket.

"If you were in the play, you'd have mica powder packed in your sleeve and when you cursed the heroine for releasing your herd of wethra-steeds you'd throw it over her to show you've frozen her in stone," Skellan explained.

Elezar required no trick powders but he did like how securely the pocket could be fastened and decided to use it to keep the Sumar grimma's signet safe and close at hand. When he dug the signet out of his traveling cloak Skellan's gaze followed it intently—like a dog watching a leg of mutton. Elezar shook his head.

"Not for you." He dropped the shining red ring into the cheat's pocket and laced it closed.

"As if I'd care about some gaudy wood witch's charm," Skellan replied. He feigned interest in a cake of face powder and Elezar almost laughed at how transparent he was. Skellan glanced sidelong to Elezar. "It's not as if I'd do it any harm just having a little closer look, would I?"

Elezar ignored the comment and turned his attention to the dressing table. Among the multitude of perfumed toiletries, powders, combs and makeup he discovered a pair of proper scissors. Between that and a fine bone comb he trimmed his beard back from looking like a bramble full of flycatchers to a more civilized, if not fashionable shape. A folded barber's razor lay beside a lather brush but Elezar decided against shaving. In northern Labara the only clean-shaven men seemed to be either Cadeleonians and witches; he didn't want to be taken for either.

Skellan settled down on the wooden stool next to the one Elezar had claimed. He picked up a tin of black oil, which Elezar guessed the actors used to darken their hair. Then he set it aside.

"I wouldn't have thought your skin was so pale." Skellan's gaze fell on Elezar's bare calf. His black leg hair stood out in sharp contrast. "Your face and arms are brown as bulls' balls."

Elezar laughed at that then asked, "Is that a common Labaran saying? Brown as bulls' balls?"

"In the north it is." Skellan nodded. "Aren't there bulls in Cadeleon?"

Elezar smiled at the question, despite himself. His family's emblem was a bull, and images of the beasts abounded throughout their estates and chapels. Bulls themselves flourished among the vast herds of cattle owned by his family. Javier had often compared Elezar to the creatures, for both his build and stubborn character.

"We have bulls, but they're generally red or white in color," Elezar explained.

"Like the one on the ring in your traveling trunk?"

Elezar opened his mouth to ask how Skellan knew about that but realized the answer himself. "You truly are a savage, aren't you? You know it's rude to go through someone else's things. Particularly right after he's just saved you from being killed."

"I know, but I was bored and curious." Skellan picked up the razor and seemed to consider it and his own reflection. Only a hint of golden red stubble showed on his chin and jaw. He set the razor aside. "Your brother's drawings of your hometown were beautiful. I think I dreamed about one of them last night."

"Strange, that," Elezar remarked, more to himself than Skellan. He never dreamed of Anacleto anymore—just the Sorrowlands... Except last night. What had he dreamed then, he wondered?

"Do you know what this is for?" Skellan held up a nail brush.

"Certainly." Elezar took the brush from Skellan and after locating a file and clipper, demonstrated on his own battered fingers. Skellan watched as though Elezar were performing some arcane rite.

"Come on." Elezar caught Skellan's right hand. "Give over. I've seen rats with more presentable claws than yours."

He expected the witch to refuse, but Skellan allowed Elezar to tend to his long callused hands, though the suspicion with which Skellan regarded the nail clipper actually made Elezar laugh. Skellan shot it a look of reproach that Elezar would have reserved for an adder lurking in his water closet.

"Unnatural thing," Skellan muttered. Then he lifted his gaze up to Elezar. "Did you learn about these devices when you attended academy with the duke?"

"You think I attended academy?" Elezar asked just to buy himself a little time.

"I wouldn't have thought so, except I spent most of the last month listening to the duke dictate his memoirs. He mentioned you a number of times." Skellan cocked his head and the afternoon light fell across his pale cheek, lighting one of his eyes to the color of an emerald.

"Ah, yes, his memoir." Elezar tried not to scowl. The memoir served to keep Atreau's restless intellect occupied and the manuscript that he mailed back to the capital city of Cieloalta, supposedly for preparation for publication, presented a perfect way to camouflage their reports to Fedeles. If only Atreau could have been convinced to be a little more discreet in his recollections all would have been perfect. As was, Elezar had to wonder, on average, how many pages of philosophical pornography Fedeles leafed through before he discovered one of Elezar's messages.

"The two of you are close?" Skellan asked.

"We are. Though under other circumstances I don't know that we'd have ever bothered to become acquainted," Elezar admitted. "But at the academy we both ran with the same group of troublemakers. After a while I came to appreciate his better qualities. He's a bit restless and tends to view orgies as a daily necessity, but you couldn't ask for a more loyal friend or a more open-minded confidant."

"Were you lovers then?" Skellan asked and Elezar almost choked.

"God no!" he gasped out. Even given the whorehouse orgies of their school days, he and Atreau had always fallen just a little too far outside each other's tastes.

Skellan studied him quizzically as if he didn't quite believe him.

"What in the three hells could make you even think such a thing?" Elezar demanded.

"The two of you are much more informal than I'd expect

of a Cadeleonian nobleman and his servant… and the way he spoke of you in his memoir… I suppose I could have misunderstood."

"You did! However poetically he may have described our friendship, there's never been anything between us. He's always been a great lover of women."

Skellan shrugged but his expression remained thoughtful. He said, "I suppose it's just that the duke reminds me of Rafale. If I didn't know better I'd even say the duke was from the same southern Labaran stock as Rafale. They look alike and all, don't they?"

"They do bear a certain resemblance," Elezar admitted. For all his rough manners, Skellan could be quite observant.

"So, you see, Rafale's always bragging about having seduced some wealthy widow or making a cuckold of his latest patron. Yet he comes slinking around my bed as often as not."

Elezar jolted like he'd been struck. His neck tensed like a fist and he felt his face burn with a flush. Suddenly he realized that he gripped both the nail clipper and Skellan's hand far too tightly. He released Skellan instantly.

"I've shocked you, haven't I?" Skellan smiled but there was regret in his eyes. "We aren't all Cadeleonians, you know. In Labara—the north at least—it's not illegal. Common practice among Mirogoths and the Irabiim, as well."

"Of course, I know that," Elezar responded reflexively. His mind still reeled with the idea of Rafale and Skellan lying together. He'd suspected Rafale but somehow hadn't allowed himself to imagine that Skellan shared the inclination. He'd seen enough of the witch's sleek body to picture the coupling far too well. His face felt hot.

"When he comes to you…" Elezar couldn't meet Skellan's gaze—couldn't look him in the face with lewd images flickering through his head. He didn't want to know and yet he had to. "Do you two…"

Elezar didn't even know what words to use to ask his question. It wasn't his business and knowing wouldn't do him any good.

"At first, of course. I was young, relieved to have the company and flattered. He's a well-made man and all." Skellan shrugged. "But after my friend Cire fell for him I realized I didn't want to do her harm and I needed to keep well clear of Rafale's affairs. These days the closest I come to his crooked dick is treating it for merrypox."

Outside the door Elezar could hear voices rising. Someone tuned a lute and the distinct scent of stewing fennel drifted through the air.

"Is it really so terrible a thing to you?" Skellan asked.

"I…" Elezar's heart pounded as hard as it had when he'd fought for his life outside the stables. Amazing, really, he thought, that a simple conversation would terrify him far worse than either a pike or sword. He couldn't seem to even get a word out.

"I shouldn't have said anything…" Skellan started to rise. "Rafale will make sure you get what you need to contact the duke. I should go."

Elezar knew that if he let Skellan go now, like this, he wouldn't likely ever see the witch again. That would be for the best, for both of them, no doubt.

He caught Skellan's hand with the speed of reflex. Skellan met his gaze for the first time since he'd admitted to bedding a man.

"Your nails aren't even close to clean enough for you to meet with the duke," Elezar managed to get out. He pulled Skellan back down next to him. Elezar's own hands trembled almost too much to keep hold of the nail clipper and brush, but Skellan let him take his time.

He eased Elezar away from the subject of his anxiety with meaningless conversation about Cadeleonian public baths and the famous hot springs in the south of Labara. Skellan was not a great believer in baths himself and went on to list several diseases that could be contracted from too much washing.

Slowly Elezar relaxed and soon enough Skellan's hands looked clean and, if not polished, at least trimmed. He was already a striking young man, given just a little care he could be handsome, Elezar decided, then immediately shied from the direction of his contemplation. Elezar didn't want to study Skellan with too appraising of an eye—he possessed neither the courage nor stupidity to follow where that course could lead him.

Outside the door Rafale's voice rose over a murmur of other conversation as he shouted about costumes and props. Elezar couldn't keep himself from looking to Skellan and wondering where he allowed the other man to touch him. Had he been tender in the same way that he'd seen to Elezar's wounded calf or had he given himself up to the same uninhibited glee that allowed him to eat with his bare hands?

Next to him Skellan spread a pinch of chalky face powder on the tabletop and traced a symbol in the surface before wiping it away and drawing another.

"Casting a spell?" Elezar asked.

"Trying to remember an old story about the forbidden flame that destroyed the Old Gods... there was a symbol for it, I think." Skellan frowned down at his powdered fingertips. "I knew it a long, long time ago but I can't quite remember now."

Several of the actresses wandered into the warm chamber to powder their bodies and dress. Under other circumstances Elezar would have been uneasy in their company. But he was far too aware of Skellan to really even notice the mostly nude women coming and going. The actresses returned his disinterest. A few exchanged a word of friendly greeting with him or Skellan, but even then their attention focused on making up their faces while reciting long, tongue-twisting monologues over and over to themselves and each other.

A naked, waifish child wandered in muttering, "Red leather, yellow leather, red leather, yellow leather, red leather, yellow leather..." He handed Elezar three pieces of cheap pulp paper, a quill and a nearly empty bottle of walnut ink.

"Thank you," Elezar said.

The boy nodded, still repeating his chant and skipped out of the room. Moments later a scrawny dark-haired woman with a sickly, unconscious infant slung over one shoulder sashayed in with a tray of food and drinks balanced in one hand. She handed the heavy tray to Elezar but turned her attention to Skellan.

"You've heard about Vieve?" she demanded of Skellan.

Skellan returned her gaze from the mirror but didn't turn from the symbol he'd drawn in front of him. Elezar remembered it. The null symbol that meant nothing.

"She's missing, Navet says," Skellan replied.

"Dead." The skinny woman shifted the infant and for the first time Elezar glimpsed the red blistered burns marring the right side of the child's gaunt face. "Her and her new man, Brand, both burned to ash and gristle sheltering our little Mirri with their own bodies."

Skellan wiped the powder aside and turned to the woman. "You were there, Clairre?"

"No, but I heard the scream and I smelled...it." Clairre wrinkled her nose as though the odor lingered still. From the way the color drained from her face Elezar thought that she might be about to vomit. He stepped back, abandoning the tray of beer and stew.

"I dug Mirri out from under what was left of them," Clairre murmured. A few feet from them two doe-eyed actresses practiced a dialogue of happy chatter, while a slender girl dressed in white chiffon painted her lips a deathly blue. All three shot pitying glances at Clairre's back but looked away when they noticed Elezar observing them.

"That was nearly a week ago," Clairre went on to Skellan. "But every day since, whenever Mirri comes full awake these little burns break out across her body. I've had to feed her drops of duera-water to keep her half sleeping but she's wasting away—"

"What does Rafale say?" Skellan asked. "She's his daughter. He must know a sister-physician who can—"

"He don't want none of it, does he? He's got you to fret over for the last month. Calling on nearly every witch in the city to try and find you. Meanwhile, I'm left to see to Vieve and Brand's funerals and care for our Mirri. "

Skellan looked terribly sad and Elezar wondered just what each of these people must have meant to him. They were only names for Elezar, but even so he found the idea of so many deaths disturbing. The burns disfiguring the little girl's face lent a greater immediacy to the threat of the violet flame. Oesir's witchflame might still be shining but that didn't mean that people weren't already suffering.

He wondered what the bishop's priests were doing to combat this demonic violet flame. In Cadeleon all priests and every monk would have rallied to fight it. Here the church seemed to be doing nothing. Perhaps they thought the witches of Milmuraille expendable or perhaps...

Elezar hated to think it, but perhaps they were simply letting it happen to be rid of the witches of this protectorate once and for all.

Skellan reached out and very gently touched the crown of the baby's tiny head. Her fine black hair looked like ebony against his pale skin. He raised a powdery finger and Elezar thought he might trace a sign over the girl but instead Skellan shook his head and withdrew his hand.

"Aren't you going to do anything?" Clairre demanded. Sneering, her sallow, thin face looked particularly ugly.

Skellan only gave another shake of his head in response.

"You're the reason he divorced her and all but abandoned Mirri, Skellan. You owe it to our family to make things right. But will you? No! Instead you swagger in here all fresh with your new flunky in tow." Clairre drew so close that Elezar could see the drops of sweat beading her brow and trickling down the back of her neck. She smelled of old milk and strong wine. "But you won't lift a finger to help Rafale's child, will you?"

"I will, but not here and not now. It wouldn't be safe for either of us," Skellan snapped back at Clairre. He paused, seeming to consider something in the distance that no one else saw. "But tomorrow night after sixth bell, bring Mirri to the Rat Rafters—"

"What? So she can see the full tour of whores her father abandoned her mother for?" Clairre's arms tightened around the limp baby. "Cire's flophouse is no place for Vieve's child."

Skellan's expression went very hard and he glowered at Clairre. She stepped back.

"If you want your niece to live, you'll bring her where I say and when," Skellan stated coldly. "If any of Vieve's coven have survived and want to stay alive they'll come as well. Do you understand me?"

Clairre's lips twitched but she said nothing. Then taking another step back she nodded. She nearly backed into Elezar and glanced to him as if she'd just noticed that he was still there.

"Fine company you're keeping, let me tell you!" she grumbled. "Thinks he's a grimma up in that rat-crap palace. Well, he don't know his shithole from a fingerbowl!"

This last exclamation drew glances and a few suppressed laughs from the group of actresses at the door. Clairre stalked out past them.

Skellan watched her go then sighed heavily.

"Is she always so gracious, or were those the good manners she puts on for strangers?" Elezar asked. He was rewarded with a laugh from two actresses. Skellan pulled a faint smile.

"Clairre's never been fond of me. Funny thing is that Vieve and I got on pretty well." Skellan lifted one of the tankards of table beer and gulped back a quick mouthful. "She had a good heart and the loudest laugh…"

"What are you going to do about that little girl tomorrow night?" Elezar asked.

"It won't just be her," Skellan muttered. "I'm going to have to find myself about thirty rabbit skins and see what I can't make of them."

Elezar wondered if that was some Labaran idiom or what passed for an answer among witches.

Skellan drank again, more deeply and then, perhaps noticing Elezar's gaze, added, "The afternoon play will be starting soon. You'd best get to writing your letter if you want the ink dry in the time for me to hand it over to your duke."

That was plainspoken enough, Elezar supposed. Best to leave the witch to his own thoughts for the time being. He took up the pen and as an afterthought tasted the table beer. Like many of the day's encounters, it was not what he'd expected— pungent with sharp, northern herbs—but he found the difference interesting and drank a little more in careful measure as he wrote his report for Fedeles.

From a wing of the stage, Skellan watched the audience settle. He held Elezar's folded letter tightly. High overhead stagehands locked heavy shutters over the ring of circular windows, blotting out the bright afternoon light. The playhouse plunged into twilight gloom. Rafale and his leading ladies already commanded the center stage, though they stood still as statues posing atop gilded pedestals, awaiting the delivery of the play's prologue.

Beyond them, a sea of common Labaran men and women, most decked out in their best clothes and looking bright-eyed with excitement, filled the cheap seats. Their chatter and laughter rolled and heaved through the deep shadows just as the heat and scents of their bodies saturated the entire playhouse with a living quality. A bun vendor and several sweets sellers wandered the crowd offering small delights for humble prices. From the attendance of Rafale's play no one would ever have suspected the number of folk who'd fled the city.

Skellan lifted his gaze.

The three tiers of box seats rising above the common crowd offered moneyed Labarans opulent accommodation as well as the privacy of heavy red velvet curtains and deep recesses. The patrons gathered up in those heights were no less noisy, excited or lovely to look upon than those below, though the men wore richer brocades and many of the women adorned themselves with strings of costly Cadeleonian pearls. Doubtless, they perfumed the air with a distinctly better-fed quality of fart as well.

Skellan was not at ease among such genteel people, but at least he recognized one face from among those assembled in the box seats.

The duke of Rauma was not hard to pick out from the general crowd of prim Cadeleonian merchants and Labaran guildsmen who'd come to be scandalized by Rafale's theatric excess. Dressed entirely in black sable and green silk, he appeared to be the only person in the audience not at all interested in the scene set upon the stage. Instead he raked the dark forms of the crowd gathered below him, searching. No doubt he hoped to spy Elezar among them.

Skellan allowed himself a private smile at that. The duke might employ his Elezar, but Skellan was the one who knew exactly where he hid.

Then the musicians on the balcony behind the center stage struck up a light tune and at once the chaotic horde of the common audience quieted. Two immense chandeliers descended from the trap doors in the ceiling high above and a fiery blaze of light slowly illuminated the actor.

"I come to remind you frail mortals that in an age long before this one, your ancestors bowed in slavery to Demon Lord Zi'sai!" Rafale's voice boomed out over the crowd as he stepped down from his pedestal into a circle of light. Gold dust and strings of costume jewels glinted across his nearly naked body—he still possessed a pleasing enough figure to display himself so. The huge golden horns crowning his head flashed like scythe blades.

"What you so easily forget in your temples and chapels is that my downfall was not assured by the courage of a Cadeleonian Savior, nor by the power of the Old Gods that set witches' cunts quivering. I was the last of the demon lords and my reign came after the deaths of Saviors and Old Gods alike. I was not defeated in battle, but by betrayal. The seeds of my ruin lay in my own faithless heart and in the spite of a concubine whose love I spurned. Look! Even now she walks before you."

As Rafale pointed, a tall actress descended from the shadows into the pool of light opposite him. Lengths of pale gauze trailed her like tattered wings.

Skellan didn't remember any concubine playing a role in the myth of the Demon Lord Zi'sai, but then again Bone-crusher's stories rarely involved romance. Instead he'd set Skellan shuddering with excitement and terror when he'd whispered to him that the demon lord's body lay coiled in stone beneath the grounds of Lundag's sanctum. The last demon's fiery soul had been stolen from him and his petrified flesh had been buried deep. Deep, but still waiting there beneath Skellan's feet to have his soul returned to him and reawaken. Lundag had raised her sanctum over his remains to show her contempt for the fear others felt of the long-abandoned grounds.

Rafale's play wasn't likely to turn travel guide, though Skellan suspected that he knew that story well enough Rafale seemed intent upon turning lore scandalous and political. He gloried in putting his own words in the mouths of mythic figures and dressing them in little more than chiffon and powder.

At the same time, he neatly side-stepped charges of heresy for his audacious plays with his surprisingly meticulous research. Nearly anything he claimed beneath his stage lights he'd gleaned from an obscure but authentic resource.

Skellan felt certain that when the parties of outraged priests and morally concerned guildsmen complained to Count Radulf, Rafale would cite his sources and perhaps receive some secret reward for his trouble. According to Rafale, the count reveled in these scandalous productions, particularly when they defied the codes of the Cadeleonian church. The count often summoned Rafale and his players to perform for him and his daughter, Lady Hylanya Radulf, in the privacy of his Sun Palace. Vieve had once joked that Rafale would end up abandoning them both to wed the count's daughter when she came of age.

Melancholy rose through Skellan at the thought of Vieve. He fought it back. Standing here, moping over Vieve's death, wasn't going to do her or her daughter any good. And Elezar's missives weren't likely to deliver themselves.

All around, the gathered audience watched in a mesmerized hush as Rafale's tale of lust, betrayal and murder unfolded on the stage. Skellan slipped from the wings unnoticed, creeping along a narrow aisle and then scurrying up the dark staircase to the third-tier boxes. A variety of armed guards and bored servants clogged the narrow corridor running behind the box seats. Skellan spied the duke's two youthful pages hunching alongside four older men, tossing dice.

"I have a message for the duke of Rauma," Skellan told them.

"You aren't his varlet," the heavier of the two pages commented. "He's expecting his varlet."

"Well, if it's only varlets that interest your duke," Skellan replied, "I suppose he'd have no use for a message from an actress, would he?"

The young pages exchanged knowing smirks and then nearly fell over each other, escorting Skellan to the duke's box.

Despite the luxury of velvet upholstery and a table laden with fruit, pastries, sausages and Labaran wine, the duke looked ill at ease. He eyed Skellan warily when he was announced, though he hid the expression behind his raised glass of wine. Skellan wouldn't have noticed it at all, if the duke's countenance hadn't changed utterly when Skellan explained that he'd brought a letter from a friend of their mutual acquaintance, the lovely actress, Cobre.

At the mention of Elezar's horse the duke motioned Skellan to the empty seat next to his own and then sent the pages away. Once the youths were out of earshot, the duke leaned close to Skellan. A perfume of roses, wine and musk drifted off him.

"Is he well?" the duke asked. "Is he safe?"

Skellan warmed to him for his concern. Another lord might have inquired after the letters or demanded news of Elezar's mission into the Mirogoth forest, but instead the duke asked after Elezar as if he were dear as a brother.

"He's both, though it nearly wasn't the case this morning. He sends you this." Skellan handed the duke the folded pages.

Skellan had attempted to read the contents while Elezar wrote but found that Elezar had secreted the true information in some code that made the pages resemble nothing more than a diary of various meals taken and enjoyed.

The duke accepted the papers without even glancing at their contents. He simply tucked them away into the pocket of his silk-slashed coat. "Where is our friend now?"

"Watching us, I think," Skellan replied. He couldn't see Elezar where he hid in the shadows of the musician's balcony, but he felt certain that he'd remained there. He seemed the sort of man who would keep watch. Skellan felt certain of that now.

The duke's attention remained on Skellan. He cocked his head slightly.

"Haven't we met before?" the duke asked suddenly. "There's something about you that looks so familiar to me… Could you be a member of Count Radulf's entourage perhaps?"

Skellan gave a dry laugh just to hide his shock. The duke couldn't possibly recognize him from the time he'd spent a dog, could he? No.

"Nothing so grand for me, I'm afraid," Skellan replied. "I do scamper about town though. I imagine you've seen me in passing at a theater or in some cockerel house. I'd remember if I'd been formally introduced to a duke." He wiped his hand on his pant leg and then offered it in Labaran fashion. "I'm called Skellan."

The duke nodded but didn't offer his own hand or given name, which was the right of nobility, Skellan supposed. But still it rankled his pride given the duke's present circumstances.

"How did you come into Elezar's service?" the duke inquired.

"I don't serve him or anyone else. I'm a free man of Milmuraille," Skellan stated.

"Forgive my assumption." The duke sounded amused and Skellan was certain he was smirking behind his wine glass again. "I sometimes forget how firm you northerners are about your independence. I meant no insult, I assure you. I simply wondered however the two of you met."

"He helped me out of a bad spot, and I was happy to return the favor when I realized he had trouble of his own." Skellan shrugged. He wasn't about to admit anything more to a smug Cadeleonian nobleman—friend of Elezar's or not.

"If he's troubled you must tell me about it." Then duke choose a walnut-encrusted sugar roll from his table and placed it in Skellan's hand. Then he pressed his hand to Skellan's shoulder and smiled quite handsomely at him. The curve of his full mouth and the warmth of his touch were very much at odds with his words.

"It would look a little less odd, I think, if you ate and we smiled at one another while we talked," the duke said. "People tend to pay a little too much attention to me and the company I keep. And while no one would mistake you for one of my mistresses, you are striking enough to be an actor who's taken my interest."

Skellan only needed to steal a sidelong glance out to the other box seats to see that indeed a number of women and a few men were observing them. None favored Skellan with any friendliness, but they were watching.

"Of course." Skellan returned the duke's pleased smile and ate the sugar roll in a single bite. Sweet, buttery flavor melted through his mouth. Just this one roll seemed so much more filling than the watery stew Rafale had fed him. But then it was gone all too soon.

The duke regarded him with an expression very like the one Elezar had worn when he'd eaten with him.

"Did you just devour that whole—" The duke cut himself off and handed Skellan a second roll. "Chew, for God's sake, and take your time so that we can seem to be speaking socially."

"Sorry," Skellan replied. For a race of great warriors, Cadeleonians seemed awfully dainty about their food. Skellan took a tiny bite—though it went very much against his instinct— and smiled as politely as he knew how while he made a little show of chewing and swallowing.

"So you were saying something about… our friend?" The duke poured Skellan a glass of wine and refilled his own as well. Skellan set the wine aside almost as soon as he received it. He much preferred beer to sweet ice wines.

"This morning, three Cadeleonian men tried to take him in an ambush. They were mercenaries, I think," Skellan told the duke. "Something to do with the murder of a man back in the Cadeleonian capital, Cieloalta."

The duke's easy smile took on a very hard edge and Skellan wondered if the murder hadn't been at the duke's behest. Certainly something like guilt caused the color to drain from his face.

"You said he was safe and well." There was no mistaking the strain in the duke's voice. "He is, isn't he?"

"Oh yes, he's tough as iron, our friend," Skellan reassured the duke. "But the three that came for him are all dead. So he's keeping out of sight for the time being."

"Three more dead. God, poor Elezar." The duke emptied half his glass of wine and Skellan contemplated his sweet roll, thinking that it was an odd thing for the duke to say. Elezar hardly seemed like the kind of man to fret over the death of assassins. He definitely hadn't been as shaken as Skellan had been after the fight. His cool demeanor had calmed Skellan and allowed him to concentrate on the larger, more troubling situation they faced.

"He's fine and well, I promise you," Skellan reassured the duke. "But look, there's a greater matter that he wanted me to tell you about. There's something very wrong happening in the city—"

"Do you mean the witches disappearing?" the duke suddenly asked.

Skellan nodded. So it was wide enough spread that even the Cadeleonians were forced to acknowledge the deaths. He wondered if the writers of their broadsheet had deemed the lives lost worthy of condolences or if they took comfort in the fact that so far only those they deemed heretics had died. Did they think it their God's work? Did the duke?

The duke leaned closer and whispered, "I don't know that this is related but last night Sheriff Hirbe called upon one of the priests in Bishop Palo's employ and when they seemed to believe they were alone the sheriff tore into the man about his machinations being completely out of hand and likely destroying everything."

Skellan frowned at the idea of Sheriff Hirbe calling upon Cadeleonian priests.

Common gossip concerning the sheriff had never made him out to be at all fond of Cadeleonians. A Cadeleonian noble was said to have murdered his granddaughter, after all. But right now Skellan was willing to consider anyone as being involved with the violet flame if it would offer him a clue as to how to defeat it.

"Do you remember what exactly he said had gotten out of control? Did either of them give it a name?" Skellan stared at the duke, willing him to have the answer.

"No, I'm sorry I wasn't paying them all that much attention at the time, and they were out on the grounds so I only overheard a few snatches of their conversation clearly. I was actually looking for a lost dog."

"Oh." Skellan took one of the sausages, wrapped the rest of his sweet roll around it and ate it in two disappointed bites.

The duke's smile wavered, but he went on, "I did approach the sheriff later just because the conversation kept going around in my head and the more I thought about it the more sinister it seemed."

"And?" Again Skellan's entire body tensed as if he could somehow simply wish all the answers he needed to erupt from the duke.

"He explained that he'd gotten a little too angry about the bishop scheduling a welcome ball for his niece the same week as the debut for the count's daughter, Lady Hylanya. Only a day apart, which made it look like the bishop is attempting to upstage the count."

"A ball and a debut party? Now? That's trimming the drapes while the house burns down, that is." Skellan took a third bun and ripped into it, belatedly remembering that he ought to make a pretense of delicacy.

"Indeed. But there was something about the sheriff's expression. A look of such utter defeat and sorrow that I couldn't believe that it was the only thing troubling him."

"More like folk burning alive in their homes and their little children being tortured by searing welts," Skellan growled into his roll.

The duke nodded as if awarding a point to Skellan in some debate but then went on, "There's something more as well. According to a kitchen maid who happens to be rather fond of me, there have been strange comings and goings in the bishop's household of late. Something's not right about the work going on in the chapel—"

Skellan half-choked on the sweet mouthful and he excitedly blurted out, "She's all too right. There is definitely something wrong with that place. I've felt it. A lurking hungry thing had been put to rest down there but by chance or design I think the bishop woke it up and I'd swear that he sent some part of it—a consuming violet flame—to Oesir to destroy his witchflame. If it isn't stopped—"

"Wait a moment." The duke held up one of his graceful hands. "You're telling me that you think Bishop Palo himself has unleashed some kind of curse against the Labaran grimma?"

"It was sent out in a golden coffer—a coffer like another I've seen being carried from his chapel," Skellan replied. "But that thing—the violet flame—it isn't satisfied with just Oesir. Maybe he tastes like the poison he is, I don't know. But the violet flame has been burning up more than witches. It's been devouring charms and spells all across Milmuraille. If it keeps up it will have stripped the city of every magical protection and have devoured Oesir's witchflame in less than a month's time."

The duke frowned then caught himself and softened the worry in his expression. He sipped his wine and offered a quick wave to a dark-haired Labaran woman in another box seat. Below them, foreboding music swelled as Rafale summoned the voracious fire-lion from the depths of the red hell—a trap door beneath the stage. But the creature did look convincing with an orange lamp light shining up onto it.

Members of the audience gasped and suppressed little cries of shock as the wild beast bounded across the stage, shaking its shining mane and baring long, ivory teeth. It was astounding to see how beautifully the Yuanese acrobats brought the creature to life. Yet as Skellan took in the scene, he felt a sudden fear for all the vibrancy and artistry around him.

If the Mirogoth grimma took Milmuraille they would slaughter the populace, tear the buildings down, and return the land to a wilderness where their enthralled creatures could thrive and hunt.

The duke turned his attention back to Skellan, his expression more curious than troubled.

"Doesn't a witch have to defeat a grimma in a duel or some such to keep a witchflame always burning over the sanctum?" the duke asked. "Isn't the Mirogoth truce dependent upon the Labaran witchflame never failing?"

"Do bears shit in the woods?"

"I believe they shit wherever they are," the duke responded. But then he added, "But I take your point. Though I never did understand why it should matter so much to them—the Mirogoth grimma I mean, not the bears."

It seemed obvious to Skellan, having lived within a sanctum, but Cadeleonians on the whole seemed to understand little of magic and nothing of spirituality outside their own church.

"Would your royal bishop be well pleased if a group of Mirogoths seized a high cathedral?"

"Of course not, but that's a holy place."

"I'll not argue, but do you know why it's holy?" Skellan replied and the duke looked uncertain. "It's the same reason that a Labaran temple is sacred, or an Irabiim grove and the very same reason that the sanctums are sacrosanct. All of them are raised where the free magic of the living world flows in abundance. Call it a church or a sanctum, the purpose is the same—to harness as much magic as possible and make it serve the will of the one who holds the place."

"So you witches have a religion after all?" The duke appeared pleased with this. "With churches that you call sanctums?"

"No, we're never so organized as that. We've all got different ways. Some teach theirs to others and make up covens. We're not all of one mind but we can hold each other to certain promises if only to keep from rousing the creatures of the demon realms ever again." Skellan paused, wondering if perhaps the duke was somewhat correct after all.

Really, what made up a religion other than the recognition of something holy and a code of conduct to protect what was sacred?

Only for witches the sacred was the living world around them.

Skellan continued, "We are all bound to the place that resonates with our witchflames—our souls—and those places we bind to the spells we craft from them. The spells holding a sanctum are the most binding of all. A sanctum grants a grimma immense power but in return she is bound to that place before all others. That's the covenant the grimma have upheld since the fall of the Old Gods. Maybe even before then."

"Really?" the duke asked. "You all possess a mythology as well?"

Skellan shrugged at the word mythology, but he'd not had anyone seem so interested in all that he knew in a long while and he went on, "They say that by raising a sanctum the first witches were able to draw all the free flowing magic of the air, water and earth to their wills. And using that power they bound the Old Gods into the very stones of the sanctums. If a sanctum falls then who knows what will be set free."

"You're saying that there is an Old God walled up in the masonry of the Labaran sanctum?" The duke cast him a skeptical look.

"Not walled up—actually turned to stone. In the Labaran sanctum Lundag only caught things like frogwives and wethra-steeds or trolls, but they're there. And there are others that she bound in their tracks around the city. Surely you have seen them."

"Do you mean the statues?"

"They are not statues. They live." Skellan grew so weary explaining this over and over again to endless disbelieving listeners. Still he persisted because it mattered. Those creatures trapped in stone mattered. "The Labaran sanctum is less than one hundred years old so Lundag could only enthrall and trap creatures from the grimma armies during the invasion. But the four sanctums of the north were raised in the age of the Old Gods. The lives they hold captive are countless. Who knows, one of the four grimma might even hold an Old God enthralled. Or maybe a demon, like that one."

Skellan gestured offhandedly to where Rafale wheeled and spun a wooden lance, making a whirling dance of his battle against frail mortal warriors. His fire-lion fell upon men in costume armor and dragged their bodies down to the gaping mouth of the red hell.

"So long as a witchflame shines over a sanctum the grimma know that the covenant is kept. Magic from the age of the Old Gods lives on, but doesn't run amok. But the instant Oesir's witchflame dies, well, there are countless creatures of wild magic that might break free and return us all to the grand days when dragons devastated cities and mordwolves devoured entire herds."

Skellan could tell that the duke didn't know how much of what he described to believe. Skellan himself felt a little mixed—though not in his belief that countless ancient creatures lay trapped within the power of sanctums. That he knew for fact, as undeniable as Bone-crusher's voice. But he despised the thought of keeping Bone-crusher and so many others prisoner. Still that was the purpose of a sanctum and the reason the grimma would not allow one to fall once it was raised.

"Well, that's all as it may be but surely the Mirogoth grimma realize that invading Milmuraille would mean war with Labara and Cadeleon?"

"If the witchflame dies, they will come. War or not," Skellan replied.

The duke stared at him in a lost way. Then he drained the rest of his wine. "Can't we find a witch? Someone to challenge Oesir—"

"The violet flame that now inhabits the Labaran sanctum feeds on magic and devours witches. I don't know how anyone even slightly magical could get past it to reach Oesir and challenge him." Skellan shook his head. He'd had nearly exactly this conversation with Elezar already. He supposed it reflected the direct way in which Cadeleonians thought and fought.

No wonder none of them were witches.

"What we need is to know just what this violet flame is," Skellan told the duke. "Don't they say that even a god may be killed by a sewing needle if it knows where to prick him?"

The duke smiled briefly at that. "My mother always said a devil could be slain with tweezers, but yes, I know exactly what you mean. We need more information about our enemy."

The duke glanced down to the stage where Rafale, as the triumphant demon lord, claimed the daughters of his fallen enemies for his harem. Their sons would serve in his armies and their parents would be slaughtered to feed to his dogs.

"You see that grim, balding man in the box to your right?" the duke murmured. Skellan glanced to the scowling, big-boned Cadeleonian. He looked well past fifty, and sour despite the attentions of two lovely young Labaran prostitutes and a mousy attendant. Skellan didn't know him.

"Zangre Lecha," the duke supplied. "The commander of Cadeleonian forces in Milmuraille. What do you think he would make of all this?"

Like every other resident of the old city, Skellan knew the commander's name and his nasty practices but had never seen him in person. Skellan resisted the urge to spit at the mention of the man's name.

"I think that whoremonger would use any excuse to drive people of Mirogoth heritage off their property and seize their belongings," Skellan answered. "I wouldn't involve him unless I had no other choice. Even then…"

The duke nodded as if he suspected as much as well. "For all we know he could be part of it. He despises the Labaran grimma and is quite friendly with Bishop Palo." The duke paused then added, "Also he's apparently a rival of mine for the hand of the bishop's niece."

"Considering your charm and his lack of it, I'd say he's already lost. He must hate you some," Skellan replied.

"Yes, but it's a dry hatred, so he just manages not to swear at me across the bishop's dinner table." The duke sighed and his amused smile faded. "You said before that the bishop's chapel has something to do with this violet flame?"

"I think so, yes."

"It wouldn't be too difficult for me to get in there and have a look around. But do you have any idea of what I should be looking for?"

Skellan didn't know why but he hadn't expected the duke to offer any help other than perhaps money. But he seemed sincere and he did have the best chance of entering the chapel unsuspected and unhindered.

"Anything you can discover about what was there before the chapel would be helpful. Look for the oldest inscriptions. If there are coffers there, particularly small gold ones, see if you can take lay hands on one—but whatever you do, don't open it. It will kill you, likely as not."

The duke nodded. "I'll do all that I can at the bishop's townhouse. Count Radulf's library might help as well. His family goes all the way back to the founding of Milmuraille; if there's going to be some mention of what was on that site before the bishop's chapel, it might be among his records."

"That's a good thought," Skellan agreed. "But you must take care."

"Must I?" The duke smiled as if indulging Skellan.

"Haven't your priests warned you?" Skellan asked. "With your history they must have. Unless the rumors about you having been possessed aren't true—"

"Ah yes, that." The duke's expression sobered at once. "Yes, I was possessed by a shadow curse for nearly three years... I try not to think about it now. Sometimes I actually manage to forget."

"Well, you should keep it in mind, now," Skellan warned him. "The fact that you held a curse in your body for years without being torn apart by it means that you're born of a strong bloodline. You may not be a witch, but you have the capacity to carry immense spells, even demons, within your flesh. As you well know, that's an attribute of great use to some."

The duke frowned but didn't appear unnerved. It had been said that he'd endured agony during his possession and had nearly been driven mad, so Skellan found this bland reaction to the threat of it happening again a little odd. Perhaps he hid his emotions better than Skellan had suspected.

"If someone needed a place to hide this thing, this violet flame." The duke set his wine glass aside. "The duke of Rauma would certainly be a valuable vessel. He could carry even carry it into the king's own court."

"Yes." Skellan hadn't even considered that possibility, but it did exist.

"Is that why he invited him?" the duke murmured.

"Who?" Skellan asked.

"Nothing. No one. I'm just thinking aloud and along uncertain lines." The duke ran a hand through his thick black hair, somehow managing to appear both agitated and attractive at the same time. "You're very right; I shall have to take great care in my investigation."

That seemed to be all there was to say. He felt almost certain that if he lingered much longer in the duke's company the pretty young woman in the east-facing box seat was going to hurl her wineglass at him. As was, she glared like she could wish pox and poison upon him. And doubtless if he remained on hand through the intermission she'd dispatch one of her stout brothers to show him to the river.

Skellan had known enough of that bitterness when he was with Rafale. He wasn't about to put up with it over a feigned flirtation with the duke. Especially since another sweet roll didn't seem to be forthcoming.

"If you discover anything, or have need of myself or our mutual friend, just send word to the Rat Rafters of the Fairwind stables." Skellan started to rise from his chair but the duke placed his hand on Skellan's shoulder and Skellan sank back down. The duke leaned so close that his lips brushed Skellan's ear.

How must this appear to an onlooker, Skellan wondered briefly, but then his attention turned to the words the duke whispered to him.

"Before you go, please, isn't there any way that I can see him? Just to know that he's alive…"

Something in his tone made Skellan suddenly remember Clairre holding Mirri and telling him that Brand and Vieve were both gone. Love could inspire such anguish. He felt almost relieved that he'd never had it in him to care so very much for anyone but Bone-crusher.

"All right, but you mustn't give him away by waving or pointing," Skellan replied.

"I'm not daft, you know." The duke arched a sharp black brow.

Skellan shrugged. How was he to know what an indulged duke might think was daft?

"Look to where the musicians are playing up on the balcony." Skellan resisted the urge to point. "Now close your eyes tightly, so that they adjust to complete darkness. Now open them and look again."

The duke did as Skellan instructed, his expression cool and impassive up until the instant he picked Elezar out from the deep shadows of the black velvet curtains. Then Skellan could have sworn the duke lit up, like he'd swallowed the moon. His expression hardly shifted, but the worry lifting from his countenance left him radiant.

"Thank God," the duke whispered. Then he turned to Skellan and smiling pressed a kiss to his cheek like the two of them were brothers. "Thank you, Skellan."

Skellan felt himself flush. He did have soft lips and the loveliest hint of rough stubble, the duke did. No wonder he'd had so many lovers that he could spend weeks recounting them all. A man might fall for him easily enough if he didn't mind the smell of rose perfume and too many women.

Skellan drew back.

"You're quite welcome, my lord, though now I really must be going." He rose and almost turned to leave, but his gaze was drawn back.

After that taste he had to ask for at least a little more. Even if he was refused, he had to ask. "I don't suppose you'd mind if I had those last two sweet rolls, would you?" Skellan inquired.

"Sweet rolls? The pastries, you mean? Have them, with my compliments." The duke handed the golden rolls over with a look of refined confusion. Perhaps he didn't realize what treasure he was giving up.

Skellan accepted them and, feeling like a fox with a hen in his teeth, he slipped away.

CHAPTER FOURTEEN

The setting sun smoldered on the horizon, casting a deceptively golden glow across the bustling streets. Radiant they might be, but the day's warmth had gone. Cool, sea-scented winds rose off the river and brushed over Elezar like cold-fingered pickpockets. The saddlebags thrown over Elezar's shoulder chafed and the gash in his ear throbbed. However, Skellan, in his now-black fur cloak hardly seemed to notice the chill or the fatigue of the long day. He snatched up small topaz stones from the dirty road and chatted, shifting from one language to another as he greeted copper merchants, dung mongers, street musicians, and herb girls throughout their walk back across the city.

A self-satisfied smile lingered on Skellan's lips and he swaggered like he was the lord of the land as he recounted his conversation with Atreau and then pointed out which of the cobblestones beneath their feet could be trusted. Some he even named. When he caught Elezar's disbelieving glance at a plain brown stone bearing the title Old Wind-eater, Skellan laughed.

"Truly that is her name! She was the griffin still flying at the end of the age of the Old Gods, born to devour storms. Most of her now lays underground, locked in stone. This here is just a patch of her great skull, but someday she will fly free and you'll see." Skellan crouched down and patted the stone. "I'm not having you on, man of mine."

He spun round and snatched up another bathwater gray pebble from the gutter. Elezar himself had found a few of the homely stones earlier and handed them over to Skellan. The activity reminded Elezar of the night Elrath had him gather particular stones from an ice cold river bed. He wondered how she and her family fared and if she'd sent Eski south with an Irabiim caravan already.

Beside him Skellan paused to dust the topaz off on his breeches and then he held it out for Elezar to admire. Its blue-gray surface bore a single symbol and not one Elezar recognized.

"What does it say, do you know?" Elezar asked.

"To embrace," Skellan pronounced in accented Cadeleonian. Then he raised his eyebrows lewdly and went on speaking Labaran. "That's what mannerly Cadeleonians like your handsome duke say when they mean fucking, isn't it?"

"I'm pretty certain he just says fucking."

"Well, I suppose he does and all." Skellan tucked the topaz away in his coin purse and scampered ahead. Elezar paused to pick up a second stone and then followed.

It annoyed him to know Skellan was beaming while thinking about how Atreau might make a proposition. More so that Atreau had so thoughtlessly embraced and kissed Skellan up in that private box. Hadn't he realized that it was Fedeles' reputation he was battering about? Such affairs might be considered fashionable vices here in the far northern reaches of Labara, but if word traveled back to the king's court it could ruin Fedeles.

And what the hell had his game been in any case? He had his choice of women to seduce—and just as many clamoring for a second opportunity to succumb to his charms. Why couldn't he just keep his hands off Skellan?

Now the half-feral young witch was grinning and giddy from the notion of Atreau's attentions and Elezar might as well have been a pack animal walking alongside him. Jealousy, as sharp and hard as steel, stung Elezar and he fought the urge to lash out. He knew his own ugliness too well to act upon it ever again. He swallowed back the bitter oath he wanted to growl out against Atreau.

If he was going to be angry it should be at himself. He'd been an idiot to even entertain the idea that there might be something, some kind of sympathy or attraction, between himself and Skellan. They'd only just met, for God's sake. What was he imagining? He certainly didn't believe Skellan's talk of sharing a fate.

Just for an instant Elezar recalled the tender sensation of holding Skellan's hand in his own. He'd felt so close to him for that moment. But that was all it had been, a moment, which had passed even before Elezar could rightly understand it. He scowled down at his rough scarred hands and made himself uncurl his big fists. The fragment of topaz in his palm bore the symbol of emptiness—nothing.

"What have you got?" Skellan called back to him.

Elezar hadn't thought Skellan was paying attention but now meeting his curious gaze Elezar tossed the stone to him. Skellan caught it and held it up to the fading sunlight then smiled.

"Another null symbol. That's the third you've found on our walk so far." He looked to Elezar. "How do you always find them and I never do? I'm the witch, you know."

"Maybe it's because I'm not a witch so I'm just looking for them instead of feeling for them, like you seem to do. What does nothing feel like, after all?"

Skellan went briefly still as he seemed to ponder the question. "To a witch, it feels like nothing. You might be right about that, my man."

Skellan slipped the stone away with the others. "The night bells will be sounding soon enough, but never fear, Cire's probably put some stew on the fire for us and we're not far from the Rat Rafters now."

Elezar nodded. This morning he wouldn't have possessed the faintest idea of where they were bound, but now he knew they would cut across the markets near the river and take a series of narrow bridges into the shabby heart of the old city.

They crossed a narrow bridge, arching over a foul-smelling stream, which much of the city population apparently used as an open-air latrine. Upwind of the stream they crossed a second footbridge and then followed narrow alleys and winding streets up to a hulking two-story boarding house.

In the surrounding crush of white-washed buildings, the boarding house's brilliant yellow walls blazed like a field of summer buttercups. A sturdy timber frame supported the jutting balcony and numerous overhanging windows of different sizes and styles. The vast reed-thatched roof hung over the eaves, providing a shelter for dozens of birds and what looked like a small colony of bats. A signpost jutted out above the door but only two scorched chain links remained of the sign. Charred symbols dotted the door frame but the painted images of frolicking rats remained. They didn't make for an inviting sight, not even laid out in paint.

"Why rats exactly?" Elezar wondered aloud.

"They're Cire's chosen familiars," Skellan replied. Something seemed to suddenly occur to him and he paused on the doorstep. "Whatever you do while in her house, don't harm any of the rats."

"Any…" Elezar repeated. "Just how many are there?"

"That's a hard number to know," Skellan said, shrugging. "They come and go on Cire's business, so it's rare to see all of them at once. But I think she keeps at least a good hundred. Certainly, that's what it sounds like when they're running through the walls."

Of course, Elezar thought to himself wryly, while every other housekeeper in the world exterminated rats with cats, traps, and poison, some northern witch would insist upon succoring the creatures. From Skellan's expression, Elezar guessed this wasn't a particularly unusual behavior. Who knew what bizarre customs other witches maintained?

"I suppose that's why the place is called the Rat Rafters," Elezar commented.

"And why the rent comes cheap," Skellan replied with a smile. "Common folk are squeamish about living with witches' familiars, I think."

"That could well be," Elezar agreed, but he would've bet good money that the fact that those familiars were rats didn't help. If the woman had kept bright butterflies or songbirds she might well have been turning prospective tenants away.

"And one more thing…" Skellan glanced to the open window overhead with a guilty expression and dropped his voice low. "Cire hates dogs."

Elezar couldn't stop the short laugh that escaped him. Skellan frowned.

"It's a serious matter. She can't know that I—" Skellan dropped his voice to the shadow of a whisper. "I take the form of a dog. She was nearly mauled when she was a child and never got over it."

"All right," Elezar assured him. "She won't hear a word of it from me, I promise."

Skellan looked relieved. He rapped on the door and Cire answered. Elezar remembered her as the pretty woman who had called to Skellan on the street that morning. Though having seen her at a distance and up in a window he'd not realized that she was closer in age to Rafale—in her mid-forties—and truly tiny. He'd seen dwarves in the king's court with more height and weight to their frames. The red-orange crown of braids piled atop her head barely rose to the height of Elezar's elbow. Her delicate frame, large dark eyes, and long pink fingers made Elezar think of a mouse. The fact that she wore a fur-trimmed gray shift only added to the impression.

Elezar could see how a dog, even one as affectionate as Skellan, could terrify her.

She greeted Skellan warmly and then cast a curious look up at Elezar. Skellan introduced him by his given name, and only offered the phrase "my man" as an explanation of his involvement and presence. Vaguely, Elezar wondered if Skellan's introduction was a common way for Labarans to introduce their servants. Or was the witch's implicit meaning more like "varlet" or even "henchman?"

His mother would have been outraged at the notion of some filthy street witch claiming to be the master over any of her sons. But somehow Elezar found that playing this part amused him and did his best to look both servile and menacing in equal measure.

"Well met." Cire held up her tiny hand in Labaran greeting and Elezar touched his palm to hers as gently as he knew how, which elicited a throaty laugh from the woman.

"Well, you are bigger than a bear, Elezar, but fear not. I'm not spun from sugar." Cire drew back and held the door wide open. "Come in. There's three-weeds soup in the kettle, black grave bread on the board, and butter to be had."

Inside, the wooden timbers supporting the building stood bare and lustrous as polished amber. The fragrance of the bundles of drying herbs hanging from the rafters infused the air. A battered wooden staircase rose on the left and the doors to small empty rooms hung open just beyond that, but otherwise the open space was dominated by a huge hearth that looked to serve both the common room and the adjoining kitchen. A long bar table, lined by numerous stools, served as the only division between the two areas. Stubs of dozens of candles lay unlit on the bar table while the last rays of twilight streamed in through a series of pretty, but oddly shaped, windows on the far wall.

An equally eclectic collection of worn but comfortable-looking chairs filled the common room as did several small tables and a variety of embroidered pillows. With so many seats, it struck Elezar as odd that no one else seemed to be in residence.

Something skittered overhead and Elezar looked up into the exposed wooden beams that supported the floor above. Bunches of green fleabane hung down on twine braids as did several dry sausages. Then a large rat leaned over the beam and returned Elezar's stare. Elezar looked to other surrounding beams and noted more clusters of the creatures observing him.

Whiskers flicked and tiny squeaks sounded through the quiet.

Then one particularly big, tawny rat bounded down, dropping first to the top of Skellan's head and then leaping out to Cire's shoulder. Skellan reached out, grinning, and patted the rat's narrow face.

"This is Queenie," Skellan informed Elezar. "She's Cire's favorite."

"Only because she's so smart and pretty." Cire beamed at the creature and like Skellan stroked it as if it were a lapdog. To Elezar's relief, she didn't invite him to pet the rat as well. Instead she went to one of the kettles hanging over the fire and busied herself ladling a greenish broth into two earthenware bowls.

Skellan dropped down into a chair near a round well-worn table and gestured for Elezar to take the seat across from him. The wooden chair groaned as Elezar lowered himself down but held his weight. He lay his saddlebags down at his feet.

"It's so quiet," Skellan commented.

Cire nodded, looking grim, and set the bowls down in front of them.

"You're my only boarder now so don't you even think of skipping your rent. I don't care that you've been gone the whole month," Cire told Skellan. She turned before Elezar could read her expression clearly. She strode to the kitchen and pulled open a low-set cupboard. "Where were you by the way?"

Skellan frowned at his bowl with a guilty expression.

"You went after Oesir, didn't you?" Cire straightened and Elezar saw that she held a small loaf of black bread in one hand and a very long knife in the other. "Damn it, Skellan, I warned you not to! You're lucky that Count Radulf doesn't have his men searching the city for you."

Skellan said nothing as Cire strode back to them and all but tossed the bread and knife onto the tabletop.

"I had to." Skellan hunched his shoulders in the defensive manner of a boy caught helping a friend crib notes during a test. He picked up the bread but ignored the knife and simply tore a hunk off of it before shoving the dense dark loaf to Elezar. Cire made another trip to the kitchen, this time scampering up one of the many wooden stepladders to an ice chest. She brought out a butter dish but then scowled at the two of them.

"Swear to me you didn't have anything to do with this violet fire, Skellan."

"I didn't," Skellan protested but then that guilty expression flickered once again across his angular face. "I was there when it started but I didn't have a hand in unleashing the violet flame that's besieged Oesir's witchflame. I swear."

"But you were there?" Cire asked.

Skellan nodded.

"Did anyone see you?" Cire demanded.

"No, not me."

Cire arched a red brow in question to the response. Elezar knew exactly what Skellan meant. They'd seen him only as a dog—a dog they thought to be a witch's familiar and had pursued until Elezar had stopped them and given him shelter.

"I don't know that you deserve any butter," Cire said. Then she looked to Elezar. "However, since we have a guest and I'm a well-mannered hostess I'll share."

Cire carried the plain earthenware butter dish like a small treasure and slid it gently onto the tabletop. Then she pulled up a tall chair with a large pillow laid across the seat and hopped up. Her rat gave a squeak but clung to her shoulder and kept its place like an expert rider.

Cire took up the knife and bread and cut several slices, before slathering one with golden butter and taking a bite. Skellan reached for the butter but Cire slapped his hand with the flat of the knife and shoved the dish and bread in Elezar's direction.

"You need a room?" Cire asked. "I can rent you one for ten—no, nine silver ladies."

"Elezar doesn't have nine silver ladies, and besides he's staying with me!" Skellan protested.

Cire narrowed her eyes, studying Elezar's face intently then sighed. She took another bite of her buttered bread then looked to Skellan.

"No offense to your giant, Skellan, but you could do better."

"No, I couldn't." Skellan shot Elezar such a sympathetic look that Elezar almost laughed. It wasn't as if he held many illusions about the image he presently presented, and in any case he found it a little amusing to be mistaken for a fellow without even nine Labaran coins to his name.

"No, really, Skellan," Cire said. "Rafale's met a nobleman with connections directly to Count Radulf. He thinks he could very much use someone like you—"

"Not you too," Skellan muttered. He tossed bits of his black bread into his bowl of greenish broth. "I've already seen Rafale."

"You have? Well, good. He was worried half out of his mind over you." Cire's expression softened. "I was too."

Elezar sliced a piece of bread, buttered it and took a bite. He knew that it couldn't actually have been milled from rocks but there was a solid, grainy quality to it that Elezar had never before encountered in a food. He glanced to Skellan, who tossed his bread and broth back like a shot of white ruin, and then to Cire who continued taking dainty bites from her buttered serving.

"So who is this count's man then?" Skellan asked.

"I've not met him in person but I know his family. He's an Eyeres. Real Labaran nobility and very loyal to the count, despite having taken his schooling as a Cadeleonian priest." Cire glanced to Elezar and added, "No offense."

"None taken." Elezar looked at his own slice of bread and noted the irregular white flecks that pebbled the surface. Chips of bone, he realized. He sipped his broth, since no cutlery seemed available. It tasted bland as boiled lettuce at first but then as he swallowed a spicy, sweet flavor filled his mouth. He'd tasted far worse, though possibly not weirder.

"Listen, Skellan, this fellow is the count's man," Cire said. "Likely he could get you out of the city. Take you somewhere safer in the south. And he might even be able to provide you with a title or introduce you to others in the count's court. This could be the making of us, Skellan."

"If he's so fine a fellow why don't you take him up on this work of his?" Skellan asked.

"You think I wouldn't if it were offered to me?" Cire buttered another slice of grave bread. "At least think on it."

Skellan grimaced, then said, "Merle and Navet think I should run north and throw my lot in with the Sumar grimma."

"What, and live the rest of your life eating pine cones and bark?" Cire looked to Elezar as if expecting him to second her opinion. Elezar nodded. Though having witnessed the bounty of the Sumar grimma's sanctum he didn't think that food would be the real problem for a man attempting to make a home there so much as the grimma's fury. That, and the bears.

Elezar scratched his calf absently.

"I'm not going anywhere," Skellan replied. Then he added a little sheepishly, "I promised Clairre that if she brought Mirri here tomorrow night I'd help her."

Cire stilled, buttered bread halfway to her mouth.

"You invited Clairre?" Again she looked to Elezar. "You've met Clairre, have you?"

"Just briefly," Elezar replied.

"It's not as though it requires hours of her company to suss out that she's a bitter hag with a grudge against half the world," Cire said.

Elezar laughed despite himself.

"That was my impression," he agreed.

"Well, obviously you are a far better judge of character than our dear Skellan here," Cire said. The rat on her shoulder batted its lashes at Elezar in an oddly womanly manner. Then it returned to preening its thick golden fur.

"They need help," Skellan protested.

"Everybody needs help," Cire responded. "But there's only so much anyone can give and at some point you have to know when someone isn't worth the effort. Clairre isn't worth the effort. She hates you."

"But she has care of Mirri, and I owe it to Vieve to help—"

"Ugh, not Vieve again," Cire groaned. "It wasn't your fault, or mine, or the fault of any one of the countless bodies who've warmed Rafale's bed. He left her because that's just who he is. He can't be happy with what he has so long as he thinks there might be something better around the next corner."

Skellan frowned down at his empty bowl and Elezar felt a pang for him. He'd made it sound as though he didn't care at all about Rafale or his affairs but obviously the other man had hurt him. The grim line of Cire's mouth made Elezar suspect that she too had suffered some heartbreak in the course of all Rafale's affairs. She broke off a piece of the bread and held it up to the large golden rat on her shoulder.

"Well, what's done is done, I suppose," Cire said. "It's not as though I called the meeting to have us band together for an old-time witch war. But we can help each other pack up or share the cost of carts among those of them that are leaving. Honestly, aside from sharing those barrels of beer that Uncle Ogmund stole from the Cradle's stores I don't know what any of us can do for each other."

Elezar cocked his head to Cire as he recollected the Cradle and more importantly that it operated inside the Cadeleonian garrison.

"Your uncle robbed the Cadeleonian garrison?" Elezar asked.

Cire shrugged as if slipping past a small army of soldiers was a minor accomplishment.

"With all the desertions I don't think it was really much more than a matter of waiting until the boy on watch had to take a shit and then rolling the beer barrels out." She handed the last of her bread to her rat, Queenie. "Folk of all kinds are leaving the city in solid numbers now that word's gotten around about the count's astrologer burning up. And those two Cadeleonian priests as well."

"I hadn't heard about the priests," Skellan said.

Elezar hadn't either but then he'd only staggered back to town last night and hadn't had time since to gather much news at all.

"Very devout, according to those who should know. And they went up while at prayer in their chapels." Cire looked to Elezar. "You can bet that shifted more than a few Cadeleonian asses. No offense to you and yours."

"None taken," Elezar responded.

"All in all I'd expect more folk to flee," Skellan opined.

"Now that's rich coming from the fellow who won't leave Milmuraille even when he has a good chance of being whisked away to a life of luxury and silk sheets by a nobleman."

Skellan gave Cire a crooked grin and then asked, "How could I leave when I'm the only lodger you have left to gouge for rent?"

Cire smiled at that and shook her head.

Skellan turned his empty broth bowl through his long hands and then said, "How many do you think will come tomorrow night?"

"Maybe fifty," Cire replied after thinking. "Why?"

"Well, I'm not sure what I can do for the full-grown witches, but I have an idea of how to help the children," Skellan said.

Elezar knew nothing of spells and magic but after seeing the infant, Mirri, he wanted to hear whatever Skellan had to say. Cire stared at Skellan and Elezar noticed that so did all of the rats.

"I think I can cast a thrall over them and hide the light of their witchflames inside animal bodies. But I'll need skins—"

"No," Cire said flatly. "You'll be devoured the instant you attempt to cast a spell that large."

"I won't." Skellan looked to Elezar as if expecting him to back him up. "I've worked out a way to use discarded remnants of abandoned spells. Broken incantations and charms. Any garbage with just the spark of power lingering in it. I've already cast two spells that way."

"He did heal a wound in my calf," Elezar admitted, though he decided against mentioning the spell that disguised Cobre.

Cire stole a glance down the length of Elezar's legs then turned back to Skellan, seeming to assess him.

"If anyone could I suppose it would be you," Cire admitted. "So, we'll get the parents drunk and protect their children for a while at least. It's a good start."

"Yes," Skellan said, and again he lowered his gaze to turn the earthenware bowl through his hands. "But the thing is that I'm going to need fur pelts, one for every child, and good pelts aren't going to come cheap—"

Cire's eyes went wide and the rat on her shoulder bristled.

"You really aren't going to pay me rent, are you?" Cire demanded.

"I will!" Skellan held up his hands. "It might just come a little… late."

Cire put her hands over her face and groaned.

At this Elezar decided that he couldn't just continue to play the impoverished varlet they both seemed to have taken him for. He leaned down and dug into his saddle bag. To his chagrin he realized that all that remained of the funds he'd packed were four silver ladies and a copper wolf. He'd thoughtlessly given away the last of his heavy Cadeleonian coins the day before when he'd been fevered and imagined his journey over.

Cire leaned over and scowled at the moneys in his hand.

"Give me two silver ladies and the wolf." Cire sounded annoyed but also resigned. "Keep the rest to buy the pelts you'll need for tomorrow."

Elezar handed her the coins, feeling slightly stunned. During all his travels in Cadeleon he'd never been without funds or credit. His name alone had assured that. But now he found himself with only two tiny silver Labaran coins and no means to trade on either his name or title. If he'd been thinking, he realized, he should have directed Skellan to acquire a full purse from Atreau but the possibility of being without funds simply hadn't occurred to him.

"Thank you, Cire." Skellan offered her a wide charming smile, which she did not return. "I'll pay you full rent as soon as I'm able, I swear."

"Yes. Well, until you do the two of you can just share your single little room and be glad I'm not throwing you out onto the street."

Skellan smiled easily, stretched, and yawned in his chair. Cire served them both and herself more soup. Outside, a woman sang a soft lullaby, likely to a child, but all three of them in the Rat Rafters sat quietly and listened to the soothing melody. The last light of the sun sank away and darkness crept through the common room.

Cire leveled her gaze to Elezar. "Close up the window shutters for me, will you?"

Elezar nodded and Skellan roused himself from his languid sprawl in his seat. Together they made short work of drawing the heavy wooden shutters closed and locking them.

The hearth fire crackled and popped, throwing a burnished luminance across the room.

Cire remained seated, though her favorite rat dropped from her shoulder to the tabletop. It gobbled up the very few crumbs left of the small meal. Cire glanced back to Elezar and Skellan.

"Go on up to bed; you both look half dead on your feet." She rolled one of the coins Elezar had paid her over the worn wood of the table and her rat scampered after it and then carried it back to her. She rolled another coin and the rat again gave chase.

"Come on, then," Skellan said, and he caught Elezar's hand. Elezar's skin seemed to hum with excitement where Skellan's fingers touched him. He followed the witch up the narrow worn stairs feeling dazed.

At the top of the stairs Skellan let him go. "I have a lamp. Wait here. It'll only be a moment."

Skellan disappeared into the gloom, and Elezar listened to the sound of his footsteps as well as the noises from the floor below. He hated this deep darkness and the ugly memories that it roused in the back of his mind. Thinking himself away from the Sorrowlands and his brother's recriminating ghost, he tried counting the different scuffling, squealing and skittering sounds of all the rats surrounding him. There was a sad sign of his state of mind he supposed, when he could take comfort in the noise of vermin.

Almost immediately a flare of soft orange light illuminated the tight confines of the hallway in front of him. Skellan smiled at him from an open door at the very end of the hall. He beckoned and Elezar joined him.

Elezar had to duck to get through the doorway, and the top of his head brushed the ceiling at its highest point. Skellan set the lamp aside on a small sill and knelt beside a mound that Elezar first took for rags, but then realized was a bed.

With its bare timber walls and sharply angled ceiling, Skellan's room would have been a beautiful broom cupboard. A small bow window offered just the glimpse of the moon. But as an abode for a grown man it struck Elezar as a very small space. For the two of them it seemed absurd. With his back to the door it wouldn't have taken Elezar more than two steps to reach Skellan where he knelt beside his bed.

In the tight confines the air warmed quickly. The scent of sweat and straw rolled up from Skellan's bedding and seemed to fill Elezar's lungs. Elezar tried to think of something else as he took in the cramped surroundings.

Aside from the low bed, with its sad heap of tattered blankets, very little else decorated the room. The deep recess of the bow window seemed to serve as Skellan's table and workspace. Beside the flickering lamp a variety of stones, some dull, others clear and bright as stained glass, lay spread out. Elezar recognized several as the ones Skellan had collected on their walk.

"Where should I…" Elezar trailed off realizing that there was hardly space in the room for him to stand and certainly no place for him to unpack or hang up his cloak.

Skellan glanced up to him.

"Hang your saddlebags on the nails. That way the rats are less likely to get into them."

Elezar scanned the bare walls in the flickering light twice before he discovered a series of four, thick, rusty nails jutting from the wood, like primitive coat hooks. He hung up his saddlebags and then his cloak and the bright theater coat Rafale had lent him. Then he surveyed the space around him.

"I could sleep on the floor," Elezar offered.

Skellan finished straightening what there was of his bedding and laughed.

"There isn't enough floor to fit you, my man," Skellan told him.

He was right, Elezar thought.

"It'll be tight but the bed sleeps two," Skellan assured him. Then without any apparent self-consciousness Skellan stripped off his clothes and rolled them up to rest on the windowsill. His leather knife belt and Elezar's hunting knife he laid out with great care. Then he removed the collar, with its dozen cheap charms, and spread it out around the base of the lamp as if it were precious treasure. Then he spread his dogskin cloak across the foot of the bed. Elezar tried not to stare at his nakedness but little else in the meager space drew his eyes so intensely.

"Aren't you tired?" Skellan asked.

"I am." Elezar could feel heat creeping up his face and blood pounding into his loins. He sat on the edge of the bed with his back to Skellan and fought with shaky hands to unwork the knots he'd tied in his bootlaces. He heard Skellan drop back onto the straw-stuffed mattress and felt him shift the threadbare blankets. Elezar didn't know how he could feel so painfully aware of the living heat of a man stretched out only a hand's length from his back.

But only a hand's length when it came to that.

Elezar jerked the knots apart and pulled his boots off with unnecessary force. Just because Skellan had taken a male lover before didn't mean that he harbored any interest in Elezar. And even if he did it would be sheer folly to involve himself with a Labaran witch who proclaimed the names of his lovers at the least provocation. Even as Elezar's thoughts turned and roiled, the hungry longing of his body seemed to only swell.

He pulled off his shirt and tossed it to the nail where his coat hung. His heart pounded in his chest. His hands went to his sword belt.

"Does it disturb you?" Skellan asked quietly from behind him.

Elezar cursed his own obvious arousal.

"Killing a man, I mean," Skellan added.

Elezar hadn't been thinking of anything remotely close to that and Skellan's question suddenly threw a chill across his feverish agitation. He looked over his shoulder to where Skellan lay stretched out on his belly, staring out the tiny window into the darkness outside. Skellan met his gaze briefly before returning to his study of the night.

"I hadn't thought about him all day, but just now when I closed my eyes I remembered the sound of him gasping as I pushed the knife in." Skellan frowned. "I don't know what else I could have done."

Elezar understood all too well how it felt to regret taking a life but not to know what else could have been done. He'd not found any philosophy to ease his own guilt, but he wanted badly to offer something like a consolation to Skellan.

"You didn't kill him for the mere pleasure of it," Elezar said. "You saved my life. I'm sorry that it came at a cost to your conscience."

Skellan sighed and rolled onto his back. Despite the grim subject of their conversation Elezar couldn't help but note the line of Skellan's red body hair leading down to his groin. The thin blankets hardly disguised the shape of his long, naked legs or the swell of his endowment. He certainly wasn't a child by any stretch of the imagination, but he possessed a relaxed easiness in nudity that Elezar himself had lost in his manhood. For all his experiences of crooked dicks and merrypox, Skellan retained an air of guileless honesty.

"I'm not sorry." Skellan said it as if making a decision. "He was given a life to forge as he wished, but he made his vei one of murder and that brought him to his ending. I didn't like killing him, but it's as you said: It was to save you and I can't regret that."

Elezar managed a grim smile. He wondered if Skellan would still have thought as much if he'd been aware of the kinds of depraved thoughts that haunted Elezar.

"We should get some sleep," Elezar said at last. He removed his sword belt, laying it close to the bedside. Skellan reached past him, his arm grazing Elezar's bare back. He leaned forward, blew out the lamp flame and then dropped back down to the bed.

Elezar stripped of the last of his clothes in the dark and then slid under the thin blankets beside Skellan. The mattress felt surprisingly comfortable and the heat of Skellan's naked skin warmed him quickly.

Still, Elezar didn't sleep for hours.

CHAPTER
FIFTEEN

The next day Skellan woke early, to the cackling of Cire's hens. The residue of a strange dream lingered with him. He'd been surrounded by the coils of a huge serpent with violet flames for scales. He'd wanted to flee for his life but instead he'd stood frozen in place by an intense fascination for a small golden ring, which floated just out of his reach. The ruby stone in its center glowed as if it were a burning ember. It seemed to call to him.

Even as Skellan recollected the dream, it faded from his mind—replaced by the thought that his Cadeleonian, Elezar, had slept the night with him.

"Did you sleep well?" Skellan asked quietly as he rolled over. But it wasn't a body that pressed against his back, only his own rolled up dog-skin cloak. He lay alone in the bed. Alone in the room. No sign of Elezar remained. Disappointment sank through Skellan.

Then he heard the man's laugh rising from the floor below.

Skellan sprang out of bed, swung open his window for a quick piss, and then dressed and rushed downstairs. He found Elezar stirring Cire's kettle for her while she directed two strapping men as they rolled barrels of beer into the kitchen and heaved them up onto the bar table. Cire's grizzled Uncle Ogmund lounged in the doorway alongside his aged badger.

He took note of Skellan first and nodded a greeting, which Skellan returned in kind. As Skellan padded down the stairs Ogmund beckoned him nearer.

Skellan joined the old witch, though he didn't stand so close that the other man could reach out and pretend to pluck off the tip of his nose, as he had been wont to do since Skellan had first met him eight years ago. Ogmund shared Cire's dark eyes and tiny nose, though he stood twice his niece's height bare foot. He dressed much like Skellan, with a tattered cloak thrown over his shoulders and low-slung breaches that had clearly been sewn for another man. Pale, freckled skin hung loose on his spindly frame and though only a faint gray stubble marked his jaw, the top of his head and his brows bristled with wild, wiry hairs. The aroma of beer and bread seemed to float always around him like a halo.

"Cire says you've got it in your head to cast a spell over the babes and kiddies," Ogmund commented.

Skellan yawned and nodded.

"Now this isn't to do with another of those troll stories you like telling so much, is it?"

"No." Skellan tried not to sound defensive. For reasons Skellan never quite understood, the old man had always seemed to take a pleasure in getting Skellan's back up. He was particularly fond of teasing Skellan over the stories he'd told all and sundry back when he'd been too young to know better.

"That big Cadeleonian seemed to think that there was some griffin living under the city streets." Ogmund's dark eyes glittered as he grinned at Skellan. "I wonder where he got such a fanciful idea?"

Skellan scowled at the old man, and in response Ogmund gave a raucous laugh. His badger even gave in to a fit of amused snorts and grunts. Elezar and Cire both looked their way just in time to witness Ogmund tweak the tip of Skellan's nose.

"Stop teasing our Skellan, Uncle, and come have your barley tea," Cire called. "You too, Skellan. Your man has traded his labor for a meal for you both."

Skellan and Ogmund joined them just as the fellows who'd moved the beer departed. At the table Ogmund scooped up his badger and settled the aged creature across his lap like a blanket. Cire cast it a brief disapproving glance but didn't comment. On her shoulder, Queenie arched and bared her teeth at Ogmund's dozing familiar. Years ago the badger would have stormed through the common room intent upon eating up every one of the rats in residence but time had mellowed the beast, allowing Cire and her uncle to see much more of each other of late. Skellan thought that the old man might even take a room here sometime soon.

He didn't know how the tip of his nose would bear it if he did.

"A very good morning to you," Elezar called to him.

"Morning," Skellan responded. He wasn't used to being greeted with more than a nod.

Elezar ladled a soup of barley flour into bowls. Cire made a show of serving six bright, yellow eggs that her hens had laid the day before. Then, to Skellan's shock, she brought out the butter as well as a tiny dish of gold pepper and another brimming with large flakes of red salt imported all the way from the Salt Islands. After setting those down, she took a roll of tattered silk from her apron pocket and opened it to reveal four of her precious silver spoons. Skellan wondered what Elezar had done to endear himself so much that Cire unlocked her ironwood spice safe and shared her spoons with him.

He frowned at the gleaming yolk in his steaming barley broth and the four different designs of filigree decorating the small spoons. Ogmund, too, stared as if stunned, then both of them grabbed up spoons and served themselves heaps of butter and spice before Cire could smack their hands with the flat of her knife.

Elezar took his share last and with so little excitement that he could have passed for a man who regularly ate red salt with silver spoons. Of course he was a member of a duke's household, so perhaps the leavings he took from his master's table were better than those Skellan dug up from behind the Brewers Guildhouse.

"Now as I recall," Cire told Elezar, "Lundag took the count's son along with some dozen other hostages. But that was eighteen years back, and I was just a girl then so I don't recollect much—"

Ogmund gave a loud laugh and his badger briefly startled awake.

"You were thirty if you were a day," Ogmund said.

Cire flushed and tossed a rag from her apron at her uncle. "I was twenty-four," she snapped.

Skellan bowed his head over his barley soup to hide his grin, while across the table Elezar somehow managed not to crack even the hint of a smile.

"But you don't know what became of the hostages?" Elezar asked.

"Oesir returned most to their parents," Skellan said. He almost went on but stopped himself. It had been ten years yet he still wasn't ready to tell anyone that he had escaped Oesir's purge of the sanctum that night. There still might be grimma guards willing to take him captive. The news wouldn't likely endear him to anyone here either. None of the street witches adored Oesir, but most folk across all of Milmuraille had despised Lundag. The entire city held a week-long celebration when her death had been announced.

"Oesir did indeed free Lundag's hostages. Though not all got safely home." Ogmund's smile faded. "Count Radulf's son was never seen again. Likely one of Lundag's champions murdered the poor child out of spite when his mistress died."

Skellan shook his head. They hadn't been there. They couldn't know that most of the hostage children had been held high up in Lundag's tower, transformed into hapless soft creatures, unable to speak or cry out for their nurses. Any number of them could have been mistaken for true animals after Lundag's murder. The count's son, along with the progeny of nobles and guildsmen, likely had ended up in their would-be liberators' stewpots.

Though, when he was feeling sentimental, Skellan liked to imagine that some had escaped like himself and been taken in by soft-hearted folk to live spoiled lives as fat pets.

Skellan glanced sidelong at Ogmund's badger.

"But as far as you know," Elezar addressed the question to Ogmund after taking a neat sip of his barley soup, "there was never a rumor of Lundag stealing away the Sumar grimma's child?"

Both Ogmund and Cire laughed. Skellan crinkled his brow trying to imagine any grimma having a child. Vast power and long life came at a price. Those of truly magical bloodlines were rare in this age and grew more rare with every passing generation. Still if the Sumar grimma had somehow birthed a live child, stealing it from her would have been a monumental task.

He might have only been a boy in Lundag's sanctum, but even he would have known if she'd captured a prize like that. She would have certainly shown the babe off to no end and taken endless joy in her power over both the child and its parent.

"None of the grimma have ever borne a living child," Ogmund said. "If one did, can you imagine what a monstrosity it would be? Those hags are older than most trees and kept alive by the blackest magics, if you ask me. If ever they were natural women able to conceive, they left that behind hundreds of years ago."

"It's true," Cire agreed. "Even Lundag was far older than she appeared."

"Naught but dust and cobwebs in her womb," Ogmund mumbled. "Can you imagine any man willing to stick his business in a tomb like that?"

"Oesir did," Skellan responded. "That was what Count Radulf sent him into her sanctum to do. Seduce her and kill her."

"Our count? Never." Ogmund smiled indulgently at Skellan. "Where do you get all those strange ideas in your head?" Ogmund held up his hand. "No, don't tell me. You've been talking to statues again, haven't you?"

"I heard it from Rafale." Only a half lie there, since Rafale did often gossip to him about the secret schemes of this or that nobleman. He'd let it slip once while in his cups. "He said that

Count Radulf is a witch himself and he sent Oesir to destroy Lundag because she was going to betray him in an alliance with Bishop Palo and the Cadeleonians."

"He was just having you on with some gossip he made up for one of his plays no doubt," Ogmund said. "That challenge between Oesir and Lundag was lawful, otherwise the sanctum wouldn't have passed to Oesir, would it? He's many a rotten thing, but Oesir's no mere assassin."

No, Skellan thought, but there hadn't been anything "mere" about Lundag's murder.

He could still remember that cold night all too well. Oesir had charmed Lundag into showing him how witches fought their challenges, and while she smiled indulgently at him from the circle of her wards, he'd reached out with his gleaming witchflame and torn her apart. She'd fallen, gutted and foaming blood from her mouth.

For all the days he'd been angry with her for forcing him into animal flesh or parading him around on a leash, he would never have wished so horrible a death upon her.

Despite his misgivings about his childhood, bittersweet nostalgia rolled over Skellan at the memory of the pranks he and Bone-crusher concocted to surprise Lundag. She wasn't often amused, but Skellan had known that she'd been secretly a little proud of him even when she caned him for his disobedience. She always tolerated him spying on her spell casting and allowed him to waste entire days in Bone-crusher's company. She hadn't been a mother to him, not really, but still he missed her and mourned her.

Skellan hunched in his seat, his appetite blunted by melancholy.

Elezar cast him a questioning glance, and Skellan quickly pulled a broad smile. Turning weak and watery-eyed was hardly going to win Elezar over to him, was it?

"Too much pepper all in one bite," Skellan said.

"Your own fault for being so greedy," Cire responded. Then

she turned her attention back to Elezar. "Is there some reason you think that the Sumar grimma did spawn some abomination into the world?"

Elezar hesitated then said, "I was traveling with a group of Mirogoth guides and they seemed to think it was the case. They said something about Bishop Palo betraying the Sumar grimma and stealing her child away to hand over to Grimma Lundag."

That pulled Skellan entirely from his reverie. He knew that Elezar hadn't merely traveled into Sumar lands on a whim. He'd been sent by someone whose commands even outranked the wishes of the duke of Rauma. Had he discovered something there on the business of one of the Cadeleonian princes that made him think the Sumar grimma truly had birthed an offspring?

And if ever there was such an abomination loosed upon the world, couldn't it take a form like that of the violet flame?

Skellan studied Elezar across the table. The entire idea seemed like a leap. Still he badly wanted to hear what it was exactly that Elezar had been getting at. He said, "You're not thinking that the violet flame is somehow the offspring of the Sumar grimma that Bishop Palo stole and hid away in his chapel?"

All three of them frowned at Skellan in silence.

"No... I was just pondering the fate of the children Lundag abducted." Elezar took a bite of egg, chewing it thoughtfully while Cire and her uncle both shook their heads and eyed Skellan with that familiar expression of disbelief.

"It must be a strange world you live in with such ideas floating around in your head all day long," Ogmund commented as he spoon-fed a hunk of egg to his badger.

Skellan glowered at him. This was just the reason that he most often kept his ideas to himself. Or at least tried to. Some simply felt too brilliant for him to hold in. Rare were the folk who agreed with him on that point, though.

"Now, Uncle, don't tease," Cire put in, though she looked to Elezar. "You never know when Skellan's going to be right about the very strangest of things. He can be quite uncanny. He found two of these very silver spoons just by listening to the whispers of the stones. Which ones were they that told you, Skellan?"

"The frogwives. They saw a maid drop them there twenty years before," Skellan admitted, but he felt utterly embarrassed now and kept his head down over his empty bowl. He scraped his spoon through the oily streaks that remained of the meal he'd wolfed down.

"You know, the suggestion about the violet flame being the progeny of the Sumar grimma isn't actually impossible," Elezar commented. "Except that there was something one of the guides said that made me think that the supposed child wasn't old. Certainly not as old as you think this violet flame must be."

Skellan raised his head, half expecting to catch a smirk on Elezar's face or worse a pitying, patronizing smile. But his expression seemed quite thoughtful. Skellan was startled to realize that someone other than Bone-crusher or one of the other trapped creatures took his ideas seriously. Not just this one grasping guess, but his solid conviction of the violet flame's age.

Elezar set his spoon aside and pushed his bowl away before looking to Cire.

"Thank you for the meal," he said.

Cire nodded then turned her attention to Skellan. "Are the two of you off to buy those skins then?"

"Yes, but we'll be back in time for tonight's meeting." Skellan nodded to Ogmund. "Leave a drop of table beer for us."

"One drop, certainly." Ogmund laughed, then bent to stroke his badger's snout. "Perhaps even two if you can make this plan of yours work."

After walking the city for an entire second day Elezar felt certain he could navigate the crowded noisy markets of Milmuraille with his eyes closed, though he'd likely be robbed of every scrap in his pockets and then the pockets and cloak as well if he tried it.

Twice since the afternoon sun dropped, casting long shadows between the crowded market stalls, beggar children had attempted to snatch his sad coin purse. Elezar rewarded the most recent lad with a smack across his curly blonde head but then was disconcerted to discover that Skellan knew the gangly boy and his fortune-telling mother. Skellan chided the scrawny boy for his clumsy attempt to lift Elezar's coins and by way of an excuse the boy showed Skellan the ugly burns and blisters that had erupted across his hands and hindered his light fingers.

A witch's child, Elezar realized belatedly as he noted the boy's dirty, bare feet.

After agreeing to come to Circ's Rat Rafters the lad scampered off to try the easier pickings near the stands of hard cider before the sun set and cold closed in.

"I didn't have the heart to tell him that even if he'd gotten your riches all he'd find are a couple copper wolves," Skellan said.

"Hardly worth hanging for." Elezar shifted the awkward bundles of fuzzy rabbit skins, goat hides and fox furs slung across his back. The pelts stank of poor curing and had cost him a pittance—not even two silver ladies—but even that tiny expenditure had depleted him of nearly everything.

"Unless of course he got his hands on that charm you brought back from the Sumar grimma's lands. Perhaps I should carry it for you, my man." Skellan gave Elezar a sly smile and Elezar laughed. Skellan had so consistently tried to convince Elezar to hand over the ring and Elezar had so often refused throughout the last two days that it could easily have become a point of contention. Instead—perhaps because Skellan possessed such a playful nature and odd sense of humor—the subject had instead grown into a private joke.

As the two of them worked their way through the narrow corridors of wagons and stalls that filled the open plaza beneath the city's aqueduct, smoke from grills rolled over them. The scent of frying onions and seared fish wafted on the cool breeze. Elezar's stomach rumbled and growled.

Bone crackers, blackened eels, pickled hare hearts, chicken feet, fried snails, lamb's tail dumplings and bowls of long noodles soaking in bright orange oil stood on display among other stands selling gleaming squid, gape-mouthed fish and spitting crabs. Such offerings wouldn't have tempted Elezar under normal circumstances. He'd always much preferred choice cuts of red-blooded game: boar, venison and elk. But as the day wore on he discovered himself considering the few coins he retained and the strange Labaran dishes on offer. Unfortunately most cost even more than he had. Elezar gazed at the hanging cuts of smoked turtle meat and sighed.

He'd gone hungry before, often while traveling between cities and most recently in the Mirogoth forest. But never before had he been surrounded by the sight of so much food heaped in baskets in front of him and been denied even a taste.

Worse, with the growing darkness, vendors all around him discarded unsold goods before his eyes. As fishmongers packed up their little carts and baskets, the market gutters ran with floods of dumped river water and hunks of grilled and raw fish. Packs of glossy rats scavenged through heaps of discarded crayfish shells. Occasionally, Elezar noticed an escaped soup snail inching up the arches of the aqueduct that sheltered the market. He felt a kind of sympathy for the homely, hermaphroditic creatures and privately wished them luck.

"Oi, Skellan! Master Elezar!" A pair of lanky blonde Mirogoth twins selling live frogs beckoned through the twilight gloom. Skellan had introduced them the day before and since then Elezar had passed by twice and made small friendly talk with the teenaged girls. Their bearded father, Gullin, offered Elezar and Skellan a nod of acknowledgment then returned to his work packing their little stall onto his cart.

One of the twin Mirogoth girls twirled her full red skirt while her more entrepreneurial sibling held up her last two brilliant green frogs like enticements to Skellan. They kicked and croaked but the girl kept her grip. Both the teenage twins were gap-toothed but a tiny beauty mark distinguished Sammi from her sister, Sarl.

"Anything already cooked?" Skellan inquired. He glanced to Elezar.

"For our Skellan and his man, anything," Sammi replied. Her twin stuffed the live frogs back into a reed cage, lined with tufts of moss. Then she brought out several long skewers of roasted frogs. The sisters obligingly sold their supper for a single one of Elezar's copper wolves. They confessed that they were well tired of frog flesh for every meal and would use the money to buy themselves a treat of two imported Kir-Zaki lemon drops.

"Don't tell your dad or he'll want one as well." Skellan winked at the girls' father as he tossed another of the topaz stones he'd collected from hand to hand. "You're all coming to Cire's tonight?" Skellan asked the twins.

The girls grinned and nodded in unison.

"We'll be there, smelling like lemon drops." Sarl whirled her skirt out around her legs again.

"Oh, and won't your Cire be delighted with her property full of all our common rabble," Sammi added and both the girls and their father laughed.

Skellan handed three of the six skewers over to Elezar before tearing into his own. Elezar bit into his share with some hesitation. Despite having been in Labara for months, he still found the snails, frogs and kelp snakes that poor Labarans sustained themselves upon somewhat disconcerting. But after a mouthful he decided that the smoked meat wasn't any worse than some of the stringy chicken flesh he'd eaten as a first-year student at the Sagrada Academy. He and Skellan stripped the skewers of nearly every glob of gristle. Then they bid Sammi, Sarl and their father good evening until they met again at the Rat Rafters.

They continued along a lane paralleled by rows of cramped cockerel houses and gambling dens, making easy conversation as they went. Skellan shared hilarious stories of playing hound in Bishop Palo's house and in turn Elezar described the oddities and wonders he'd witnessed during his years of travel throughout Cadeleon. Skellan listened with fascination when Elezar explained how he'd spent one night clinging to the rafters of his jail cell while a herd of ergot-addled swine rutted and squealed below him.

"The sheriff's deputy forgot about me entirely and the next morning while he was occupied dragging the pigs out of the cell and arguing damages with the pig herder, I slipped down and made my escape."

"Was that a better adventure or worse than the one you just returned from in the Sumar grimma's lands?" Skellan asked.

"Hard to say. Certainly it involved more pigs, but fewer bears."

Skellan nodded. He'd treated Elezar's leg and had probably guessed what had caused him the injury.

"Was it…" Skellan paused, seeming to weigh his words. "I know you can't tell me the details but did you accomplish what you set out to do?"

"I don't know," Elezar replied. "I hope so."

"Never hurts to hope," Skellan said. "I hope you don't have to be sent back there."

"You and me both." Elezar couldn't imagine surviving a second visit to the Sumar grimma's sanctum.

Despite the growing darkness, loud crowing cries rose from one of the noisier venues. Cheers and hooting followed. Elezar guessed that some rooster must have slashed another to death and money would be changing hands. Rising above the cockerel houses were three much more sturdy gaming houses where, Elezar surmised from their brightly painted Cadeleonian signs, men and women could witness dogs, pigs and even stallions fight and die under bright lamplight.

Though he'd often willingly fought in tournaments and duels, surrounded by onlookers, Elezar had developed an intense distaste for the idea of forcing creatures that neither chose nor consented to battle for their lives. It struck him as degrading to the nature of the animals and demeaning to what honor there was for men who lived by their swords.

"Stupid, stinking waste," Skellan muttered and Elezar realized that he, too, eyed one of the gaming houses. Then he glanced to Elezar and seemed to misread his expression because he added almost apologetically, "I know plenty of people enjoy it—Cadeleonian national pastime and all. And I guess there are probably worse ways for dogs to die. But—"

"There probably aren't many worse ways for human beings to entertain themselves," Elezar stated.

"You don't enjoy the sport?" Skellan asked. "I thought all Cadeleonians loved it."

"Most do," Elezar confessed. "I don't know why, but my sympathies are too much with the animals being torn to pieces and not enough with the folk enjoying the sight."

"Mine as well, though the reason is probably obvious," Skellan admitted. He smiled a little shyly. "Once, when I was twelve, I very narrowly escaped being in one of those fighting pits."

"As a dog, you mean?" Elezar asked, to clarify.

Skellan nodded.

Now there was a whole world of experience that Elezar hadn't ever considered. And he thought he'd had a hard time of it as a child.

"You witches truly lead strange lives," Elezar commented but Skellan was already bounding ahead of him, his attention focused on something that Elezar couldn't see.

"It's gone." Skellan stopped suddenly, craning his neck back to stare up at the height of a bell tower, one of many built by Labaran gentry and dedicated to ancestors whom they worshiped like guardian saints. Weathered figures of a plain-faced woman ringed the base of the tower. Higher up, Elezar noticed the silhouettes of Labaran priests pacing the open space where a great bronze bell should have hung. Their exact words didn't carry down to Elezar, but their tone of alarmed dismay reached him clearly enough. Even so it took him a moment to accept what he saw—or didn't see.

"How can the bell be gone?" Elezar wondered aloud. "It was ringing only an hour ago."

"The violet flame." Skellan's expression went grim. "If it's grown strong enough to devour guarding bells, then Bone-crusher and Wind-eater won't be safe for much longer. We have to find a way to stop it soon."

Even through the gloom Elezar recognized the distress on Skellan's face. He felt stunned and adrift. It was one thing to be told that invisible charms were being destroyed, or even to see a bit of tin blacken and burn, but staring into the empty void where a three-hundred stone, bronze bell had burned away in less than an hour... It certainly cast the fragments of topaz that they'd spent half the day gathering in a rather desperate and pathetic light.

"Perhaps one of the other witches at this gathering will know something more about destroying the violet flame," Elezar suggested.

"True," Skellan said. "You never do know everything about other folk, particularly not other witches. And at least the Columbe Bell is still there." Skellan stared out across the dark skyline of the city, picking the bell and its tower out from chaos of silhouettes by means that Elezar couldn't discern.

Skellan continued walking, but the glee had drained from his steps. Now he moved with focused speed and Elezar quickened his strides to keep apace of him.

CHAPTER SIXTEEN

When they arrived at the Rat Rafters they found Cire's boarding house already overrun with women and children. Not only were all the seats in the common room filled, but several children sat atop tables, while grown women settled in groups on cushions on the floor. The majority of the women looked like fair-haired, big-boned descendants of Mirogoth stock. But several dark-haired, wasp-waisted Labarans proved to be witches as well. An air of hardship and poverty pervaded the company.

The few who looked up greeted Skellan with little more than nods before returning to their private, subdued conversations.

A white-haired old woman tended the kettles hanging over the hearth fire, while a spindly young Irabiim girl prodded the firewood below with a poker.

A circle of six blonde women sat nearby on the floor, sipping from simple earthen cups. Most cradled sleeping infants in their free arms or kept slightly older children at their sides. Many of the children bore ugly burns on their faces, hands and arms. One naked little boy lay across his mother's lap, glassy-eyed as a dead fawn. Black scabs and bandages were wadded around the stump that should have been his right hand. Neither the bunches of herbs hanging from the ceiling beams, nor the many open pots of pungent medicinal salves, quite covered the distinct odor of sickness that hung over them all.

Ogmund crouched next to a plump Labaran girl of nine or ten, whose head bore a ring of ugly burns as if she'd been crowned with a molten circlet. She smiled as the old man encouraged her to scratch the badger dozing at her feet.

"Is that our own Skellan and his man Elezar here now?" a woman called from the kitchen. Glancing up, Elezar saw Navet wave and then he caught sight of Merle's steel-gray hair and ruddy face as she tended from an oaken ice chest. Flakes of sawdust clung to her hair. She held aloft a huge block of what looked like pressed butter. Elezar wondered if that, too, had been stolen from the Cadeleonian garrison.

"We are here indeed," Elezar called back. "Is there anything I can help either of you with?" He knew full well he didn't belong in any kitchen, but it was only good manners to offer some help and there was nothing he could do for the women gathered in the common room with their injured children.

"Aren't you a man of fine manners, our Elezar?" Merle replied with a grin. "But we're all done here and coming to join the rest. Just you have yourself a seat."

"Here, beside me." Skellan beckoned Elezar up the staircase, where he perched on one of the higher steps. As Elezar went to join him, a loud knock sounded at the door.

Elezar caught sight of Cire at last, as she rushed from one of the first-floor bedrooms to the door. Clusters of yellow flowers decorated her ornately braided hair and she'd discarded her simple gray shift for a brown one embroidered with small gold circles. Images of coins, perhaps.

Cire offered him and Skellan a greeting flash of her open palm in passing. Then she drew open the door and welcomed another large group of women and children. Sammi and Sarl sauntered in followed by their bushy-bearded father, Gullin.

Behind them came two brightly dressed Yuanese women wearing their black, kinked hair in thick braids and escorting four children between them. The pickpocket who'd talked earlier with Skellan skittered inside as did several women who, after the past two days, looked familiar but Elezar couldn't have named. A few men trailed after them. Fathers and husbands Elezar guessed, from the way they watched the injured children and conversed with each other and the women.

Cire bade them welcome but craned her head as if expecting someone else. Then just as she started to pull the door closed another party arrived.

Another dozen people poured in past the stairs. Some of these Elezar recognized from the Mockingbird Theater. Clairre arrived with Mirri in her arms, but if she noticed Skellan or himself she didn't bother to greet them. Instead she made straight for the crowded bar table where the beer kegs stood. Ogmund offered to tap the bung hole and received a loud burst of laughter and several teasing responses as he went about it.

The beer flowed freely. Though Elezar suspected that he wouldn't taste any himself until the second cask was tapped, he couldn't think of a time when he'd seen so many women looking like they needed drinks so much more than he did.

Merle and Navet emerged from the kitchen to take up one of the black kettles from the hearth fire. They made their way around the room and finally came to where Skellan and Elezar sat on the steps.

Merle hefted the kettle and poured out a stream of liquid that steamed with the perfume of strong Yuanese spices as she filled the small clay cups she'd handed to Skellan. All the while she balanced the remaining stacked cups on the fingers of her left hand like a tower of thimbles. Then with a flick of her knife, Merle dropped a thick yellow slice of butter into the small servings. A gold sheen melted across the tea.

"Our thanks." Skellan took two cups and handed one to Elezar. Navet glanced to the bundles of furs that Elezar had rested on the step below his feet.

"You do what Cire says you can do and you'll deserve far more than a cup of butter tea," Merle told him.

"Oh, I'll do it, don't you fear." Skellan grinned at the two gray-haired women and their expressions brightened. Smiling at each other, they turned with their kettle, butter slab and cups.

Though after they'd moved farther into the gathered crowd, that haunted expression Skellan had worn when he'd studied the missing bell returned to his face. He cast a nervous glance to the twilight view outside the windows. Yellow lamp-light from across the lane flickered, but Elezar saw nothing else.

"Can you really do this?" Elezar asked in a whisper.

For just an instant, Skellan seemed startled, as if he'd forgotten Elezar sat beside him. Then he grinned and tossed back his butter tea.

"Absolutely." Skellan stretched out on the stair, leaning his back against the railing and allowing his legs to sprawl against Elezar's. The contact was almost nothing. Skellan's shins just crossed beneath the curve of Elezar's knees and brushed against his calves. Yet Elezar's awareness of the contact felt utterly out of proportion. Skellan's skin seemed to blaze through the thin fabric of his cloths and burn against Elezar's. Contradictory urges surged through him: the guilty reflex to pull away and the unseemly desire to reach out and stroke the heat of Skellan's thigh. Resisting both impulses, Elezar sat still as a stone and forced himself to think of anything else—count the people gathered in the Rat Rafters.

Including the three Irabiim who trailed a pack of Labaran herb sellers and rushed to the beer cask, the gathering now numbered fifty-four adults. Most talked among themselves, though several women simply drank in silence or stared forlornly into emptiness. The children numbered around two dozen and were harder to count since they darted about and disappeared between the women and men looking after them. Many of the older children seemed to know each other well enough to gossip and strike up hand games. Sarl flirted with the freckled pickpocket but Sammi appeared intent upon winning a round of thumb wrestling.

Despite the distractions Elezar's nerves hummed with awareness of Skellan's proximity. He felt it the instant Skellan straightened, drawing closer.

"You should drink your tea before it goes cold," Skellan told him.

Elezar took a sip and found it very strange—hot with pepper, honey sweet and so buttery that it coated his mouth—but also satisfying. With the evening chill creeping in he could see why this would be a northern favorite and even found himself pondering a second serving. But his recent experience of feeling hungry and having no means to secure food gave Elezar pause. This kind of privation wasn't just a passing happenstance for the folk gathered around him. For them a second serving of butter meant much more. So he left extra portions for others who needed them so much more than he did.

Next to him, Skellan toyed with his empty cup, rolling it over his knuckles. His dexterity reminded Elezar a little of his old school friend Javier. But where Javier had flaunted his skill, intent upon impressing and intimidating every other youth in the Sagrada Academy, Skellan performed the feat with offhanded ease—as if this were simply how he kept his hands occupied while he pondered other matters.

"What does nothing feel like?" he murmured. He glanced to Elezar and shot him a sly conspiratorial smile. "Nothing feels like nothing. Isn't that right?"

"The topaz you mean?" Elezar replied. "Do you think those stones could be useful?"

"They might be—" All at once Skellan went silent and still and so did every other witch in the room. The companionable murmur of conversation died all at once and every one of the witches looked to the darkness beyond a small, round window on the east wall. Several woman pulled their children and infants to them. Sammi and Sarl both bolted to their father's side, wide-eyed as fox kits sighting a hunter's hounds.

Elezar peered into the dark, but discerned nothing other than a distant carriage lamp burning far away on the winding road.

"The violet flame?" Elezar whispered to Skellan. "Is it here?"

"Outside," Skellan whispered. "There are too many witches gathered here." He glanced over the assembly and then suddenly his expression hardened and he stood. "Are any of you here known to the Columbe Bell?"

For an instant all the gathered witches seemed too fearful to even respond, but then Cire raised her head. "Not me or mine."

And then a flurry of negatives arose in quick succession.

"Columbe, it is then." Skellan's gaze went distant. He raised his hands as he had that first morning at the travelers' inn, seeming to pluck the strings of some vast, invisible harp. The gathered witches looked on in fascination. Elezar noted that, like himself, most of the men bore bewildered expressions.

One child peered hard at Skellan's hands and then suddenly his eyes went wide. "I can see it, Mama! I can see Skellan's soul! It's so red!"

The woman beside him patted the boy's head but remained silent and tense. Elezar couldn't see what magic Skellan performed but he guessed from the worried faces of those who could that it was neither safe nor simple. Navet held her hand over her mouth while Merle glanced back and forth between the violet flame that crashed invisibly outside the window and Skellan's manipulations.

Into the quiet, Cire whispered, "Steady... Steady... Oh, Skellan, steady!"

Skellan shuddered and hissed under his breath as if he'd singed his finger, but he didn't stop his work. Beads of sweat rose across his brow and along his outstretched arms. He looked fevered—almost luminous. The shadows at his feet trembled and jumped, and Elezar realized that now even he could now discern the faintest ribbons of purple light swirling and rolling around Skellan.

"He can't..." someone whispered. Out of the corner of his eye, Elezar saw Sammi hide her face against her father's chest. Sarl had her hands over her eyes.

Skellan hissed and flinched again but then smirked, as if mocking his unseen opponent's attack. He smacked one hand on the railing of the stair. Thin plumes of smoke rose from the wood. Overhead, the rats lining the rafters scurried away.

"Come on then," Skellan whispered, "catch me." He drew back his arm and then swung forward as if he were hurling a lance with all his might. He threw open his hand and some immense force rocked through him and into the air, hissing like an arrow slicing the wind. Again Elezar thought he glimpsed the purple light as it shot away after Skellan's shot.

Looking both worn and dazed, Skellan swayed on the step. Fearing he would tumble down the stairs, Elezar caught his arm. Skellan's stiff body fell against Elezar's chest. He felt blazing hot as if he was a wooden soldier Elezar had snatched out of a fire.

The evening quiet broke as a distant bell suddenly clanged and boomed. The distorted notes rang like the howls of a wild creature. Individual cries of relief and wonder rose through the room like a cheer. Still in Elezar's grip, Skellan seemed to return to his senses. He slumped down and leaned into Elezar's shoulder.

Elezar asked, "What did you do?"

"Lured it to me and then set it on the Columbe Bell. The wards there are among the oldest in the city and won't burn easily. It should buy me some time."

"Well done, Skellan!" Cire rushed up the stairs and threw her arms around him, despite the fact that he already slumped against Elezar. Her slight weight hardly made an impact, though the gold rat that had been crouched on her shoulder veered so far forward that her nose and flicking whiskers brushed against Elezar's sleeve.

"This is exactly why you ought to be introduced to Count Radulf's court," Cire exclaimed. "I wish the count's man could have seen you!"

"It's not for his sake or the count's that I did it." Skellan pushed Cire off him gently and straightened out of Elezar's arms. He stared out the window with a concerned expression. Outside the bell continued to pound out weird, lowing notes.

"That was a fine show—we're all impressed, no doubt," Clairre called from where she leaned against the beer cask.

"But what does it accomplish? Mirri's still dying in my arms, isn't she?"

"Now, Clairre—" Navet objected.

"It buys us enough time to hide Mirri and the rest of the children," Skellan replied. "Which is more than blubbering in table beer will do for any of them."

While Skellan made a good point, he certainly hadn't presented it in a diplomatic manner. Elezar supposed that it was to Clairre's credit that instead of berating Skellan further she just offered him an obscene finger then said, "Well, hide them then. You and Cire can plan your appointments to the count's court after you done something for the rest of us."

"I'll need the children in a ring and a guardian to stand before each." Skellan pointed to the middle of the room.

"But Skellan," Cire said quietly, "couldn't you wait just a little longer—until Rafale arrives with the count's man to witness your work?"

"You invited him?" Skellan demanded.

"It is my house." Cire planted her tiny fists on her hips.

"Rafale's not coming," Clairre shouted. "He was gone from the theater all day. He's probably safe in his carriage halfway across the country by now."

"He swore he'd come!" Cire snapped.

"Swore he'd come in your cunt maybe, but not to a meeting of street witches," Clairre muttered. "He and his courtly friends are already fleeing the city in droves. If it gets much worse the Cadeleonians might even notice."

Cire ignored her and looked to Skellan. "Columbe's wards are strong. They could hold all night."

"Maybe, but I can't risk it," Skellan said. "Sorry, Cire. But as much as it pains me to say this, Clairre is right. We must look to our own."

"But you will hear the count's man out when he gets here?" Cire cast Skellan a skeptical look. "Instead of sneaking out the back?"

"I'll listen to what he has to say," Skellan replied, though when Cire started down the steps he added, under his breath, "Unless he starts jabbering about the joy of serving his liege. Then we're out, my man."

Elezar found it interesting and odd that Skellan didn't aspire to a position in Count Radulf's court, but then so much about the witch went counter to Elezar's expectations. He had to wonder what aspirations Skellan did harbor—beyond a full stomach and a fistful of dusty stones.

"You go ahead and make sure every child gets one of the furs, will you?" Skellan asked him. "They'll need the hides to keep them safe and their power hidden."

"I'll see to it." Elezar stood and hefted the bulging saddlebags onto his shoulder.

After that the course of action seemed decided. Although Cire appeared disgruntled, she didn't argue with the few instructions that Skellan called down to them from where he slumped on the stairs.

In fact, the only disagreement arose when Sammi protested being included in the circle of children. Her father whispered something in her ear and nodded to where Sarl stood looking abandoned and forlorn. Sammi bounded to her sister's side and gripped her hand in her own.

Elezar distributed the animal skins. One for each child. Larger children like Sammi and Sarl received goat hides, whereas he blanketed the majority of the infants with rabbit furs. The youth Sammi had flirted with took a tattered fox skin.

The adults formed a circle around the children, either cradling the infants in their arms or placing their hands on the older children's heads. They stood shoulder-to-shoulder with each other but gazed only at the child before them.

Elezar noted that it wasn't Clairre who held the girl Mirri's limp body, but Merle. Cire came forward to place a delicate hand on the brow of the pickpocket clutching the fox skin to his chest and one of the Yuanese woman took a badly burned infant from his mother and rocked him in her dark arms as she took her place beside Cire.

Skellan hunched on the stairs, watching in silence until, without a word, he stood and pulled the hood of his fur cloak up to shadow his face. He bounded down the steps, pieces of topaz gripped in his right hand. Elezar wondered which ones Skellan had chosen.

Skellan looked like a runner at the end of a marathon, moving by sheer force of will alone. He circled the ring of guardians and children once, throwing down the topaz in a manner that reminded Elezar of the way Elrath had taught him to cast the stones of his vei. Skellan completed the first circle. Then, taking in a deep breath, he raced around again, this time turning and twisting so that the air rose in his wake as if he were summoning a night wind. He whispered softly under his breath and every few steps spun to snap the palm of his hand against one of the guardian's backs.

Elezar expected to see nothing, but for just an instant a molten red symbol seemed to flicker up from the stones on the floor and then rise to hang like the faintest wisps of smoke where Skellan's hand had been. He gathered the drifting smoke in his hands and hurled it up in spinning arcs over the guardians' heads. With the release of each new smoky symbol Skellan moved faster, spinning them around each other and catching them before they could slowly descend or dissipate. His arms glistened with sweat and his bare feet left damp prints against the floor as he cavorted, swinging his arms and spinning a tapestry of countless fine lines of smoke over the heads of the guardians.

It was exhausting to watch him and eerie to hear the Columbe Bell, still pealing the dissonant long notes of it undoing as though accompanying Skellan's manic dance.

Though Elezar couldn't see the growing blaze of light rising over the circle of children, his eyes reflexively narrowed and flinched away as if he were facing into the heart of a noonday sun. Navet shielded her eyes with her hand and Elezar followed suit. Beneath the shadow of his fingers, he glimpsed Sammi. She looked faded as if blazing sunlight had burned away all the detail and color of her form leaving only a pale silhouette, which curled and twisted like paper burning to ash before his eyes. Then suddenly her figure grew saturated with color and more solid, but at all the wrong angles. Elezar realized that he was staring into the yellow eyes of a speckled goat. Sarl, too, sported a gold hide, dappled with black spots. A white rabbit lay in Merle's arms. Cire's hand now lay across the russet red brow of a shockingly large and long-limbed fox.

An instant ago Elezar had looked out over some twenty-five children and now all he saw were animals in the arms and under the hands of their guardian witches. The bell rang out twice but then no more. A disturbing silence settled over the city.

Skellan staggered to a halt then stumbled back. Elezar moved quickly, again catching him as he sagged back.

"Now where would I be without you, my man?' Skellan grinned. Despite the sheen of sweat glazing his skin he felt cold.

"Flat on your face twice already, it seems," Elezar replied. As the other man regained a little more of his strength, Elezar eased his grip though he stayed close. Skellan still looked like he might not keep his feet in the face of a strong breeze. Around them the transformed children lolled, hopped and staggered, while their parents and guardians tried to shepherd them.

Sarl bleated loudly and then jumped as though shocked by the sound of her own voice. The gangly fox kit dropped back onto his haunches and stared at his paws as if unsure of what they were. Cire knelt beside him, stroking his head and speaking too quietly for Elezar to pick out her exact words. But from all around the room, reassuring voices floated through the growing chorus of confused and frightened animal noises.

"Have they lost the ability to understand what's happened?" Elezar asked.

"They still have their intellects. But knowing a thing and experiencing it are different," Skellan told him. "It's shocking to suddenly lose your human senses and plunge into the raw scents, sounds and sights of an animal mind. The whole world feels foreign. It'll be hardest for the older children to adjust since they're most used to traversing the city in human form."

Elezar pondered this, while watching the Yuanese woman hand a huge lop-eared rabbit back to the woman who had given it to her when the animal had been her son. Despite the utter strangeness of the situation, the rabbit seemed at ease and relaxed into its mother's arms, just as a human infant might have been. Though he remembered that this child had been badly burned and missing a hand, the sleepy rabbit in the woman's arms looked healthy and whole.

"When he changes back will he lose his hand again?" Elezar asked.

Skellan gave a confused, drowsy murmur and Elezar realized that he'd been almost asleep on his feet. He blinked then followed Elezar's gaze to the rabbit.

"I don't know," Skellan admitted. "He's very young, so he may grow into the flesh enough to reclaim his hand, though it might be a little oddly formed… The real question is: If he spends too long in animal flesh will he ever completely come back from it?"

"Do you mean in body or in mind?" Risking either seemed daunting to Elezar, though he suspected that nearly anything was better than watching the child be burned alive by the violet flame.

"Bringing his body back will depend upon the witch who transforms him—but if it's me then it won't be any trouble. His temperament afterwards might be another matter." Skellan lowered his voice. "Living in the flesh of an animal affects you after a while. Rabbits tend to become jumpy, deer turn quiet, goats get more curious, bears become bold. Most of the effect wears off after a little time back in your own skin and society, but not all and not always. You hear stories about Mirogoth warriors and even witches who never come back from being beasts and who have to be driven out into the forest to live as savages."

Elezar nodded. Even in Cadeleon tales spread of men whom Mirogoth witches had transformed into voracious and monstrously clever predators. Fur traders swore that these pathetic creatures prowled the darkness of the Mirogoth forests. A few were said to have returned to human forms, but their brutal bestial natures always betrayed them. For a time, Elezar had even wondered if he could have somehow been one such beast and not have known it. But now he recognized the absurdity of that idea.

"Does it affect you when you change into a hound?"

"Some, I suppose. A man can't turn into a dog and not realize how different the world is from that perspective. It does alter a person." Skellan pulled a tired smile. "I've gone back and forth so many times, since I was a snot-nosed babe that I think I'm much the same creature in nature whether I'm in my own skin or a dog's."

"Really?" Elezar remembered the dog lying across his lap, licking his hand and nuzzling him playfully. Imagining Skellan doing the same thing as a man—it didn't bear thinking about.

"Maybe I'm a little more impulsive, perhaps little more affectionate when I'm under the influence of a dog's flesh," Skellan continued. "But there are any number of men who change just as much and for far worse when they're deep in their cups or they've smoked themselves dumb with black poppy."

"I suppose you're right at that," Elezar agreed. Watching the scampering rabbits and nervous kids that had once been children, he found Skellan's insight a helpful way to think about these transformations. These were still the same children but now acting under the influence of animal instincts, in just the way he might act oddly under the influence of wine or white ruin.

By comparison, the children were behaving rather well, really. Had Elezar been the one transformed into an animal there was no telling what kind of monster he might have become.

The fox boy padded up to Sarl and Sammi and all three hesitantly sniffed each other. An excited gekkering bark erupted from the fox, and all three of them jumped at the strange noise. Then both goats broke into soft grunting sounds, almost as if they were laughing. The fox joined them and this time they all seemed to enjoy the sharp noise of his calls.

Skellan smiled at them, but looked tired to his very bones. Elezar could see why; it had been a hell of a day.

"You should make use of your bed now," he commented.

"Maybe you should come with me," Skellan replied and then he yawned, offering Elezar a view of his long teeth and pink tongue.

Before Elezar could respond a loud knock sounded from the front door. Cire answered and gave a warm greeting to not only Rafale—who now sported bright silken garb befitting a Labaran courtier—but also to a sturdy Labaran draped in the black and violet robe of a Cadeleonian priest.

A dagger with an over-long, fantastically ornate hilt and gilded scabbard jutted like an awkward erection from Rafale's brocade sash. Elezar suspected that it, like the oversized gold spurs strapped to his immaculate knee boots with thick ribbons, served more as ornament than instrument. The short sword that hung from the priest's belt struck Elezar as just the opposite. The leather grip of the hilt showed the wear of constant use as well as attentive care. Sweat stains darkened the stitching but not a thread was split. The scabbard, too, was well worn and even better made. Elezar doubted that he, himself, possessed anything finer. Northern Labara was known to be a dangerous place for Cadeleonian priests, still it made Elezar uneasy to see so professional a weapon hanging over holy robes.

Five brawny, bearded blond men wearing the liveries of the Labaran grimma and carrying gold spears followed them in. In trepidation, Elezar scanned the faces of the guards, but the men who'd sold him Skellan from weren't among them.

"Master Rafale!" Cire beamed as the handsome playwright brushed her cheek with a kiss. "And you must be Brother Bois Eyeres." She offered her palm to the priest. "It's an honor. Do come in."

"It is a pleasure to meet you in person at last, madam. Rafale has done nothing but sing your praises the whole way here," Bois replied with a smile. The expression didn't seem natural on his lean, tanned face.

Rafale's gaze swept over the gathered witches and small animals until he found Skellan. When he did, the smile that lit his face struck Elezar as self-congratulatory.

Elezar didn't have to look to Skellan to sense the other man's agitation. The sleepy ease dropped from his stance. He straightened and went very tense—all but vibrating with alarm.

"What is he doing here?" Skellan studied Brother Bois. He obviously knew the man. Elezar wondered if he could be another of Skellan's lovers but then he realized that he, too, recognized this Labaran courtier who'd studied as a Cadeleonian priest.

He was one of the many priests who served Bishop Palo. The bishop's sacrist, if Elezar remembered correctly.

During his time in Milmuraille, Elezar had spent more time in taverns and the Mirogoth wilderness than in the bishop's house, so he doubted that he and Bois had exchanged more than two words, but he tended to remember well-made men.

Yes, he recollected seeing him near the chapel and again in the stables. The fact that he was apparently keeping the company of Count Radulf's favorite playwright and traveling with an escort of Oesir's guards made him suddenly all the more remarkable.

"Skellan," Cire called brightly. "This is Brother Bois Eyeres. You remember me mentioning him."

Skellan remained still and silent. Elezar guessed that he wasn't the only one who registered Skellan's uneasiness, because Navet stepped forward.

"Brother Bois hasn't just come to call upon Skellan," Rafale announced. "He's journeyed here to discuss solutions to this... trouble you've been having."

"Well, now that's a relief after all the trouble we've been having," Navet said. "And doesn't it lift our hapless spirits just to look upon such well turned out gentlemen standing in our shabby company. It makes me proud to pay my butter taxes, knowing you two made the treacherous journey all the way across this dark town with only a carriage and five of the grimma's guards for protection."

Several of the other women laughed outright, while most of the others snickered behind their hands. Obviously, the rift between these weathered witches from the streets of Milmuraille and the elegantly clothed upper classes ran deep. The fact that Clairre stepped up to stand shoulder to shoulder with Navet and block Rafale's path to Skellan seemed proof enough that street witches' resentment of the court outweighed any animosity amongst themselves.

Clairre resettled the tiny white rabbit sprawled over her shoulder and glowered at Rafale like he was a ne'er-do-well husband looking for a handout. "You think you have any business here, do you?"

"I do actually," Rafale replied. His attention and that of the priest fixed upon Skellan.

"A third of the city's gone and all you've got on your mind is pimping that boy off to some mocked-up priest?" Clairre demanded.

"Don't be absurd," Rafale replied. "I'm as worried as any of you about what's going on. More folk have fled the city than have been struck down, and if we can settle all this I have no doubt that most of them will come marching right back to their homes and my theater. But we must stop these attacks first."

"Oh, there's where your concern lies, I see." Clairre rolled her eyes.

"We're all concerned! And it's in everyone's interest that we work together." Cire smiled hard and stepped between Navet and Clairre, opening up the way for Rafale and Bois. "So let's all do be civil if only for one evening."

The big guards remained at the doors and watched the gathered witches as well as the assortment of little animals with expressions of bored disregard. What kind of things had they witnessed in Oesir's sanctum that the bizarre scene before them could seem banal, Elezar wondered.

Cire walked to Skellan's side, beaming. Then, with a very pretty smile, she turned to Rafale and offered him and Bois the vacated stools near the fireplace. Rafale accepted, though he eyed the assembly of animals in the center of the room with uncertainty. Several of the rabbits thumped the floor hard with their hind feet. Others clung close to their guardians. The goats studied Rafale with sidelong glances but the young fox seemed mesmerized by the enormous yellow plumes decorating the playwright's velvet hat. An Irabiim girl had to place a hand on his shoulder to keep him from trotting after it.

"Master Rafale has something to say to us all," Cire announced, and then she stepped back and claimed a chair among the rest of the witches.

"Yes, indeed. It is my honor to bring you greetings from your liege lord, Count Hallen Radulf, Lord of Milmuraille, Protector of northern Labara and Radulf County. Firstly, the count wishes to reassure you all that he will not abandon the city." Rafale addressed the group in the dignified, courtly tones that were not unlike those he'd used while walking the stage as a demon lord. Elezar wondered if now, too, the man was playing at a part. Certainly his foppish dress seemed at odds with the clothes he'd worn the previous afternoon, as was the light dusting of gold powder that gleamed across his skin.

His pompous formality drew eye rolls and sour expressions from this group of tired, surly witches gathered around the beer barrels and tending the hissing teakettle. If Rafale noticed their enmity he gave no sign. He went on—chin high, gaze focused upon some great distance as if he were posing for some heroic portrait or delivering a soliloquy to a distant audience.

Elezar thought he caught the slightest smirk briefly lift Rafale's lips, as if he found his own flamboyant performance absurd.

Behind him, Brother Bois sat on his stool observing each of the witches in turn. He raked them and their children with a dispassionate, assessing gaze. Elezar immediately recognized and distrusted the predatory quality of the sacrist's scrutiny. Reflexively, he stepped closer, blocking Bois' direct view of Skellan.

"Count Radulf is fully prepared to call upon all of his prodigious resources to repel the aberration afflicting our city and you witches in particular," Rafale pronounced, drawing all attention to himself. "You need not fear, you will be looked after—"

"Oh, now that is a relief to know," Navet broke in. "Here we were afraid to our bones that we might have to get up off our helpless asses and take care of our own, weren't we?" That drew a fair number of cackles from the gathered witches. Even Sarl and Sammi let loose with peals of grunting laughter.

Rafale smiled gamely but appeared otherwise unfazed—and once again Elezar couldn't help but think that this was the reaction the playwright had wanted. He held their attention this way and roused them to responding, even if they thought it was only to spite him.

"There is, of course, something you can do to help yourselves as well as your city and liege," Rafale stated as if Navet had asked a genuine question of him. "Brother Bois and other scholars have discovered references to this very abomination in Count Radulf's family library, as well as directions to dispelling it. But with the count's astrologer lost to us, his liege will require another witch to perform the incantations."

Rafale turned and looked directly at Skellan. "One of you."

"Of course, one of us." Fon, the Yuanese noodle seller, shot back her little cup of butter tea and glared at Rafale. "You expect us to believe that in all of Count Radulf's lands, not a single courtier, minister, healer or sage could be found who could read a damn incantation?"

"Rafale isn't saying anything like that!" Cire objected, though Elezar felt certain that it had actually been Rafale's meaning and from his expression Rafale seemed to think so as well.

"He's offering us this opportunity to step up and prove our prowess," Cire declared. "It's easy enough to grumble and whine about how we're given no respect and how Count Radulf so wantonly indulges Grimma Oesir's every whim at our expense. But now the day has come for us to show the count the courage we possess. Our city—no, our entire county—stands on the brink of ruin. This is our opportunity to prove that we are neither wretched nor cowardly. We can save ourselves and our city!" Cire glowered at the assembled witches like a little queen. In the rafters overhead, shadows flickered in the firelight but didn't quite disguise the glossy black forms of the hundreds of rats gazing down. She might not have stood higher than Elezar's elbow, but for just this moment she seemed that largest presence in the entire building.

Elezar felt almost as if he ought to clap, but then he saw Skellan shake his head.

"Exactly," Rafale said, nodding. "This is your time! This is your opportunity to not only save yourselves, but to win Count Radulf's favor and rise above the filth and deprivation of your beginnings."

Even Cire looked annoyed by Rafale's choice of words. He unapologetically maintained the haughty air of a man who knew all too well the difference between this rickety wooden hovel and the count's Sun Palace. Elezar could see that despite themselves, the gathered witches were beginning to be swayed by Rafale. Here he was, shining with gold and offering them not only salvation, but glory.

Hell, Elezar wanted to know more about this deal himself.

"If Count Radulf knows so much about all this, then why can't you give us the name of the thing attacking us?" Skellan demanded.

"The count knows exactly what it is called." Rafale scowled at Skellan. "He knows everything that there is to know concerning it. However it is not my place—"

"How?" Skellan broke in.

Out of the corner of his eye Elezar noticed Bois shift to fix his hard gaze on Skellan. But the witch took no note; all his attention remained on Rafale. In fact, nearly everyone seemed so attentive to Rafale that the priest had become almost invisible.

Bois going so unnoticed while Rafale drew all eyes made Elezar a little uneasy. It reminded him too much of when he and his friends had employed distractions at the Sagrada Academy to filch answer sheets, beer and pies. Often he and Javier had feigned some argument and had played at fighting while Atreau and the rest of the Hellions had slipped across the school grounds unseen.

What was it Bois and the grimma's men wanted to get away with when no one watched them?

"How does Count Radulf know everything when none of us can even give it a true name?" Skellan continued his interrogation of Rafale. "We call it the violet flame but none of us know what it really is. Not even Oesir knew how to restrain it, much less destroy it. So how does the count come to know it so well?"

"From his library," Rafale replied, though Bois made a motion as if to render him mute.

And suddenly Elezar realized where Skellan must be going with his questions and why every witch in the room watched Rafale with nerve-jangling intensity.

"That puts the count in rare company then, doesn't it?" Skellan went on. "Since only he and whoever summoned the monster would know so much of something that has confounded even Grimma Oesir."

"Skellan, are you seriously thinking…" Rafale trailed off as if the idea were unutterable. "Are you implying that Count Radulf had anything to do with this?"

"Can you swear to me that he didn't?" Skellan challenged.

Rafale opened his mouth but Bois cut in quickly, "Such a question is unworthy of acknowledgment."

"Or perhaps you're just afraid to lie in the company of so many witches," Skellan taunted.

Bois' hand dropped almost casually to his knife belt. All at once the guards lounging at the door came to attention. Elezar met their hard stares and purposefully caught Skellan's arm and pulled the witch back behind him again. If Bois or the grimma's guards wanted a fight he'd give them one. From the look of the other witches in the room he wouldn't be the only one.

"Oh, now this is just absurd!" Rafale threw his hands into the air and several of the rabbits startled. He rolled his eyes. "Of course Count Radulf didn't have anything to do with this violet flame—or whatever it's called. Milmuraille is the count's ancestral home. Why would he endanger his own city so recklessly? Why would he kill his own astrologer?"

"Someone unleashed the violet flame—" Skellan replied.

"Yes, well argued, lover," snapped Rafale. "You've worked it out. Someone committed this terrible crime and the count is someone. For fuck's sake, Skellan, use that brilliant mind of yours. There are thousands of people living in the city. Any one of them would have a better motive for destroying Milmuraille than Count Radulf does."

Skellan started to open his mouth but Cire silenced him with a glare.

"No one believes that the count is to blame," Cire stated. "We've all just been under a great deal of strain and tempers are short… But I think Skellan was just trying to make a point about how important the information in the count's library could be. We're all probably quite curious about the details."

Elezar appreciated Cire's intervention but remained stationed between Bois and Skellan. The sacrist's tan, toned body had not been forged by hours of copious letter writing. Elezar had no doubt that he knew how to use his blade.

"Then you and he should come and see for yourselves," Rafale replied. "That's all the count is asking of any of you—of all of you, in fact. Come and help him to save our city."

"How exactly are we to do that?" Skellan stepped forward to glare at Bois, ruining all of Elezar's careful defensive positioning. "Why is it that you and your bishop know so much more about all of this?"

"I know the same as the rest of you," Bois replied. "This violet flame, as you will, is killing Grimma Oesir and if it is not stopped very soon we will face a Mirogoth invasion."

"You could tell me more than that, I think." Skellan stared hard at the other man and raised his hands. A flicker of fear showed in Bois' face, but he hid it well and this time he made no move for his short sword. "Shall I call the truth from you?"

"Skellan! Don't you dare!" Cire growled. "These men are as much my guests as you are. I will not have you enthralling any of them."

"Never fear on my account, Madam Cire." Bois' expression barely changed. "The boy is bluffing. We all know that violet flames would consume him if he attempted any magic."

If he and Rafale had arrived much earlier, Elezar thought, Bois might not be so confident about how little magic Skellan could manage.

But Elezar also knew Skellan was exhausted. He wasn't surprised when Skellan dropped his hands back down to his side.

Bois allowed himself a flicker of a smile.

"If you know that none of us can perform a spell, then how exactly do you expect any of us to speak this incantation of Count Radulf's?" Merle only glanced up from the keg, as she poured herself another beer.

Bois turned his attention to Rafale and Cire. "You spoke rather highly of many of these people and yet when I come to them in good faith, it seems that all they will do is grumble and make wild accusations. I understand that many of your children are being burned alive by this violet flame but all you're doing is sitting around drinking cheap table beer."

"Now don't go red in the face about it, boy," Navet replied. "We can't help ourselves if we're just a bunch of hapless cowards, willing to do fuck-all for our own good, can we?"

Bois ignored Navet's provocation, preferring to glower at Cire as if she had promised him a bed of roses and sold him nothing but thorns. Rafale, on the other hand, seemed to be contemplating engaging the beer barrel himself.

"When does Count Radulf wish us to come calling upon him?" It was Cire's uncle, Ogmund, who inquired.

"Pardon?" Bois asked.

"You said that the count wishes us to come to him and look at the incantation," Ogmund said. "But you didn't say when or where this should occur."

"I thought you weren't—" Bois began then seemed to think better of it. "Three days from now. Sacreday. Count Radulf will have returned from his spring hunt then. You should call upon him first thing at the Sun Palace. The documents are in the library there."

"Three days then." Ogmund gulped back his beer.

"Three days," Navet agreed. "We'll come early as the sun rises."

Ogmund simply nodded.

"So is there anything else we need to discuss?" Merle asked after taking another swig of her beer.

Skellan drew in a breath but Cire shot him a murderous scowl. He exhaled heavily, hunched his shoulders and scowled down at his bare feet like one of Elezar's teenaged brothers sulking after confession.

"I hate to see you so downcast, Skellan," Rafale said. "Why don't you accompany Brother Bois and me to dinner. Cook has several fat ducks—"

"Yes, the boy will come with us," Bois pronounced.

Skellan's head came up fast then and Elezar thought he actually saw Skellan's pulse pounding in his throat. He caught the hood of his cloak and pulled it up over his head.

"I don't think—" Cire began but Rafale already moved toward Skellan.

"He could see the palace and clear up these his wild suspicions of his." Rafale reached out as if to take Skellan's hand. "And we would certainly house him more nicely and securely than—"

"Don't push your luck here." Elezar stepped toward Rafale, standing nearly chest to chest, towering over the other man.

Rafale blanched and went as stiff as if he'd come upon a slavering wolf in a dark wood. But it was Bois whom Elezar watched. Bois studied him in return, he realized—not with any personal recognition but with a duelist's assessing gaze.

Elezar's fingers curled around the hilt of his sword.

In these close quarters with so many other people and skittish animals underfoot a fight would turn clumsy and bloody fast. If Bois had any sense he'd realize that.

Bois offered Elezar a sneer of a smile. Then he caught Rafale's eye and gave a shake of his head. Rafale withdrew back and Elezar let him go.

The waiting guards seemed disappointed, but when Bois called them away they followed him out onto the dark street. Cire crossed the room and quietly barred the door behind them. She paused then slid the bolt and secured a chain as well.

"You played that a little strong, didn't you?" Cire demanded and it took Elezar a moment to realize that she was talking to him. He'd grown used to being ignored in the company of all these witches. "What would you have done if the count's man called your bluff?"

"My man doesn't bluff," Skellan answered for him. He shoved his hood back from his face and grinned at Elezar with open admiration.

"It's a good thing that Rafale does then," Merle muttered. She knelt beside a small black rabbit and stroked it reassuringly.

"What the fuck did that priest want our Skellan for so badly?" Navet asked Cire.

Cire frowned as if the same question troubled her. Then she shrugged.

"I suppose Rafale oversold our boy to the priest and made it sound as if he might be gagging to serve Count Radulf's court." Cire scowled at Skellan. "Like any sane witch would be. But honestly, after the way you behaved, I have no idea why they still wanted you."

"It's because I was there in the sanctum challenging Oesir when the violet flame broke free," Skellan told her. "I saw the golden coffer that the violet flame was kept in and the Cadeleonian carriage that delivered it to Oesir. And I've seen Bois use the same carriage since then. Maybe they found out and don't want me spreading word of it."

Elezar stared at Skellan. Couldn't he have mentioned this earlier?

"If that's the case then they're more than a little late, aren't they?" Merle muttered.

Cire scowled at the locked door and then looked back to Skellan. She wasn't the only one studying him. Most of the witches watched him, though it wasn't exactly concern for him that Elezar read in their expressions, but uncertainty and annoyance.

"Are you absolutely sure of what you witnessed?" Ogmund asked. He absently patted his badger, which, Elezar realized, had clambered up beside the beer kegs, to lap up the liquid spilled beneath the tap.

"Nearly certain… I didn't see Bois himself in the sanctum that night," Skellan admitted. "But I did see the carriage and I know that the violet flame has something to do with the chapel on Bishop Palo's property."

"It wouldn't be some bit of statue that told you as much, would it?" Ogmund inquired. He refilled his beer and let a little extra fall for his badger.

"No." Skellan's jaw clenched so hard that Elezar could see the muscles straining. "I felt it in the stones of the place."

Ogmund shook his head. "A tingle from a rock is no grounds to go throwing accusations in every direction; you need to think about it. Now, I suppose I can imagine a Cadeleonian churchman deciding to unleash the violet flame to kill Oesir in the hope of driving witchcraft out of Labara completely… maybe."

Ogmund drained his beer then went on, "Though Bishop Palo hasn't been known for hating witches. In fact, back in my day he was said to be quite close with Grimma Lundag. He took her death badly, they say. Never did warm up to Oesir…"

"Sure, I remember all that," Navet commented. "I suppose he could have decided to murder Oesir with the violet flame to avenge Lundag. But if that's the case he sure took his time getting to it. And with his niece coming to Milmuraille to marry that Cadeleonian duke, seems like the last thing he'd want is to risk a Mirogoth invasion."

Skellan hunched his shoulders and muttered something too softly for even Elezar to hear.

"And where did that accusation against Count Radulf come from, then?" asked a younger woman with two white rabbits curled up in the folds of her full red skirt.

"Indeed!" Ogmund nodded and filled two more cups of beer for other witches. "Everyone knows Oesir and he are close—he gives the grimma every favor he asks. And the last thing he'd ever want was to endanger Milmuraille. Rafale was dead right on that."

"I know." Skellan scowled down at his hands. "It's just that Rafale's claim about the count possessing an incantation to destroy the violet flame didn't ring true. How could a mere incantation destroy something that all the wards in the grimma's sanctum can't stop? If it's just a matter of reciting a few spells, why hasn't Count Radulf done it already?" Skellan glowered out the small circular window across the room. "The violet flame is too ancient to have been recorded with pen on paper. It comes from the age of the cairns, from the time of the Old Gods and demon—"

"Now let's not get carried away into troll stories, Skellan," Ogmund cut him off with a kind, if patronizing, smile. "We all know how you love those old rocks, but this isn't some fable, boy. It's real trouble."

Skellan's pale cheeks flushed, though whether it was with more embarrassment or anger, Elezar wasn't certain. Seeing him color, several witches burst into laughter. Elezar scowled at them but could hardly enter into the debate. He knew nothing of witchcraft, except what he'd seen Skellan accomplish. That, as far as he could tell, had been more than most of these older witches had managed for themselves.

But perhaps there was something larger going on here that he didn't yet understand.

Skellan glowered at the floor and then lifted his head in challenge to Ogmund. "All right, if I'm just spinning floss then why were Rafale and Bois so excited to take me with them? You think they just wanted to share the pleasure of my company?"

Ogmund made a sour face but said nothing.

"Rafale and Bois make an oily pair, true enough. And they meant to make some use of you, Skellan. That's certain, but what they wanted and why we can't know." Navet pushed a wild wisp of her gray hair back from her face and sat down beside Merle. "That said, I don't think we can ignore Count Radulf's invitation."

"Agreed," Cire stated. "We may not like everything about all of this but something must be done about the violet flame and soon. Right now Count Radulf seems our best hope. At the least we should go to him and see what we can do."

Some fifty voices rose in soft agreement.

"I've been gathering topaz fragments and there's something in them..." Skellan mumbled.

"We'll see Count Radulf first thing Sacreday and we'll be able to see this incantation for ourselves then," Cire stated firmly. "In the meantime, I think we just need to make everyone as comfortable and safe as possible."

Skellan bowed his head. It was obvious to even Elezar that the gathered witches were in no mood to hear him out. Most seemed to want only to calm the animals that their children had become and drain the last of the table beer. In their eyes, Skellan's usefulness had come to an end.

"I imagine a number of you are spending the night," Cire commented. "I'll see about blankets and we can discuss the cost of a day's board in the morning."

That inspired a number of grumbles as well as a consensus that, though it was dark, if they traveled in groups it would not be too dangerous to travel across the city to their homes.

"You're not as likely to be robbed on the street as you are here in Cire's company, that's for sure," Clairre muttered.

"Skellan," Cire called out brightly as if she'd overheard none of them. "Be a dear and fetch that second cord of wood from the kitchen, will you? It's going to be cold tonight."

Skellan sighed so heavily that Elezar almost laughed.

"I'll get it," Elezar told him. Both Skellan and Cire seemed surprised that he would offer, but honestly he couldn't imagine Skellan lifting kindling much less lumber in his current state.

Elezar found his way back into the shadowy recesses of the kitchen, where the smell of dried herbs turned strong and harsh. Small rodent eyes gleamed from the rafters and followed him as he moved. He hefted up the stack of split logs and brought them back to the fireplace.

In his brief absence several of the witches had already departed. Sammi, Sarl and their father were nowhere to be seen. Nor were either of the Yuanese women. Merle and Navet stood at the door, saying their goodbye to Skellan. They offered Elezar a wave and then left. Skellan locked the door behind them and headed up the stairs alone.

"Here." Ogmund came up beside Elezar with two large clay cups of beer. A thick animal smell rolled off the old man and up close Elezar could see that red scorch marks and a few blisters marred his right arm and gaunt chest. "For you and the boy."

"Thank you." Elezar accepted the cups and, after wishing Cire a good night, he followed Skellan up the worn stairs, through the low hall and into the dark warmth of Skellan's room.

"What a day," Skellan muttered. Quite offhandedly he tossed aside the coat he wore. He then took one of the cups from Elezar and sat down, patting the space beside him on the bed. "Come sit and join me for a drink."

"I... all right," Elezar agreed though he felt unreasonably nervous. It wasn't as if he hadn't already seen Skellan naked and slept beside him in this very bed.

"Take off those bloody boots, before you even sit on my bed," Skellan ordered. Elezar smirked at the thought of Skellan being so fastidious but was glad enough to take off his fetid footwear. He put the boots outside the door. Then he returned and dropped down onto the straw-stuffed mattress. Skellan raised his own cup.

"Here's to you, my man," Skellan said, smiling. "I think that between them, Rafale and Cire might have auctioned me off to that Brother Bois if you hadn't been there looking murder at him and the grimma's guards."

"You do me too much credit. You were well ready to bolt out the back before any of them laid a finger on you."

"Well, that was my plan." Skellan took a deep drink of the table beer and sighed contentedly. "But to be honest I'm near dead on my feet. I don't know how far I would have made it if I had to run for it again."

Elezar contemplated Skellan's smiling face and lanky sprawled body.

"If that's the case, when you went after Bois, what did you think was going to happen?" he asked.

"There was a chance he'd give something away. And he did in a manner." Skellan yawned and then gulped down more of his beer. "You saw how he went all prickly when I implied that Count Radulf could have summoned the violet flame."

Elezar gave a reluctant nod. He didn't understand witches or witchcraft enough to follow Skellan's intrinsic logic—if such intuition could even be described as logic.

"Now that told us something, didn't it?" Skellan set his cup aside and stretched out on the bed. "He was half-shitting himself at the thought of swearing before a room full of witches that Count Radulf wasn't involved. Now we know that he must be."

"But how did you know to suspect Radulf?" Elezar asked.

"I didn't." Skellan laughed. "I was just kicking shit to see where it stuck. But Count Radulf... I wouldn't have guessed that, ever. And I still have no idea why he would do something like this. I can't see the sense in it." Skellan folded his arms under his head and gazed up at the slanting ceiling as if he were gazing after a distant star.

"So, you just went after Bois on the off chance that he knew something? Despite the fact that you were already exhausted and they'd brought five armed guards with him?"

Skellan frowned slightly. "Well, when you say it like that it sounds a little…"

"Daft?" Elezar provided.

"Daring, you mean?" Skellan responded with a laugh. "Your Labaran's good but some words obviously still elude you, my man."

"Why don't we split the difference and say you acted brashly." Elezar tasted the table beer. They tended to drink it bitter in the north but surprisingly he found he didn't mind. This brew wasn't strong. Still Elezar drank slowly, carefully. He felt Skellan stretched out beside him on the bed far too keenly to trust himself completely. God only knew how he was going to sleep through another night of feeling naked skin against his own.

The lamplight flickered and rolled low. Through the window Elezar could just make out the black spires of dozens of bell towers, backlit by the shining ribbon of the distant river. All those towers and yet the night seemed so quiet.

"Just seeing me you wouldn't take me for a dog, would you?" Skellan asked.

"Seeing you as you are now?" Elezar asked. "Or as I first saw you, because I did take you for a dog that time."

"No. As I am now."

Elezar made a show of looking him over; Skellan lay still and relaxed, jacket abandoned to the floor, shirt open to show the pale expanse of his chest. His red hair spilled out across the patched bedding and he wore an easy smile. Elezar's heartbeat quickened. Before he could stop himself he reached out to touch Skellan's chest, to feel the solidity of bone and muscle sheathed beneath delicate, warm skin. Then he caught himself, pulling his hand up and making a show of patting Skellan's head.

"You know, I think I can see the dog in you."

"Really?" Skellan frowned.

"Indeed," Elezar replied. "You're just like my mother's favorite little rat hound, a ferocious ball of fur, named Baladron. He weighs about as much as a fart. But you'd think he was a fire-breathing bull with cannon shot for balls from the way he'll go in for a fight with just about any living creature."

Skellan laughed and Elezar marveled at how trusting he was. It would be so easy—Elezar drew his hand back and drained the last of his beer quickly.

"I weigh a little more than a fart," Skellan stated. "But you are right about my balls. They could very well knock down a castle wall."

"I have no doubt of that," Elezar said. "I didn't realize until tonight, but you really are a skilled witch, aren't you?"

"Here in Milmuraille, I'm the best you could find. Out where the land and air don't know me..." Skellan shrugged. "I don't know."

"What would you have done if I'd taken you back to Anacleto?"

"What, when I was still a hound? I'd have caused you no end of trouble," Skellan replied lightly.

"I suppose it's for the best that I didn't, then." A soft laugh rumbled through Elezar's chest. "We wouldn't want to have any trouble."

In the depth of the night, Elezar woke with a shout, bringing Skellan up with him from sleep into the darkness of the small room.

"A bad dream?" Skellan asked.

"A memory..." Elezar's skin felt damp with sweat despite the chill in the air. "I was back there again..."

"Where?" Skellan's voice drifted out of the darkness, sounding relaxed, half asleep.

"The Sorrowlands," Elezar muttered. "No, it was that fucking barrow..." It was all over and yet the damn dreams never seemed to let up.

"Was it bad?" Skellan asked.

Elezar wanted to lie, to claim that it was a meaningless nothing but hunched in the darkness and still shaking he couldn't.

"You don't have to tell me," Skellan said. "But if you want to, I'll hear you out."

Elezar had only ever told one other person. But lying here in a foreign land beside Skellan, maintaining his reticence seemed strangely childish. Elezar blew out a breath and stared up at the shadows of thatch and wooden beams that made up the ceiling. Skellan felt warm and relaxed beside him.

What was there to fear of that past here and now?

"Six of my eldest brother's friends murdered him in a barrow." Elezar spoke slowly, hearing the words aloud for the first time since he'd been a boy. In the years that had passed, the events had taken on a kind of horrific vastness in his mind and memory, as if they were too immense and shameful to ever be spoken of. Yet words came to him as he told the story. "They were all swordsmen whom I admired, and they used the excuse of my eleventh birthday to lure Isandro away with me. They gored my leg and threw me in a corner like a heap of trash while they tortured him to death. And I watched them..."

A long silence stretched between them, and Elezar felt relieved that he couldn't see the disdain that no doubt showed on Skellan's face. How could anyone respect a man who let his brother die like that? Elezar clenched his hands against his eyes, wishing he could scrub the images from them.

"That wide scar across your thigh?" Skellan asked quietly.

"They thought the wound would kill me but it didn't. Still, I let them slaughter Isandro in front of me. I should have done something... stopped them somehow..."

"Stopped them?" Skellan sounded incredulous. "How does a wounded eleven-year-old stop six men? Can you imagine any child capable of stopping you—much less six of you?"

Years of guilt flared within Elezar, instinctively resisting Skellan's argument. He had been big for his age, stronger than other boys and even then used to thinking of himself as responsible. But he'd never once considered the assault from another perspective. Never would he have imagined himself as one of the bastards set upon murdering Isandro. But if he had been, could any mere boy have stopped him?

No, not even a weeping wife had stilled him from seeking vengeance for his brother. As terrible as the comparison felt, it also served to lift a portion of Elezar's guilt.

"Why would they do something so cruel to you and him?" Skellan's hand touched his shoulder. His skin felt dry and warm.

"Because he broke with the Cadeleonian faith and secretly married a Haldiim woman," Elezar admitted. It all seemed so much easier to talk about in the darkness and to Skellan.

"What's a Haldiim?"

"They're the Irabiim's cultured southern cousins. They live in a walled district in Anacleto," Elezar said.

"Your brother's friends killed him for only that?" A tone of outrage sounded in Skellan's voice. "What utter bastards! Look, Elezar, when this is settled in Milmuraille I promise you I'll do all I can to find those men and make them pay—"

Despite his misery Elezar laughed. Not because he didn't believe Skellan would try to do as he said, but because this was all so similar to the only other time he'd confessed the truth of his brother's death. He'd been twelve then and his best friend Javier had sworn an oath on his pricked finger that he would see justice done.

"There's no need. They're all dead," Elezar said. "It took me years, but I hunted all six of them down and killed them in duels."

"Oh." Skellan sounded a little defeated. His warm hand stroked Elezar's shoulder again. The contact sent a shiver of longing through Elezar. "Well, then you should let the dreams go."

"You think I don't want to be free of them?"

"Of course you do," Skellan replied, yawning. "But at the same time they are part of your memories of your brother and perhaps you needed them once upon a time to drive you to avenge him."

It disturbed Elezar to consider how the nightmares that had tortured him for years had also served to harden his resolve, but he couldn't deny that there was a truth to that.

"I used to have nightmares all the time," Skellan said easily. "Bone-crusher once told me that dreams and nightmares are our souls reminding us of what we already know."

"It's not as though I needed reminding," Elezar replied, but he couldn't summon any vehemence.

"No. But maybe there's something about your brother's death—I mean beyond the horror of it—that your soul is still fighting with." Skellan shifted. Elezar thought he might be rubbing sleep from his eyes. "Even terrible memories can hold wisdom if—"

"Wisdom?" Elezar growled. Just the idea of using Isandro's death as some lesson angered him. "Such as not to tell anyone ever if I break Cadeleonian holy law? Or maybe not to ever let six armed men lure me into a black, fucking barrow again? What more fucking wisdom could I want?"

"That's not what I meant... Just that the past stays in us no matter what we might wish, and we have to find a way to... use it. Or to understand how it makes us who we are even if we hate it," Skellan said, sighing. "I'm not saying this right. I'm sorry, I'm too tired..."

Hearing the exhaustion in Skellan's voice Elezar felt suddenly like a boor. What kind of man woke his bed partner with violent nightmares in the dead of night and then lashed out when the groggy fellow tried to console him?

"I told you, you didn't want to sleep beside me." Elezar slid his legs off the edge of the bed and gripped his thigh. How could a scar so old still pain him?

"Don't go." Skellan's hand caught his hip. He didn't pull at Elezar and yet just that gentle touch stilled him.

Silence stretched between them again. Elezar's heart raced in his chest. He told himself that only a fool allowed the mere touch of a man's hand to affect him so deeply.

"Come back under the blanket and warm me up," Skellan said.

Elezar found himself sliding back down against the mattress and soaking in the sensation of that long warm ribbon of contact where his body brushed against Skellan's. He wanted to wrap his arms around him and pull him closer—to taste his skin and mouth. Elezar realized that he needed to find something to distract him from this line of thought. Then he noticed the scratching and scrabbling noise just beyond him. Something squeaked.

"How do you sleep with all these rats skittering around in the walls?" Elezar asked.

"Well, they're friends, aren't they?" Skellan replied. "They'd be the first to raise a warning if there was trouble."

"I suppose they would." Elezar relaxed slightly. How strange it was to take things in from Skellan's point of view. Strange and yet at the same time it seemed refreshing and even beautiful.

Elezar closed his eyes. He didn't think he would sleep and yet somehow he drifted off. To his chagrin he woke hours later as Skellan twitched and tossed in the obvious throes of his own troubling dream. He wondered if the story of his own haunted dreams had given Skellan a nightmare. Then again a young man who'd nearly been thrown into a fighting pit for dogs and who could see some gigantic violet fire hunting the city likely possessed troubling enough thoughts to have nightmares of his own.

Elezar touched Skellan's shoulder and he seemed to calm. He shoved his angular face into the crook of Elezar's neck and curled one of his hands across Elezar's chest. Elezar allowed himself to run his own hand along the curve of Skellan's waist. His fingers lingered on his hip, soaking up the feeling of the fine skin and hard muscle beneath.

He was killed for breaking Cadeleonian holy law.

The thought slithered through Elezar. He withdrew his hand.

Maybe Skellan had been right about him needing to remember the lesson of his brother's brutal murder.

And yet he couldn't bring himself to withdraw from the loose grip of Skellan's hand on his chest.

The faint light of sunrise already filtered in through the bow window but Elezar remained a little time longer, simply lying beside Skellan and absorbing the sensation of the other man's sleeping body curled next to his own.

CHAPTER
SEVENTEEN

From the heights of the crumbling tower, Skellan watched his city burn. The violet flame poured over the black sanctum walls flooding the streets and engulfing people and buildings at once. The water of the harbor did nothing to slow the fire. Ships ignited like casks of black powder as the bay boiled and steamed.

The roar of flames struck Skellan like a blow, swallowing the screams of the dying below. He stumbled at the edge of his precipice, choking on soot and feeling his lungs sear with each scorching breath. Seeing Navet and Merle trapped on a bridge, Skellan turned them to birds—so that they could fly to safety—but the flame arced up and tore them from the sky. Sarl and Sammi, still trapped in animal guises, shrieked as they burned in their paddock. Cire scrabbled across thatch rooftops with her rats, but they couldn't outdistance the engulfing fire.

Skellan howled curses down upon the flame, calling every shred of his rage and power, and pouring it out until his throat bled and his voice broke.

But it was to no avail. Below him Bone-crusher writhed and howled in the fire. The Mockingbird Playhouse collapsed and at the foot of Skellan's tower, Elezar's body blackened to char.

There was nothing Skellan could do—not for any of them. Not even for himself.

One immense geyser of fire twisted up from the rest, climbing Skellan's tower like a huge viper. Searing heat rolled off the serpentine creature in waves, and then Skellan saw its molten yellow eyes staring straight at him.

You feeble-minded creatures deserve to burn for making an enemy of a demon lord then daring to forget me! You will remember when I rise again and devour all your world!

The serpent opened its jaws and fire gushed up the tower walls, charring the stone and engulfing Skellan in agony and flames.

He jerked and knocked his knee against the wall of his cramped room. Briefly his eyes fluttered open. Morning light streamed in through the small window, warming Skellan's cheek and exposed shoulder. The sun always woke him too early in the spring, though today he seemed to have held out longer than usual. Lively conversations and loud honks of excited geese rose from the street outside. Skellan thought he heard someone mention his name, and he groggily wondered if Cire was already gossiping to the neighbors about being summoned to Count Radulf's Sun Palace.

He didn't even want to think about that. None of it.

And no wonder he was having such rotten dreams: sun burning into his face, half-overhearing the conversations below him and his whole body still aching from where the violet flame had seared so close to him last night.

He clenched his eyes closed and rolled away from the light. A body, built like a solid wall halted him from sprawling across the entire bed. He liked the masculine smell that floated over him. Skellan nuzzled deeper into his thin blanket and began to drift back to sleep.

"Are you going to sleep the whole day away?" Elezar's low voice drifted down to Skellan. He was sitting on the edge of the bed, Skellan realized. Which meant that this was Elezar's hip that Skellan had his faced mashed up against. He'd already dressed and from the slight chill that lingered on his cloak, Skellan guessed he'd been out on the streets already. He would be an early riser, wouldn't he? Or maybe he hadn't been able to return to sleep after his nightmare.

"Skellan?" Elezar asked quietly but Skellan decided against offering a reply. The strain of crafting so many spells without ever calling upon his own witchflame still churned through him worse than any hangover. He'd earned the right to a lay-in, and the least his man could do was to indulge him. Elezar seemed to draw the same conclusion. He didn't speak again but remained there at the bedside. Skellan drifted back to sleep.

Curled up against Elezar, Skellan hardly dreamed at all, except of a small red stone in a gold ring, which seemed to sing a lullaby to him. He wanted to hold it but instead found himself trying to pry open a strange puzzle box painted with scarlet bulls and Cadeleonian stars.

"It's not what you think," Elezar told him in his dream, but Skellan just kept pulling, knowing that he'd never wanted anything more.

When he woke again, the room seemed far warmer and he guessed he'd slept at least an hour past noon. He didn't feel so unwell now, just lazy and suffused with a longing to lounge in his bed the rest of the day.

Then he felt a callused finger brush over his brow, pushing his hair back from his face. Skellan cracked one eye enough to reassure himself that it was Elezar who watched over him. Indeed, his Cadeleonian crouched at the bedside looking too large for the confines of the tiny room. Ever so lightly he drew the corner of Skellan's blanket up over his bare shoulder. Such a careful touch and tentative expression. Skellan wouldn't have expected that after witnessing him dispatch two men so brutally two days before.

"You have good hands," Skellan told him. Elezar startled at the sound of his voice and, meeting Skellan's gaze, he drew his hand back suddenly as if caught filching a sausage from common soup.

"I'm not going to hurt you, my man." Skellan assured him. "You needn't be afraid."

"You think I'm afraid of you?" Elezar's expression hovered somewhere between embarrassment and amusement.

"Were you jumping from the joy of hearing my voice,

then?" Skellan teased but even as he spoke Skellan found himself thinking that it hadn't exactly been fear that he'd read in Elezar's expression—but a something nearer to guilt.

"I thought you were asleep, that's all," Elezar said. He met Skellan's gaze with a look that struck Skellan as both hopeful and guarded at once. The hesitant expression brought to mind an evening, years ago, when he'd trotted down a dark alley and nearly collided with a rangy, gray-eyed wolf. He'd thought that the beast shouldn't have been there—not lurking so deep within the civilized heart of a city. Then Skellan had realized that the creature regarded him with much the same expression. That evening Skellan had backed away and the other man, clothed, like himself, in animal flesh had fled away toward the city gates.

Now too, Skellan caught that reflection of a deep affinity buried beneath tense muscle and fear. Whether Elezar knew it or not, longing flickered there in his dark gaze—but he was more wary than a wild animal, Skellan thought, more likely to lash out if pushed too far. A wise witch would have left Elezar's unspoken desires well alone.

But then if wisdom had been one of Skellan's gifts he would have surrendered to Oesir rather than endure that first terrible winter on his own on the streets of Milmuraille. No, foolish daring served him well and he wasn't one to flinch away from what he wanted just because it might hurt him some.

"If you're not frightened, there's no reason to pull away is there?" Skellan reached out and laid his own hand over Elezar's.

Elezar tensed at the contact and just the slightest flush colored his face.

"It's late…" Elezar began, only to trail off.

"I won't harm you," Skellan said softly.

He drew Elezar's hand to his bare chest. Skellan felt slight tremors shaking through Elezar's arm but he didn't resist as Skellan pressed his warm palm to his heart.

"You see," Skellan smiled into Elezar's stony expression, "I'm not so bad to touch, am I? And you, you're a well-made man." He ran his hand up the thick muscle of Elezar's straining arm. Elezar's shoulder felt like chiseled rock beneath the fabric of his shirt. The exposed skin of his throat flushed hot beneath Skellan's fingers.

"It wouldn't be so bad to keep each other company for a little while, would it?"

Elezar stared down at Skellan, still as a statue. But his pulse hammered beneath Skellan's fingers as he curled his hand around the nape of Elezar's neck. Thick, dark hair brushed against his knuckles. With deliberate slowness, Skellan drew Elezar's head down to his own. He expected to feel the other man resist but Elezar didn't fight. Instead his gaze remained locked upon Skellan's even as their mouths met.

For an instant Elezar remained unmoving against him and Skellan almost released him. But then Elezar closed his eyes and Skellan felt a shiver pass through the straining muscle of his body. His hands curled around Skellan's shoulders and his restraint seemed to shatter.

He pulled Skellan up against his chest and held him as he kissed him deeply, teasing his lips with his teeth and thrusting his tongue up against Skellan's own. The heat of Elezar's mouth and the power of his embrace flooded Skellan with arousal and ignited a voracious yearning.

Skellan ran his hands over Elezar's back and down his flanks, feeling the strength of those long bones and all that hard muscle. Elezar responded to his lightest caress with a soft gasp. His big hands curled through Skellan's hair and he kissed the tender expanse of Skellan's neck. His teeth grazed Skellan's skin, sending shivers through him. With just a stroke of his hand, Skellan brought Elezar's mouth back up to meet his own.

Skellan didn't know that he'd ever held such influence over another man—certainly never such a powerful man. He forgot the playful pecks that he'd planned to bestow—forgot his own earlier hesitation at the thought of provoking and arousing a man as dangerous and strong as his Cadeleonian. Now all he wanted was to meet Elezar's might and drive with his own longing. A kiss was not enough, he wanted everything Elezar possessed.

He tore at Elezar's sword belt and kicked the tangled blankets aside, desperate to remove all barriers between their bodies. As the heavy metal buckle knocked against Skellan's knuckles he let out a growl of frustration.

Elezar drew back, releasing Skellan at once. He looked flushed and wild but also so very worried. Gently, he caught Skellan's hand. "I'm sorry, did I hurt—"

"Don't apologize." Skellan pulled from his careful grip, jerked open Elezar's belt buckle and traced the hot, straining flesh beneath Elezar's breeches. "Just get out of these damn clothes!"

Whatever reason there might have been for Elezar's reluctance, it seemed to evaporate in that instant. He tore off his clothes and gave himself up to all that Skellan desired of him throughout the languid hours of the afternoon.

CHAPTER
EIGHTEEN

At dusk, gnawing hunger roused Skellan. As he extricated himself from beneath the hot weight of Elezar's legs, Elezar mumbled something soft and inarticulate. His hand brushed across Skellan's shoulder.

"I'll see if I can't find something to feed us. It shouldn't take long," Skellan whispered to him and received a mumbled response that sounded a little like "good" but might well have also been "food." Then Elezar settled back into a deeper sleep.

Skellan pulled on his cloak and trousers and padded downstairs. He wasn't accustomed to so much quiet in the boarding house and found it eerie. What if Cire had fallen to the violet flame while he'd slept? The anxiety arose from the remnants of that terrible dream. But as he descended, reassuringly familiar voices drifted up to him and he noted Cire's brood of rats frolicking along the ceiling supports.

Cire and her uncle sat with an old white-haired woman and her moon-faced daughter at a table. Skellan suspected that he knew Cire's guests far better than they knew him. As a dog he'd often attempted to sneak mouthfuls of smoked and cured meats from their market stall. Often as not, the old woman drove him off with her cleaver. The round-faced daughter and her little son often tossed him odd remnants, however. If he'd had a tail Skellan thought it might have wagged as he took in the rich aroma of meat, brine and smoke that saturated the women's hair and clothes.

The flickering gold glow of hearth light lit them as they all sipped frothy table beer and discussed how best they should turn themselves out to meet Count Radulf.

"Merle and Navet are offering very fair terms for the use of their goat carts and ponies," Cire commented. "I'm thinking of bringing a gift as well. Maybe a clutch of my hens' finest eggs."

Then Cire cast an appraising glance to Skellan as he sauntered up to them.

"Breaking in your new man, eh?" she asked.

Skellan grinned. He couldn't help himself. But then thinking of how the exchange would mortify Elezar he said, "In my dreams. The spells from last night knocked me flat. I snored the whole day away. Only got up now because I'm half starved."

"Well, your timing is perfect," Ogmund informed him.

"Mother brought one of her blue-brined drake breasts, and I brought my cider for you as thanks for all you did for my son last night," the round-faced woman told Skellan.

"My thanks in return." Skellan's mouth began to water at just the mention of the meat.

"Duck is to your liking, I hope?" the old woman asked.

Skellan nodded vigorously.

"You've made him drool too much for speech," Ogmund declared, drawing a round of laughter from all assembled.

Skellan didn't mind. He rushed to the kitchen where the dark, cured duck breast rested, wrapped in a braid of dried herbs. He started to snatch it up but then paused and glanced back at Cire.

"Oh, go on. Take it all. You earned it," Cire told him. "And anyway, if things work out we might all be feasting on pork and cherries at the count's table come this Sacreday."

A formless anxiety shivered down Skellan's spine at the mention of their invitation to the Sun Palace but Skellan ignored it. No one would want to hear more of his wild speculations, and in any case there was duck to be had. Beside it stood a large clay jar of cider, still steaming up wisps of spice and apple perfume.

Cire and her guests returned to their discussion of how they would dress to meet Count Radulf—whether wearing the count's colors of gold and scarlet would show their loyalty to him or seem too presumptuous.

Skellan took the duck and cider then added a few pickled onions and two slabs of grave bread to round out the fare. Arms full and feeling happy as a thief carrying off a cask of diamonds, Skellan hurried back upstairs.

When he entered he found that Elezar had lit his lamp and now sat on the edge of the bed gazing out the small window. The smells of sweat and sex lingered in the little room. One of Skellan's blankets flopped on the floor, while his clothes and Elezar's hung together from nails on the wall. It struck Skellan as a homey sight.

Elezar turned Skellan's way and rose to make room for Skellan to lay their feast out on the windowsill. Standing, Elezar hunched low to keep his head from knocking into the ceiling supports. Skellan couldn't help but note that he didn't fit in so confined a room, or indeed in such shabby surroundings.

But on the other hand, Skellan had earned them a blue-brined duck breast and that was a meat fine enough for Sheriff Hirbe to dine upon every Auguiday, according to the market gossip.

Elezar crouched back down on the bed and Skellan joined him, enjoying the feeling of their bare legs brushing against each other. Elezar's thick, black hair tickled through Skellan's curlier red hairs.

Skellan tore a hunk of the duck breast off and placed it on the hard grave bread and handed that over to Elezar.

"Onion?" Skellan offered.

Elezar declined so Skellan took the onion for his own serving of ragged meat and hard, dark bread. He downed a mouthful then remembered himself and handed the jar of cider Elezar's way.

"Cider. Still warm," Skellan explained around his mouthful of food. Elezar accepted the drink.

As before Elezar ate and drank more slowly and with a fastidious precision while Skellan wasted no time filling his belly. Elezar declined the offer of the breastbone, so that, too, Skellan devoured while Elezar watched with an expression Skellan took for amazement. Skellan sucked grease from his fingers then flopped back onto the bed and belched.

"I'm full. Actually full, can you believe it?" He caught Elezar's hand and pulled it to his stomach. "Feel!"

Elezar obligingly rubbed Skellan's taut stomach and smiled. But he didn't lie back on the bed. Instead he frowned out the window and then glanced to where the collar he'd bought Skellan rested beneath the low-burning oil lamp.

"Thinking about adding that charm of yours to my collar, I suppose?" Skellan asked. He'd not forgotten the charm, but he'd grown used to the warm feeling it radiated. More than that he'd come to enjoy pestering Elezar over it and almost looked forward to hearing how Elezar would rebuff him.

"I wouldn't want to ruin so fine a piece of work as your collar with some Mirogoth charm." Elezar offered him an easy teasing smile. But as his attention returned to the window his expression grew more serious. "It isn't just the night and darkness out there, is it?"

"No," Skellan admitted. He pushed himself up onto his elbows and took in the view outside. "The violet flame lights the sky like a bright sunset. I can see the Lyoness Bell Tower outlined in its light."

Elezar squinted intently then shook his head.

"I thought I glimpsed it last night and again just before you returned. But it was gone before I could be sure."

"It's growing stronger. Soon it may be visible to everyone." Skellan fell back, preferring the view of his own ceiling to the writhing violet flames outside. "At the height of their power, some witches cannot only raise their souls up from their bodies to take action but ignite them to forms that every living creature can see and feel... or at least that's what I've heard. Lundag was the most powerful witch I've ever known, but even she couldn't embody her witchflame—"

"Her soul, you said before," Elezar commented.

"They're one and the same thing," Skellan answered, though it struck him as stating the obvious. Then he realized that a Cadeleonian would know none of this. "We witches call our souls witchflames because they flicker up sometimes when a witch is young. Makes it easy for elder witches to recognize those with potential for teaching, though I think that it's also those flickers that violet flame was attacking in the children."

Elezar considered silently for a time then asked, "So your soul leaves your body to practice magic?"

"No. That would be truly dangerous. I might never find my way back." Skellan ran his hand over his precious full gut. He didn't want to even imagine the horror of losing his body right now. "I sometimes stretch my witchflame far up above my body, but I always hold a thread back within my flesh. But it's safest to just..." Skellan flexed his fingers and toes trying to think of a word that would sum up the sensation he knew innately. "Just to reach out. When I do I feel the whole city flowing over me, like the river current flowing across a bare hand."

"That sounds truly strange," Elezar commented. Again he studied the view out the window. "So, is the violet flame some kind of witchflame then?"

Skellan started to assure Elezar that it wasn't but then caught himself. He rose up onto his elbows and stared at the huge, furious flames as they engulfed the bell tower. Could it be a kind of witchflame? Not the soul of a mortal witch but the raging spirit of some immense and ancient creature? An Old God or even—all at once Skellan's heart began to pound hard in his chest—a demon. Suddenly Skellan remembered his dream—that huge serpent, smoldering with violet fire for scales and furious yellow eyes.

...burn for making an enemy of a demon lord then daring to forget me!

Only one demon lord had been stripped of his soul. As a boy Skellan had walked over the grounds where the huge demon's body coiled deep in the grip of stone. Skellan tried to remember exactly what Bone-crusher had told him. The demon lord's soul had been trapped and locked away... not destroyed, but locked away. None of the Old Gods had remained to destroy him.

"The ancient stones beneath Bishop Palo's chapel were set there to guard something terrible..." Skellan whispered and fear shuddered down his spine.

"Something wrong?" Elezar asked.

"Only that I've been an idiot and should have thought of this sooner. I should have seen it after all the tales Bone-crusher told me. You are exactly right, my man. The violet flame is a soul just like a witchflame only it's the soul of the Demon Lord Zi'sai... I'm certain of it."

"Zi'sai from Rafale's play?" Elezar sounded somewhat skeptical, but Skellan didn't fault him. He hadn't been the one who'd seen the demon lord's true face in his dreams.

"Yes, the one and the same."

"You're certain? Not just throwing shit to see what sticks again?" Elezar asked.

"So certain that the knowledge resonates through me." Skellan held his shivering hand out and pressed it against Elezar's bare muscular chest. "This truth blazes like the stones lighting my vei. I feel it to my bones."

"All right." Elezar ran his hand gently over Skellan's fingers. "You see and sense so many things that I can't that I don't really need to know how you know. If you're certain then I believe you. But you do realize that this means that it's either an amazing coincidence that Rafale wrote that play or very suspicious."

Skellan hadn't thought of that. He was so accustomed to using intuition to understand the secrets his surroundings carried to him that he never considered the source of any particular fact. Stones told him stories, and his dreams showed him what he had already absorbed from the earth and air around him.

But Elezar was right again. Rafale was no ancient stone that might have witnessed Zi'sai's downfall. Nor was Zi'sai's story a common tale known to all and sundry. Some traces of it perhaps existed in Count Radulf's library, but otherwise the story was one told only by petrified frogwives and trolls.

"Rafale is a regular guest of Count Radulf's; perhaps he came across someone at the count's palace looking over the old story and that inspired his play. He might not..."

Elezar cast him one of those stern, skeptical glances that assured him that he wasn't fooling anyone but himself.

Skellan frowned at his own impulse to defend Rafale. He'd been comfortable accusing Count Radulf, whom he knew nothing of personally, as well as the priest, Bois, whom he didn't particularly like. But even he had to recognize that Rafale was the link that connected the other two. Rafale had brought Bois to the Rat Rafters. He'd extended the invitation to the Sun Palace on the count's behalf. He had to be up to his neck in this mess.

Yet even knowing all that, Skellan he didn't want to think a man he liked—a man he'd once loved—capable of deliberately unleashing something so terrible.

"Perhaps they didn't mean to release it at all," Skellan said. "What if Bois just came across the golden coffer while making repairs to the bishop's chapel and he sent the coffer to Oesir for identification and Oesir opened it by mistake?"

"Did he?" Elezar asked. "You said you were there. Did he open it by mistake?"

Skellan thought back, trying to remember those few minutes before everything had turned to horror. He closed his eyes.

"Oesir stood by the water garden and he was holding the coffer. I waited for him to notice me and then got annoyed and he—" Skellan recalled the surprise in Oesir's face and that strange, brief expression that was so like joy. Then the coffer had slipped from Oesir's grip and burst open. Skellan went rigid with horror.

"Skellan?" Elezar's hand curled around Skellan's. His skin felt so warm compared to the icy chill that spread through Skellan.

It's my fault. The coffer slipped from his hand because I startled him. It's my fault that the demon lord has been set free.

Skellan couldn't say the words aloud.

"Skellan?" The alarm in Elezar's voice made him open his eyes.

He pulled his hand back from Elezar's grip as if just his touch might somehow contaminate Elezar.

"What's wrong with you?" Elezar demanded. "Damn it, talk to me! Is the violet flame here in the room?"

"No." Skellan almost wished that it were, if only to keep him from feeling this terrible guilt. Vieve's death was his doing as were countless others. How could he ever make amends for that? "I didn't mean to worry you. We're safe just now. But I…" He flicked his gaze from Elezar's intense dark stare. "I think that Oesir was so shocked by seeing me again that he lost his grip on the coffer. I think I may have made him drop it, and when it fell open the demon lord escaped." Skellan tried again to meet Elezar's gaze but couldn't. "It's my doing—"

"No," Elezar cut him off.

"I startled him and it fell—"

"Did you dig the damn thing up?" Elezar demanded.

"Obviously not, but—"

"Did you deliver it to Oesir?"

"No, b—"

"Were you the one holding it when it fell?"

"No—"

This time Elezar placed his finger over Skellan's lips, silencing his protest.

"You are not to blame." Elezar held his gaze intently. "You might have been there when the plot of other men fell apart, but you aren't to blame for what they set in motion."

Skellan tried to consider Elezar's words. He wanted to believe them so badly. He wanted to be innocent. But he kept remembering Oesir's expression and the coffer falling, over and over. Oesir saying his name—his true name—and the coffer slipping from his hands, crashing to the ground. Those terrible flames rising up.

"Would you say that I was to blame for my brother's murder?" Elezar's demand broke into Skellan's fixation.

"What? Of course not!"

"Then you can't blame yourself for this, because much the same thing happened to us both, if you think about it," Elezar said. "I was there, witnessed it and even served as a kind of accomplice by helping my brother's killers to get him alone and far from any aid. If I hadn't been there, they never could have lured him to that barrow." Elezar paused and Skellan could almost see him considering his own words. "But I didn't want his murder. I wasn't party to the plotting or the planning of it. The men responsible embroiled me, just as you stumbled across something already in progress. You can't take the blame for something other men set in motion. You mustn't. It will ruin you."

Skellan recognized the parallel, strange as it seemed. And he realized, in his own sense of responsibility, how badly the murder must have wounded Elezar's spirit as well as his body.

"You truly are not to blame," Skellan told him firmly and with absolute conviction.

Elezar nodded his head just slightly.

"You aren't to blame, either," Elezar answered him with equal assurance.

It was as if he'd invoked a spell. The wretched sick feeling of guilt lifted from Skellan. He felt completely relieved, in no small part because he'd thought that if he really had unleashed a demon lord upon his dearest friends and their helpless children, he might just vomit up his precious duck dinner. As was, he pulled Elezar close in his arms and back down onto the bed. He didn't know any words that would convey his elation at having Elezar here with him now. So instead he kissed him, first on his lips and then lower down his body. He took time to make much of his man and reward him with all the skill he'd learned in other beds.

Elezar's hands tangled in his hair, and Skellan felt Elezar tensing and fighting back the joyous shout of his released ecstasy.

Had it been another man Skellan might have made a joke about the danger of downing such a large dessert so soon after his supper. But with Elezar he kept quiet and simply stretched out beside him.

He slept a little and woke to find the lamp sputtering low and Elezar gazing up at the ceiling. Skellan yawned and shifted to a slightly less damp bit of his mattress.

"I know so little about you," Elezar commented, though his gaze remained on the shadows dancing across the ceiling beams.

"I don't know much more of you, do I?"

"You've read my letters and overheard a month of memoires," Elezar retorted.

"Very well, ask me a question and I'll see if I can't give you an honest answer," Skellan replied. People rarely concerned themselves with his history. Perhaps because seeing him, half-starved and of no obvious honest occupation his history likely seemed straightforward as any foundling tramp's.

"All this talk of yours about trolls and growing up in a walnut orchard—is any of it true?"

Skellan weighed his response and decided that he owed Elezar honesty. "Yes. Only the walnut orchard was in the Labaran sanctum. I lived there until I was eleven."

"You were one of the children Lundag abducted?" Elezar rolled onto his side to look Skellan in the face.

"She'd have gotten fuck all for a ransom," Skellan replied. "She found me and took me because even as a little grub I had a bright witchflame."

"You've no family at all?" Elezar seemed to find this incredible, though as far as Skellan could tell orphans and abandoned children were common enough.

"I don't have any blood kin, but there's Bone-crusher," Skellan added. "He's a troll."

"A troll? Not one of those ones lurking under the Fardee Bridge, is he?"

"No, those two are just babes." Skellan met Elezar's languid gaze and went on. "Master Bone-crusher is the huge troll who holds up the east wall of the Labaran sanctum. He was first enslaved by Grimma Naemir and sent to fight here, but Lundag trapped him in her sanctum and there he's been for a hundred years," Skellan said. Then when Elezar kept quiet he added, "I know it sounds like I'm telling tales, but I swear I'm not. If it weren't for Bone-crusher I wouldn't likely be a witch at all. He's the one who taught me how to hear the stones and to change myself back into a boy after Lundag transformed me into a hound. And he kept me warm on the cold nights..."

Skellan fell into a reverie, remembering Bone-crusher holding him and whispering promises that had reverberated through his whole body until they seemed to shake his very bones.

One day, my Little Thorn, you will claim the stones of this sanctum and they will know only you. I wonder, when all of this is yours to command and you hold my life in your hands, will you free me at last?

And always Skellan swore he would. No matter the cost, he would set Bone-crusher free.

Elezar's voice broke him free of memory. "Wait, did I hear you right? You were a dog before you were a boy?" He looked a little alarmed and Skellan laughed.

"I was born a human being, never you fear. You've not taken up with a dog wearing a man's skin," Skellan said, with another chuckle. "No, Lundag liked to keep me as a pup though. Actually, she preferred to keep the hostage children enthralled as well. I didn't see many of them, but I know that if they cried or vexed her she often turned them into kittens. Sometimes she carried them in the pockets of her coat when their parents came to parlay. It amused her, I think, when the parents couldn't recognize their own."

"She sounds cruel," Elezar commented. Skellan supposed that she had been but not always. On the rare occasion, particularly when she'd indulged in poppy smoke and wine, she had sat him in her lap and stroked his head.

"I think she was very lonely," Skellan said. He'd not told anyone any of this, and it felt both odd but also relieving to share what he knew. "At one time she'd lived in a sanctum herself, you see. She'd studied under Grimma Ylva—called her Auntie Wolf-Bitch. She fell in love with one of Ylva's prisoners. And instead of killing the man Lundag fled with him back to Labara, and according to her that's what sparked the war a hundred years ago."

Elezar seemed interested so Skellan went on. "They fought the grimma together but after the war Lundag's lover left her. He died soon after and the children born of his Labaran wife refused to acknowledge Lundag. Nor would many of the guild masters and courtiers. She grew bitter and lonely."

"And so she found you and kept you as her dog?" Elezar asked.

"I was meant to be more," Skellan said. Then, noticing the rats gazing down from the rafters overhead, he lowered his voice. "I've never told anyone else this but Lundag meant me to be her champion—her great scarlet wolf. The cloak I wear is from her. That changed when Oesir murdered Lundag. After he killed her he had to break countless spells that hung in the sanctum. It was absolute chaos. The child hostages you were asking about earlier—I think more than a few were lost while they were still transformed. Probably Count Radulf's son lived out his days as some old lady's pet cat. The Sumar grimma's child too."

"And you?" Elezar asked. "Is that how you survived? By becoming someone's pet?"

"If only I'd been that clever," Skellan replied. "No, when I first fled I was too shy of people to be taken in. I'd never been around folk before, and it didn't help that Oesir sent men to hunt me down. I rolled in oil and soot to hide the color of my coat from them. That didn't make me attractive to the few folk who might have taken it into their heads to tame me."

"But how did you eat? Where did you sleep?" Elezar asked.

"There's food and shelter enough in the alleys if you're not too picky, and you know for a fact that I'm not."

"How long did you live like that?" Elezar looked stricken.

"Five years about. Then I started to want to go with fellows and... Well, I wasn't all that interested in the sorts that were interested in me when I was a dog. So I started slipping out of the dog flesh more and more." Skellan pulled a wide grin. It hadn't been so easy as he made it sound, but he didn't want Elezar to look at him with pity or think him pathetic. He wanted Elezar to believe him to be strong and brave, a man deserving to hold his knife and share his bed. "Worse strays than me have lived on these streets just fine. Anyway, I knew I wouldn't die. Even when I was whoring myself for dry sausage I knew that I would return to take the sanctum someday and fight the grimma. That's my vei. Even Bone-crusher thinks so. It was only the violet flame that stopped me last time."

Skellan reached out and wrapped his arms around Elezar, feeling him tense and then slowly relax.

"Once I take the sanctum I'll be a grimma so you might want to consider resigning your service to the duke, because I'll need a champion."

"Oh yes? Is that the vei we share, then?"

"It could be indeed, my man. We'll wear furs and silks as fine as Duke Quemanor's. Finer even. And we'll have all the duck we could wish for, no matter the season. It will be a fine life for me and my champion. You should consider it."

Elezar's still silence stretched so long that Skellan almost lost his nerve. Then Elezar's strong arms curled around him, gathering him closer.

"And what duties might be required of your champion?" Gentle humor sounded through Elezar's voice. Skellan knew he didn't believe him, but at least he wasn't pitying him or pushing him away.

"Much the same as you've already provided today." Skellan slid his hand down Elezar's hard stomach.

"Perhaps I should have a little more practice." Elezar's lips spread in a rare, unguarded smile. "Just to ensure that I'm prepared when the time comes for you to fulfill your vei. "

It's not mine alone, Skellan thought, but he didn't need to say as much. For now just this between them was enough.

❧

The next morning Skellan's whole body ached in a pleased, used way. Early morning sun lit his naked skin with a golden light. Elezar lay half atop him, snoring contentedly. Skellan shifted, pulling his shoulder free before his arm went numb. Their legs still tangled, Elezar's heavy thighs all but pinned Skellan's own. Taking in Elezar's sleeping form, Skellan felt a kind of pride, as if he'd summited a great mountain, or ridden a wild stallion the entire night through.

Or more aptly, he'd ridden a wild mountain the whole night through. Skellan smirked at himself.

Elezar was not a small man by any measure or in any aspect. Skellan understood that full well now and felt a little chagrined at his own reckless appetite and aching muscles. He didn't know what he'd been thinking, urging Elezar so hard and deep. But in the moment he'd only felt a kind of molten joy in driving himself and Elezar up against the limits of endurance.

Thankfully, Elezar had possessed far greater restraint than Skellan himself. Or perhaps at his very core, he was simply more gentle than Skellan could have imagined a swordsman so deadly to be. Certainly he took more time and more coaxing than any other man Skellan had bedded, and seemed—up until the abandon of ecstasy—if not wary then watchful of Skellan's limits. Skellan felt certain that it was only thanks to Elezar that he was in any condition to rise from bed and go about the day.

Not that he could do either with the man sleeping on him. Skellan considered jabbing Elezar's ribs to make him roll away, but couldn't bring himself to do it. Even now something about the way he lay naked with his large hands curled around Skellan seemed oddly tender. So instead Skellan contented himself listening to the chatter of morning gossip from the street below.

An unusual cadence of Irabiim conversation drifted up to him. Travelers from the far south, Skellan guessed. They were arguing with a Mirogoth who appeared to serving as their guide. The travelers were saying something about: "The implausibility of finding any sort of emissary in this unsavory section of the city."

Well spotted, Irabiim traveler, Skellan thought and smirked to himself.

Hopefully they hadn't paid their guide up front.

One of Cire's cockerels let out a string of crackling crows.

Elezar sighed in his sleep and Skellan gently traced the dark line of his black body hair. It stood in stark contrast to the pale skin of his chest and thighs. Only the wide, white scar that ran the length of Elezar's thigh interrupted the sharp pattern of thick hair. Skellan stared at the deep furrow of the wide white scar. He'd glimpsed it before when Elezar had washed at the Mockingbird Playhouse and he'd wondered, if only in passing, how a man recovered from so ugly a wound. Elezar's leg must have been laid open from hip to knee.

Now that he knew the truth behind it, Skellan felt awed. Not by the scar itself. That only bespoke the cruelty of the men who'd attacked Elezar and his brother. No—Skellan thought with admiration and a touch of envy—Elezar's whole being seemed a testament to a ferocious strength of body and will. He'd not just survived a crippling injury, but afterwards he'd honed himself into a magnificent weapon in spite of it.

Though now that Skellan was able to look more closely he also noticed another small, strange scar just to the right of Elezar's heart. Skellan had only ever seen one other scar that lay so flat and black.

Lundag had sported such a mark on her forearm, the remnant of an assassination attempt against her where a dose of Cadeleonian muerate poison had burned its stain into her flesh. She'd survived the poison only by calling up a purging magic and driving the muerate into a flock of sacrificial doves. Skellan didn't know who had purged the poison from Elezar, but he felt deeply thankful.

He placed his hand on Elezar's chest, taking in the living warmth of him and feeling his strong heartbeat. The small silver pendant lying against Elezar's chest caught Skellan's eye and he briefly inspected it. He'd thought it was just a Cadeleonian star but now he realized that a Bahiim tree had been etched into the back of the necklace.

Odd that.

The closer he came to knowing Elezar the less he seemed to fit the simple image of the coarse brigand that Skellan had first taken him for. Of course Skellan had hardly presented all he was to Elezar on their first meeting either.

"You are not what I think you are," Skellan whispered, only half recalling the words from his earlier dream.

"Oh?" Elezar's low voice rumbled. "What am I, then?"

Skellan glanced up to see Elezar considering him from only half open eyes. Fine lines of tension already creased his brow.

"When I first saw you I thought you were a brigand." Skellan snaked his fingers down Elezar's broad chest, teasing his dark nipples before following the dark trail of hair down to his groin. "You say you're the varlet of the duke of Rauma, but now I think you might well be a catamite fleeing from some Yuanese prince's harem."

"So you've found me out, at last." Elezar smiled and closed his eyes again. "What gave me away? My flawless courtly Yuanese, my soft, delicate hands, or my tiny, girlish figure?"

Skellan laughed and Elezar opened his eyes.

"You have a good laugh." Elezar raised his rough, calloused hand and gently stroked Skellan's cheek. "And a handsome smile."

Despite his warm words, melancholy edged Elezar's expression, as Skellan had feared it might.

Elezar was a Cadeleonian. It would be in his nature to regret the joy they'd given each other. Still Skellan wished that it could be otherwise—if only there was some spell he could speak that would release Elezar from his heritage.

"Are you all right?" Elezar frowned at Skellan but not with disgust. If anything, he seemed genuinely concerned.

"Me? I'm fine." This Skellan hadn't expected. His lovers didn't, as a rule, concern themselves with his well-being. He was tough as a tick and they all knew it.

Rafale tended to wax long and prosaic after sex, but generally on the subject of his own prowess and pleasures. The others he often parted from after no more than the secure exchange of coins to pay Skellan's rent.

"You looked troubled just now," Elezar said, though he seemed uneasy broaching the subject. His gaze dropped to Skellan's hips. He touched Skellan's waist so lightly that it felt like a breath against his bare skin.

Then Skellan realized just what worried Elezar. He found it funny that a man who could cleave another fellow's head in two with a splitting maul couldn't actually say these words.

"Do you mean to ask if your great dick has split my ass in two?" Skellan laughed despite himself. "Nearly, nearly. But not in any way I'm not glad for." On impulse he leaned forward and kissed Elezar lightly on the lips. He was rewarded with the slightest flush coloring Elezar's tanned face. He wasn't certain if it was the kiss or the fact that he'd spoken explicitly of Elezar's endowment—he guessed the later. But what was the use of euphemisms when Elezar's heavy prick lay warm against his thigh and both of them knew well enough what pleasure Skellan had had of it?

"Never fear," Skellan told him, "I'm made from tougher stuff than whatever little boy ran away crying from you and made you think you were some kind of a monster."

"Little boy?" Elezar scowled. "I assure you there was nothing like that."

"But there was someone." Skellan pulled himself up onto his elbows, so that he could better see Elezar's expression. The bright morning light shone along the harsh angles of his face, but also lit his dark eyes to amber. He looked younger than Skellan had first thought.

"Not like this," Elezar admitted after a long quiet. "Nothing like this. I just…"

"Just?" Skellan prompted.

Elezar shook his head.

"Well, if you won't say then that leaves me no choice but to make up my own story," Skellan told him. "So I say that some tarty boy with a noble title at that academy you attended took a fancy to you. He did all he could to get at the prize in your pants—"

Elezar snorted. "I already told you that it was nothing like what just happened between you and me."

"I'm a tarty witch, not a nobleman," Skellan replied. Seeing that Elezar's sense of humor had returned, he went on with his absurd conjecture. "One stormy night after you'd finished your work grooming the duke's hundreds of horses you stumbled exhausted to your cot—"

"I slept on a cot?" Elezar asked.

"The duke didn't make you sleep on the floor, did he?"

"No, not at all." Elezar looked oddly smug but also relaxed.
"So, my spindly little cot it was then."

"Yes. You collapsed naked onto your cot when suddenly
from the shadows a cock-crazed noble runt pounced upon
you"—Skellan paused dramatically—"and in a terrible flurry
of sucking and slurping the brat lost all common sense and
choked himself to death on your huge rod. From that day on
you lived in fear that your immense endowment might someday destroy another tarty boy's life." Skellan studied Elezar's
amused expression. "Pretty close to the mark?"

"Not even near. Though your version of my love life makes
a far more entertaining tale than the reality of the matter,"
Elezar replied.

"It hasn't been long enough that you can speak of it, I suppose," Skellan said.

"Now who's turning whom into a melodrama?" Elezar
seemed to consider his words. "The truth is that I was taken
with a classmate, but he had someone else and when I discovered the two of them..." The warmth drained from Elezar's
voice and his expression went hard. "I nearly killed the man
I thought I... loved. I realized then that deep down, I'm quite
ugly, possessive and jealous. I can hurt the people I care for as
easily as the ones I despise."

Elezar shook his head and pulled a grim smile. "But it also
turned out that I'm damn good with a sword, so there's that
consolation, I suppose. I've put my rage to good work in the
years since then."

"Did he die? This boy you fell in love with?" Skellan asked.

"He was hardly a boy—"

"This was when you were at the Sagrada Academy?"
From what Skellan remembered of the duke's memoir, even
the oldest of the boys at the academy hadn't reached his majority. Certainly none of them had yet lived on their own like
grown men. They'd played at war and romance but not a one

of them even bought their own bread. "Weren't you both just boys then?"

Elezar didn't respond right away. He gazed up at the ceiling and laid his hand over his silver pendant. "We'd both just turned nineteen. And yes, he survived, but that was a miracle of Bahiim magic. It had more to do with his lover's bravery than any decency on my part."

"So because of that you're a monster?" Skellan pondered the notion, testing its veracity. "I watched you kill two men in a matter of minutes—but then that same day I drove a knife into a stranger's back without more than a second's hesitation myself. I don't know of anyone who's never inflicted harm of some kind upon someone. But compassion and courage— those are rare qualities."

"Compassion?"

"No lover has ever asked me how I felt the next morning," Skellan admitted.

Elezar regarded him then said, "You need to find a better class of man to lay down with."

"What do you think I'm trying to do now?" Skellan said, laughing. "Before I met you, I would never have believed that a stranger would stand against the grimma's guards just for the sake of a battered dog. You've made all the difference in my life, and I won't countenance anyone calling you a monster including yourself, my man. So hush."

Elezar sighed heavily then sat up on the edge of the bed. He fished Skellan's fallen blanket up from the floor, folded it neatly and then laid it at the foot of the bed. Skellan could almost feel restlessness rolling off him.

"Yesterday was wonderful... more than I could ever have hoped for. It was better than anything..." Elezar didn't seem able to make himself go on.

"But?" Skellan asked. The pang in his chest told him that he already knew what Elezar would say. Yet he still held out hope of being wrong. They shared a fate, after all.

"I'm not Labaran, and I don't know how to do this," Elezar said quietly. "I don't know that I can…"

Skellan sat up as well.

"You don't have to do anything," Skellan told him. "What's between us is just what it is."

"You sound like Atreau." Elezar shook his head.

"Who?"

"No one. Never mind." Elezar glanced to Skellan and after a moment's hesitation he reached out and wrapped an arm around Skellan's shoulders. "Thank you for… letting me…"

"My pleasure. Really," Skellan replied in his best imitation of a Cadeleonian gentleman. "I haven't told anyone else, not even Cire."

Relief showed plainly on Elezar's face. Skellan turned away and pretended to busy himself arranging the charms on the collar Elezar had given him. They looked bright and cheery spread out around the base of the lamp.

Eventually the sounds of the day passing them by outside filled the quiet between them. Elezar glanced to the window, attracted by something. A noise or a scent, perhaps. Skellan could see the tension building through Elezar's body.

Skellan listened to the rumble of conversation and animal sounds. Suddenly Elezar sprung to his feet and paced to the window. Light glowed across his naked body as he peered down into the street below.

"That voice… It can't be." He looked stricken.

Skellan rose more gingerly and joined him. The usual clusters of loitering actors, fortune-tellers and gossips congregated in the street below. Two pigs trotted out from an alley, their bored swineherd following with his stick balanced over his shoulder. Then Skellan caught sight of an unusual figure—a youth of eighteen or nineteen who had to be the palest Cadeleonian he'd ever laid eyes upon. He wore a typical Cadeleonian sword and boots but also sported a faded leather cloak more suited to a Bahiim holy man. His ink black hair hung in braids long and thick enough to make a Salt Island cross-dresser proud.

A handsome Irabiim man with skin like polished walnut and cropped ringlets of golden hair walked close beside the youth. Though the Irabiim seemed to be directing his heavily accented comments at the rangy, white-blond Mirogoth girl stomping ahead of the two of them.

"Look, this is the third time we've been up this street. I'm not implying that your aunt's magic stones don't work, but it's been my experience that if one of them is cracked it can create a misleading path."

"This is the way," the Mirogoth girl insisted.

"Forgive my incredulity," the Irabiim replied, "but this is obviously a very unsavory section of the city. What on earth would a royal emissary be doing—" The rest of his words were drowned out by another burst of wild crows from the young cockerel housed across the yard. Then the three of them drifted around the corner of the Rat Rafters.

Elezar stepped back from the window and stood looking stunned. Then he snatched up his clothes and began dressing in a wild rush.

"Do you know them?" Skellan asked.

"Yes." Elezar belted his breeches and then pulled his shirt over his head.

Very faintly Skellan caught the sound of someone knocking on the front door downstairs.

"Friends?" Skellan asked.

"For my part, yes," Elezar replied. "But we did not part on the best of terms. I should go to meet them."

Skellan tossed Elezar his stockings and then pulled on his own pants. "Then we'll both go down and greet them, shall we?'

"It could mean trouble—"

"Yes, I gathered as much, my man. But I'd be a cad if I had my way with you and then just tossed you out all alone."

Skellan noted the tension in Elezar's expression and quickly left behind any further mention of the intimacy they'd shared. "And in any case, I'm curious about this royal emissary they think they're going to find."

CHAPTER NINETEEN

Skellan pulled his cloak around his shoulders and raced from his room, catching up with Elezar halfway down the worn wooden staircase. There, in the deep shadows, his big Cadeleonian had drawn to a halt. Skellan didn't ask why. The last time men had come looking for Elezar it had been to ambush and murder him. Skellan kept silent and waited with his hand curled around the hilt of the hunting knife Elezar had entrusted to him.

On the floor below Cire strode to the door of the boarding house and pulled it open.

The gangly Mirogoth girl, a dark-skinned golden-haired Irabiim man and a tall, deathly pale Cadeleonian youth all stood at the threshold. At closer range Skellan noticed the mud and road dust from at least a week of travel spattering their worn clothes. The Mirogoth girl looked the worst. Skellan thought that the two men must have ridden while the girl walked ahead of them. She dressed like a forest guide, though she seemed too young to be working alone. The Irabiim man also wore the battered leather tool belt of a professional tinker and carried a light pack on his back, along with a short bow and quiver. Taken altogether, they seemed a very unlikely threesome.

"He's here, I swear it!" the lanky Mirogoth girl proclaimed. She clenched a polished white stone in her hand. Skellan thought it might be a stone of passage. The other two didn't appear convinced or even inclined to step inside. They studied the doorway with deep suspicion.

In fact, Skellan distinctly recalled Elezar giving the Rat Rafters the same sort of uncertain look while eyeing the motif of rodents decorating the overhanging sign. The pale youth made a gesture with his hands as if warding off misfortune, while the handsome Irabiim man managed a belated, but polite, smile at Cire.

"Good day to you, madam." The Irabiim man's accent reminded Skellan of Elezar's. Perhaps they hailed from the same region of Cadeleon? That followed, since this man was known to him. He didn't seem like a mercenary, though appearances could be deceiving.

"Good day to you as well," Cire replied. "Welcome to the Rat Rafters, strangers."

Skellan couldn't see Cire's face but from her tone he knew that she didn't like the look of these three anymore than they seemed to appreciate her boarding house. Queenie scuttled up Cire's shoulder to perch in the shadow of her bright red braids. Several other rats fanned out behind her, crouching in her shadow like tiny footpads. Another pack of black rats sat watching from rafters.

Skellan, too, felt uneasy. Some chill breeze began to creep in through the open door and curl down the nape of his neck.

"Who are these people?" Skellan whispered to Elezar.

"The Cadeleonian is called Javier, and the Haldiim is Kiram Kir-Zaki. He hails from one of the wealthiest and most refined merchant families in Anacleto. You wouldn't know it from seeing him now, though."

Skellan remembered Sammi and Sarl going on at length about the delights of imported Kir-Zaki candies, but this man certainly didn't match Skellan's own visions of a delightful candymaker.

Elezar leaned forward to peer down at the wispy, silver-haired Mirogoth girl. "And unless I'm very mistaken, that's Eski with them. How in hell they met her is anyone's guess."

Skellan scratched at the back of his neck. Out of the corner of his eye he noted Queenie's shudder. Something wasn't quite right about these three. Javier, in particular seemed too fair skinned, almost as if a faint light glowed up from his flesh, lending him a luminous quality. His hair and eyes were black pools in comparison.

"So what brings you good travelers to my boarding house on this fine day?" Cire asked. "You are lost, perhaps?"

"We're here to call upon Prince Sevanyo's emissary to the Sumar grimma." Eski lowered her voice as she crept over the threshold. Even hunched down, the Mirogoth girl towered over Cire. "We know he's here. Probably escaping the crowds at Count Radulf's palace." She glanced uncertainly over her shoulder at the two men behind her, then looked back to Cire with an expression somewhere between hope and desperation. "He'll want to see us, I promise you. Please just tell him that his good friend, Eski, has come to call on him with a warning of calamitous events."

"Prince Sevanyo's emissary?" Cire's scowl carried clearly through her voice. "Here at the Rat Rafters?"

Elezar sighed. Then, to Skellan's shock, he stepped out from the shadows and said, "I'm here, Eski, but you should stop announcing it to everyone."

Elezar started down, taking the stairs two steps at a time.

Catching sight of Elezar the Mirogoth girl grinned and bounced up and down in an excess of youthful joy. The two men with her both stared at Elezar as if he'd unexpectedly burst to life from a tapestry.

Skellan eyed his man as well—a royal emissary? Really?

"Elezar!" The Cadeleonian youth, Javier, bounded past both Eski and Cire and rushed to the foot of the staircase just as Elezar reached the bottom. The youth's wide smile lent warmth to his otherwise deathly pale face. "God's tits, is it really you under all that beard?"

"The last time I shaved it still was," Elezar replied.

Javier stood quite tall and was well built. Even so, Elezar loomed over him. Javier craned his head back slightly as he looked Elezar over. Then, without warning, he threw his arms around Elezar in a hearty hug.

Skellan could have sworn that Elezar had been bracing himself to take a blow. He seemed stunned and only belatedly returned the embrace. However, when the two of them stepped apart, Elezar seemed much more relaxed.

"You bastard!" Javier said, laughing. "How in the three hells did you ever get yourself appointed an emissary?"

"Less my doing than your cousin's," Elezar replied.

"Even so, why are you boarding here of all places?" Kiram frowned at Elezar from the doorway then he added to Cire, "I mean no offense to your property, madam. But this isn't really the district in which one would expect Prince Sevanyo to house his personal servants or courtiers."

"Noticed that, did you?" Cire gave a hard laugh.

"It's because he's in disguise, I tell you," Eski said. "But if you saw his horse you'd know right away."

"Somehow it seems to have slipped our good Skellan's mind to mention any of this when he first introduced us." Cire glanced up the staircase.

Skellan suspected that she was trying to pick him out from the shadows. She obviously wasn't inclined to believe all this talk about any of them knowing Prince Sevanyo but couldn't refute it either. He felt the same way himself.

Elezar was far from what Skellan pictured as a royal emissary—nothing like the wan, gold-powdered dignitaries that he remembered calling upon Grimma Lundag. At the same time the revelation explained why Elezar had ventured into the Mirogoth wilds despite the danger and over the duke of Rauma's objections—he served an even more illustrious master with a greater purpose.

Skellan scowled at the thought. There was nothing he could offer Elezar that a prince could not—except his own company in bed. After their morning conversation Skellan thought even that might seem a detriment to Elezar.

"It is a weird choice of lodging though, you must admit." Javier took a quick step back as a troop of juvenile rats scampered past his feet and rushed up the stairs.

Cire said nothing, but Skellan read her expression clearly.

She'd decided that if Elezar were actually an important emissary then the only reason he would slum in Skellan's company at the Rat Rafters was to hide rampant indulgences in sexual escapades that could land him in prison in his homeland.

"Suffice it to say that I'm not interested in attracting attention," Elezar replied. Then he added, "You mentioned something about bringing a warning?"

"Yes," Javier replied, though he seemed a little distracted. He turned slowly in a circle, with his pale hands spread. "But I think now that there's more going on here than we first thought. The violet haze lurking over the Labaran sanctum has been growing in my awareness. It troubles me."

"You and every other witch for twenty miles, I have no doubt," Cire muttered.

Skellan glanced to the front window. To his eyes the demon lord had not grown overnight, but retracted. Only faint streaks of violet light tinted the sky beyond the sanctum. A note of suspicion rang through Skellan's mind. Why, after rampaging so wantonly after even the smallest crumbs of magic, should Zi'sai hang back? It struck him that Zi'sai lurked, like a cat waiting in ambush for a passing mouse.

"Well, if you three good travelers wish to keep the emissary company I imagine that you'll want to rent rooms?" Cire addressed the question to Kiram, clearly reading him the same way Skellan did.

Skellan couldn't have said whether it was the solid quality of his weathered boots and long gray coat, or his cool, appraising demeanor but something about the Haldiim man conveyed at a glance that he was the one carrying the coin purse and making the sensible decisions.

"Two rooms. One for Javier and myself, another for Eski," Kiram requested. "With views of the street preferably."

"And your mounts?" Cire asked.

"They have two, and the white stallion bites," Eski announced. "Neither of them are as big as Elezar's though. He's huge!"

Javier nudged Elezar in the ribs. "No news there."

True enough, Skellan thought but he didn't like the fact that this Javier seemed as aware of it as him.

"You can't find bigger or better than those bred in Anacleto," Elezar whispered back to Javier.

"Our animals are already stabled, thank you," Kiram told Cire. He shot both Javier and Elezar a disapproving glance before returning his attention to his hostess. "But we will want supper and what warm drinks you might spare us."

Cire nodded. "How long do you three expect to be staying?"

"Not long," Kiram replied. "A week at the most."

While he and Cire fixed the exact price for the rooms and board, the Mirogoth girl investigated the common room with a kind of curious fascination that made Skellan suspect that she'd never seen the polished surfaces or embroidered fabrics of a Labaran house before. Or maybe not the interior of any house.

Nearer to Skellan, Javier leaned against the staircase banister and spoke in a quiet tone to Elezar. Skellan noted that Queenie had abandoned Cire's shoulder for a post close to the stairs where she strained forward, trying to hear their conversation just as Skellan did.

"Don't take this the wrong way," Javier murmured to Elezar, "but have you really come as an emissary of peace or were you sent to take command of the troops when they're deployed for the war?"

"Sevanyo honestly wants peace, but I could serve him in another capacity if it were necessary," Elezar responded.

"A war would be utter madness," Javier said. "You realize that."

"I do, and I'm taking what steps I can to pacify the Sumar grimma, but this has gone far beyond her dispute with the church."

"Yes, it would seem to have wakened something far more." Despite his youth Javier looked suddenly very knowing.

Elezar simply nodded. Then he asked, "Are you safe here?"

"From Cadeleonian law or from the scourge that is hanging over the Labaran sanctum?"

"Both. Either." The concern in Elezar's face was so plain to see that it sparked a flame of jealousy in Skellan's chest. "It can't be wise for you to be here now."

"Admittedly, it isn't the best season for a man like myself to tour Milmuraille." Javier glanced to Kiram and his carefree expression slipped. "But I couldn't let Kiram come alone and he would have. You know how recklessly upstanding he is. Once he realized what was happening, nothing could have stopped him from coming even if only to ensure that the city is evacuated before it's overrun by the grimma—" Javier broke off, raising his gaze to where Skellan stood.

Skellan felt a chill rush over him. Javier's sharp, youthful features momentarily seemed to burn away and Skellan saw the radiant, white face of death blaze from beneath his flesh.

Skellan jumped back despite himself. Javier might look like a pretty boy of nineteen, but this pale youth was obviously a true Bahiim—a ghoul neither wholly of the living world nor of the dead, who traveled the Old Road and walked among common men like an omen of ruin.

"We're being watched," Javier whispered.

Elezar turned back, took in Skellan, and then beckoned him to join them. Skellan straightened and slunk slowly down the stairs.

"This is Skellan." Elezar patted Skellan's shoulder but his hand didn't linger. "He healed an injury of mine and has been kind enough to share his lodgings with me the past few days. If it's the violet flame that concerns you, you should speak with him. He's been fighting it for days now. And he thinks he's worked out just what it is."

"Really?" Javier raised a black brow in the manner of some courtier casting his gaze upon a beggar. Skellan considered responding with an obscene gesture but Elezar spoke up.

"You of all people should know better than to judge a man by his coat." Elezar's tone resonated with warmth despite the rebuke.

"I should, shouldn't I?" Javier flashed a smile then offered his palm to Skellan in Labaran fashion. His skin felt cold and dry as ash. Beneath it a radiance of power blazed with frigid light. Gazing at Javier's face, Skellan again glimpsed the black hollows of death lying behind his dark eyes. He held his ground despite the chill that coursed through him at the Bahiim's deathly touch.

"Well met, Skellan. I'm Javier."

"Well met, Bahiim."

"My name is Eski," the Mirogoth girl called, though she hardly looked up from her study of the flaxen ponies prancing across one of Cire's many cushions.

"My companion there with the golden hair and tight fist is called Kiram." Javier provided the final introduction.

The Haldiim man cast Javier an indulgent look and nodded in Skellan's direction but his attention remained upon his negotiations with Cire. He handed her a pittance of coins. Cire appeared more pleased with the transaction than Skellan would have expected. But then any boarders were better than none. She secreted the money away in the folds of her shift.

"Cire will suffice for me," Cire offered as an introduction. Then she added airily, "Skellan, do me the kindness of showing your man's friends the first rooms above while I'm out, will you? Gullin sent frog tea for you as well, so you might share that with them too. I would stay but I have business at the Fairwind Stables. Merle has promised me a good price to let a fine horse and cart for my ride to the Count Radulf's Sun Palace tomorrow morning."

She collected her squirrel fur hood and cloak. Queenie dashed to her and slipped quickly into her pocket. Most pickpockets in Milmuraille knew better than to delve after Cire's coins, but occasionally someone still extended a hand too far and drew back bitten, bleeding fingers.

"What of their board?" Skellan asked. "Bread and a dry sausage or two, don't you think?"

"Of course, but try not to beggar me in an afternoon." Cire only offered him a glower and then glanced meaningfully to where another of her rats perched among the bouquets of drying herbs.

In Cire's absence, the rats kept watch over the larder. From bitter experience Skellan knew that they would deliver vicious bites if too many sausages went missing, though occasionally a dish of beer went a good way toward relaxing their vigilance.

"Oh, but I want to go to a stable! Please, can I?" Eski called out. Strangely, she addressed her request to Elezar. "Unless you plan on taking me to see Cobre tonight?"

The Mirogoth girl gazed at Elezar like he was her best man. Elezar regarded her in return with the indulgent smile of an elder brother—which relieved Skellan more than it should have.

"I'm not likely to visit Cobre until much later today," Elezar informed the Mirogoth girl.

Eski deflated visibly but then glanced to Cire. "May I follow you then, good mistress? I only want to see the horses. I won't cause any bother."

Cire frowned at the girl and then held out her hand and said, "One copper wolf to show you the way."

Skellan almost laughed at the notion of a Mirogoth this wood wild possessing any kind of currency other than the supple leather over her bare skin. Eski looked stricken.

Elezar fished two Labaran copper wolves from his pocket and flipped the coins into Cire's outstretched palm.

"To take her there and bring her back," Elezar said. "With my thanks."

Cire made a face like she'd bitten on an aching tooth, but witches kept their word and so she took her leave of them with the delighted Mirogoth girl bounding behind her.

"Nicely played," Javier commented after the door had fallen shut. "Who knew you'd have such a way with women, Grun—"

"First names are fine among friends." Elezar cut Javier off with a smile, but Skellan didn't miss the nervous glance in his direction.

"Oh true indeed." Javier seemed quite amused by Elezar's uneasiness. "We wouldn't want to bog down the conversation with too many lordly titles, now would we?"

Elezar smacked Javier on the back of his head. Javier laughed but Kiram shot Elezar a very hard glance. The playful smile dropped from Elezar's countenance at once. He stepped back from Javier's side and turned toward the large hearth.

"Why don't the two of you make yourselves comfortable." Then Elezar glanced to Skellan. "I can fetch water from the well for the tea, if you'll serve the bread and sausages."

The kettle still held water enough for a few cups of tea, Skellan thought but he didn't argue. He followed Elezar into the kitchen, but before he could even open his mouth, much less ask why Kiram had shot him such a cold look, Elezar disappeared out the back. If he hadn't known better he would have said that his Cadeleonian looked shaken by the whole exchange.

What, he wondered, did this Kiram have on his man? Could he have been the boy Elezar had been in love with at the academy? Elezar had said boy had been resurrected by Bahiim magic, so perhaps Javier was the lover who'd saved him.

Skellan played at exploring Cire's cupboards, while he watched Javier and Kiram settle. They took a table near the fireside. Javier commented on how pleasant it was to sit once more at a table, even one so shabby as this. The two of them shed coats, cloaks and packs but kept all close at hand, as if they were well practiced in taking their leave at a moment's notice. They sat across from one another, easy in each other's company. As Kiram bowed his head over some small device that he'd taken from his work belt, Javier plucked a yellow catkin from a curl of his companion's hair.

"You're blocking my light," Kiram said.

"Shall I provide you with another?" Javier held out his hand as if offering Kiram something in his palm.

"Don't you dare." Kiram caught Javier's hand and folded his fingers closed. "You have some gall calling me reckless."

"I believe I referred to you as recklessly upstanding." Javier's tone sounded light and his expression brimmed with fondness. "I, on the other hand, am a reckless show-off. Particularly when I'm being ignored in favor of some mechanism."

"It's the minute locket you requested," Kiram replied. "And you're still blocking my light—as charming as your shadow is, my lord."

Javier snorted and then shifted slightly so that the firelight fell brightly over Kiram.

He watched Kiram tinker with the glinting coil of tiny gears. Then Kiram snapped the locket closed and handed it to Javier, who slipped it into his pocket.

Skellan felt sure they were lovers but still wasn't certain of their relationship with Elezar.

"So, did you both school with Elezar?" Skellan asked. He'd already found the jar of dried frog tea as well as half a loaf of grave bread. "I recall Duke Quemanor mentioning you, Javier, but I can't remember what he said about you, Kiram."

Both of them regarded him with expressions of disbelief.

"You're a friend to Fedeles as well as Elezar?" Javier's sharp black brows rose. Kiram simply eyed him like he was trying to peer straight through Skellan's face into his skull.

"I don't know about being friends," Skellan admitted. "I'm more closely acquainted with Elezar than the duke. But I spent a month in the duke's company at Bishop Palo's townhouse. I heard a good deal about his young life."

Both Javier and Kiram still wore expressions of deep skepticism.

Skellan glanced to the rats crouched over the hanging dry sausages. He didn't relish the thought of having his fingers bitten to the bone but at the same time he wanted to impress

Elezar's friends. He tapped a goodly pool of old table beer into a saucer and set it on the bar table. The rats began to drop from the overhead beams and gather around the beer at once.

Skellan snatched four of the fattest sausages.

"The duke and I walked together frequently," Skellan went on with his explanation. "He often read to me from the memoir he's penning."

"Fedeles is writing a memoir?" Javier spoke as if such a thing were somehow impossible.

"Yes." Skellan found it strange that this would be the detail that Javier found hard to believe. Perhaps the duke hadn't seemed the literary type back in school—maybe due to the sheer amount time he must have spent in brothels.

"It's an account of his many sexual conquests." Skellan felt that might clear everything up but if anything it seemed to confound Javier even more.

"Sexual conquests—Fedeles?" Javier sputtered as if he were choking on the words.

"He is a grown man," Kiram commented, but he too frowned at Skellan. "Though it sounds distinctly unlike him to put anything of an intimate nature to paper much less recite it before an audience…"

"It's the truth, I swear on the stones at my feet," Skellan replied. Who would make something like that up? "He's writing a memoir, and he regularly read it aloud to me and his two page boys."

Skellan tore the bread and cut the meat into large pieces— he didn't want to present Elezar's old friends with those stingy thin little slices he always saw Labaran taverns serving their patrons. He piled his small feast of black grave bread and sausages onto a platter, then snatched up the jar of frog tea as well as a jug of goat milk and carried it all out of the kitchen before the rats took notice of him.

"I remember that he wrote about swimming with you, Javier. You and Elezar and the duke as well as a number of other young men went swimming in the streams under the apple trees at the Sagrada Academy." Skellan sat the platter down in front of them, then darted back to the kitchen to find cups. He couldn't expect them to drink from the kettle as he would have done.

"That's true enough. We all swam together." Javier admitted though he looked all the more perplexed. "What did he look like—the duke, I mean?"

"Handsome, like yourself," Skellan admitted, studying Javier. "Fair-skinned with black hair and dark eyes. I'd say he was a little shorter than you and a good five years older. He smells like roses."

Kiram cocked his head to the side, studying Skellan. "And how was the duke's Labaran? Last I heard he was quite displeased with his strong Cadeleonian accent. He even engaged a half Labaran friend to tutor him, as I recall."

"The tutoring must have taken." Skellan wondered if the leading question was meant to trip him up in some manner. Fortunately he'd overheard the duke speaking flawlessly in both Labaran and Cadeleonian. "If I didn't know better I'd have said he was born Labaran. The only hint of any accent was a slight Cadeleonian cadence."

Kiram nodded and a look of realization seemed to light his face. Then he asked, "The duke didn't mention any one woman particularly in his memoir, did he?"

Skellan paused, clay cups in his hands. Why would Kiram ask after a particular woman? Then he recalled the widow that Elezar had mentioned and how pained the duke had looked at the recollection of her husband's death at Elezar's hand. Perhaps Kiram was attempting to sound out how much he knew about the affair and the price on Elezar's head.

Remembering the cold glance that Kiram had cast Elezar, Skellan decided that the less he said the better.

"Most of the women seemed to be professional types. I don't think that any of them meant anything to him beyond the satisfaction of sex," Skellan replied honestly. "Only when he spoke of his fellow Hellions did I get an impression that he truly cared about any other human beings. Maybe the whole memoir is a flight of fantasy that he's concocting for his own amusement. He never mentioned anything about the years he spent being possessed."

"No, he wouldn't." Kiram looked as smug as a cat with a stolen squab in her belly watching a dog take the blame. "Now that I think about it, this all does sound very like our old classmate. The handsome Hellion, always faithful to his friends though not his lovers."

"We can all hear the gears clinking away in your head. But what are you thinking?" Javier asked. Kiram simply gave a shake of his head.

"If Fedeles is here, why didn't he send word to me?" Javier asked.

"Why didn't who send word?" Elezar asked from the back door.

Skellan felt relieved; he'd begun to fear that Elezar would never return.

Now as he crossed the kitchen, Skellan saw why he'd taken so long. He hadn't filled the moldering pail that Cire normally used to carry water from the well. Instead he walked in carrying both the huge bronze pitchers that had remained from the days when the property had belonged to a whoremonger and been staffed with brawny Mirogoth servants.

"Fedeles should have contacted me," Javier called back to Elezar then he asked. "Do you want a hand with those?"

"How could I ask a maiden in long braids to haul water jugs for me?" Elezar returned.

Javier rolled his dark eyes.

"It would be a sight easier than asking me to stop laughing at you after you throw your back out, I imagine." Javier sprang up from his chair and sauntered to Elezar who handed the smaller of the two pitchers over to him. To his credit, Javier took the burden gamely and lugged it to the hearthside where he placed it next to Kiram with a small groan.

"Are you showing off for my sake or Elezar's?" Kiram inquired.

"Elezar, always," Javier replied, and he grinned back at Elezar playfully.

Skellan tried not to feel envious of the affection that Elezar shared with Javier. He noticed two of Cire's rats watching him and hoped that they just wanted more beer and weren't serving as Cire's eyes.

Skellan tipped them out another serving of the table beer. Then he took the cups and joined the others in the common room.

As he drew near he caught just the end of a conversation between Kiram and Javier. Elezar stood behind them holding the bronze water pitcher as if he'd forgotten its weight.

"It's Atreau," Kiram told Javier, but then seeing Skellan's approach he tapped the water pitcher in Elezar's arms. "There's a frog crouched down on the bottom of this pitcher."

"There are frogs everywhere here and snails as well," Elezar replied. "Happily, this frog is bronze."

"They're for good health." Skellan told them. "You know the Mirogoth proverb?"

"Why on earth Atreau?" Javier asked, though the question seemed addressed to himself more than anyone. He dropped down into his seat across from Kiram, still looking thoughtful.

"That's not even close to being a proverb," Elezar replied. "The saying goes 'not even a bronze frog will stay in a poisoned pitcher,' doesn't it?"

"That it does," Skellan responded.

"I take it from the frog in the bottom of this pitcher we'll not all be poisoned." Elezar hefted his pitcher up and poured a neat stream of water into the kettle. Then he set the pitcher aside. Skellan suspected that it would remain where Elezar left it for years if it fell to himself and Cire to move the thing.

"This frog tea Gullin left for you," Elezar glanced to Skellan, "tell me it's not actually a brew of frogs."

"Dried frog-reed leaves and toad blossoms," Skellan assured him. He passed the jar to Elezar. "Pour it all into the water and let it boil."

Elezar did as he instructed and then sat in the chair that Javier pushed out for him. That left Skellan the seat across from Elezar, with Kiram to his left and Javier on his right.

The meal that Skellan had prepared was spread out before them all. Skellan started to grab for a hunk of dry sausage but then stopped himself as he remembered Cire once telling him that civilized hosts always let their guests take the first, best servings.

"Those are Yuanese spice sausages I cut up with the bread. They're the very best in the city," Skellan announced.

"They look delicious," Javier commented, but instead of taking one he turned his attention to Elezar. "We were just discussing how friendly the duke of Rauma and you are with Skellan here."

"Were you?" Elezar shot Skellan a sidelong glance.

"They don't believe me that the duke is writing a memoir—"

"I do, actually." Kiram offered him a kind smile then looked to Elezar. "I just don't understand why our fellow Hellion would be penning a memoir here in Milmuraille, during a time of such political upheaval."

Skellan stared at the oily, fragrant cuts of spice sausage, hardly caring that he'd just learned that Kiram had indeed schooled with Elezar and the duke at the Sagrada Academy.

"He's come because this is where he needed to be. The details make for a messy, complicated story, and they're beside the point right now. He's here to protect the peace, as am I," Elezar said. "What about the two of you? What calamitous news were you going to bring the emissary?"

"Well, first my offer to help him anyway because I had thought that the appointed emissary would be Fedeles," Javier said. "But secondly, we bring news of the grimma armies. They're marching southward even as we speak. Kiram has numbers."

"They're already marching?" Elezar scowled.

"Oh yes," Kiram replied. "Whole forests of men and beasts like you've never seen all advancing at the command of their grimma. Nothing has united the Mirogoth tribes in a hundred years but the fall of the Labaran sanctum just might."

"You've seen them with your own eyes?" Elezar asked.

"Not by design," Javier replied. "Normally we skirt the domains of the grimma but last fall Grimma Naemir took it into her head that she wanted an astrolabe. She sent her champions to attack the Irabiim caravan we were traveling with and they carried Kiram off into the bitch's sanctum." Skellan felt the cold anger that surged beneath Javier's words. Kiram placed his hand over Javier's.

"I was relieved that you weren't there when it happened. It would have become a bloodbath if you had been," Kiram said. "In truth, Grimma Naemir wasn't a cruel captor so much as... bizarre and pitiable in a way."

Skellan noted that he and Elezar both frowned at the description. He had no idea how the grimma who ruled the far north like a goddess of ice and snow could be deemed pitiable.

"Once I'd built the astrolabe for her she warmed up to me and even offered to have me back any time of my choosing." Kiram gave a soft laugh and caught Skellan's eye. "Needless to say I fled as soon as the gates of her sanctum opened far enough for me to squeeze through. Javier found me within the hour. But by then we were truly separated from the surviving remains of our caravan. It was while we were making our way back to the trails between the grimma's domains that we began to see the forces gathering."

"What we didn't see for ourselves," Javier took up the story, "we gleaned from a clan of Mirogoth guides whom I'm on good terms with."

"Eski's family?" Elezar asked.

"The very same," Javier said.

"We know that Grimma Ylva alone commands some thousands of archers and foot soldiers. They aren't armed with forged steel, but they're still hardened warriors," Kiram informed Elezar.

"They're fierce," Javier also addressed Elezar. "But it's the hundreds and hundreds of mordwolves running alongside the troops and the wethra-steeds flying overhead that I fear will easily overrun this city and then all of northern Labara."

Skellan felt as forgotten as his plate of bread and sausages, despite the fact that of them all he was the only native to Milmuraille. It was his home that these armies marched to destroy.

"The numbers of wild animals only seemed to be growing," Kiram said. "Last I counted there were at least three hundred mordwolves, and likely sixty or more huge snowlions."

"They have trolls with them as well," Javier added.

"Trolls?" Elezar sounded a little stunned.

Skellan's gut twisted with dread. If it had been possible, his appetite would have fled entirely. But hunger persisted grinding at the sick feeling in his stomach. He'd worked hard magic, and he needed to eat. Even now he felt as if his body was burning away to bone and skin.

"How long before they arrive?" Elezar asked.

"A month. Two if the rivers flood, but I wouldn't count on that," Javier replied. "I'm actually surprised that the Sumar grimma isn't here already. If she acted quickly she could seize a second sanctum before the other grimma arrived."

"She won't come alone. She'd find herself facing down a devouring demon lord all on her own," Skellan muttered.

"What?" Javier looked at Skellan like he'd forgotten that he was even sitting with them.

No surprise there, Skellan supposed.

"She hasn't come because she fears that she can't take Milmuraille on her own while a demon lord has taken over the sanctum," Skellan said.

"What demon lord?" Javier asked. Kiram too turned his attention on him.

"Eat," Skellan said, "and I'll tell you."

To Skellan's exasperation, all three of his guests hesitated.

"Forgive my rudeness in inquiring," Kiram asked, "but are we to eat with our bare hands? It's hard to know what's proper etiquette going from place to place as much as we do."

Skellan didn't know why he would even ask, after all he'd already cut the bread and meat so that there was no need for any of them to draw a knife. But then he remembered the great silver displays of cutlery that always lay across Bishop Palo's dinner tables.

All three probably expected to eat their meal with silverware and finger bowls and their own painted porcelain plates as well. As commonly as they might dress, these three men had schooled at some great Cadeleonian academy with a duke and knew a prince well enough to call him by his given name.

He didn't want to, but Skellan felt humiliated by the meager fare he had offered them and embarrassed of himself for thinking that it was a feast. Was it any wonder Elezar wouldn't introduce him as a friend, much less a lover? But Skellan went on as gamely as he could, pulling a smile.

"You can dip your fingers in the water pitcher if you'd like," Skellan offered. "But otherwise, yes, take what you will. It isn't as if at one time or another we haven't probably all had mouths full of much dirtier cock—"

Seeing the color rising in Elezar's face Skellan caught himself but had precious few directions to take the comment back. "—cockerels… or other meat that's hit the ground in the market and gone back on the table. Quibbling over greasy fingers when your ham's rolled in a gutter. No point in that."

Javier and Kiram eyed him uncertainly and Skellan gave up on playing at good manners. He snatched up a large hunk of sausage in one hand and a slice of bread in the other and jammed both into his mouth.

The Bahiim reacted by making the expression that Skellan was growing to expect from all Cadeleonians, while Elezar looked just short of mortified. To Skellan's surprise, Kiram seemed far less affronted. He warmed to Kiram for that.

"Well, I wasn't raised dining at a duke's table, was I?" Skellan muttered. "Even if I had been, you Cadeleonians eat so damn slowly, I'd die of starvation if I just waited for each of you to take a dainty little serving."

Still, he did wait to take more. Kiram helped himself first, then Javier and Elezar. All three made themselves neat little sandwiches of sausage and black bread. Elezar served the steaming green frog tea. Once they'd taken goodly shares Skellan wolfed down four more large chunks of sausage in quick succession.

"I worked on several spells the day before yesterday and the day before that," Skellan said, feeling self-conscious but also so hungry that he couldn't help himself. "I need to eat."

He bowed his head over his mug and slurped up his soupy frog tea. He didn't add goat milk to his serving, but Javier nearly emptied the entire pitcher into his cup.

"I thought it might be something to do with practicing magic," Kiram said, and nodded. "Javier gets the same way. He'll deny it but I've seen him devour half a sack of dry oats and then blame it on my gelding."

"I—" Javier sounded like he was going to object but then he gave Skellan a wry smile. "So, this demon lord?"

Skellan told them what he knew of Zi'sai's defeat and explained how he'd witnessed the demon lord's release from the golden coffer. He didn't bother informing them of his earlier history within the sanctum, and they didn't seem to require an explanation for why he would think he could defeat a grimma, though Javier did appear amused by the fact that he attempted a challenge. When Skellan mentioned the vision from his dream, Kiram commented that dreams didn't constitute evidence.

To Skellan's surprise, Javier spoke up, arguing in a friendly tone that they didn't know enough of the intuitive quality of witches and their veis to discount Skellan's insights out of hand. By default, Skellan's story soon lead to his meeting with Elezar. The revelation brought a wide, very boyish grin to Javier's face.

"So you came to Elezar's notice as a dog?" Javier asked.

Skellan nodded and ran a hand over his cloak. "Wearing this fur cloak of mine."

"There's luck." Javier nudged Elezar's ribs. "I can't imagine any man more likely to take pity on a sad mongrel or more prepared to pulverize the men pursuing you."

"It wasn't luck. It was my vei and Elezar's too," Skellan said. "We share a fate, I think."

"Divining a man's fate lies well outside the realm of my expertise." Kiram's gaze flickered over Elezar then back to Skellan. "But you do seem to have done each other some good."

A quiet passed over them all. Skellan looked out the window and took in the expanse of calm and blue of the sky. It had been months since the air had seemed so harmless. He hardly felt the Zi'sai's presence. Skellan should have found the demon lord's retreat relieving but instead it put him on edge.

The immense violet flame coiled up behind the sanctum walls like waiting snake. The finest tendril of the flame flickered out over the streets, tasting the stones like a hungry tongue.

Kiram spoke into the afternoon quiet. "If the demon lord is feeding on spells and magic, I don't think that Javier should linger here."

"Skellan seems to have cast a number of spells, without any harm done him," Javier replied.

"Not easily," Skellan admitted. He stole a quick glance to Elezar and, catching the man's brief smile in his direction, his dwindling confidence rebounded.

"You do yourself a discredit," Elezar said then he addressed Javier and Kiram. "He's the only one in the entire city who's been able to outmaneuver the demon lord. I would never have believed it if I hadn't been here and seen it happen with my own eyes. One instant I was looking at twenty-five children and the next they were each transformed into animals."

"Really?" Javier's expression seemed skeptical.

"Their witchflames—the brilliance of their souls—drew Zi'sai's attention so I hid them deeper inside animals. Of course the animal flesh mutes their power as well but for now they should be safe. And the demon lord has been deprived of more sustenance."

"If this thing feeds on sorcery and magic, then a shajdi would offer it sustenance without end," Kiram remarked pointedly to Javier.

Skellan had heard of shajdi before. They were the blazing forges of raw magic that sprang from the very heart of death's realm. A witch coming upon one paid it respect but left it alone, just as she did not trespass upon the kingdoms of demons. But the Bahiim were arrogant enough to believe that no realm should be closed to them and that even the stars should be theirs to grasp in their hands.

Skellan frowned at Javier and said, "If the demon lord seizes you he will have everything he needs to free himself completely and summon his armies into this world."

"But that's only if he can seize me," Javier replied.

Arrogant, Skellan thought; all Bahiim were so arrogant, and it got them into trouble. But then that was their calling. Their order went seeking monstrosities to pit themselves against.

"You shouldn't have come here," Skellan told Javier.

The Bahiim frowned as if he knew as much but didn't offer to leave. Then he said, "I can keep the shajdi hidden. Don't worry. And it wasn't as if I was going to just send Kiram off on his own."

"I did try to leave him behind a number of times, but I couldn't outdistance him when he followed on the Old Road," Kiram complained. He took another sip of his tea.

Despite himself, Skellan shuddered at the thought of a man willingly opening the gates to the Old Road, much less traveling that way. It would be like deciding to sleep in a crypt full of ghosts.

"There's no point in arguing. I'm not leaving while a demon is on the loose," Javier stated. He drew himself up straight and gazed out the window as if already posing for the portrait that would depict his eventual triumph. "If nothing else it would be a gross dereliction of my duty as a Bahiim."

Kiram's reply came not in Cadeleonian, but in a strongly accented dialect of Irabiim that had to be the Haldiim tongue. He said, "Sometimes I hate being in love with you."

The words seemed to make Elezar uncomfortable. He stood, turning away from them to check on the tea, and then offered to refill their cups. When he sat again Javier turned his attention to Skellan.

"So what does Zi'sai want ultimately? Do you know?" Javier asked.

"He wants to gather enough power to break the spells that hold his flesh trapped in stone. Once he's reclaimed his own body he wants nothing more than to punish all life in this world and burn our whole land to desolation," Skellan replied. The fiery image from his dream washed over him again. He couldn't look at Elezar, remembering the sight of his scorched remains. "After he's destroyed Milmuraille he will reach out in all directions to consume all the magics of our world and make himself a god."

At first the snapping of the logs in the hearth and the muted noises of Cire's hens clucking from their henhouse was all the response Skellan got.

"No hope of him simply returning to his own realm then." Javier smiled and stretched in his chair as if he found this all somehow relaxing. His dark gaze remained on Skellan. "Tell me about how exactly you've managed to work spells since he's been free."

Skellan's pride rankled at the Bahiim's casual order, but he told him anyway.

"By scavenging, mostly." Skellan explained the trick of building spells from remnants of discarded and forgotten magics. Javier asked him pointed questions about the types of abandoned spells he used and he explained that any would work but that it was wisest, and kindest, to only choose those that no longer held a connection to any living soul.

After a few minutes of interrogation, Skellan realized that it might be easier to show the Bahiim than to explain. He leapt up and dashed up to his room where he snatched up the stones he and Elezar had gathered—as well as a few baubles he'd found in his wanders through the city—and brought them all back down to show to Kiram and Javier. Elezar cleared away the platter, and Skellan spread the broken charms and dull pebbles out on the table.

"Broken bits of spells and charms are what I've been using more or less like decoys," Skellan explained. "But these small, etched topaz stones are the ones that seem somehow immune to Zi'sai. There's something about them."

Javier squinted at the stones. He reached out but seemed to have difficulty landing his hand exactly on one of them. Skellan understood. Even now he felt that he had to know where the stones were before he could see them. At last Javier picked one up. He frowned as he turned the homely rock in the light. Then he handed it to Kiram.

"This is a Mirogoth mathematical symbol scratched into the surface," Kiram said. "It's a naught. A placeholder."

"In Labaran it means emptiness or nothing. In spoken spells it's called a null sign," Skellan said. "It represents the pause of a drawn breath."

"Is it ironic or meaningful that this tells us nothing?" Elezar wondered aloud. He took another drink of his tea.

"No idea." Kiram set the topaz back down on the table gently.

"Well, they're certainly very old," Javier commented. "And somehow difficult to see, though they are obviously right here in front of me."

"That's only you and Skellan," Elezar said. "The rest of us can see them just fine."

Skellan nodded. He felt like they'd been talking for hours now but the sun pouring in through the windows had hardly reached past noon. He fiddled with his cup of frog tea.

"I can't say that I'm coming to any conclusion about how to use these stones, interesting as they are," Javier announced finally.

"Maybe there's something to them being placeholders?" Elezar murmured. "Somehow something powerful could occupy their place? Kiram, isn't there a type of math where a symbol stands in for an unknown number?"

"Are you suggesting ancient witches practiced a form of magic based on algebra? Because I'd love—"

Skellan didn't hear the rest of Kiram's words. Instead his senses were suddenly filled with the roaring blaze of violet fire as it gushed up on the street, outside the Rat Rafters. The entire view burned away before a wall of writhing purple fire.

Javier leapt to his feet. The light within him flared like a radiant star. Skellan saw in Javier's proud expression that the Bahiim fully intended to open the full force of his power and battle the violet flame.

That was exactly what Zi'sai wanted.

Oesir had fought in exactly the same manner, but he'd only fed the demon lord.

Skellan bounded past Kiram and over the table. As the violet flame came crashing through Cire's windows, Skellan hurled his cloak over Javier and threw his arms around him, using all his strength to mask Javier's brilliance beneath fur and flesh of an animal form. The violet flame crashed down over them—so cold that it burned—and tore into him with teeth like a ravaging frostbite. Its roar filled his mind. He hardly heard his own scream of agony as spears of ice plunged into his flesh like savage teeth.

Skellan flailed out frantically for the stones scattered on the table, blindly gripping a fistful. They were nothing, but that was exactly what he needed.

In the throes of wrenching pain, the tiny flecks of emptiness clenched in his fist felt like an oasis. Skellan pushed all of his will and awareness—all the heat and strength of his witchflame—into those topaz pebbles. He sank into the emptiness they offered. His body went suddenly limp and numb. A silence, like the grip of deep water, enfolded him, carrying him down into a deadening tomb of stone.

Skellan lay there lost in dark, in emptiness. Then like a seam of gold buried within dull basalt, the warm whisper of a lullaby seemed to drift up to Skellan and though he had no reason to, he felt safe. A ring of gold with a shining red stone seemed to float above him. He reached up after it.

Dimly he felt a hand digging into his ribs. Voices buzzed at the edge of his awareness, sounding angry as shaken wasps. The smell of wood smoke filled his lungs.

Skellan didn't hear his name so much as a distant, ragged growl. What he could feel of his body hurt badly and hung at a strange angle. He managed to crack one eye open only to realize that Elezar clutched him with one arm while extending his other to hold Kiram at bay.

Elezar had claimed that Kiram was civilized, but right now

he looked as murderous as an Irabiim bandit. The edge of his long curved knife gleamed in the afternoon light and the only thing holding it back from Skellan's flesh was Elezar. He stood, protecting Skellan with his own body and blocking Kiram's knife with only his open hand.

"What the fuck did he do to Javier?" Kiram shouted. Out of the corner of his eye Skellan saw a glossy black hound lying prone across a wide swath of charred floorboards. The table and chairs lay toppled and shards of shattered cups scattered all the way to the hearth. The hound didn't move. Skellan feared that he'd acted too late. Had the violet flame stripped Javier of his life and the shajdi he possessed? If so, Zi'sai would destroy them all. But then the hound lifted its head and clumsily kicked his long legs.

"He saved his life," Elezar bellowed back at Kiram. "Look at the damn windows and floor, Kiram! If he hadn't acted, Javier would've been as shattered and burned as those! So, just calm the hell down!"

Kiram stole a glance to the black dog lying on the floor and then slowly sheathed his blade and stepped back to kneel at the beast's side. He stroked the hound's muzzle.

"Javier?" Kiram whispered. The dog's long tail slapped against the floor weakly. "Why did you have to come? Why do you always have to be so..." He didn't finish but simply bowed his head against Javier's.

"He'll be all right." Skellan's voice hardly rose from his numb lips, but Elezar glanced down to him.

"Skellan? Are you going to be all right?"

Skellan attempted a jaunty nod but his head lolled more than he would have liked. He put a little more focus into the motion and managed a tight bob of his head. What the display of control cost him in a pain, it won him in self-respect. He managed to get his feet back under himself and take most of his own weight.

"I'm fine, my man." Skellan's voice still rasped from his throat but at least this time it carried. "No need to haul me around like a sack of drowned cats."

"You went down so damn fast." Elezar's expression turned starkly grim for an instant, but then he simply shook his head and asked, "You're certain you can stand on your own?"

"I've been doing it for years. No fear."

Elezar cautiously released him though he kept his hand at Skellan's back and steadied him when Skellan wobbled. But he was doing better than Javier, who tried and failed twice to rise up onto two legs. Kiram caught Javier and held him as he looked around in dazed confusion. Skellan understood the shock of being suddenly transformed. He'd been terrified the first time Lundag had bound him up in an animal. But the confusion generally passed.

"He doesn't understand that his body has changed," Skellan muttered. Then he called out, "Javier, I had to hide you and your shajdi in an animal's flesh."

Javier swung his head around to meet Skellan's gaze, and Skellan was shocked to see the faintest white glow rising from his dark eyes. Wisps of steam rolled from his open mouth as he barred his teeth. He was burning his way out, Skellan realized.

"Don't! Don't fight the spell! It's all that's keeping the violet flame from finding the shajdi inside you." Skellan staggered to his side. "I know it's frightening to be trapped in another form. But it's to keep you and the rest of Milmuraille safe. Don't destroy the only protection any of us have!"

Javier closed his mouth and his eyes dulled. He knelt back down to the floor. Slowly he looked down at his body, taking in the hide, tail and big paws. He opened his mouth and managed a garbled half bark, then looked to Kiram.

"Swear to me that you can and will change him back!" Kiram demanded.

"I will, I swear." Skellan took a quick step back, remembering how quick Kiram was with his knife. "If Javier wishes, he could free himself. He's no hapless orphan taken off the street, is he? But if he does the violet flame will be back and at his throat. I'm certain that the only reason Javier wasn't assaulted the moment he set foot in Milmuraille was that Zi'sai wanted to lure him deeper in, closer to the stronghold of the sanctum before trying to tear the shajdi from him."

Kiram gazed down at Javier with a miserable expression. Oddly, Javier's tail began to wag. He butted his head against Kiram's hand.

"You find this amusing now, don't you?" Kiram asked. Javier rolled his shoulders in a good approximation of a human shrug. "Yes, well, perhaps in this state you will at last learn to stay put where you're told to."

Javier produced a recognizable laugh though his smile looked decidedly weird on a hound's face. He might have gone a little wild for a moment, but it seemed Javier wasn't one to fall apart in the face of strangeness. Skellan could see why Elezar seemed to so admire the man.

Then he noticed the rats gaping at him and he again took in the shattered windows and burned wall and floor of the common room. Cire was going to be mad as a cat stuffed in a doll's dress. And that wasn't even taking into account how badly she'd responded to seeing a dog right in the middle of all this wreck.

"I think we may all have to find somewhere else to stay tonight," Skellan said.

Elezar just blinked at him. Then he gave a grim smile. "Practical as ever," he commented.

"Merle and Navet might put us up at the Fairwind for one night at least. Tomorrow we'll go with them to see Count Radulf." Skellan glanced to Kiram and Javier's belongings. "At least your friends' things are still packed."

"We have to get word out about the approaching armies." Kiram straightened up. He looked as if he'd aged a year in the last few minutes, and when he spoke frustration rang through his voice. "That's the whole reason I came here in the first place."

"All right." Elezar held up his hands. "We'll do both… somehow."

After only a brief discussion they all agreed that Skellan should keep Javier with him and take all their belongings to the Fairwind. He'd explain the situation to Cire while he was there and hopefully Merle and Navet would keep her from tearing his ears off.

While he was moving all their belongings before Cire could burn them, Elezar and Kiram would call on the commander of the Cadeleonian garrison as well as Sheriff Hirbe and warn them of the imminent attack.

"For whatever small help he'll be, Commander Zangre Lecha will likely be at the garrison all night. It's when business at the Cradle is best," Skellan informed them. Over the years Ogmund had shared with no end of stories about the commander's habits.

Kiram nodded as he absently stroked Javier's glossy black head with one hand.

"Sheriff Hirbe's fine house isn't far from there. It's halfway down Revi Street and flies the banner of his fireguard," Skellan went on. "You aren't likely to find him there till late in the evening. Since the deaths of his wife and his granddaughter the sheriff's become famous for patrolling from first light till well past dusk."

"We'll try our luck at the garrison first." Elezar's distaste sounded in his voice. Then he looked to Skellan. "If we make good time perhaps we can swing through the market and fetch something more substantial for your supper."

Skellan felt almost light-headed at the promise of a meal. Another day like this one and he'd be nothing but a sack of bones.

Kiram nodded though he didn't seem much concerned with sustenance. Instead he looked at the charred floor and then studied the cracked and blackened windowpanes.

"Please assure Cire that we will pay her for the damages done to the boarding house as soon as possible," Kiram said.

Considering the state of all four of them, Skellan didn't

hold out much hope for any immediate or immense financial windfalls, but he assured Kiram that he'd pass the promise along to Cire.

After Elezar and Kiram departed, Skellan glanced into the kitchen. Dozens of dazed-looking rats peered back at him. If Cire didn't already know of what had happened, she'd have a full report soon enough. In his battered and exhausted state, Skellan found it almost amusing to ponder whether the subject of pilfered sausages would come up.

CHAPTER TWENTY

Folk might have been abandoning the city in hordes, but Elezar wouldn't have suspected so from the crowds out this afternoon.

He led Kiram through the Theater District, past the resplendent white walls of the Mockingbird Playhouse and then along the southern streets that were lined by brashly affluent gaming halls and discreet brothels. Here the city's Cadeleonian population mingled with the highest and lowest of Radulf County's folk and indulged in local vices as well as costly meals and business speculation. Between the clusters of warmly dressed courtiers and guildsmen, groups of ragged beggars and gaunt cripples sang for copper wolves. A Cadeleonian priest who looked as though he'd just stepped off the boat from Cieloalta paused to draw out his coin purse and root through the heavy Cadeleonian gold for a single Labaran copper. In a flash one of the beggar girls snatched the entire purse from him. Then she and her compatriots disappeared into the bustling crowd.

Elezar didn't laugh, but it was difficult. Beside him Kiram bowed his head, hiding a guilty smile. The priest called to a Cadeleonian soldier, but the swaying private only stared at him blearily and then staggered into a brothel.

Elezar and Kiram continued on their way. Both of them received curious glances from all classes of people, as neither of them seemed to belong to any. A young Labaran woman dressed in silver sable dispatched her maid to inquire if Elezar was performing as the stormgiant in a nearby theater. He supposed that was what came of dressing in the disused costume from a celebrated playhouse. Kiram, on the other hand, received at least two whispered solicitations. That, Elezar thought, was what came of being beautiful while walking on a street famous for its actors and whores.

Kiram paid little attention to the advances, ignoring one and informing the other that he was happily married. He held up his hand, displaying the oath ring he wore.

"You're really married?" Elezar asked once they were away. "To whom?"

Kiram raised a brow with an expression that told Elezar that only an idiot would need to ask.

It had to be Javier, Elezar realized.

"You and he are… married." Elezar couldn't help his startled tone. Cadeleonian men didn't wed one another, so he'd made the error of assuming that Kiram had taken a wife.

But Kiram was Haldiim and Javier had converted. Elezar didn't know why, after witnessing the two of them fucking in a field, he should feel so shocked by the thought of them exchanging vows. It just seemed so… banal, considering that Javier had once prided himself on being called a Hellion.

"Congratulations," Elezar added belatedly.

Kiram shrugged as if it was nothing, but his proud expression gave him away. He all but beamed as he gazed at the ring on his finger. "It's only been a few weeks. Grimma Naemir gave me enough gold to make the rings as a reward for my work. I cast them myself."

"Now I really will have to buy a feast at the market, so that we can celebrate," Elezar told him, though he had no idea how he'd pay for anything. He'd given the last of his money away to Cire. Still he felt he needed to make up for his gaffe and to assure Kiram that he'd left his old animosity behind.

The market lay to the west of them and Elezar could hear vendors calling out the delights of their wares. Elezar recognized voices from amidst the cacophony, Gullin's booming call in particular. As they walked on a white-haired old woman caught his sleeve. Elezar glanced down at her and seeing the rabbit in her arms knew at once that she had numbered among the witches who'd gathered at the Rat Rafters.

"Skellan's man, Elezar, aren't you?" She smiled broadly at him with only a few teeth. Elezar nodded.

"You come anytime to my cider stand and you'll have your fill free," she told him and then just as she started across the street she smiled back over her shoulder and called, "Bless you."

"That was nice," Kiram commented.

Again Elezar nodded, feeling stupid for being so touched by the old woman's warmth toward him.

Farther south the massive gray walls of the Cadeleonian garrison came into view. Watchtowers jutted into the sky like spears, and two black cannons stood high on the wall in plain sight. But Elezar spied neither soldiers on watch duty nor gunners attending the cannons. The most soldierly looking men in view appeared to be a party of five mercenaries lounging outside, perhaps looking for pay in the service of the garrison.

The heavy stone walls looked every inch the imposing garrison that Labaran butter taxes supposedly paid to maintain. Nothing—not the Labaran sanctum, the Sun Palace, nor even the vast Labaran market—occupied more of Milmuraille's land. The training yards for cavalry and infantry were said to accommodate one thousand men and six hundred mounted soldiers. The central headquarters had been designed by a royal architect and was rumored to be a fortress in itself.

But to hear most of Milmuraille tell it, the garrison had served as little more than a venue for Commander Lecha's private business enterprises for more than a decade now. The pink peaches sloppily painted on the wall were advertisement to any well-traveled man as to what entertainment he could purchase beyond the foreboding front gates.

"Is this a whorehouse?" Kiram muttered under his breath. "Why is it that wherever Cadeleonians settle there's always an abundance of chapels and whorehouses?"

"Because patronizing one is most often a remedy for too much of the other and vice versa."

Kiram gave a quiet laugh. "I'd forgotten how funny you can be, Elezar."

"Well, I wasn't all that amusing during the last days we spent together."

"It's all right. I don't recall any of us being very prone to laughter," Kiram said.

Elezar paused at the gate of the garrison but didn't step into the courtyard. Neither could he bring himself to meet Kiram's clear blue eyes. "I never got the chance to tell you—honestly— how goddamned sorry I was for... everything."

"You're apologizing?" Kiram asked lightly. "Only an hour ago I drew a knife and nearly skewered your arm. If anyone should apologize, it's me."

"You were defending Javier. And besides, you hardly pricked me." Elezar drew in a deep breath. He didn't want to have this conversation and yet he knew that he might never have another chance to clear his conscience. He'd made the mistake of thinking it could wait once already, and then Kiram and Javier had simply been gone from his life and from all of Cadeleon in one day.

Back then he'd foolishly imagined that the six of them— Hellions of Sagrada Academy all—would have been lauded as heroes for defeating a curse, freeing both Javier and Fedeles from its grasp, and stopping an imposter from seizing control of a dukedom. They'd suffered an ambush, poisoned wounds and a harrowing journey through the Sorrowlands for their cause. But Kiram had risen above them all in courage and sacrifice to ensure that Javier and Fedeles were saved. He'd been all but torn in half. Javier had revived him but only at the cost of revealing himself to be a Bahiim.

Still, when Elezar had left them recuperating and escorted his young brother, Nestor, back home to Anacleto, he'd thought the king would be moved by all that they'd endured and sacrificed. He'd imagined that there would be feasts and celebrations and more than enough time for him to make amends for slandering Kiram and attacking Javier in a fit of near madness.

But neither accolades nor feasts came. Instead, Javier had been excommunicated, stripped of his title and clapped in irons for committing heresy, and Kiram had broken him out of prison before news of the arrest even reached Elezar. Outlaws, the two of them had fled, leaving Elezar with only his guilt and regret.

Now Elezar forced himself to look at Kiram's delicate face. He still possessed the winsome countenance of youth but something in his expression had altered, grown calmer—or perhaps more weary. The pale crescent on his cheek had faded, but Elezar couldn't imagine that the terrible scars hidden beneath Kiram's tunic ever would.

"I don't know if this matters to you at all anymore," Elezar said. "Five years ago, I did and said terrible things to you. I just want to tell you that I was wrong. I was wrong about you and about Javier and what you were to each other. When the moment came and Javier needed someone, you were the man who sacrificed everything, while all I could do was watch."

Only the hint of a flush colored Kiram's dark cheeks. He looked almost shy.

So something of the schoolboy did remain in him.

"You didn't just watch, Elezar. You practically rebuilt an entire mechanical cure to my specifications in less than a day. And more than that you kept me from dying when we crossed through the Sorrowlands."

Elezar shook his head.

Kiram sighed. "Look, if we're clearing the air between us, then you should know that I'm sorry as well. Back then, I thought you were just a stupid, jealous beast."

"You weren't wrong."

"Of course I was," Kiram snapped. Elezar smiled at the flippant tone. He'd forgotten Kiram's predilection for offhanded dismissal of any opinion he felt to be erroneous. "I hardly knew anything about you, except what I could see. You were big, strong and every inch an ideal Cadeleonian man. So, I assumed that you must be simple as an ox and that your actions were without thought or nuance."

"I'm still not all that nuanced."

"Hear me out. You brought this up and I'll say my piece," Kiram stated. "When we heard about how Lord Grunito was going through the country challenging apparently random men to blood duels, Javier told me about your brother's murder."

Elezar didn't even know how to respond to Kiram's words. He felt almost as though Kiram had knocked the air out of him. Then Elezar recovered himself. Had he really imagined that Javier would keep a secret that he'd sworn when they'd both been only twelve years old? Why would Javier keep any secret from a man he'd sacrificed an entire dukedom to live with?

"You thought that I was seducing Javier and would lead him to the same fate Isandro met. Naturally, you hated me." Kiram spoke with casual ease, as if their bloody fight had taken place in ancient history. "And I believed you were just brutish. But then you saved my life and I realized that there was more to you."

"Perhaps," Elezar admitted. "But I was envious of you."

Really he'd been something much worse. For those brief minutes when he'd seen Kiram and Javier laying together in that open green meadow, he'd turned as savage and repulsive as the men who'd murdered his brother in that dark, ancient tomb.

"Well, if you're still madly covetous I'd be willing to let you sleep with Javier tonight," Kiram suggested with a wry smile. "I'm not all that fond of dog breath."

"Thanks for that generous offer." Elezar found it a relief to change the subject. "But I think I'm past that now. We've all moved on."

"And yet somehow we still end up walking into a brothel together," Kiram replied.

"Say it like that and Javier might be the one who ends up feeling jealous."

Kiram laughed but then gave Elezar a questioning look. "Any chance we'll find Atreau in there?"

"None, and not just because he struck the commander a few months back. The girls here are far too young and green. And I've never known Atreau to put a premium on virginity. Not even as a curative for merrypox." Elezar started through the gates, offering a cursory nod to the two sloppy Cadeleonian soldiers keeping guard. Then he and Kiram made their way to the main building of the garrison.

Kiram followed close and looked wary.

Elezar had no doubt that he'd seen more than his share of trouble in the five years since they'd last met. Elezar could read as much in the way Kiram moved. Gone was the curious, carefree scholar who'd pick up and tinker with anything that caught his eye. Now Kiram kept his hands close to his knife belt and walked lightly as a thief.

At the doors they stated their business, which took the doorman by surprise. Elezar wondered how long it had been since anyone had bothered to come looking for Commander Lecha with any concern other than the commerce of chattel and comely children.

It pained him, as a Cadeleonian, to see this garrison representing his nation so poorly. No wonder Labarans resented the Cadeleonian soldiers in their midst. They cost Labarans dearly in taxes and in return only provided them with half a barrack of listless men-at-arms and perhaps the ugliest whorehouse in the city.

"You're here to see Commander Lecha about Mirogoths?" the skinny dark-haired doorman clarified. "The wild kind from the woods?" Despite his tidy dress uniform and proper tone Elezar wondered if the doorman wasn't drunk or addled with poppy smoke.

"Yes, the armies of the grimma," Kiram repeated in exasperation. "The foreign threat that this entire garrison was built to defend against. They are marching on the city, and I have ridden here to give your commander their distance and numbers."

"God in heaven…" The doorman paled slightly, then he beckoned them in. Inside, the garrison was no more lovely or welcoming than it had seemed from the street, but the bare gray walls did offer cover from the afternoon winds rising off the Raccroc River.

"I'll inform the commander at once," the doorman decided. Then he tottered back farther into the dim recesses of the hall, leaving Elezar and Kiram standing in the stone entry under the flickering light of a single lamp. Elezar could see sconces that should have held further lights but seemed to have been forgotten.

"This place looks vacant," Kiram commented.

Distantly, Elezar could hear men hustling through the courtyard. It wasn't the noise of soldiers at practice or changing shifts but the bustle of wagons being loaded and carriages rolling away. Beneath the clatter of hooves he caught the sound of a drunk crooning about a spider spinning gowns for flies.

"…dressed in silk so fine, we shall dine. And you'll be mine, swathed in silk, so fine…"

"There's a cheery melody," Kiram muttered. "Fitting for the cobwebs up on the walls."

"It would suit a spider wooing a fly, wouldn't it?" Elezar replied. He squinted through the gloom, picking out the clean spaces where portraits and mirrors must have once hung, but had all been stripped from the smoke-darkened walls.

"Not even a fire in the hearth," he noted.

Then the doorman returned and escorted them up a staircase and into a cramped study where Commander Lecha sat behind a heavy writing table, balancing sums in a ledger. Costly perfumed lamps blazed and silk decorated the ornate furniture as well as the bright tapestries that insulated the walls. Neither Elezar nor Kiram sat and the commander didn't seem to expect them to.

Elezar had seen Commander Lecha in passing before, twice at Bishop Palo's table and once riding through the cloth market on his plump, white stallion. The man was well into his fifties, his hair thinning and his waist thickening but neither to excess. His features were unremarkable and his expression bland. Even dressed in tawny velvet and sporting a dramatically waxed mustache he reminded Elezar of nothing more than a peeled, boiled potato.

"I'm told that you have urgent business?" Commander Lecha glanced at Kiram only briefly before turning his attention to Elezar. He narrowed his gaze. "But don't I know you already?"

"Indeed," Elezar replied. "I am in service to the duke of Rauma. He dispatched me to the forest to seek a gift for his bride-to-be—"

"Bishop Palo's niece is not yet his bride and she may never be." Commander Lecha pinned Elezar with a hard glare. Obviously, the commander fancied himself as Fedeles' rival, though in what realm this plain-faced, miserly degenerate imagined that he could outshine a man of Fedeles' qualities—or even Atreau's impersonation of those qualities—Elezar couldn't hazard a guess.

"Perhaps I misspoke." Elezar bowed his head. "I meant only that the duke sent me to fetch a pelt fine enough for any woman worthy of becoming his duchess."

"And this boy? Certainly he's not for the duchess as well." Commander Lecha eyed Kiram with a very speculative gaze. "Irabiim guides come at quite a cost, I've heard, and aren't easy to lure off from their mothers. A little old this one, but still… exotic."

"He's not for sale, if that's what you mean," Elezar replied. Whatever indignation Kiram must have felt at being discussed like a stud at auction, he hid well.

"A treat for the duke, perhaps? I've heard that his taste is rather… indiscriminate." Commander Lecha gave Elezar a look of sordid knowing, but then went on coolly enough. "If the Irabiim isn't up for market, why drag him before me? Come to the point."

"The point of our intrusion upon your business is simply to inform you of what this Irabiim has seen." Elezar decided against offering Kiram's name. Javier was still a wanted man and many who hunted him knew of Kiram Kir-Zaki as his constant companion. "He has recently traveled from the Blue Forest and over the Eagle Hills. On his journey he saw armies of Mirogoths all marching toward Milmuraille."

"Really?" Commander Lecha glared at Kiram. "All on his own?"

Kiram regarded the commander in return with an expression of indifference.

"What caravan he traveled with hardly matters," Elezar stated. "He saw the Mirogoth armies."

Commander Lecha swore under his breath and snapped his ledger closed. Then he returned his attention to Kiram. "How many men in these supposed armies of yours, boy? Or can't you Irabiim count higher than your ten fingers?"

If the situation hadn't been so dire Elezar might have laughed. Asking a man like Kiram if he could count was like wondering if a hawk might possess the aptitude for flight.

"I have small learning," Kiram replied in a stilted and rather authentic Irabiim accent. "But I am good at number. I count men and beast and I make marks on birch bark."

"And?"

"Five spear men in orders of eight hundred and four archers by orders of six hundred. All running on foot. On the gray steed maybe three orders of thirty. Then four times that number of wild beasts—"

"Eight hundred what?" Commander Lecha cut in. The faintest smirk twitched at the corner of Kiram's lips.

"Four thousand men at arms," Elezar clarified, though the numbers chilled him. "Two thousand archers, ninety riders mounted upon wethra-steeds, and some three hundred and sixty mordwolves and snowlions."

"He does keep good count, doesn't he?" Commander Lecha muttered. "Still that's no reason to parade him across my carpet. I'm a busy man and I have very little interest in Mirogoths marching to war."

"They are coming for Milmuraille," Kiram stated.

"So what?" Commander Lecha shrugged.

Elezar scowled at Commander Lecha. Was it possible that he didn't know Oesir's witchflame was dying? That a violet flame was ravaging the city? That people had burned alive and more were fleeing the city? That entire bell towers were reduced to ash?

"You heard the Columbe Bell crumble apart, didn't you?" Elezar asked.

"Yes, it collapsed. At least three of their bell towers have fallen recently, I'm told. Shoddy Labaran workmanship." Commander Lecha opened his ledger again. "What does any of that have to do with the Mirogoths? And more to the point, what do you imagine any of this has to do with me?"

Elezar wanted to roar with frustration. How could this man be allowed to command when he was so utterly incompetent and corrupt? Did the king and his courtiers truly care so little about the Labarans under their protection and the soldiers sent here to lay down their lives for this land?

Even as the thoughts occurred, Elezar recognized his own naivety. Cadeleonian kings had not cultivated dominion over Labara for the sake of Labarans. Nor were soldiers rare enough for most nobles to value them for their own sakes.

"Hasn't anyone told you that the witchflame is dying?" Elezar asked. "The truce is breaking."

"Certainly," Commander Lecha replied. "But our priests will see to it that the light is maintained long enough for persons of importance to properly decamp. I spoke with Bishop Palo's man, Bois, only this morning."

"Sacrist Bois?" Elezar asked. That priest certainly got around, didn't he?

Commander Lecha only offered Elezar an imperious sniff as if such ought to have been obvious.

"He mentioned something else, which I think is much more interesting." Commander Lecha smiled at Elezar with all the warmth of an adder. "Apparently, Lord Grunito, there is a noblewoman offering very good money to have your head delivered to her."

Kiram glanced to Elezar only briefly, and Elezar answered him with the slightest silent nod.

"According to Sacrist Bois, three men have already died attempting to win the lady's reward. Seeing you in person, I can well imagine that a few more will fall before the lady has her way with you." Commander Lecha hardly shifted in his seat. He simply sat there smirking at Elezar. "Mind you, I don't intend to number among them. Assassination doesn't often turn much of a profit once you consider the investment and risk involved. And I haven't the time in any case."

"Because you're going somewhere," Kiram said.

"Indeed. After I've totaled this last ledger, I and my household will be traveling very far south to take the springs in Chaudvent."

"You're abandoning the city?" Elezar wasn't sure if he felt more outraged or relieved. He certainly wouldn't have trusted Commander Lecha to lead anyone against Mirogoth invaders, but to simply abandon his post? "Your men—"

"Don't waste your outrage on a pack of malcontents and deserters." Commander Lecha sneered at Elezar as if he were somehow to blame. "They ran like rats from a house fire at the first sign of trouble. Afraid of their own shadows and a few dying witches."

"There are still men on the grounds," Elezar began, but again Commander Lecha cut him off.

"The six men remaining are following me south, and that's only because I have their payroll. And how dare you look at me like that! You think you can do better? You think you could control this wretched city full of heretics and witches? Well, go ahead, then!" Commander Lecha suddenly darted a hand into his pocket and withdrew a ring of keys. He tossed them to Elezar.

"I entrust the Milmuraille garrison to your care, m' lord. After all, you've already got this pretty Irabiim boy to give you accounts of the Mirogoths—"

"You cannot just abandon your post!" Elezar glowered down at Commander Lecha.

"It's not my post any longer," Commander Lecha snapped, though Elezar glimpsed as much fear in the man's face as anger. "I've resigned!"

Elezar had to fight the urge to grab the self-satisfied man by his throat and throttle him. His fingers clenched reflexively, and he felt the ring of keys in his hand biting into his palm. With a single blow he could knock the teeth out of Commander Lecha's head or crush his throat and watch him slowly choke to death on his own blood. Elezar had to look away from the commander's smug face. His gaze fell across a small trunk standing to the side of the commander's desk. Its stonewood walls were banded with iron and the lock holding it shut bore both the stamp and seal of the king's treasury. It had to be the garrison payroll. And then Elezar knew exactly how he would hurt Commander Lecha. He shoved the garrison keys into his pocket.

"We should speak to the sheriff." Kiram cast a disgusted glance at the commander, but then turned and pulled the door open.

"We'll go, but not empty-handed." Elezar grabbed the trunk, almost enjoying the terrible weight of it. Nothing but gold could be so small and so heavy at once.

Commander Lecha started to his feet but stopped as Elezar spun on him, glaring.

"Sit, you coward!" Elezar kicked Commander Lecha's desk hard enough to knock the man back into his chair. Commander Lecha stared at Elezar and his face seemed to drain of color.

"You gave me this garrison so I will take what is now mine," Elezar told him. "If I see you again after tonight, I will kill you with my own hands! Do you understand me?"

Commander Lecha nodded.

Elezar turned and followed Kiram, though he hardly registered their walk to the gate and out onto the crowded street, his thoughts were so consumed with fury at Commander Lecha's utter betrayal of his responsibility to all the people under his protection and under his command.

"Is that what I think it is?" Kiram asked quietly.

A small party of revelers sauntered past them and Elezar waited until they were out of hearing to answer.

"King's coin," Elezar replied. A quick glance at the unbroken seal assured him that he was correct.

"It's not every day I walk into a garrison and steal the payroll, so I might be confused," Kiram remarked. "But don't we look more than a little conspicuous just lugging that trunk around on the open street?"

"We do," Elezar admitted. They both doubled their pace to a quick clip. Overhead, brilliant orange and scarlet streaks of sunset climbed into the darkening blue sky. The wind gusted and reeled. Bells should have rung out the late hour. The trunk, balanced on Elezar's shoulder, dug in like a granite boulder.

"This much money doesn't travel light," he said.

"If only Javier were here to engage in a weight-lifting contest with you. Oh, but wait. He's a dog, now." Kiram ran his hand through his dusty hair and coughed. "This day just keeps getting better."

"We're not too far from the market. Sammi and Sarl's father will be there. We should be able to at least borrow a frog net from them to throw over this trunk." Elezar spoke the plan as it came to him. "I'll send a runner boy to fetch a horse and cart from the Fairwind Stables…"

"And then we'll call on the sheriff with a trunk full of stolen—"

"Appropriated. If the garrison is mine, then so is its gold." Elezar couldn't help but think that Skellan would have grasped this intuitively. On the other hand, Elezar couldn't argue that it wasn't a damn pain to be lugging around this cumbersome trunk, all plastered with royal stamps, seals and ribbons. "I couldn't let Lecha just take everything. I had to do something to make him pay."

"Yes, I grasped that," Kiram replied. "Though, I really thought that you were just going to beat him bloody."

"For a minute so did I. But it would have been too easy to kill the man if I set on him in a fury. Right now, I could do without the murder of a worthless shit like Zangre Lecha weighing down my soul." If Elezar had to suffer guilt, then he preferred that it should be for a death that he truly regretted.

Elezar had to step to the side as a drunk staggered past, dropped to his knees and vomited in the street. The man's companions heaved him up, but not before Elezar heard the man cry out that they were all going to die.

"The bell towers have fallen and soon Mirogoths will be wearing our skins for cloaks," the man slurred.

Kiram eyed the fellow as he was dragged back into the shelter of a tavern.

"It seems word is traveling around town already," Kiram commented.

"Most of the street witches have known that the sanctum has been losing its light for weeks now," Elezar told him. "The local Labaran nobility are aware of it as well. It's hard to believe, in the midst of this crowd, but I've heard that nearly a third of the city has already fled. I suspect a good number of these people are indulging in a last binge before their escape."

"Considering the kind of protection Commander Lecha was providing them, they might have the right of it, getting out before the whole city falls."

"Maybe," Elezar said. "But nothing will ensure that Milmuraille does fall faster than abandoning it. The surest way to lose a fight is to give up before it even begins."

"Our sainted teacher, Warmaster Ignacio, would be proud to hear you say as much," Kiram responded, but he sounded as if he were only half-listening. He drew a large silver locket from his coat pocket, opened it and scrutinized the contents. Elezar glanced down and realized that the locket contained a small, polished mirror. Kiram shifted his attention from the mirror to Elezar. "How close is that market?'

"Just around the corner. What did you see?"

"We're being followed—don't look back. They'll only come down on us all the sooner if they think we've noticed them."

"How many?" Elezar asked.

"Five men, all Cadeleonian and well-armed. Three swordsmen and two spears."

"Archers?"

"No. They mean to do this at close quarters."

Elezar remembered the party of men he'd noticed lingering outside the garrison. Commander Lecha's comment about learning of the price Lady Reollos offered for Elezar's head came back to him as well. No wonder the man had looked so smug.

"I noticed the big swordsman just outside the garrison when we first went in. At a glance I'd say mercenaries... Perhaps working for a certain lady?" Kiram closed the locket and slid it back into his pocket. "How shall we handle them?"

Five against one were not odds Elezar liked in the least. But he also had no intention of endangering Kiram.

"We keep moving," Elezar replied.

All around them groups of tradesmen filled the walkways, most leaving their shops for the day and making for their homes or taverns. Workmen, maids and matrons bustled between clusters of merrymakers just beginning their evening revels.

"Should I ask why a noblewoman has placed a price on your head?" Kiram cast him a curious look.

"Lady Oasia Reollos," Elezar supplied. "Her husband caught her dallying in Atreau's bed. He meant to murder Atreau but I killed the husband before he could. I didn't mean to."

"Sometimes it can't be helped." Kiram's expression was somber. "Did the lady love the husband she was unfaithful to, or is there another reason that you've earned her wrath?"

"If I stand trial the details of her affair will come out and she'll be ruined. For the same reason she's put a price on Atreau as well."

"I see..." Kiram nodded slowly, as if confirming something to himself. "So that's why you're here in Milmuraille and why suddenly the duke of Rauma is developing a reputation as a libertine."

"Yes, he sent us," Elezar admitted. "Those men behind us don't have any interest in you. The sheriff lives only three streets from here—"

"I don't think that witch boy would ever forgive me if I let you fight five men alone," Kiram informed him. "And I'm rather hoping to keep on his good side until he turns Javier back into the man I married."

A dry laugh escaped Elezar, but he shook his head. "And since you're a wedded man, that's all the more reason for you to stay well clear of this mess. Javier wouldn't make a pretty widow, you know. No one else would have him with all that hair."

"I'm not planning on getting myself killed," Kiram responded.

"Few men are and still it happens. Look, Kiram, you're the cleverest man I know but you aren't a fighter."

"I know," Kiram agreed. Still walking, he swung his pack from his back and fished out two strange little devices that looked to Elezar like gilded goose eggs, each with a glass window cut in one end. "I'm an inventor, and these are mechanisms that I've been cobbling together using flint and a few Bahiim spells."

"What do they do?" Elezar eyed the small spheres suspiciously.

"I'm attempting to create compact lamps that won't require oil to give light," Kiram replied with a weak smile. "Though so far I've only gotten them to flare up with a blinding pulse of illumination, though when they hit hard against something they do often burst into flames."

"All right, I can see the application," Elezar said, nodding. "But the fact that there are spells in there worries me. Skellan said that a spell can lead the violet flame back to feed upon the caster."

"Javier." Kiram sounded frustrated and fearful at once.

Elezar had feared as much. They couldn't take the chance.

Ahead of them the street opened into the wide plaza of the fish market. Rows of wooden stalls and brightly painted stands created a maze beneath the high arches that supported of the city's aqueduct. Most of the patrons had already left, and nearly all the fishmongers and merchants were in the midst of packing up their wares for the day. Elezar caught sight of Gullin, and picked up his pace to reach the man.

"Your friendly frog seller?" Kiram asked. "You think he might give us more aid than the use of one of his nets."

"Possibly. I know him—well, Skellan does, but I think that might be enough." Elezar waved to the blond man and to his relief Gullin grinned and waved in return.

"Elezar," Gullin called and when he did several other vendors turned from their work to take him in. Elezar recognized several of them from the night before, but a few he didn't.

"What brings you here?" Gullin inquired. Worry tinged

354

his features. "Is it Skellan?"

"He's fine," Elezar assured the man. "I was hoping that you could look after this trunk for me." Elezar swung the locked box down to the ground, where it sank several inches into the muddy soil. Gullin eyed the dark trunk but then his gaze shifted to something farther back beyond Elezar. "This wouldn't have anything to do with those five uglies marching up our way, would it?"

"The uglies are my trouble," Elezar replied. "But they don't have any claim on this trunk even if they kill me in combat. This trunk goes to Skellan."

He didn't know why he choose Skellan except that for the briefest instant he'd imagined how stunned and delighted the witch would look beholding a trunk loaded with Cadeleonian gold. And after everything Skellan had given Elezar the previous day, he owed Skellan something.

"Are you going to start running or face us like a man?" A deep baritone voice called from behind Elezar. Kiram started but Elezar stopped him with a motion of his hand.

"Let's hold on to what element of surprise we still have," Elezar whispered. Then he drew his sword and turned to take in the five men closing in around him.

They were plainly mercenaries, but dressed in good leather and all wearing cloaks emblazoned with three gold skulls. Their crisp haircuts and handsome boots suited court assassins more than the ordinary roughs who hired themselves out. The three swordsmen stood nearest and all wore the long, lighter blades favored by professional duelists in the Cadeleonian capital. Their blunt noses and long faces made Elezar guess that they were close relations, most likely brothers. The spearmen crept out to the edges of Elezar's peripheral sight, no doubt hoping to get behind him and skewer him like a boar. Elezar guessed that Lady Reollos had dispatched these men personally. They wouldn't be scared off with a good bluff, but the duelists at least might possess some grain of honor.

"Shall we draw up dueling circles and make honest combat of this?" Elezar asked. "Or would you have me slaughter you all at once?"

The spearman to Elezar's left actually stilled at the threat. That would make him new to this work and most likely to hesitate. He did look young and, noting the way his eyes darted, Elezar guessed that he was scared—his heart probably pounding in his chest and sweat making his grip turn slick. Elezar knew exactly how that felt, but today he couldn't afford to feel pity.

The eldest of the swordsmen, the stocky brother with a wide scar across his tanned cheek, sneered at Elezar.

"You tell us where Atreau Vediya is and we'll put you down easy."

So much for honor among swordsmen, Elezar supposed.

"You're none of you pretty enough for Atreau's tastes. He'd only send you away with your hearts broken. But let me make you an offer," Elezar said lightly, as if he hoped to banter for a little more time. The mercenaries relaxed just a little, expecting the promise of riches, no doubt. Instead Elezar charged hard and fast. He took the young spearman off guard and cut him down with a blow that nearly severed his head. Elezar ripped the youth's spear from his dead hands as his body fell to the ground.

The other four mercenaries charged Elezar, with anguish and wrath in their expressions and ringing through their voices. Their rage was what he wanted, because it made men rash and foolish. It made them misstep—charging at once when they should have taken the time to get behind him. They should have staggered their charge, compensating for the greater reach of the spear in Elezar's left hand.

But their brother was dead and fury consumed them. Elezar understood that.

He met their rush, with a low, hard thrust, taking the swordsman to the left through the gut with the stolen spear and punching its shaft through the man's back. As the man fell convulsing, Elezar released the spear.

Still three left and all of them much too close now. Elezar bounded back as the eldest of the mercenaries thrust his sword in for Elezar's hammering heart. Elezar parried the blow and tried to drive the man back, to win himself a little space, before the other two mercenaries could get behind him. In particular, he didn't want the remaining spearman to get a clear thrust with his longer reach.

But the scar-faced elder brother was fast, and it took all of Elezar's focus to drive him back and protect himself from becoming pinned against the wall of some snail vendor's stall. Out of the corner of his eye Elezar noted the spearman creeping to his left, while the second swordsman edged to the right.

Then without warning a heavy black kettle came hurtling past Elezar's shoulder and took the spearman directly in the face. He fell and immediately two Labaran women—one a white-haired granny and the other a round-faced matron—hurled heavy fishing nets over him while an older man wrenched the spear away. The younger swordsman on Elezar's right suddenly shrieked and collapsed back howling. A fox and a grizzled badger darted away from the mercenary's bloodied leg.

The thought that he knew the fox and badger came to Elezar like a memory from a fever dream, leaving him momentarily as startled as his remaining opponent. But Elezar had seen stranger things in his life and recovered faster. He thrust past the mercenary's guard and drove his sword deep between the ribs and into the man's heart. The mercenary jabbed back, slashing Elezar's doublet. Elezar jerked his own blade free of the man's body and bounded out of his reach. The mercenary staggered forward, managed one more clumsy thrust and then fell to the ground.

Elezar spun to subdue the remaining swordsman before he could regain his feet. But the man simply remained on the ground where he'd fallen. He dropped his blade and held up his empty hands in surrender. Elezar stepped back from the man feeling both relieved and stunned. Free of an opponent, he took in his surroundings.

To his right Gullin made quick work of binding the remaining swordsman with a heavy rope. On his left, the spearman lay too still beneath the fishing nets, the crushed shell of his face hardly recognizable. Only a pace from Elezar, the eldest of the mercenaries lay dead. Beyond him a huge pool of blood marked where Elezar had felled the first two men.

Merchants, vendors and beggars stood all around, many staring on in silence. Others collected the winnings of hastily placed wagers.

Kiram glanced to Elezar with a questioning expression, his knife half drawn from its sheath. Clearly he hadn't had time to draw before half the market had turned on Elezar's attackers.

Gray and nimble, Ogmund strode up to Elezar, his big badger trotting proudly around his scrawny legs as he walked. "I'm not sure you needed our aid, our Elezar, but we're glad to offer it. Would have done it sooner but you charged in so fast."

"I wasn't expecting anyone to..." Elezar realized that wasn't what he needed to say. "Thank you."

"Oh, how could we do anything else? We may argue, but we look after our own." Ogmund grinned at him. "Of course there is still the question of dispersing these would-be murders' goods."

"That can wait until the sheriff arrives," Gullin called. He picked up the big kettle from the dirt and handed it over to the white-haired cider seller and her partner who together hauled it back to their cider cart. A young man joined them, taking a fistful of straw and scrubbing the blood and gore off the kettle.

"Claude's run to fetch Sheriff Hirbe. The sheriff's a good man and he'll hear you out." Gullin offered Elezar a broad grin from beneath his thick yellow beard. "The girls are watching your trunk, by the way."

Back by the frog baskets, nibbling at one of the seals on Elezar's trunk, stood two pretty young goats. Kiram eyed the girls curiously but then turned his attention to Elezar. He pointed to Elezar's chest.

"Are you all right?"

Elezar glanced down to the gash in his doublet. He didn't feel any pain but that meant little in the giddy rush after a fight. A fatal wound could register as only a little pinch when his blood coursed so wildly through his veins. He slipped two fingers into the slash and felt where the mercenary's blade had sliced through his under shirt as well. The warm flesh of his chest bore only the faintest scrape.

"Fine," Elezar assured Kiram.

"Last time you told me that you died of poisoning." Kiram lowered his voice. "Alizadeh isn't here now to bring you back."

"Last time I was lying," Elezar admitted. "This time I'm not. Truly."

Kiram accepted that and then looked up at the darkening sky. Elezar followed his gaze. Sunset colors still streaked the horizon, but directly overhead stars sparkled against the dark blue expanse like chips of ice floating over a frozen sea.

Despite the complaints around them, Elezar was glad for the evening chill. Any warmer and flies would have been buzzing all over him and the corpses at his feet. In the midst of his fallen brothers, the bound swordsman hung his head and sobbed like a child. Elezar couldn't look at him.

Kiram shook his head. "Well, it seems we'll be speaking to Sheriff Hirbe, if not exactly in the manner we'd planned."

"Not much ever does go as I've planned," Elezar muttered. He wished the swordsman behind him would stop crying.

An elderly woman whom Elezar vaguely remembered as one of a cluster drinking table beer with Cire's uncle, Ogmund, tottered up to Elezar and handed him a rag.

"There's so much blood on your hands and face, my dear. You don't look half a fright."

Elezar took the cloth and wiped away what he could of the blood. His hair was sticky with it and no doubt the doublet he wore was ruined. Elezar held the bloody rag in his hand, unsure if it would be more rude to offer it back to the elderly woman or to throw it away. Fortunately, she reached out, took the filthy cloth and tucked it away into the butcher's apron she wore over her red skirts.

"Who knew our Skellan had such a champion of a man!" She smiled at him and Kiram as well. "Even a coffin-dodger like me feels stronger knowing that you're fighting for us."

Elezar could have told her that he wasn't fighting for her, or for anyone, really. He simply fought because he didn't know any other way to keep himself and the people he cared for from harm. Perhaps Skellan had seen right through him when he'd accused Elezar of fighting for so long that he didn't know how to do anything else. Elezar didn't want that to be true. He didn't want the rest of his life to be nothing but the stench of blood and the sound of someone sobbing.

He offered the frail little woman a smile and a bow, and simply asked, "You wouldn't know of anywhere nearby that I could purchase Yuanese spice sausages, do you?"

CHAPTER
TWENTY-ONE

Sheriff Hirbe arrived on horseback accompanied by six mounted Labaran men wearing light armor. The sheriff sported only a chest plate for protection, but otherwise nothing heavier than a lined leather coat and a modest woolen cap shielded him from the elements or attack. He wasn't a large man nor was he young, but something about his calm manner—even as he took in the decapitated, mangled and bludgeoned bodies strewn across the muddy grounds of the plaza—made Elezar think he had seen and survived far worse carnage. His curled white beard whirled up on the evening wind like the fog rising off the river. The flickering torchlight of the half-empty fish market lent a gold glow to his deeply lined face.

Gullin greeted the sheriff respectfully and then explained what had happened, as he understood it. The sheriff studied Elezar as he listened.

Elezar kept quiet.

Further back in the shadows of the cider stall Kiram lingered so still and silent that he almost passed for a trick of flickering firelight. That, if nothing else, told Elezar just how much the last five years of eluding the royal bishop's bounty hunters had affected him. Once, he would have immediately come forward to educate everyone present as to just what had occurred as well as which mathematic principles the battle had demonstrated. But no longer.

Elezar waited, feeling aimless and awkward, his coat pocket stuffed with links of bright orange Yuanese spice sausages. The white-haired cider seller had bought them for him, which had saved Elezar the embarrassment of admitting that he hadn't a coin to his name. At least not any coins he wanted to bring attention to. He could only hope that Gullin and the surrounding merchants had been too startled by the bloody fight in their midst to pay much mind to that dark trunk, half sunk in the mud.

Elezar didn't look at it or at Kiram. He simply waited, tense as the taut string of a bow, and hoped that he would not need to be released into another battle.

That would depend upon the character of Sheriff Hirbe and his men. If Elezar could have had his wish he would have wanted an honest bunch of idiots—the kind of law he'd encountered a few times in the Cadeleonian countryside—men who never solved a mystery outside of what they would have for their suppers, but who meant well and did no one any particular harm.

The worst possibility would be men both quick witted and corrupt: assassins clever enough to take regular pay and exploit a city's resources to fund their own indulgence in blackmail, extortion and bounty hunting. Such men wouldn't hesitate to attempt to claim Lady Reollos' money and Elezar's life.

Elezar watched the sheriff as he questioned Gullin. The old man spoke too softly for Elezar to quite catch his words, but he treated the frogmonger politely and seemed to listen to all Gullin had to say. While the questioning went on, two of the sheriff's deputies took the single surviving swordsman away to the city jail. The remaining four deputies made brief inquiries of other merchants. They returned to the sheriff, reporting their findings in hushed whispers.

Then the sheriff dispatched one of the men to the west and the other to the east.

The other two deputies stripped the dead mercenaries and laid out their goods on the cleared table of a cockle seller. The sheriff glanced over the assembly of coin purses, dueling knives, amulets, family rings and silver pox-charms but indicated that his men bring him only a small envelope and the letter inside. He read it over and then slipped the letter into a coat pocket. At last he turned his attention to Elezar, gazing at him with an expression very like recognition.

It was then that Elezar began to worry that this sheriff was no dullard.

"So, you're the wanted man," the sheriff said. He remained seated astride his bay gelding, so that he could look down just slightly at Elezar.

"I'm not wanted by the law. The only bounty placed upon my head is there at the behest of a lady who bears me a grudge." As far as Elezar knew that much was still true, though he wasn't certain how much longer Fedeles' machinations would keep the king from bringing charges against him for Lord Reollos' death.

"I understand that you serve the duke of Rauma?" Sheriff Hirbe asked.

Elezar nodded. What had been in that letter? A missive from Lady Reollos describing him? A promise of gold for his death?

"And yet to hear our friend Gullin tell it, you're a street witch's man," Sheriff Hirbe commented.

"I've helped him out and he's helped me," Elezar replied. "It's no crime to know two men."

"No, but it is peculiar to know men of such differing rank. Cream rises and stones sink. It's a rare thing that bobs between the two."

"I travel in broad circles," Elezar replied, and the sheriff smiled as if he were appreciating a private joke.

"Of that I have no doubt," Sheriff Hirbe replied. "You're called Elezar?"

"Yes, I am, sir."

"And these aren't the first men who've come hunting for your head. There were three others two days ago." Sheriff Hirbe said it without uncertainty or accusation, as if repeating a recorded fact.

"There were." Elezar thought it pointless to lie to this sheriff. "They ambushed me at a stable."

"You knew they were there but you wouldn't leave your horse. The boy there told us about it. Doue was his name, wasn't it, Magraie?" The sheriff glanced to the taller of his two remaining deputies and the young man nodded. "You made quite an impression upon young Doue. A lone Cadeleonian who traveled into the Mirogoth forest and returned with a scarlet wolf at his side. He half-thought you'd wooed and bedded the Sumar grimma."

Having seen and spoken to the Sumar grimma, Elezar couldn't imagine any man wooing her and couldn't help a snort of laughter at the idea.

"You did just return from the Mirogoth forest, didn't you?" Sheriff Hirbe asked.

"I did," Elezar admitted. "The duke sent me to find a pelt befitting his future bride."

Sheriff Hirbe nudged his horse and the big animal brought the weathered white-haired old man a step closer. The sheriff studied Elezar's face. He lowered his voice as he spoke. "I've heard rumors recently from the Mirogoth lands. Wild guides and displaced witches are fleeing for ships here in the city, hoping to sail as far from these lands as they can go. All of them fear for their children, all of them warn of a coming war."

Elezar had not thought to expect anything like this and yet in a way he couldn't have hoped for a better chance to warn the sheriff of all that Kiram and Javier had seen and what he knew himself.

"One of my Mirogoth guides said something similar. At the time I thought that she was worried about a Cadeleonian invasion." Elezar, too, kept his voice down. "But since then I've met other travelers, who've come from lands much farther north, and they told me that the grimma and their armies are marching south."

"These travelers were?"

"Irabiim," Elezar answered. He wouldn't give Kiram away in this uncertain situation. He didn't even look to see where Kiram had melted back into the shadows of the aqueduct. If this all turned bloody, Elezar just hoped Kiram would be able to find his own way back to Javier and Skellan at the Fairwind.

"An Irabiim too! But you do travel in a wide circle, Elezar. Witches, nobles, Mirogoths and Irabiim." Sheriff Hirbe raised his curling white brows. "And what is it that you do for a living?"

"I serve the duke of Rauma."

"Oh yes, you told me that, didn't you?" The sheriff smiled and then glanced over Elezar's shoulder. "But that chest laying there in the mud, that isn't the duke's, is it?"

The sheriff pointed to where the little trunk slumped in the mud. One of the sheriff's men went to it and after attempting to lift it alone called his compatriot to help him. The two of them hauled the trunk to the sheriff, dropping it only two strides from Elezar's reach. The sheriff studied the dirty ribbons, chipped seals and stained stamps that festooned the wooden exterior. Elezar didn't move a muscle, but his whole body trembled with restraint. If he needed to he could swing the trunk up with one hand and use it like a murderous bludgeon to bring down even a warhorse.

The sheriff wouldn't expect it. Neither would his men. But a sea of merchants surrounded them and as far as Elezar could tell they seemed friendly with the sheriff. Probably more likely to take the old man's side than Elezar's if it came to a fight.

So Elezar remained still and waited to see just what kind of character a trunk filled with gold would reveal.

"Care to explain how the payroll for the Cadeleonian garrison came into your possession?" the sheriff inquired.

"Much the same way I came into possession of the garrison itself," Elezar replied. "I even have the keys. Shall I show you?"

"All right, but slowly," the sheriff said, allowing it.

Elezar used his left hand to dig the garrison keys from his coat pocket. He held them out for the sheriff to inspect.

"Commander Lecha turned what little is left of the place over to me."

"To a varlet?" Again the sheriff's white brows rose. "It seems more likely that he'd give them over to a street witch's man, but not by much."

"You don't understand," Elezar answered in a whisper. If word spread that the garrison had been abandoned it might provide that final spark of despair that at last ignited panic across the city's entire populace. "Commander Lecha has dismissed what few soldiers remained on guard at the garrison and has abandoned his post. I think I just happened to be the first Cadeleonian who came by."

The sheriff scowled at Elezar but then beckoned one of his men to his side.

"Go call on the Cradle and see what's there. Be quiet about it," Sheriff Hirbe ordered. The young man nodded, and mounting his horse, rode away.

"It still doesn't quite follow that Lecha would turn keys, much less coin, over to some rough in a theater coat."

"I'm telling you." Elezar had to fight not to raise his voice. "He didn't care—"

"But he would have." The sheriff cut him off with a tone of perfect certainty. "Commander Lecha is a coward and a pig, but he's a Cadeleonian pig through and through. He'd never place a symbol of his own authority in the hands of a common man. He'd throw those keys down a shit-hole first."

Being a Cadeleonian nobleman, Elezar hadn't even questioned the fact that Commander Lecha had given him the garrison. He'd only railed against the commander's incompetence and gutlessness. Suddenly he realized that the sheriff was right. Commander Lecha had even addressed him as Lord Grunito.

"So who are you, really?" Sheriff Hirbe asked. "And why are you here?"

Elezar considered lying but saw no profit in it, not when he wanted the sheriff to trust him and hear him out when he told him of the numbers of Mirogoths marching on the city.

"My name truly is Elezar, and I am a friend to a duke and to a street witch. But I also know a third man called Sevanyo Sagrada, who appointed me to be a Cadeleonian royal envoy. I was sent to broker peace with the Sumar grimma. That's why I went into the Mirogoth forest."

Elezar didn't know whether the sheriff would believe him. After all he was dressed in a blood-spattered theater costume and wore no emblems of rank or nobility. The sheriff simply nodded.

"And did you find her?" the sheriff asked.

"I did," Elezar admitted.

"And?"

"She warned me then that Oesir's witchflame was dying and that the Mirogoths would come to take Milmuraille, whether it meant war with Cadeleon or not."

All mirth disappeared from the sheriff's face and he looked terribly old. He drew in a slow, calming breath and straightened his shoulders as if shaking off a blow he'd expected. Then he glanced to the merchants gathered around them and immediately that unconcerned affectation returned to his features.

There was something so familiar to Elezar in that mix of care and concern that he couldn't help but feel a shred of kinship toward the sheriff. He was not a man who, like Commander Lecha, would flee and let the people depending upon him fall into lawlessness and chaos.

"These Irabiim travelers you spoke of," Sheriff Hirbe asked, "what did they tell you of the Mirogoth armies?"

Elezar recounted the numbers Kiram had supplied. "They are still a good month from the city but moving fast."

"But why did you not go to Count Radulf?" the sheriff asked. "He maintains two companies of two hundred men at arms."

Elezar scowled. Count Radulf had been one of the first men he'd considered contacting—if only for the resources of his ancient library—up until last night when Skellan had challenged the count's servants, Rafale and Brother Bois, and thrown the count's involvement with the violet flame into question. But that wasn't anything he was about to admit to a man appointed by the count himself.

"I went to a fellow Cadeleonian first, hoping that he could vouch for me." Elezar held out his arms to better display the costume he wore. "I don't present the most respectable of appearances as I am now. Not knowing the kind of cur Commander Lecha is, I had hoped he would help to alert the right men without throwing the whole city into chaos. After meeting Commander Lecha I discovered that I was wrong and thought I should approach you, since I'd heard that the count wouldn't be back from his hunt until tomorrow."

"I hadn't heard that he was expected back at all," the sheriff replied.

"The night before last the playwright, Rafale, swore that the count would return to the city and meet with the remaining street witches at his Sun Palace tomorrow morning."

"Our Rafale told you that?"

"He said he represented the Count Radulf." Now that Elezar thought about it, it did seem strange that any count would dispatch a random thespian to do his bidding. But Rafale was known as one of Count Radulf's favorites.

Sheriff Hirbe looked deeply troubled by this news. "You're certain of this?"

"Ask the others if you don't believe me. Fon, Gullin and Ogmund were all there." Elezar glanced across the plaza, taking in the faces of the men and women gathered around who pretended not to be straining to overhear them. Unlike the rest, Cire's uncle, Ogmund, waved to Elezar.

"Ogmund!" Elezar called to the man. "You remember last night. Didn't Rafale promise the count would be back in the city tomorrow?"

The grizzled, bare-chested old man nodded and came trotting across the plaza. Elezar still found it astounding to see a how witches walked barefooted through icy mud. Ogmund held out his hand to the sheriff's gelding and the horse, seeming to know him, allowed him to draw alongside the sheriff.

"It's true and all, Master Hirbe," Ogmund said. "Our famous playwright came last night to my niece's house in the company of a Cadeleonian priest and the two of them were dressed fine with the grimma's guards attending them like lords of the realm. Rafale said plenty of pretty things to my Cire and all the company of us gathered there. He swore the count knew a way to save the sanctum, and he asked that we should gather in the Sun Palace first thing tomorrow morning. Which we are all planning to do, so have no fear."

Sheriff Hirbe didn't look any less skeptical of Ogmund's claim than he had when Elezar had answered him.

"I swear by the North Wind's bite and my badger's tail," Ogmund insisted. "It's the truth. You can ask any of us that were gathered. I remember like I was sober. Cire wasn't serving beer strong enough to addle even an infant."

"I believe you, Ogmund. I do," the sheriff assured Ogmund. He stole a sidelong glance to Elezar. "Is there an hour when this gathering of street witches is supposed to take place?"

"We'll be there by first light, you can be certain of that. We may not claim holdings or belong to any great guild, but Milmuraille is our home as much as anyone's and we'll defend it."

"Of that I have no doubt," Sheriff Hirbe commented.

Elezar wondered why the sheriff had been so dubious of the meeting with the count. Certainly in times as perilous as these even a lord as illustrious as the famed Hallen Radulf would deign to speak to street witches if they could save his capital city.

The sheriff asked, "Rafale didn't bring Lady Peome with him, did he?"

Elezar didn't know the woman but her name sounded familiar. One of ladies of Count Radulf's inner court, he thought.

"That would be the day, wouldn't it? My Cire rubbing shoulders with the noble sister-physician who raised the count's daughter," Ogmund said, laughing. "No. We were just street witches, gathered to hold our own council and have the wild one do what he could for the children—"

"The wild one?" the sheriff asked.

"Our Skellan. As born to magic as a dog is born to bark. But he'd be of no use to a cultured man like you, Sheriff. He's hardly human." Ogmund grinned as if his words weren't thoroughly insulting. "A filthy lad with the manners of a mongrel and foul—"

"I think you are confused, sir," Elezar growled despite himself. "The Skellan who attended that meeting was indeed a skilled witch, but he was also more brave and clever than anyone else in the place. And as I recall he risked his life to protect children of no relation to him at all."

"Oh yes, my mistake! He's just as his man Elezar says. Like a spring breeze, the boy is, and handsome enough to charm a savage beast with a glance." Ogmund gave a laugh and winked at the sheriff. "But still I think it would be a cultured girl like my Cire that a widowed gentleman such as yourself would rather have to his table, if he was looking for a witch's company."

The sheriff shook his head. Elezar wasn't sure if it was at him or Ogmund or perhaps the absurdity of them both.

"Thank you, Ogmund, I'll keep your Cire in mind," the sheriff said and then he added in a friendly but distinctly dismissive tone, "Please don't let me distract you from your business any longer."

Ogmund offered the sheriff a quick bow and then retreated back to his stall. In the falling darkness the sharp barbs of the eel hooks that the old witch plied glinted like rows of ragged teeth as he packed them away.

Night shadows fell from the aqueduct in long black arches and the world surrounding the plaza receded to pools of orange torchlight. Now Elezar could only glimpse Kiram when he shifted his head and light caught on the curls of his pale hair. Elezar didn't stare after him but instead tracked departing vendors as they passed beneath fish-oil lamps. Their voices and the creak of wagon wheels mixed with frog songs. From the gloom Gullin and then the white-haired cider seller wished Elezar and the sheriff a good night and they both returned the farewell. Elezar noted the luminous gold eye-shine of two goats glancing to him and offered them a wave of his hand. Then all of them disappeared into the night, taking with them the trills of their few unsold frogs.

Elezar heard the clatter of horse's hooves before he saw the rider come trotting down the wide lane toward them. It was one of the sheriff's deputies, carrying a storm lamp to light the way for himself and his mount. He picked up his speed as soon as he caught sight of the torches where Elezar, Sheriff Hirbe and the remaining deputy waited.

"And what news, Magraie?" the sheriff asked when his man drew close by his side.

The deputy looked fine-boned enough to be Haldiim, but his pale skin and dark hair made Elezar think he was of pure Labaran stock, but too young to sport a mustache. He seemed disgusted and ill but made his answer in an even tone.

"The Cradle is nearly empty, sir. The gates were unlocked and unguarded. Within the forecourt I found a drunken doorman whom I could not wake." Magraie bit his lip as if loathe to go on. "In the kennels I came upon litter of starving mastiff pups crying and found their mother chained to a wall. She looked to have been dead a day or more. The stables are worse—foul from neglect, and the horses that are still living are walking skeletons. When I ventured below I discovered men locked in the holding cells. They'd been flogged and then left down there to die. I couldn't get them out, sir. The locks were too sturdy."

"I might be able to," Elezar offered at once. "Lecha gave me the keys. I should go—"

"Yes, we'll see to them, but not just yet." Sheriff Hirbe silenced Elezar with a wave. He then looked back to his deputy, Magraie. "Go to Wisdom Temple, call upon Mother Solei and tell her what you have seen, but keep it quiet for now. Assure her that I will join her at the garrison very soon with keys and money enough to pay for her services and those of her sister-physicians."

The deputy offered Sheriff Hirbe a salute and then was off again, riding into the darkness.

"The Cradle is only a few streets away. If the keys to the jail are among the ones Lecha gave me then I could get those men out right now," Elezar protested.

"Perhaps, but we have yet to prove who you really are."

"I told you—"

"Now I wouldn't be much of a sheriff if I allowed a man to vouch for himself, would I?" The sheriff smiled indulgently at Elezar. "Fear not, I'll have my answers soon and in the meantime the sister-physicians will have brought those men food and beer as well as blankets and bandages. They will be fine."

Elezar almost demanded to know what would be done for the horses, what for the pups, but he stopped himself. A sheriff facing possible invasion of his city and some kind of sinister, creeping magic wasn't going to put the welfare of a few animals before his inquiries.

Then came the beat of more horse hooves. Elezar caught sight of another lantern, this time approaching from the west road. Silhouetted forms bounded up before the lantern, blotting its light as they raced for the plaza. Suddenly Skellan came into sight, running like a wild creature with a glossy black dog at his side. Skellan's loose red hair shone like flames and his pale bare chest gleamed with sweat. He drew to a sudden halt in the center of the plaza, ringed by torches. Elezar saw his pale eyes dart over the stripped bodies of the dead mercenaries. Then Skellan looked to the sheriff.

"I am the witch, Skellan! You summoned me, and I have come to vouch for my man, Elezar." Skellan drew the curved Haldiim hunting knife that Elezar had given him only a few days prior. Elezar tensed, wondering what on earth Skellan meant to do with the weapon. Certainly he didn't imagine he could attack the sheriff. Not only was the man mounted, but one of his deputies stood only a few feet away and another came riding up behind Skellan and Javier with a lantern.

"I am entrusted with Elezar's knife. I am his protector and I take responsibility for his actions," Skellan stated. "Your grievances against my man are mine to answer for. You will release him to me!"

This Elezar had not expected, and he felt both embarrassed and touched that Skellan, as exhausted and ragged as he was, would stand before armed men for his sake. The witch was an idiot—he shouldn't have come at all—and yet Elezar didn't think anyone had ever stood up for him like this before in his life. Heat rose across Elezar's cheeks and he felt glad for the surrounding darkness.

"A blade oath? Now that is old law," the sheriff muttered. He leaned forward, squinting at Skellan and looking amused, but then his expression went suddenly serious. "You say your name is Skellan?"

"It is." The witch drew himself up taller.

"Come closer. Let me see our Skellan a bit better," the sheriff commanded.

Skellan hesitated. Elezar thought he knew why. Skellan had been hunted by Oesir's guards. Perhaps he was wanted by the sheriff as well. If that were the case then matters were likely to get ugly and bloody very soon.

Bloody idiot, Skellan. You shouldn't have come.

Guilt as much as annoyance flared through Elezar. Skellan had come for his sake, obviously. But he, more than anyone, must have known what danger he risked making himself known to the city authorities.

Skellan slunk nearer to the sheriff, drawing to a halt just out of the man's reach. He glanced to Elezar and seemed to take some assurance in what he saw. He lifted his face to the sheriff with a defiant expression.

"How old are you, Skellan?" the sheriff asked.

"I'm a grown man of twenty-one and within my rights to lay my protection over Elezar."

"You would have been born in the year of the wolf then." The sheriff's tone was conversational, but he still kept Skellan under his unwavering scrutiny. "What of your parents?"

"My mother is the South Wind, my father is a stone; I call the cobbles my friends, and my name is my own." Skellan recited the words like they were a well-known rhyme, and the sheriff smiled broadly at him.

"Now, now, I'm not going out of my way to call you a foundling," the sheriff said. "It's only that you have such a face… You look very like a man I know."

"Perhaps he was a man my mother knew as well," Skellan said, shrugging. "I'm grown now with no need of parents any longer. I've come to vouch for my man as your deputy called me to do."

"Yes, yes, certainly," the sheriff replied. "But tell me this, what is your man's full name?"

"Elezar," Skellan replied.

"But he's Cadeleonian and they are always twice named. Such a quick-witted witch as you should know as much. Cadeleonians bind their bloodlines by name just as Labaran nobles do."

As Elezar saw uncertainty break across Skellan's expression, guilt flared through him for all he'd withheld. But he would have been a fool to confess the truth to some street witch whom he hardly knew. Though the fact that Skellan had come to face-down the sheriff and his deputies for Elezar's sake made him wish that he'd admitted his true identity when they'd lain so close that morning.

"He is a foundling, too, abandoned to a quiet death in the winter snow and taken in by chance to serve the house of a lord," Skellan replied. Elezar felt certain that the history must have been Skellan's own—one he imagined that Elezar shared with him. "He was brought up in service of the duke of Rauma but the duke's name is not his to claim."

"Fairly answered. But perhaps the duke will have something more to say on the subject," the sheriff responded. Elezar frowned at the older man. It was his obligation as sheriff to find out what he could, but did he have to go as far as he could to prove Elezar a liar in front of Skellan?

Then Elezar heard the distinct noise of an approaching carriage and a feeling of dread gripped him. The sheriff had sent out two of his deputies right away. One had brought back Skellan to vouch for him because he claimed to be a witch's man. That could only mean that Atreau would soon appear.

Indeed, he arrived forthwith in an ornate gold carriage, drawn by four white stallions and attended by two neatly groomed footmen. The carriage hardly pulled to a halt before Atreau leapt out, swathed in green silk and black sable. Elezar only caught a glimpse of the two startled pages whom Atreau abandoned to the luxurious confines of the carriage.

"Ah, speak his name and he will appear," the sheriff murmured. He bowed from his seat in the saddle. "Lord Quemanor, I presume. I do beg you to forgive my intrusion upon your evening, my lord."

"You have my varlet, Elezar," Atreau called, but then he went mute as he took in the corpses laying at his feet. He looked to Elezar directly and Elezar understood at a glance how afraid he was. This fate could have been his own had the mercenaries found him instead of Elezar. But Atreau recovered quickly as he always did.

"I would thank you to turn my varlet over to me at once," Atreau told the sheriff.

"I'm hoping for that as well, my lord," Sheriff Hirbe responded. "But I do need to know who this man truly is—"

"I told you already!" Skellan called out, and Atreau seemed to take note of him for the first time. Seeing the witch, Atreau appeared oddly unwilling to look away from him. Elezar suddenly recalled Atreau kissing Skellan and felt the scowl deepening on his own face. Now was not the time for Atreau to stand around ogling Skellan. No time would be.

Next to Elezar, the sheriff nodded.

"How observant the duke is," Sheriff Hirbe whispered. He glanced to Elezar with an expression close to camaraderie, but then frowned a little. "But still he doesn't realize, neither of you do, do you?"

"Realize what?" Elezar asked.

"The resemblance," Sheriff Hirbe replied. Then he raised his voice to Atreau. "I need the man's full name, Lord Quemanor. I need to be told his true name and rank."

"Why?" Atreau demanded, drawing himself up straight and imperious. "What business is it of a petty sheriff in a far-flung protectorate like Milmuraille? On what grounds do you even claim the right to question a man of my standing?"

"On the grounds that I am the law here in this far-flung county, my lord," the sheriff replied. Elezar didn't know if he liked the old man, but he had to admire his calm temperament. "Is it so hard to tell me what I already suspect? Am I looking at a scarlet bull upon a blue field?"

Elezar didn't gape at the sheriff, but he felt that he should have. Atreau went wide-eyed, while Skellan scowled between the three of them as if he'd missed a private joke. He even glanced questioningly to Javier, who stood at his side in the form of a black dog. For his part Javier seemed to be paying them all only half attention. He gazed into the dark where Elezar knew Kiram stood watching them.

"If you know that then why do you need me to tell you?" Atreau demanded of the sheriff.

"Because I cannot entrust a high duty to a man who is not named before me in full truth and that man must be vouched for by another of equal or better standing."

Elezar understood all at once. This had become more than just a matter of picking apart a mystery. If Sheriff Hirbe was going to entrust Elezar with command of the garrison and its payroll, he had to know that he was turning a royal Cadeleonian garrison over to a Cadeleonian and one of rank.

"Tell him," Elezar said.

Skellan demanded, "Tell him what? What is there to tell?"

"He is Elezar Grunito, Baron of Navine, Count of Idara and heir to the earldom of Anacleto." Atreau announced Elezar's minor titles like they represented vast kingdoms and not sea cliffs and wilderness, though from the point of view of deputies, fishmongers and witches, perhaps that might constitute a kingdom.

Skellan made an strange, garbled sound as if he were swallowing back some cry of disbelief and for just an instant he eyed Elezar as if he were mad but he said nothing.

Atreau went to Elezar and in the sight of Sheriff Hirbe he returned Elezar's signet ring to him. The gold band felt cold but it fit Elezar's finger perfectly. It was nearly too dark to pick out details, but Elezar's memory let him see the crest, a red jasper bull rearing up against an inlay of bright blue lapis lazuli.

Elezar looked to the sheriff and wondered just how he'd known exactly who he was. Had it been the contents of the letter or something more obvious in Elezar's own demeanor?

"When did you know?" Elezar asked the sheriff.

"As soon as I got a good look at you, though the beard nearly did fool me. You look older than you did before, but then that follows with the passing of years."

"We've met before?" If they had, Elezar couldn't remember when.

"In a manner of speaking." Sheriff Hirbe grinned at Elezar's curious expression and went on, "Being a Cadeleonian, you may think this is only a coincidence or the foolish fancy of an old man, but you, Lord Grunito, and I have been walking the same vei for some time now. Three years ago I visited Cieloalta for the first time in my life. I went with a warrant for the arrest of a murderer named Degaro Elota. I had little hope that the Cadeleonian court would turn him over to me. They protect their own, and I had learned that he was a nobleman. And indeed no judge would recognize my claim upon the man. But I couldn't give up because the girl he killed was my granddaughter, Poisette. Only fourteen years old..." The sheriff paused to draw in a slow breath. His eyes glistened in the lamplight. "I thought that if I could not bring him to justice any other way I would murder him with my own hands. But then like an answer to my prayers a young swordsman challenged Elota to a duel and cut him down like chattel And do you know what he said when he called that murderer out?"

Elezar did. At the time, Elota had been only the second of his brother's attackers whom he'd tracked down and challenged. He hadn't yet grown used to killing and when he'd faced Elota, the duel had drawn a huge crowd of nobles and commoners alike. They had gathered to cheer, hoot, wager and above all to see blood spilled. Elezar had not disappointed them, though they had very much disappointed him. He never would have imagined that anyone in that mob could have understood why he stood before them, intent upon taking another man's life.

"You said 'I have come to deliver justice for those who cannot take it for themselves,' and even if you didn't know it, that day you were my Poisette's champion. I never had a chance to thank you until now." The sheriff offered Elezar a warm smile.

"It seems strange to accept thanks for a killing."

"But not for justice," Sheriff Hirbe replied. "At one time or another we are all thankful for justice."

Elezar couldn't keep himself from stealing a glance back to Skellan. He stood very still and despite being a witch, Elezar thought he saw him shiver. He wore nearly nothing, owned nearly nothing, and couldn't even claim a mother's name much less a father's. Among Cadeleonian nobles such a man was a joke at best and a crude offense at worse. What he thought or felt shouldn't have mattered. Yet meeting his stunned gaze, Elezar understood that he'd hurt Skellan's pride, and probably crushed that tentative bond that had seemed to be growing between them. Skellan turned away and scowled down at the hunting knife in his hands as if he wanted to hurl it into the mud.

"Will you swear on your name and honor to fulfill the duties of Commander of the Milmuraille Garrison, Lord Grunito?" Sheriff Hirbe asked. Elezar looked back to him at once.

"I will." Elezar accepted the responsibility automatically, as he'd been brought up to do, from his earliest days.

"Then we do indeed share the same vei, Lord Commander Grunito," Sheriff Hirbe stated. "And with that in mind, I would like to accompany you to your garrison and offer you my full support."

CHAPTER TWENTY-TWO

Skellan brushed against a garrison wall as he hurried toward the dark structure of the stable, hauling yet another bale of hay from the supply cart that stood in the center of the courtyard. All across the vast grounds, torches blazed from sconces and storm lanterns threw wild shadows out from the dozens of busy figures. Deputies and grooms from Sheriff Hirbe's house bustled between clusters of red-robed sister-physicians—all of them unloading goods, from bedding to fodder to bandages. Cool night winds played through the courtyard, moaning and whispering like lost spirits. The air smelled strange to Skellan. He drew in a breath and tasted the pungent herbal steam pumping up from the infirmary chimney in the main building.

But above all else he sensed how barren of magic the air moving through his lungs felt. No sting or sweet snap of even the most minor ward. Only the faintest gleam of dull gold seemed to glint from the small Cadeleonian chapel and that might as well have been a trick of starlight reflecting across the steeple.

The surrounding barracks stood empty and dark, but across the yard the armory shone with torches and Skellan recognized Kiram's distinct silhouette passing between the black masses of the garrison cannons.

One of the newly freed garrison soldiers stumbled past Skellan, cursing the darkness as he steadied sloshing water pails in his hands. Skellan stepped aside. The night was not so dark for him—not with the blaze of Zi'sai's violet witchflame shining over the sanctum like a second moon. Only the faintest wisp of Oesir's green witchflame burned from within the purple heart now. Skellan gazed warily up at those hungry, searching ribbons of light.

His bare skin itched and pricked where the bale of hay rubbed against his back and shoulder, reminding him of his immediate concerns. Skellan lugged his load to the oaken doors of the massive stable.

More than anything else, the state of the stable made Skellan realize that though the garrison had only been completely abandoned today, it had suffered from weeks, perhaps months of neglect. When Elezar had first dragged open the doors a rank stench of horseshit, infected wounds and decomposing flesh had poured out. The starved animals inside neighed and cried piteously as torchlight fell over them. Several had been too weak to stand, and two foals lay dead and rotting.

One rawboned gray stallion had bared his teeth and screeched like he was half mad when the deputies drew close to him.

Somehow Elezar had managed to settle the creature with soft words and a relaxed approach. At last, the big stallion had accepted grain from Elezar and allowed him to lead him out of the filthy stall. Over the last two hours they had mucked the stable and summoned grooms to care for the horses. Now the stable stood decently clean, well-lit and bustling with activity.

As Skellan trudged inside, he glimpsed Elezar kneeling beside that gaunt gray stallion to tend the festering wound on the animal's leg. The duke of Rauma and Sheriff Hirbe looked on. The duke appeared to be near tears at the pitiful sight of the animal, and he stroked its jaw and neck to distract it. The sheriff stood farther back and appeared indifferent to the mount, but he watched Elezar closely. Perhaps he'd realized, as Skellan had, that regardless of darkness, exhaustion or hunger, Elezar would not rest until the garrison soldiers, horses and dogs had been seen to.

Only briefly had Elezar even spared Skellan a word and that had only been to tell him that he looked half dead and ought to get himself back to his bed at the Rat Rafters. In response Skellan had reminded him that he no longer had a bed at the Rat Rafters.

"Merle and Navet are stowing all our belongings at the Fairwind. They agreed to put Eski up for the night as well, but that's all the room they can spare," Skellan had told Elezar.

He'd taken the information with a scowl and started to say something more to Skellan but then had been called away by a haggard, bruised garrison soldier, who had begged him to find and free his daughter whom he knew Commander Lecha had locked away in a storeroom.

Elezar had rushed off at once, and when he'd found that none of his keys unlocked the store room, he'd simply kicked the door down and carried the unconscious, dark-haired girl out in his arms. Sister-physicians had taken her delicate, shuddering body from Elezar and promised to tend her. After that the entire garrison needed to be searched for further unknown people imprisoned and abandoned by Commander Lecha. Two men nearly dead of exposure were soon discovered shackled in stocks behind the latrine. Another room held the bloated corpses of three little girls. Grotesque burns inflicted by Zi'sai covered their naked bodies.

Then a lantern left burning in the dry storage sparked a small fire. Elezar rallied those garrison men who were strong and sober enough to douse it.

That had been at least three hours ago; since then Elezar had been constantly in demand. Skellan had found little he could contribute aside from the strength to haul bales of dry hay into the stables.

"This is the last of it," Skellan called.

One of Sheriff Hirbe's wiry grooms waved Skellan over to the clean stall. "Throw it into the manger there, will you?"

Skellan did as he was told. Beside him a beaten, emaciated Cadeleonian soldier emptied water pails into a trough. The man looked ragged as a beggar, though the insignia of a captain still decorated the jacket of his filthy uniform.

"Your mare will be pleased now, I think," the groom told the soldier and he led the bony, frail horse into the stall. She knew the soldier and greeted him with a nicker. As she drank greedily from the trough, the Cadeleonian soldier stroked her scabbed, mangy shoulder and leaned his gaunt face against her neck. Skellan thought the man might have been weeping.

He withdrew from the stall and the groom followed him.

"She's still got good teeth and feet. She'll pull through." The groom brushed his bushy mustache from the corner of his lips. No doubt the man normally used wax but he and his fellow grooms had been called to the garrison well past the hours they would have expected to be presentable. "All we can do now is wait, I suppose."

Skellan nodded. But there was nothing for him to wait for here so he wandered from the stable. As he walked out he caught both the sheriff and the duke watching him, but Elezar didn't look his way once.

Outside violet light streaked the sky like the fire of an endless sunset. Skellan noticed one of the duke's page boys trailing a pretty, plump sister-physician and scribbling down the names of medicines and supplies needed in the infirmary. Both of them disappeared into the two-story main building. Shafts of yellow lamplight shot through the narrow slot windows of the armory. Kiram would still be inside taking inventory for Elezar. Skellan had liked the Haldiim well enough that he wouldn't have minded spending a little more time in his company, but numbers weren't Skellan's strong suit and he imagined his own counting would only interrupt Kiram's.

A cold wind drifted over Skellan's bare shoulders and reflexively he reached back to draw his cloak close. But he wasn't the one wearing it at the moment. He thought Javier might still be in the kitchen with the mastiff pups but then he noticed a canine silhouette standing in the armory near Kiram. Skellan thought the dog watched him in return but then both he and Kiram moved away from the window.

Skellan wandered to the kitchen steps at the back of the main building, where both the infirmary and mess halls stood. He knew he should go inside and claim the shelter of the building and the warmth of the kitchen fires, but he didn't trust all this lifeless, cold rock that stood before him like a tomb.

The unknown stones felt like a trap that he didn't possess the resources to escape. He'd been in better condition when he'd been only eleven and fleeing from Oesir. At least then he could call upon his witchflame and wrap himself in his cloak. Now only an uneasy awareness of how worn and weak he was coiled around him.

He was vulnerable and surrounded by strangers without even a familiar cobble to help warm his bare skin. So instead of entering, he crouched down on the steps, in the shadow of the towering main building.

He ran his fingers over the cold rock and curled his toes against the flagstones at the foot of the steps. No witch before him had touched the stones beneath his hands or those under his feet. The rock felt frigid and desolate. If it hadn't been for the violet flame Skellan would have reached down into the stone and lit it with his own witchflame. He would have made the cobbles beneath his feet feel warm and welcoming and would have given sheltering names to the great slabs of granite that formed the garrison walls. Had he been strong and free to work his will he could have even pulled the wild, whispering wind and down to clothe it in the rock the way he'd enfolded Javier in a hound's flesh—binding the elements, be they wethra-steeds or trolls to serve him.

Skellan didn't think that he would have done so, not knowing Bone-crusher as he did. No, even if he hadn't been worn and shuddering, even if he stood at the height of a sanctum in full command of the earth, water and wind surrounding him he would not enslave those free spirits or lock them away in the stones of his domain.

Normally Skellan felt proud of himself when such a thought came to him, but tonight he wondered if his resolve wasn't more a sign of tender-hearted weakness. All grimma made slaves of men and spirits alike. He felt suddenly childishly naïve, crouching here on dead, cold rock and trying to convince himself that he could somehow defend a sanctum without trolls or beasts to call upon.

He was just tired, he told himself. He'd overextended himself transforming Javier and holding off Zi'sai, and now exhaustion dragged his mood down like a black undertow. It wasn't like him to feel so disheartened. He looked for some distraction and dug the battered topaz pebbles from the coin purse at his belt.

Nothing, they each told him. Again Skellan noticed that the absence that was cut into the topaz was not the same as the lifeless, cold rock beneath his legs. The granite of the surrounding steps and buildings felt unremarkable but was easy enough to see and feel. The topaz, however, faded out of his awareness. He could know that he was looking at them and yet still not really see them.

Without the multitude of tiny wards, blessings and charms that littered the rest of the city humming through his senses, Skellan recognized just how very magical the emptiness contained within each of these stones was. They were like shards of invisibility and silence. They amounted to nothing, but only through an immense exertion of magic.

Vast magic amounting to nothing, Skellan thought dourly. Much like me.

Skellan scowled back at the stable. He remembered how comfortable Elezar had looked in the duke's company, and then wondered what confidences the duke and sheriff and Elezar were sharing. He thought he caught the sound of laughter, but the wind carried it away.

Skellan bowed his head. How proud he'd felt when he'd raced across the city and held up the knife to claim protection over Elezar. What an idiot he must have seemed: a scrawny, mud-spattered street witch crowing like an underweight cockerel that Elezar was his man. No wonder Elezar had looked so pained at the sight of him and no wonder that Sheriff Hirbe had at first stared as if unable to believe the absurdity before his eyes, and then smiled like he could hardly keep from laughing in Skellan's face.

It wasn't as though Elezar had even known what it meant when he'd given Skellan his hunting knife. Elezar probably had hundreds of knives. Certainly he possessed many more powerful and important friends to speak for him before Sheriff Hirbe. Elezar was himself an important and powerful man, wasn't he? He commanded more lordly titles than Count Radulf himself. Baron, count and even earl, Skellan remembered the duke saying as he named Elezar, or more rightly, Lord Grunito.

Skellan smirked at himself. He too possessed a secret name, but where Elezar's conferred wealth, importance and power, Skellan's own was worthless. To think he'd considered confiding it to Elezar this morning as if he were contemplating sharing a treasure. Skellan almost laughed at the pathetic comparison that would have presented to Elezar. How absurd and stupid he must have seemed to the Cadeleonian nobleman, as he pointed out all the ragged details of "his" city.

Elezar had probably been snickering at him silently half the time they'd been together. The other half—well, it wasn't as if a Cadeleonian nobleman was going to brag about bedding a creature like Skellan—Elezar probably would have rather forgotten or at least kept his peers from ever suspecting.

There Skellan had been telling him that he would look after him and that they shared a fate, and all the while Elezar already possessed all the resources of a lord and kept the confidences of Prince Sevanyo. Among such men what could Skellan be to Elezar but an embarrassment?

Skellan felt suddenly humiliated and sick with himself. He glanced down at the hunting knife that he'd carried with such pride and then furiously unworked it and its sheath from his knife belt. He lifted it to hurl it from him but then stopped himself. It wasn't his to throw away. He set it down on the stone step and glared out at the empty grounds.

If he possessed even a shred of dignity he'd leave this place. He'd slink back into the streets and try to pretend that he'd never even met Lord Grunito, much less convinced himself that the man was part of his vei. If anything, he felt like a cobble that Elezar had been fated to step across on his journey from the Sumar grimma to the company of Labaran courtiers and Cadeleonian dukes, where he took rightful command of a huge garrison.

Skellan's line of thought broke as he heard someone call his name questioningly. He glanced out to the carriage house where the second, more boyish of the duke's pages stood with a bundle in his arms. The youth scanned the grounds with wide, unseeing eyes, looking past Skellan twice before finding his way through the darkness into the armory.

Skellan wondered if he ought to go to the youth, but then realized that Javier and Kiram were there in the armory. Between them they probably knew as much about magic as Skellan and that would be the only reason anyone here would bother to call for him. But soon Kiram and Javier appeared in the doorway. Kiram held the bundle that the page had carried earlier as well as a bright-burning lantern. He scanned the grounds with a narrow gaze. Instinctively, Skellan hunched deeper into the shadows. It wasn't that he feared Kiram or Javier, only that he'd kept himself in hiding too many years to stop the reflex. Javier, in the black hound's body raised his head, drew in a breath and then trotted out immediately towards Skellan. Kiram followed him. At last catching sight of Skellan, Kiram frowned at him curiously.

"Whatever are you doing out here in the cold?" Kiram asked.

A number of answers came to Skellan's mind, but they all amounted to much the same thing in truth.

"Moping, I think," Skellan replied.

"Really?" Kiram looked a little surprised at the response and then asked, "Would it be too impertinent of me to ask why?"

"Because none of this is how I imagined I'd be spending the night." Skellan gazed down at his bare arms, taking in the mud that flecked his pale skin. "I thought Elezar was someone he isn't, someone more like me."

Javier moved closer to Skellan, mounting the steps and then settling down to Skellan's left. His body blocked the worst of the cold wind.

"Cadeleonian titles can sound intimidating," Kiram replied. "But the truth is that if you know a man, he is who he is regardless of accolades or signets."

Easy for Kiram to say, Skellan thought. Kiram shared his life with a landless, wandering Bahiim, not a man who obviously owned great tracks of property and was in the confidences of princes. Still, he did have a point and Skellan didn't think that Elezar had altered as a man just because he was suddenly revealed to be a nobleman. The fact that he protected the hounds and horses of this garrison as well as the men proved that.

"I know Elezar hasn't changed," Skellan replied. He was only half sure of why he was telling so much to these two, except he had no one else to confide in and he wanted to be talked away from the unhappy direction of his own thoughts. And yet they persisted like certainties even now. "But a title means an obligation, doesn't it? It means that he has a place within the Cadeleonian court and duties to his king. He isn't someone who could just go…"

Or stay here, Skellan thought but he couldn't bring himself to say that aloud. He remembered Elezar's hesitance after their morning together.

"I thought I knew his vei. I thought we…" Skellan shut his mouth before he went on and made more of a fool of himself. He shook his head at the sad sympathetic look Kiram offered him and forced a hard smile. "I'm just having a sulk. You shouldn't take it seriously. I'm glad for him, really. He's got a bright future ahead of him when he gets back home. I mean, if any of us get through this mess with the Zi'sai and the grimma."

"Well, perhaps this can help there. Atreau wanted you to see it." Kiram held out the bundle of expensive brocade cloth.

"Atreau?" Skellan asked. He remembered Kiram mentioning an Atreau before and Elezar too had spoken of the man.

"No." Kiram looked a little annoyed but not with Skellan. "I'm tired and misspoke. I meant Fedeles, the duke of Rauma. One of his pages went to a great deal of trouble to procure this for you. Apparently, you asked for it the last time you and the duke spoke?"

Skellan cautiously unwrapped the bundle. The brocade fell back to reveal a small golden coffer. Skellan recognized it at once and nearly dropped it in his horror. His heart pounded in his chest. The last time he'd seen this coffer, the violet flame had leapt from it to consume Oesir.

"The page said that the priests in the chapel were creating reproductions of this and late yesterday they sent them all to the Sun Palace." Kiram lifted his hand to shield his eyes from the yellow lantern light. "What is it, do you know?"

Skellan couldn't make himself respond, or even move. All he could remember was the violet flame rushing up.

Kiram stepped closer holding the lantern up over the coffer. At his side, Javier cocked his head to regard the coffer as well. The light reflected off the coffer as if dancing across the surface of a brass mirror.

"It's empty," Kiram commented offhandedly, "but I noticed when I opened it that there are two very small moving pieces on each of the four walls. I suspect that they're false doors."

Empty, Skellan thought. Relief swept through him, though he tried not to let it show.

Of course it was empty. Zi'sai's witchflame had already escaped. Taking in the battered state of the coffer, he felt certain that this was the original that had fallen from Oesir's hands. Most of the delicate Cadeleonian stars had broken away to expose the much more ancient Mirogoth symbols beneath, which formed spells of summoning and binding.

"You see, just below the lip of the lid there's a catch of some kind." Kiram reached out and, flipping the lid back, ran his finger across the lip of the coffer. Skellan felt a tiny click pass through the coffer. A sheet of beaten gold sprang up over the symbols, like an actor popping up from the trap door of a stage.

Kiram gave the coffer a fond look and then went on, "There's another set of catches and springs on the underside of the box, which seem to retract the false walls back into the base. The mechanisms look very old and haven't been cleaned in ages. But I imagine that when they were first made they moved well. It's beautifully crafted."

Skellan stared at the false wall that now hid the old Mirogoth spells. A single symbol decorated the surface, declaring it nothing. Despite the fact that he held the coffer in his hands, Skellan sensed his awareness of it dimming. If all four of those little golden walls had been sprung the coffer would have been nearly invisible to him.

"It's a trap," Skellan said. "A trap to lure the demon lord's soul inside and then lock it away from his body."

"Really?" Kiram's expression brightened. "Isn't that exactly what we need right now?"

"It could be," Skellan agreed, but a sick, sinking feeling twisted through his gut. "But a trap has to be baited." He turned the coffer around in his hands. The spells etched over it were very old and the droplets of solder used to adhere the Cadeleonian stars to the lid had deformed several of them. Even so, Skellan could feel much of the spells' purposes just running his fingers over them. They stung and nipped at his skin. "Did the duke's page say how many copies had been sent to the Sun Palace?"

"Two dozen, I think," Kiram replied. He glanced to Javier and the glossy black dog nodded. "So, does this help?"

"It could," Skellan said. "But I need a little time to work this old conjuring out exactly."

Kiram's gaze moved over the glinting etched letters, and Skellan suspected that he was attempting to read them. He scowled in slight annoyance and then nodded.

"I have an armory inventory to report to Elezar, but if you need me for anything just call on me." Kiram started to turn but then paused. "If you aren't going to venture inside, should I leave the lantern with you for light at least?"

Skellan appreciated the consideration but shook his head. "Thanks, but I won't need it."

"I suppose you're like Javier, able to see the light of every spark of magic surrounding us?" Kiram glanced up at the sky. "Is it bright and beautiful up there or just terrible?"

"A little of both," Skellan admitted. "There's a blazing violet sunset overhead. It would be a lovely enough sight if it weren't destroying the whole of my city."

Kiram frowned at stars that Skellan could not see through waves of violet light. Then he glanced down to Javier.

"Staying to study the coffer as well?" Kiram inquired.

The hound nodded.

"All right, but please don't get into any more trouble. Today's been… too long already." Kiram gazed down at him and the hard light of the lantern carved deep lines in his face, making him look worn. "I still can't believe that you've gotten yourself turned into… this." He reached out and very gently stroked Javier's jaw and brow then shook his head. He said, "You're an idiot, and sometimes I don't know why I married you."

Javier's responding expression was at once lewd and arrogant, or at least that was how Skellan interpreted the dog's toothy smirk and cocked brow. Kiram gave a tired laugh and kissed Javier's forehead. Then he left them.

Skellan couldn't imagine any lover he'd ever taken accepting the same situation so well. Javier seemed to expect as much of Kiram, so perhaps they'd been through worse together.

Here on his own, Skellan felt a little jealous and deeply lonely by comparison.

He sank back down to the steps and continued to study the coffer. Running his fingers over the spells, he felt as much as read the malevolence of their meanings. Words slithered and hissed through him—bind, bleed, crush and imprison—and all of them intent upon the Demon Lord Zi'sai.

I was the last of the demon lords and my reign came after the deaths of Saviors and Old Gods alike. I was not defeated in battle, but by betrayal.

Skellan remembered the quote from Rafale's play. Skellan wondered if Rafale had discovered the gold coffer that imprisoned the demon lord's soul while researching his play or if he had been unable to resist penning the drama after someone—Sacrist Bois, most likely—discovered the artifact hidden beneath the remains of a Cadeleonian chapel.

Costumed as the demon lord, Rafale had certainly looked far more handsome and human than the flames that now scorched the sky overhead. The demon lord's true flesh doubtless had been even more horrifying, though flesh and bone at least could be injured—killed. But the demon lord's soul—his magnificent, oppressive witchflame—was no doubt bound to the world by some fine thread of connection to Zi'sai's body. A body that lay trapped and undying beneath the Labaran sanctum. Otherwise the soul would have passed into the next life.

Skellan glanced down into the coffer and for the first time noticed the spell written there. An enticement. The promise to feed upon the witch holding the coffer and calling out to the demon lord.

A shudder passed through Skellan and he closed the coffer, quickly, and set it down on the step.

Javier crouched beside him and Skellan reached out to place a hand on his shoulder. As he had with Bone-crusher, Skellan felt a low voice rising from Javier.

What was it you saw?

"The bait for this trap, it's meant to be the witch who holds the coffer and reads the summoning spell that calls Zi'sai."

Javier cocked his head, studying the coffer, then extended a paw and touched the side of the coffer. He drew back right away.

I see. The open coffer offers a sacrifice while the secret panels hide the binding spells that are meant to trap the demon lord's soul once he takes the bait. Clever, though I wouldn't want to be the witch who called the demon to feed upon him.

"It won't just be one witch." Skellan realized this all at once. "At least twenty-four. That's what Rafale and Bois want all us street witches to do for them. 'Come to the Sun Palace and recite an incantation,' that's what they said. They mean it to be a mass sacrifice."

Fury welled through Skellan. They'd presented it as if it would be salvation for Skellan and his friends. Rafale had smiled at Cire and made it sound as if coming to the Sun Palace would assure her a position in court, all the time knowing that this would be her death—hers and every other witch who came to serve Count Radulf in the morning.

"It won't even work," Skellan realized. "Not only will Zi'sai remember these coffers but now that he has possession of an entire sanctum he'll be able to rip these spells apart. He might have to draw upon every ward in the sanctum but he'll still be able to tear free of a coffer like this one as easily as you could burn through the cloak I've wrapped around you."

Those witches will die for nothing, then.

Javier sighed and Skellan didn't know if that was the man's nature or the dog's.

"I have to warn them." Skellan started up to his feet only to sink back down. "None of them will believe me, though."

Even if he could run down every street witch in the city, most wouldn't want to hear him out. The night of the meeting they'd scoffed at his suspicions, and he didn't think a day spent dreaming of all the rewards their services might garner would make any of them too keen to hear his further belligerent ramblings. There was too much allure to the idea of a personal audience with Count Radulf, too many hopes of gold and titles, of respect and resplendent tables. Even if he warned them, most would go.

Skellan remembered his dream of a violet flame consuming the city of Milmuraille. He'd seen his friends burning and been helpless to save them. The anger in him churned, but he had nothing to vent it against, except his own powerlessness.

Skellan glowered at the coffer. It was a heartless, conniving monster that gave a thing like this to an unknowing innocent...

But it had to be the bravest soul that Skellan could imagine who, knowing its purpose and the price, accepted it.

Once, long ago, someone had been that brave—not a famous grimma, nor a lord whose name had been remembered through the ages. The witch who had sacrificed everything and defeated Zi'sai had not been of enough importance to name in any ancient lore. The whole world likely owed its survival to a nobody.

Skellan ran his thumb over the symbol of nothingness and thought of all the anonymous wards, spells and spirits that were bound to the sanctum. He thought of his own unimportance among all these aristocrats, warriors and scholars. When princes died nations suffered, but who suffered at the demise of a vagabond using a borrowed name?

No one.

The direction of his own thoughts frightened Skellan and yet he couldn't stop them. Worse, he felt them fill him with an absolute truth. He could have cast stones and they would have all fallen in a circle around this little golden coffer. This was his vei, he realized with a terrible certainty. He had met Elezar and had been brought to this place to have this coffer placed in his hands for a reason—for a purpose that was greater than anything he could have ever imagined.

If he'd known—even suspected—for even an instant before now, he felt sure that he would have done anything to escape this fate. But now he simply held the knowledge the way he might have clutched his hand over an open wound, and waited to come to grips with the pain of it.

His hands trembled and his throat felt almost too tight for breath.

He'd been willing to die in battle against Oesir, so why was he so afraid now? Skellan knew the answer even as he wondered. Against Oesir he'd held the hope of winning the sanctum and claiming everything he could want. Pitting himself against the violet flame he could only hope that his death would come at an equal cost to the demon lord. Only an idiot would sacrifice his life for nothing.

Skellan lifted his gaze to the burning sky and remembered the horror of his dream. Sammi and Sarl shrieking as they burned, Navet and Merle torn apart, Cire engulfed, and Elezar lying defeated and dead before him. And in the end he'd perished as well, helpless and useless.

"If you had to die," Skellan asked, "wouldn't you want it to be for something? Or at least for someone?"

Javier's ears pricked up but Skellan took little note. He was too deep in his own thoughts.

He'd promised Bone-crusher that he would set him free... But what if he could release every spirit bound to the sanctum? What if he could use Zi'sai's ravenous hunger to shatter the very incantations that locked so many ancient creatures into the stones of the sanctum? Even those scattered across the city. Among the bodies trapped in stone lay Zi'sai's native flesh—a mortal body.

And if one witch with a little golden coffer had defeated him before, Skellan could do it again now. He only needed to accept that this was his vei and follow the path of his life to its end.

Only after he slipped back out from the grounds of the Fairwind Stables, dog collar in hand, did Skellan notice that Javier had followed him from the garrison. The sleek black hound prowled across the street and then trotted at Skellan's side as he made his way toward the black granite walls of the sanctum.

This close the violet flame rolled across the night sky like an immense oil fire spreading across dark water. To Skellan's eyes the streets seem brilliantly lit but the purple-blue cast of the light turned the warm colors of the cobblestones murky and lent the guards of the city's night watch the deathly pallor of hanged men. Skellan dodged past them as they peered and squinted down dark streets, making their rounds through the half-abandoned city.

When he and Javier neared the Brewers' Guildhouse building, Skellan drew to a halt.

"You shouldn't come much further," Skellan said. "Even with my cloak shielding your presence, the demon lord may sense you if you are so close to the sanctum."

Elezar asked me to look after you.

Skellan hadn't expected that to be the reason for the Bahiim's interest. He felt touched but then he put Elezar out of his thoughts. He already felt too anxious about the prospect of challenging the Demon Lord Zi'sai. Allowing himself to think of anything or anyone else at this point would only weaken his resolve.

"Well, then look after me then." Skellan scowled at Javier. "But don't follow after me. I'm not a babe in need of a coddling nanny."

Javier didn't appear particularly convinced.

I assure you, I'm no sort of nanny at all, witchling. But Elezar asked and you've made me curious. What exactly is it you hope to accomplish with that battered coffer and a dog collar?

"I'm going to use the Zi'sai's own avarice to break the spells of the sanctum. When that happens, all those held captive will be freed. That includes the demon lord's original body. The violet flame of his soul will be drawn back from this blaze overhead." Skellan flicked only his forefinger up at the streaked, glowing sky. The way those long coils of purple light lashed and curled above him made Skellan feel unreasonably furtive. He lowered his voice. "He'll be forced to recede into his mortal flesh and then I'll have a chance of destroying him."

Of course, how very simple. Irony sounded through Javier's words and it exasperated Skellan.

"I may not be a lord or a duke or even a scholar like your handsome man, but I promise you that there is no one who knows that sanctum better than I do." This time Skellan gestured openly at the towering black walls and their halo of violet fire. "Demon lord or not, I will destroy that fucker. Even if it kills me, I will not let him have my city!" Skellan hissed the last in an annoyed whisper.

Do you even know what the demon lord's mortal form is? Javier cocked his head and contemplated Skellan with large dark eyes.

Skellan thought back on his dream: the immense serpent encircling a tower in its fiery coils, those huge jaws gaping wide enough to swallow him whole and the roaring flames that poured forth from the black chasm of its throat. His palms felt damp and his guts tightened. He made a show a shrugging but the motion felt stiff.

"I do, as a matter of fact." He met Javier's gaze. "I also know how this whole city and everyone in it will die if he isn't destroyed. It's my vei to choose between facing one or the other, and I've chosen. Simple as that."

Simple as throwing a dog collar around the demon lord's neck and teaching him to fetch? Is that what you're thinking?

"No, this is for me," Skellan replied.

He glanced down to the collar he'd brought from the Fair-wind. It was the handsome one that Elezar had given him when he'd still had a place for Skellan, if only as a hunting hound. That obviously was not the way of things and just as well, but the collar still had a use.

Skellan had stripped the frail little charms and blessings from it and snapped them apart. He hid away those copper and tin shards of the broken charms in the gold coffer.

Then, using the wires, he adorned the collar with eight of the nine dull topaz pebbles he'd collected. Each of them was etched with the null symbol.

Skellan turned the one remaining loose topaz through his fingers, feeling the almost negligible scratches in the surface of the stone. For the first time, he sensed beyond the shell of rock to the immense emptiness coiled at the heart of the smooth pebble. Something deathly cold and utterly dark brushed through Skellan's mind, and he nearly hurled the stone from him. But then the awareness was gone.

Skellan pocketed the stone away into his coin purse.

He guessed that there was a good reason that these stones had been erased from history. Probably for the same reason that the spells summoning demon lords and calling down the fires of stars had been banished. Despite their danger, there would always be someone—like himself—desperate enough to unleash them.

Something foul? Javier asked.

"Nothing beyond me," Skellan replied. He glanced back to Javier. "Listen, when the sanctum breaks, every cloud imp and frogwife in the city will be unleashed. I think Elezar and the sheriff might have need of you then."

As a lapdog?

Skellan smiled at that.

"By then Zi'sai will be occupied with me and you should be able to tear yourself free and fight as a Bahiim… If you can, leave a little of my cloak, will you?"

Skellan didn't know why he bothered to ask. He wasn't likely to make it back from the sanctum to collect what shreds would remain.

I'll take what care I can with your coat.

Skellan nodded. Then he lifted the collar and buckled it around his neck. He ran his fingers over the stones, as if he were brushing the fur of a sleeping cat and felt the faintest shiver of something trying to wake. But locked away in the confines of the dull topaz the spells of nothingness conferred only a quiet kind of invisibility.

Javier swung his head about, searching the street, though Skellan still stood at his side. Skellan needed no other evidence that the collar worked as he'd hoped it would, at least for now. Who knew what would happen once he entered the sanctum?

"Here we must part ways," he told Javier.

Javier turned at the sound of Skellan's voice, but Skellan had already moved. He sprinted down the winding street, racing beneath oppressive waves of cold violet light to reach the east wall of the sanctum.

He clambered up Bone-crusher's cold stone form, finding finger grips and toeholds with the sureness of recognizing scars on a familiar body. Despite the reassuring presence of those well-worn cracks and corbelling, Skellan sensed a difference in the granite beneath him. That deep hum that often resonated through him at contact had faded to little more than the buzz of a biting gnat. The stone felt almost dead in his grip. Bone-crusher had gone quiet and sunk himself deep into the rock to escape the violent flame.

Skellan didn't know if Bone-crusher could even sense him now. Still, Skellan briefly paused on the old troll's shoulder and pressed his face up against the rough surface of the troll's earlobe.

"Tonight you will be free," Skellan whispered.

A biting wind whirled up from the river but nothing else stirred in response to Skellan's words. Alarm skittered through

Skellan but he refused to think that he'd come too late. Instead he fed his agitation into motion. He scrambled up between the turrets and raced across the oaken boards of the wall walkway. The last time he'd come this way, brawny guards in fur cloaks stood guard and snatches of conversation had drifted on a spring breeze.

Now no guards remained within the sanctum, and a quick glance across the courtyard told him that neither Oesir's servants nor his few students had survived. Ash and charred bones spilled across the grounds. Some were not even human, but the remains of livestock. All around the stable and pig pens, dead bodies of animals, women and men lay split and cracked. Sand and dirt beneath the remains formed black pools of fused obsidian. Where willow, beech and walnut trees had grown in decorative groves now-crumbling columns of charcoal stood. Ash and soot blackened the pools of the water garden.

The doors of the grimma's palace hung like shattered kindling, and a wall of violet fire engulfed the great black tower rising all the way to the pinnacle. At the very height of the tower Oesir's emerald witchflame fluttered like a moth caught in the blaze of a hearth fire.

The cold wind brought Skellan a breath of burned hair and charred gristle. Skellan shuddered. He wished desperately that he still had his cloak to wrap around himself.

Even more he wished that he didn't have to descend into the barren scorched remains of the grounds he'd once known so well. But he couldn't just hunch here, letting his fear gnaw him hollow, so he descended to the grounds.

With shaking hands he chose several bits of broken charms from the coffer at his side. For each charm he removed he made certain to keep one matching fragment in the coffer.

He crouched down at the corner of the east wall and laid the charms out at the foot of the weathered wards carved deep into the stonework. Only ash remained of the velvet moss that once hid the symbols. Now the spells lay bare against the face of the black granite wall. Skellan traced the weathered recesses of the carved symbols and felt their purposes whisper through his mind. Iron hooks the size of ships' anchors and vast lengths of steel chain flickered before his eyes as he touched the ward that bound Bone-crusher and enslaved him to the service of the sanctum.

Skellan withdrew the last topaz from his coin purse, licked it and with his saliva drew a ring of null symbols around Bone-crusher's name, hiding the troll's presence. At the foot of the wall he scraped another circle across the cold cobblestone and placed one of the cracked charms inside it as a decoy and substitute for Bone-crusher. Then he moved on to the next ward.

He worked quickly but not easily, having to suppress the reflexive flare of his own witchflame each time he strung a shiny gold charm into the dull red links of the wards. He crushed his inner fire and instead drained a little pulse from his own heartbeat or stole a spark from of his living breath. He glanced to the roiling violet fire overhead. How slow, small and insignificant his own magics seemed in comparison. But then that was the entire point, and for now the demon lord appeared more interested in feasting upon the gilded eagles of the Orneldur Bell Tower.

Skellan darted across the courtyard and dashed from wall to wall, steadily remaking every ward that held a spirit captive both inside the sanctum and throughout the city.

From Wind-eater who lay with her long wings folded beneath Market Street, to the aged wethra-steeds standing guard over the remains of abandoned temples and all the way down to the frogwives and the tiny cat-eyed imps that graced the roofs of so many costly houses in the guise of waterspouts, Skellan whispered their names. As a child he'd run his fingers over every ward on these walls—stroking the strange skins and hearing the voices of those trapped within.

Fearful of attracting the notice of the demon lord, none of the creatures returned his greeting this night. But that didn't matter. It was enough that he felt even the slightest hum, heard the faintest sigh. The knowledge that they still lived kept him moving even as his heartbeat slowed and his breath grew ragged. The witchflame within him knotted and kicked against his will like a rat swallowed live that now gnawed and thrashed at his gut as he tried to keep it down.

After he'd done with the last ward, Skellan sank to his knees and laid his face against the cold ground of the sanctum courtyard. He gasped in slow deep breaths and waited for his pain to dull. Frost on the cobblestones melted against his skin. Patches of ice glittered with violet light.

The wards weren't going to break themselves for him, nor was Zi'sai going to withdraw like some contrivance from one of Rafale's plays. Wretched as he felt, Skellan knew he had to rise and go on.

He pushed himself to his feet and walked, slowly but steadily across the courtyard and through the broken doors of the grimma's palace. Soot caked the entry, making the walls look like those of a giant's hearth. Ash rose and floated on the cold air as Skellan's steps disturbed the incinerated remains of the dozens of servants who must have huddled behind the doors praying for protection. Skellan thought he recognized the charred shape of Oesir's cat hunched beneath the crumbling cinders of what might have been a delicate chair, but he couldn't be sure. Only a dim glow of the violet flame's light now filtered through the cracked doors, and the ash in the air muted even that.

As Skellan stumbled farther into the remains of his childhood home he spied the forms of more burned bodies and did his best not to disturb them. Many lay spilled out at the foot of the massive stone staircase that dominated the great hall.

Granite columns, carved in the motif of huge trees, rose from the floor to support the spiraling staircase, while arching buttresses sprouted from the walls, all lifting the monument of stone up to the very height of the sanctum's pinnacle.

Here Skellan's eyes drank in the finest shafts of green light.

With his first step onto the stair, Skellan felt Oesir's presence. It was far fainter now than it had been the night Skellan had come to challenge Oesir, but the fragrant warmth of summer still hung in the flickering beams of pale green light. As Skellan ascended, the glow of Oesir's witchflame grew more constant but not more intense.

He was so very weak. Skellan would hardly need to whisper more than a single spell to kill him. The temptation of at last taking his revenge upon Oesir filled Skellan with something like anticipation. He'd fantasized and comforted himself with the promise of Oesir's demise so often that he couldn't help but think of it now. Each step up the narrowing stairs brought him closer.

He felt drafts of cold wind filter down from the open hatch above him. He could taste Oesir in every breath he drew in, and though he was exhausted his heartbeat quickened with instinctive anger. He took the last steps fast, charging up onto the twenty-foot circle of stone that capped the pinnacle of the sanctum. Neither decorative masonry nor rails offered protection from the elements. Ice slicked the roughhewn rocks beneath Skellan's feet. Frigid winds buffeted the towering walls of the pinnacle and whirled up over him like breaking waves.

An arm's length from him, Oesir hunched on his knees with a white bearskin cloak pulled tight around his gaunt body. His burned face was bowed against the icy stones. The green light of his witchflame rolled over him and reached up into the violet fire that raged just above Skellan's head.

The violet flame pushed inward and Oesir's witchflame flared, punching into the writhing purple mass. A whimper of pain escaped Oesir, but he didn't move or make a sound otherwise. Skellan crept nearer but Oesir didn't spare him a glance—didn't move a muscle. Skellan wondered if Oesir even realized that he was here. More than likely Oesir's awareness focused entirely on the demon lord. Skellan glanced up at it with the feeling of a minnow gazing up at the immense hull of a ship sailing overhead—an immense ship in flames.

And for the first time, Skellan perceived that Oesir's witch-flame didn't just hold the demon lord back, but fine lances of emerald light speared into the violet flames like harpoons and blades. Oesir was not dying quietly. Nor had he, like Skellan, hidden his witchflame away. He fought the demon lord, though his body was hardly more than blistered skin and bone. All he was—strength, will and soul—he had poured into his battle against the violet flame.

As much as Skellan hated Oesir yet he could not keep from feeling awed, witnessing Oesir sacrifice every shred of himself. Truly, he was a great grimma. He fought, no doubt, for his own life but his life was the only one that kept the city from falling to the violet flame; his existence was the one thing that could stop a Mirogoth invasion. No matter how easy it might be, no matter how tempting it felt, Skellan couldn't kill Oesir.

He turned to look out over the dark skyline of the sur-rounding city. Milmuraille needed Oesir to survive. Skellan drew in a steadying breath, knowing that once he took his next steps there would be no going back.

CHAPTER TWENTY-THREE

Only during their very brief carriage ride to the garrison had Elezar managed something of a private conversation with Atreau despite the two page boys riding with them. Atreau seemed to trust them completely and Fedeles had promised that they were both faithful. Still, knowing they were listening had made Elezar hesitant to just blurt out confidences.

Atreau, on the other hand, had guiltily informed him that he'd lost his dog. Elezar had laughed out loud.

"Not to worry," Elezar had replied. "He found me. I think he may have even saved my life."

Elezar had glanced out the small window but only caught sight of Kiram and Javier, though he could hardly credit that glossy black hound as being the man he knew Javier to be. Atreau had leaned close to Elezar, following his gaze out the small window.

"Am I going mad or is that Kiram Kir-Zaki trailing us?" Atreau had asked. "I would swear that's him."

"It is. He's come to Milmuraille from the Mirogoth lands with a report of the forces marching upon the city, and he didn't come alone." Elezar dropped his voice low. "That black dog with him is Javier. Our own Javier."

"Our own Javier? Spoken like a native Labaran, Elezar." Atreau's smile shone even in the dark confines of the carriage. "But wait... You mean the dog is Javier?"

"That's what I said, isn't it?"

"Yes, but... How? Why?"

"It's dangerous for him to be here. He has to be hidden, and Skellan is a genius at such disguises." Elezar tried again to catch sight of the witch but hardly glimpsed more than a flash of his red hair before a wall of horses and riders blocked his view. Sheriff Hirbe's men had surrounded the carriage, which could have been an offer of protection. Elezar had hoped it was, but he'd been waylaid and nearly killed twice since he'd returned to Milmuraille and he wasn't feel particularly trusting of strangers right now. Not even kindly ones who reminded him of his own grandfather.

"We haven't much time," Elezar told Atreau. "You need to tell me why you were staring like that at Skellan."

"The red-headed youth?" Atreau asked.

Elezar nodded.

"I've seen him before," Atreau said. "But I don't know where."

"Not the Mockingbird Playhouse, where you kissed him, perhaps?" Elezar tried not to sound sour. He noticed one of the pages glancing his way curiously. Meeting Elezar's gaze the youth looked away at once.

"I did kiss him, didn't I? I was just so relieved. Well, it's a common enough custom this far north." Amusement faded from Atreau's tone. "But no, I had the recollection of seeing his face even then. I thought I must have recognized him from some gathering at Bishop Palo's house."

Elezar scowled at him and then had ask, "You're not thinking of my red dog, are you?"

"The dog? No, why would—" Atreau quieted as realization came over him. He could be quite quick on the uptake when he was sober. "I told you that animal looked too knowing, didn't I? I said it was enchanted."

"Indeed you did, and had we wagered I'd be in your debt," Elezar admitted. "But that's not how you recognized Skellan?"

"No, not as a dog. It's his face that I've seen before, and not from a theater or brothel either."

"I would swear I knew him as well," one of the pages whispered. He held a brocade bundle on his lap and absently smoothed the fabric as he tried to remember. "I thought… I mean, I seem to remember him from when Count Radulf brought his daughter to the bishop's townhouse two months ago."

Elezar had not been in attendance, but he couldn't imagine how Skellan could possibly have numbered among the count's courtiers—and if he had, how he have kept himself from bragging about it later?

"He's a street witch, not an aristocrat," Elezar replied.

"The sheriff knew him as well." The other page suddenly spoke up. "Didn't he say from where?"

"No, and that's why I need to find out as soon as possible," Elezar replied.

Unfortunately, the carriage had reached the garrison before the conversation could progress. Once inside, Elezar had been faced with more immediate troubles. Not the least of which had been securing the payroll in a strong room and hearing out the story of the beaten Cadeleonian soldiers who'd attempted, in the weeks prior, to wrest control of the garrison from Lecha. After that he'd turned his energy to ensuring that the men, the girls, and their surviving animals were cared for. A sudden fire hadn't made the task any easier, nor had this shambles of a stable.

The whole time Sheriff Hirbe kept close and offered up his resources. He sent for grooms and workmen—though Elezar couldn't help but notice how quickly their numbers swelled and how many wore leather armor and carried themselves like soldiers. The sheriff had claimed that he commanded only six deputies but by Elezar's count no fewer than fifty armed men occupied the garrison now. And if Elezar were right they had come from Count Radulf's personal guard and would take the garrison by force if Elezar did not take care.

Elezar was beyond tired. He wanted nothing more than to find a bed and lay down. He would have liked it if Skellan managed to be waiting for him in that bed, though in their current circumstances he didn't know how profitable or wise it was to allow himself to even contemplate that desire, much less to act upon it.

He stroked the shoulder of the big gray charger standing before him, while out of the corner of his eye he watched Skellan traipse across the stable with a heavy bale of hay thrown over his bare shoulder. Elezar noted that he wasn't the only one observing Skellan and that alone made him very uneasy, though he knew now why Atreau felt so certain that he'd seen Skellan before—and why no matter how long Elezar had stared at or studied Skellan he still hadn't placed him. He also knew why Sheriff Hirbe's gaze lacked uncertainty.

"He's interesting," the sheriff commented when Atreau remarked upon Skellan's dogged work in the stable. "It's not every street witch who'd swear to defend a man like our Elezar here and truly mean it."

"He does seem an odd mix of pride and poverty, doesn't he?" Atreau replied. "I still can't quite credit that his toes haven't turned black and fallen off from going barefoot in this cold weather."

Sheriff Hirbe only nodded. Elezar kept his head down, wishing he could find some way to casually take Atreau aside and tell him what he'd learned. But Sheriff Hirbe was clever in keeping a close vigil over them while maintaining the air of a concerned grandfather.

Skellan drifted from a stall and stood for a while with an older groom. Elezar kept his head down as Skellan passed by seconds later. Sheriff Hirbe struck him as all too observant, and Elezar knew that it wouldn't do to let the man suspect more of what was between himself and Skellan than he probably already did. Even so, Elezar couldn't help but steal a glance at Skellan's bare back as he reached the stable doors.

Stripped of even his tattered cloak, Skellan shuddered as he stepped out into the chill night. Elezar want to shout for him to put on a damn coat or at least go curl up in front of a fire. But he resisted the urge. He'd already tried to send Skellan away only to have Skellan glower at him and then inform him that none of them had anywhere else to go.

Throughout the exchange Elezar had felt incredibly aware of Sheriff Hirbe's attention upon them. He'd wanted to say something to Skellan to reassure him that he would find a way out of this mess for both of them, but then another of Commander Lecha's misdeeds had intruded and Elezar had been forced to leave Skellan in an attempt to locate the daughter of one of the Cadeleonian captains whom Lecha had locked away in a storeroom.

Ironically, it had been in that storeroom that Elezar had finally discovered why the sheriff had known Skellan at a glance. There, he'd also realized the full precariousness of his own position.

He'd broken down the door to get to the girl, and she'd hardly been moving when he'd found her. Elezar couldn't guess for how long the commander had deprived her of food and water, but she'd felt cold and fragile as frost when Elezar had carried her out to her father and the sister-physicians.

Elezar had returned to the storeroom to make sure that another child didn't lie unconscious somewhere in the mess of moldering straw targets, cracked fencing dummies and broken lances. Elezar had dug through the last stacks of splintered wood heaped in the back.

Then the light of his flickering lamp had caught the gleam of eyes staring out at him. Elezar had rolled aside two sodden archery targets, to find himself standing before a life-sized portrait painted on a wooden panel. Dozens of arrow marks had pocked the chest of the figure and a few had peppered the brow, but the image had been still quite recognizable and beautifully rendered. Elezar had gaped at Skellan's likeness while the painting had stared back at him with an expression of serene authority. The painted figure had worn a lustrous red fur cloak and shining rubies had decorated his many rings as well as the ornate dagger he'd gripped in one hand. Brocaded red silk clothes had clung to his angular body while the leather of his black boots had gleamed as brightly as the eyes of the hunting dogs crouched at his feet.

Only as Elezar had drawn nearer had he realized that the man's hair looked too fair to have been Skellan's. Otherwise the portrait had resembled Skellan so perfectly—sharp jaw and clear pale eyes—that Elezar had felt strangely pained and angered as he'd taken in the broken shaft of an arrow jutting from the figure's cracked chest.

A gilded banner had floated over the figure's head, naming the subject of the portrait as Count Hallen Radulf and declaring the young count's pleasure in welcoming the newly appointed garrison commander to Milmuraille. Obviously the portrait had been painted decades earlier, before anyone in Milmuraille had become acquainted with Commander Lecha in person.

Elezar had reached out and touched the cold wooden surface of the count's cheek. He hadn't met the count in person and the only seen a small portrait of the man hanging among many other miniatures in Bishop Palo's library. It had shown an older man, all traces of his seductive smile hidden by a flowing white beard and his bright eyes hooded beneath a furrowed brow. Elezar had recalled thinking the count handsome in a rawboned, hard way but also melancholy. He would not have immediately imagined that some thirty years before the count had been this vibrant youth in the painting before him.

Sheriff Hirbe, on the other hand, had been of an age with the count and would have known him in those days. Elezar hadn't doubted that he would've recognized this painting of the count just as quickly as he had recognized Count Radulf's long-lost son.

Elezar had stood there as the realization had sunk into him. Skellan, a ragged street witch who had lived as a feral dog for some ten years, was Count Radulf's only son and heir. If it hadn't been for the undeniable physical resemblance, Elezar would never have believed it.

Little surprise, then, that neither of Fedeles' pages, nor Atreau, could quite place Skellan's familiar features. They'd been looking at them on the bearded countenance of a man a good thirty years older than Skellan. Or perhaps it had been in the angular face of Count Radulf's young daughter that Atreau had glimpsed the resemblance. It didn't really matter now.

What was important was that fact that Sheriff Hirbe had known Skellan straight away but when he'd perceived Elezar's ignorance, he'd kept the knowledge to himself. Was that because the sheriff had an interest in ensuring that the count's rightful heir not be discovered? Or was it because the sheriff didn't want two Cadeleonian nobles—himself and Atreau—to realize who Skellan was and seize him? Either way Elezar expected that the sheriff would want Skellan in his own grasp.

Elezar had known that he must proceed with deliberation. He must feign continued ignorance while finding a way to keep watch over Skellan and at the same time sound out the sheriff. If Hirbe's only motivation was to ensure that Skellan returned to his father and reclaimed his rightful place, then that was a greater good than Elezar could have done for Skellan. Elezar wouldn't stand in the way of it... though the idea of Skellan simply being whisked away from him did cause Elezar a kind of ache, like a tooth pulled from its root. He scowled at his own turn of melancholy. He should hope that the sheriff did intend to take Skellan to his father. It would be best for everyone.

That, like the sheriff's story about Lord Elota, seemed too good to be entirely true. Elezar wanted badly to trust Sheriff Hirbe. He wanted the story of his bringing inadvertent vengeance for the sheriff's granddaughter to have been a fact. But he couldn't afford to rely upon a complete stranger just because he looked kind and spun an appealing tale.

Elezar had turned the portrait around to face the dark wall and withdrew from the musty storeroom.

His personal resources in the garrison were few, but he would put them to all the use he could. Only a few minutes later, out in the courtyard, he'd caught hold of Javier. Playing at a master's affection by scratching and stroking Javier's head and neck, Elezar had whispered his confidences to his friend. The sheriff and his men looked on, but with far less interest than Kiram.

"Will you watch him for me?" Elezar lifted his face from Javier's silken ear. Javier answered him by lapping his slobbery tongue across Elezar's face.

Elezar glanced to Kiram but couldn't read his expression in the faint lamplight.

"I'm counting on you for a proper inventory of the armory, Kiram," Elezar had called. "No pun intended."

Kiram flashed him a quick smile and a loose salute then turned to the armory. Elezar expected that while he was there, Kiram would not only appraise the number and condition of the weapons remaining but better arm himself. Elezar felt almost certain that Kiram had already helped himself to a store of black powder. He'd caught the smell of the stuff on Javier's fur.

But it wasn't as if he could inquire, so he had turned his attention to the stable and his need to secure a mount.

Now Elezar tended the healthiest of the chargers, making certain that if he needed to ride the stallion it would hold up long enough to carry him and Skellan out of the garrison and across the city to the Fairwind Stables. Javier and Kiram he would entrust to the protection of Atreau's carriage, though he still needed to find an opportunity to convey that information to Atreau.

"I see that the Cadeleonian reputation for their love of their horses isn't an exaggeration in your case, Lord Grunito," Sheriff Hirbe commented. No doubt he grew tired of lingering here in the chill of the stable, while Elezar inspected each and every mount. That suited Elezar. If he was very lucky the sheriff might grow bored enough to leave him alone with Atreau.

Though it seemed more likely that Atreau would wander off before that. He'd already strolled away twice to chat with his pages and then returned carrying the leather-bound volume of poetry that he now glanced up from.

"Oh, it's not just horses," Atreau addressed the sheriff in a conspiratorial tone. "Nor is it only Elezar. The entire Grunito family is mad for hounds and horses. More varieties of dog than you could imagine populate their townhouse in Anacleto and their stables might put an army to shame. I've even heard that Lady Grunito insisted upon having her favorite rat terrier blessed in the family chapel to ensure that the creature can accompany her into golden bowers of heaven."

The sheriff shot Elezar a quizzical glance at that.

"She did," Elezar confirmed. He straightened from his inspection of the big gray stallion's leg. Cleaned and bandaged, the horse's injury didn't look too serious. Cold had kept the worst of the flies out of the flesh. The stallion was thin and dirty but hadn't come up lame despite the neglect he'd endured. Of all the mounts in the stable this stallion's health and spirit struck Elezar as most suited to charge a line of armed men.

Elezar stroked the horse's jaw and was rewarded with a soft exhalation of its breath across his cheek. He led the stallion to a clean stall and lingered just to see the charger's pleasure at discovering the bounty of feed in his manger. He didn't want to drive this handsome horse into an onslaught of spears or pikes, and yet he knew he would if he had to. He noted exactly where the animal's bridle hung before turning back to the sheriff and Atreau.

Behind them, two grooms traipsed out through the stable doors and Elezar glimpsed the bare walls of the garrison rising from the black night. Yellow lamplight flickered from a few windows on the ground floor of the main building but the rest of the compound appeared abandoned. Nearly everyone would have withdrawn to the barracks to sleep.

Skellan had probably found himself some warm spot by the fire and fed on the cutlets of the cured ham that Elezar could smell perfuming the kitchen smoke. Belatedly, he remembered the sausages stuffed in his coat pocket.

Elezar supposed they could eat the sausages together tomorrow morning.

Aloud he said, "The stable looks suitable enough for even Cobre now. I think we've done all we can for one night."

"Shall we sup, then?" Atreau closed his book of poetry with a hopeful expression.

"Certainly," Elezar agreed, and glancing to the sheriff added, "I imagine that your own household awaits you anxiously, sir."

"Oh, my household is well accustomed to the long hours I keep. But thank you for the consideration." Another of those amused smiles briefly lit the sheriff's lined face. Had Elezar not known that all of Count Radulf's sprawling northern holdings could be at stake he might have mistaken the sheriff for a playful and friendly old fellow. But the men-at-arms in the garrison weren't a joke any more than the sword Elezar carried was a toy.

"It's surprisingly interesting keeping your company, Lord Grunito."

"Interesting…" Elezar smiled despite himself. Hadn't the sheriff said the same of Skellan earlier? "Shall I take that as a compliment?"

"I hope you will," Sheriff Hirbe answered. "It would certainly make our dinner conversation more amiable, don't you think?"

"It will indeed," Elezar responded. He couldn't help but wonder why the sheriff didn't just use the men-at-arms to seize control of the garrison. Was he hesitant to move openly against two Cadeleonian noblemen because his own country might soon need Cadeleonian armies to resist an invasion of Mirogoth grimma?

Perhaps he hoped to secret Skellan away and had summoned the count's soldiers only in case of complications. Hirbe seemed the sort to plan for many scenarios at once.

Elezar started out the stable doors. Sheriff Hirbe fell into step with him but walked at a sword's length away. Atreau caught up, taking the open space between them. Elezar had no doubt that he sensed the edge of tension—probably even recognized the physical distance as the safe range two duelists would maintain. Atreau could always be counted upon to supply social grace in uneasy situations. Now he fostered comfortable conversation as the three of them crossed the frost-covered grounds of the open courtyard. For his part Elezar made a few attentive noises while only half-listening to Atreau's lively chatter about pretty girls and Labaran theater.

At the front doors of the main hall they met Kiram, who looked nearly as tired as Elezar felt. He handed over a neatly written tally of the armory's depleted inventory. Elezar thanked him and then asked after Javier.

"Around back on the kitchen steps," Kiram replied. "I'm not sure if he thinks he's looking after Skellan or if Skellan is looking after him. Either way I suspect they'll be out there a while longer."

Kiram appeared happy to join them for supper and took time to reminisce with Elezar about the thick yoghurts and spicy lamb that they had both left behind in Anacleto. Walking with both Atreau and Kiram through fortified halls, Elezar more readily remembered their school days. His recollections of an atmosphere alive with the scents and sounds of hundreds of rowdy young men in uniforms made for a bleak comparison to the empty tables and stale air of the garrison hall. Despite the fire crackling in the hearth and oil lamps throwing halos of yellow light across the oaken tables, a dark chill hung over the dining hall.

Three white-haired sister-physicians sat far across the room at a table heaped with dry herbs and the desiccated remains of several toads. They spoke among themselves as they sipped table beer from clay mugs. Near the fireplace, two Cadeleonian captains hunched at a long oaken table in silence. Both looked as hollow-eyed and harrowed as mourners keeping vigil in a crypt. Across from the two of them, the young

Labaran deputy—Magraie, Elezar thought his name was— looked up from his own grim study of his bowl of stew and grinned at the sight of their company.

He called an invitation to the sheriff who extended it to the entire party. Elezar invited the Cadeleonian captains to their table as well. They seemed relieved to be drawn from the gloom of their own thoughts. Between mouthfuls of hard biscuits, fatty stew and table beer, the group made light conversation. Hours ago the captains had described their attempt to decry Commander Lecha and their subsequent punishments and imprisonments. Now they did their best not to think on their fellows who had not survived Lecha's reprisal.

Their tired expressions brightened as Atreau entertained them and the young deputy with tales of his more ridiculous romantic adventures. Very briefly Elezar answered one of the captain's questions concerning the duels he'd won and his choice of blades.

Elezar hadn't thought that his reputation would have traveled so far north but then most of these men had only recently left Cadeleon behind to serve their king's interests in Labara. Fortunately, the conversation soon returned to Atreau's travails in wooing a particularly devout nun. Even the three sister-physicians across the room laughed at Atreau's satire of his own poetry. The women seemed charmed enough to accept Atreau's invitation to join the table, and the eldest shared her own stories of hilarious failure in seduction.

Under the cover of so much laughter, Elezar spoke with Kiram and Sheriff Hirbe. First Kiram explained what supplies he would require to repair the disabled cannons housed in the armory. Then, inevitably, their discussion turned to the numbers of the combined armies of the four grimma as well as the battle formations and tactics favored by Mirogoths. Sheriff Hirbe agreed with Elezar that the city walls would not withstand a long siege without significant reinforcement.

"The work must get underway as soon as possible." Elezar scowled at his stew and then took another bite. He was hungry, but not enough to enjoy of the texture of snails. "How soon do you think Count Radulf could have workmen out on the walls?"

Sheriff Hirbe looked troubled, and Elezar didn't think it was just the stew.

"You talk as if you truly mean to stay," Sheriff Hirbe replied.

Oddly, before the sheriff's comment Elezar hadn't even considered flight as an option. He'd come to stop a war and if he failed at that then the least he could do was fight it.

Elezar said, "Why would I go through all the trouble of cleaning up this garrison if I was just going to let the Mirogoths take it?"

"Should I answer that question or did you ask it rhetorically?" Kiram broke in, then went on, without waiting for a clarification, "Because it's going to take more than fifteen rusted-out cannons to hold this city against four Mirogoth armies."

Elezar didn't miss the tension Kiram's comment produced in the other people at the table.

"You forget that we also have your ingenuity, Kiram," Elezar replied.

"You think I'm staying? I've seen the beasts and giants that are coming for Milmuraille. And I've been the prisoner of a grimma. Honestly, I'm not certain that we shouldn't be discussing how to manage an orderly evacuation of the city. That's why I rushed all this way to warn you all—to give you time to escape."

True as that might be, it wasn't going to inspire any kind of morale among the soldiers who were duty-bound to stay and fight.

"Giving up before a fight isn't any way to win it," Elezar replied.

"Neither is dying in an all-out massacre," Kiram responded.

"That's why I'm not planning on doing that either." Elezar couldn't keep from smirking at Kiram, knowing presumption and faulty logic would peeve him.

"I swear, you're as bad as—he is," Kiram snapped, but then he gave a dry laugh. "I don't know why I even try to have this argument. I'm almost certain that no Cadeleonian nobleman actually knows the meaning of the word 'retreat.'"

"Perhaps if you explained it to them in terms of a reverse charge," Sheriff Hirbe suggested with a sly grin. "Or call it an advance up the rear? The maneuver can't be entirely unknown to such worldly men. Not unless I misunderstood that last poem the duke just recited."

At this, Kiram snickered like schoolboy and despite himself Elezar laughed as well. He hadn't been paying much attention to Atreau's recitation but obviously the sheriff had been. The captains snorted and the sister-physicians giggled. Only the beardless deputy, Magraie, appeared unamused. He sighed, an exasperated youth who'd apparently just realized that the adults around him were no less bawdy than his peers.

"You took my meaning perfectly, sir! Sadly, I fear I must inform you that the glory of such hind wise maneuvers is nearly unknown among the Cadeleonian rearguard." Atreau grinned at the sheriff and then winked at the sister-physicians. "Fortunately I am a rare man among my countrymen. For I am endowed not only with the heart of a Cadeleonian, but the soul of a Labaran, and the manhood of a stallion—though perhaps you might be more interested in my two galleons docked in Milmuraille's harbor, which between them carry eight great cannons and forty men; all of which I gladly volunteer for the protection of the city."

Elezar, too, had considered commandeering men and arms from the ships in the bay. Fedeles could easily afford the loss, but many merchants and lesser nobles might not feel so generous. Even so he didn't miss how Atreau's words lifted the expressions of the young deputy, the beaten captains and even the three aged sister-physicians.

"That stallion's manhood will come in handy when we have to pack the powder in the cannons, no doubt," Elezar replied.

"Any and every cannon you need packed, Elezar," Atreau replied. "Just promise you won't let fire before I do."

This response inspired an unlovely snort from Elezar as well as exhausted snickers and chuckles from the rest of the men and women gathered at the table. It felt good to laugh and let go of his anxiety if only for a short time.

The captains and sister-physicians bandied a few more innuendos between them before draining the last of their drinks and excusing themselves for the evening. Atreau seemed to be pondering his own possible retreat to a bed, while Deputy Magraie eyed Kiram quite longingly and then asked, "Are you going to finish that stew?"

"Please, help yourself." Kiram pushed the bowl to the younger man.

Elezar considered the remains of his own meal but then went very still as he recognized several faint but very familiar noises.

Horses and carriages, he thought, drawing into the front courtyard. Heavy doors creaked open and boot heels clattered against the stone floor. Elezar rose and turned in time to startle the young guard who bounded through the mess hall doors.

"Who's here?" Elezar demanded.

The young guard glanced to Sheriff Hirbe for just an instant, but when Elezar took a step toward the guard he snapped his attention to Elezar and saluted him.

"Master Rafale and Sacrist Bois Eyeres, sir! They said they were sent for."

"Yes, yes." Sheriff Hirbe nodded from where he sat at the long oak table. "I asked them to come here. Though they did take their time, didn't they?"

"Why did you send for them?" Elezar demanded.

"Because it seems we all have a common interest, and it would be wise if we could manage not to work at cross purposes."

"I will not allow them to take Skellan," Elezar stated flatly, and this time he caught the way the sheriff's light eyes narrowed in hard assessment.

"Now that would be our Skellan's decision to make, Lord Grunito. Not yours, theirs or mine."

"As long as that's the truth, then you'll have no argument from me," Elezar replied.

"S-so... shall I invite them—" The guard began to ask but Elezar cut him off.

"Since they're already standing just outside the dining hall door, you may as well." Elezar glanced to Kiram and noted with grim reassurance that Kiram's right hand had already dropped to the hilt of his long knife. Atreau pulled a handsome smile but drew himself up straight, at the ready for a fight if one came.

With a great show of reluctance, Deputy Magraie pushed his bowl aside and rose to stand at the sheriff's back as the young guard escorted Rafale and Sacrist Bois to the long oak table.

Rafale wore an even more extravagantly plumed gold hat than the one he'd sported at the Rat Rafters. His waxed mustache formed dainty curls over his upper lip, which echoed the gold pattern of his silk brocade coat. A different ornate dagger hung from his hip, this one studded with pearls. Elezar guessed that he'd been involved in some festivity before he'd come here. The slight flush of strong alcohol colored his nose and cheeks.

Bois, on the other hand, looked as if he'd come directly from a penning some dour service. His violet robes were a little rumpled and ink stained two of his fingers. His well-worn short sword hung from his thick leather belt along with a string of wooden prayer beads.

"What is he doing here?" Bois demanded when he caught sight of Atreau.

"I asked the duke to come," Sheriff Hirbe replied in the same reasonable tone he'd used to answer Elezar seconds before. "He has promised the use of his men and cannons to the city's defense."

"But your message—" Rafale began but seemed to think better of continuing. He turned to Elezar and gave a charming, if forced, smile. "So, we meet again and, if I understand correctly, you've taken command of this garrison?"

"I've stepped in for the time being," Elezar answered.

"And this lovely Irabiim youth?" Rafale favored Kiram with a flirtatious smile, though he addressed the question to the sheriff.

"He's a confidant of Lord Grunito's. And he's brought intelligence concerning the grimma's armies." Sheriff Hirbe beckoned the new arrivals closer. "Come, let's sit ourselves down and have honest words between us, shall we? You too, Lord Grunito. No point in standing when everyone else has his ass in a chair. You'll still be two heads taller than every man here."

Elezar grudgingly took a seat. He chose a spot at the foot of the table with the hearth fire at his back, where its light would cast his expressions in shadow while illuminating the faces of the men seated around him. With Kiram and then Atreau to his left he'd be free to draw his sword with his right arm. Bois settled across from the sheriff on Atreau's left, while Rafale dropped down across from Kiram and next to Hirbe. Only deputy Magraie remained on his feet, though he withdrew to the door, where he stood guard.

At first the six men watched each other in silence. Then Sheriff Hirbe chuckled to himself and said, "Now, this is why my daughter never allows me to choose which guests to invite to supper, I suppose."

"You're the one who said you wanted us to talk, so why don't you begin with your interest in Skellan?" Elezar suggested.

The question met another protracted silence. Then the sheriff asked, "How much do you know of Count Radulf's history with the former Grimma Lundag?"

"I know Lundag's been dead a good ten years," Elezar said, shrugging. Atreau and Kiram remained silent as well. Let the Labarans do the talking, Elezar thought.

"Well, long before that Lundag was a bit taken with the young count." Sheriff Hirbe's smile showed in his eyes, as did the sadness that followed it. "He was such a charming man, and brave. But for whatever reason old Lundag took a keen fancy to him when he was hardly more than a boy and decided that he should be her man."

Elezar frowned a little at that exact turn of phrase, but he didn't interrupt the story.

"The count had other ideas and he choose another woman but he kept the affair secret, for fear of Lundag's jealousy. Hallen and this other woman had a child, a son who by Labaran law would be the count's heir. That couldn't be kept from Lundag and when the boy was only three years old she stole him away to her sanctum."

The sheriff fell quiet and Elezar wondered if this was all he planned on saying. Then he realized that the sheriff's expression was far away, his thoughts caught up in some memory.

"What happened after that?" Elezar prompted.

"You don't have a child, do you?" Hirbe asked.

"No," Elezar replied. Kiram shook his head. Atreau did as well but didn't look entirely certain as he did so. The sheriff didn't seem to notice.

"Even if you did, I don't suppose you'd understand how precious and rare a child is in a bloodline like the count's," Hirbe said.

"Mirogoth, you mean?" Kiram asked.

"Nothing so common as that. A lineage descended from the Old Gods of the wilds and waters. The blood of the scarlet wolf flowed in his veins." Hirbe's hushed tone struck Elezar as almost religiously reverent. He'd known that ancestors were worshiped in Labaran temples. Now he thought he understood whose ancestors and why.

"Children couldn't be that rare to the count's family," Kiram commented. "He's fathered a daughter, after all."

"Yes, but she isn't full-blooded," Rafale said offhandedly, as if it were common knowledge. "Her mother, Ynes, didn't come from one of the ancient bloodlines and even so, bringing the count's child into the world killed her."

Bois made a sign of blessing with his right hand but said nothing.

"So, what did the count do after Lundag whisked away his full-blooded son?" Atreau asked.

"He went to Lundag," Sheriff Hirbe continued the story. "He went down onto his knees and begged her to spare his son. He offered her anything, everything he had, even his own life in trade for the child. But what she wanted was to see the count suffer. She had him stripped, strung up to her pillory and lashed like a thief. Even after that she didn't return his son—she only promised to keep the boy alive for one year's time. And that was the ransom Lundag demanded from the count every single year of the boy's life. And the count endured it but not haplessly."

"No?" Atreau leaned forward, caught up in the story.

Sheriff Hirbe offered Atreau a grim smile. "Count Radulf, of all men, knew of Lundag's weakness for pretty youths from old bloodlines, and by the luck of his ancestors he met just such a young man one spring—a student of astrology named Oesir. The count brought Oesir into his house and the two of them grew close and after a year at the count's side the young man resolved to enter Lundag's sanctum and free the count's son."

"So, Oesir challenged Lundag and took over the sanctum?" Atreau lit up as he made the realization but then raised his brows. "But what became of the son, then?"

"He fled." Bois spoke at last, his tone exasperated. "He'd spent his entire life under Lundag's tutelage and when she was killed he fled into the mazes of Milmuraille and disappeared."

"But why wouldn't he come forward?" Kiram asked. "He stood to inherit the entirety of Radulf County."

"He didn't come forward because he didn't know his true parentage or the real reason he was being hunted," Elezar said, remembering what Skellan had told him of his life. "A better question might be, why didn't the people searching for him make his true identity known? Why not announce it throughout the city? A few frauds would have responded, but the boy would have been easy to pick out if you knew what to look for, eh, sheriff?"

Sheriff Hirbe inclined his head but offered no explanation. Bois and Rafale kept silent as well. Atreau glanced to the Labarans then to Kiram and Elezar.

"Does someone actually know the answer?" Atreau inquired.

"I think I do. It's for the same reason," Elezar responded, "that throughout this entire narrative all three of these well-informed gentlemen have failed to mention the boy's name—"

"It's Skellan, isn't it?" Atreau guessed.

"It's Skellan, but that isn't his birth name." Elezar could see the color draining from Rafale's face. Bois glared at him, while Sheriff Hirbe simply bowed his head.

"The name his mother gave him was Hilthorn," Elezar explained to Kiram and Atreau. "The reason the count, his trusted courtiers and even Grimma Oesir wanted to keep that a secret is because Hilthorn's mother is the Sumar grimma. And his birth wasn't the result of some youthful romance. I've met the Sumar grimma." Elezar skewered Hirbe with a glance. "No, by uniting his bloodline with the Sumar grimma's, Count Radulf was forging a blood alliance. With an ally as powerful and close as the Sumar grimma, the count would be able to break his ties to Cadeleon and possibly even drive all Cadeleonian influence out of the north entirely."

"That's pure speculation!" Rafale cried out.

Elezar didn't even bother to argue. He was just glad that Skellan wasn't here to hear this. It could only hurt him to know that he'd been conceived and used throughout his life as a pawn in a power struggle to control northern Labara.

"When Grimma Lundag discovered the child's birth she flew into a jealous rage," Elezar said. He knew all too well what it was to lash out in jealousy. "She made an alliance of her own with Bishop Palo and then waited for an opportunity to seize Hilthorn because he was the count's greatest secret."

Elezar looked to the sheriff for confirmation. The old man nodded.

Elezar continued, "Did the count give into her demands because he wanted her to free his son or was it to keep her from revealing the boy's existence to the Cadeleonian king and sparking a war?"

"You will not speak of the count in that manner, cur!" Bois rose to his feet, his hand curling around his short sword. Elezar sprang up as well.

"Bois! Don't be an idiot." Sheriff Hirbe's voice boomed out with a harsh authority that Elezar hadn't heard since his training days in the Sagrada Academy. "Lord Grunito will kill you. And Lord Grunito, I have no doubt of your prowess but there are fifty men-at-arms surrounding this building and they will cut you down on sight if I give the order. So, let's everyone just sit back down and have this discussion like the reasonable men we are. As I said earlier, I think that we share a common goal and I don't see the point of us working at cross purposes."

Very slowly Elezar sank back down as did Bois.

With a quick, quiet motion Kiram sheathed his hunting knife and across the room, Magraie returned his sword to its scabbard.

"You're correct about the alliance," Sheriff Hirbe admitted. "But you couldn't be more wrong about Count Radulf's feelings for his son. He submitted himself to Lundag to save his son. He loved that child."

Despite himself Elezar felt inclined to believe the sheriff—
or at least to think that the sheriff himself was convinced of the
count's devotion to his son. But what kind of loving father left
his eleven-year-old son to struggle on the streets like a stray
dog? The thought infuriated Elezar.

"Loved?" Kiram asked. "But not loves?"

"Indeed!" Atreau shared a conspiratorial glance with Kiram. "There is a telling difference in the meaning, isn't there?"

"I warned you word would get out," Rafale groaned. He
cast an accusing look at Bois. Sitting next to Rafale, Sheriff
Hirbe's expression went grim.

From somewhere far across the city a single bell began to
sound long mournful notes.

"The count—" Rafale began.

"Shut up!" Bois snapped.

But it was already too late. Elezar looked to the sheriff for
confirmation of the suspicion that now bloomed through him.

"Has he fled or is he…" Kiram trailed off.

"Dead," Bois stated coldly. He glowered at his own tanned
hands. "He died trying to stop the violet flame from taking
hold over the city. He died in my arms."

That Elezar had not expected. He felt momentarily at a
loss. Then the greater implications struck him. "That's why
you're all so very keen to have Skellan now. He's not just the
count's heir anymore. He's the count."

"That's right," Sheriff Hirbe said.

"But I saw the count only days ago," Atreau protested.

"No, you saw an imposter. An actor in my employment."
Rafale flashed a rueful smile. "He wears the count's clothes
well enough and can pass for him at a distance, but I assure
you he's no leader of men."

"That sort of deception might work on a foreigner, but it's
not going to fool the count's courtiers or close supporters." The
sheriff shifted his gaze to Elezar. "Hilthorn must take up his

father's mantle. You appear to have gained his trust and confidence, Lord Grunito. You could persuade him—"

The rest of the sheriff's words drowned under a sudden boom of thunder. A tremor passed through the ground, rocking the garrison floor enough to make deputy Magraie stumble and to dash empty stew bowls and bundles of dried herbs from the table. Elezar lurched but then caught himself. The deputy at the door and the rest of the men at the table looked as startled as Elezar felt.

Then all at once Milmuraille's remaining bells rang out in an ear-splitting cacophony. Beneath the wild peals of the bells human cries of shock and alarm filled the air. Elezar recognized the disturbed screams of horses and the howls of distant dogs, but near at hand he caught the shout of a guard just beyond the dining hall door.

Then the door swung open, nearly knocking deputy Magraie off his feet a second time. Javier bounded past the young deputy.

Skellan's cloak hung in tatters from his broad shoulders and streaks of what looked like ash and blood stained his ragged clothes and pale skin. Kiram started toward him immediately.

"It's Skellan!" Javier shouted. "He's gone to the sanctum to fight the demon lord and all hell is breaking loose in the city!"

CHAPTER
TWENTY-FOUR

At the pinnacle of the sanctum tower, Skellan loosened the collar from around his neck and placed his one remaining topaz in his mouth. Then he lifted the golden coffer and flipped the tiny catches near its lid to expose the binding spells adorning its surface. The gold spells flared up like oil fires.

All at once the sky above Skellan went still. Then suddenly the vast sea of violet flame curled in like a fist over Skellan's outstretched hand. Skellan had to clench his eyes closed against the blinding illumination. Even so, he felt the demon lord's fury pour over him.

Tearing, howling rage blazed as intensely as light within the flames. The drive to sear the coffer to vapor and devour every spell within radiated from the Zi'sai's violet flame.

The air hissed as the flame descended. Skellan hurled the coffer off the pinnacle. It fell and the whole of the violet flame shot after it, lashing the tiny gold box like lightning, tearing into it before it even struck the ground. And then it enveloped the cracked bits of charms that Skellan had hidden inside the coffer. They were nothing in the face of such profound power and yet the demon lord could not resist. He followed the charms to their missing pieces, and the wards of the sanctum began to tear apart as he fed.

The violet flame crashed and twisted across the sanctum walls, chasing the lines that Skellan had woven through the wards like a viper wriggling down the tunnels of a rabbit warren. While the sanctum walls cracked and the courtyard burned with a furious violet light, the dark night sky enfolded Skellan. Far across the city, bell towers rang out as wards broke. Ancient creatures and wild spirits burst from their confinements.

Skellan moved quickly. Already the violet flame had destroyed half the wards of the sanctum and cracked the great walls as well. Turrets collapsed and flagstones shattered. He pulled the collar from his throat and rested it over Oesir's bowed back. He felt Oesir shudder slightly at the contact, though he didn't lift his head.

"I've come to help," Skellan whispered around the tiny stone in his mouth. It clicked against his teeth.

"Thorn…"

Skellan felt more than heard Oesir's dry rasp.

"Yes," Skellan said quietly, though he didn't want to answer to the name. He didn't know that he could think of that name or the life he'd lost along with it and still protect Oesir.

"I didn't…" Oesir shuddered. From the edge of his white cloak he extended the charred, blistered remains of his hand. He brushed against Skellan's heel but then his hand fell away. "I didn't… mean to…"

Below them, shards of granite exploded as the sanctum gates wrenched apart and a flock of shadow hawks rose into the night sky. The portcullis crashed to the ground. Through the noise of city bells and thunder of bursting rock, Skellan caught voices calling out in alarm.

"None of that matters anymore," Skellan told Oesir. "We have to save the city, but to do it you must trust me. You must stay very still and quiet. We have to keep him from finding you again."

Oesir said nothing, and hardly moved to draw a breath. His pitiful hand remained curled at Skellan's foot. Very carefully Skellan caught his thin wrist and tucked his hand back beneath the protection of the thick, white cloak. Then he straightened and stepped back from Oesir.

In the courtyard the violet flame still fed, though with each ward he consumed he also released another spirit from the sanctum, depriving himself of its power and capacities. And then, when the flame ripped through the oldest of the wards— the one laid down even before the sanctum was raised—the ground split apart in a huge arc. The violet flame descended as an immense body rose. Luminous flames turned to glossy scales and huge flexing coils. Zi'sai's violet receded into his mortal body and yet he was not small, not by any measure. The demon lord's serpentine head was wider than an ox cart and his coils arched higher than the sanctum walls as he wound and curled through the courtyard. Charred trees flattened beneath his girth.

He swung his huge body across the grounds, hungry even now for the last remaining wards. The ground shuddered and timbers shattered. The eastern wall collapsed, throwing up plumes of black dust. Skellan thought he could just make out Bone-crusher's form. He stood too near the demon lord.

Skellan couldn't wait any longer. He swallowed the topaz that he'd kept in his mouth. Then he forced himself to bellow down at the demon lord.

"Zi'sai, you idiot! Look up here!" Skellan waved his arms and to his horror the huge serpent did look up at him with blazing gold eyes. Skellan forced himself to grin, though it felt like a death grimace. He played at dancing from foot to foot on the pinnacle, his motions as stiff and jerky as a marionette's.

"Look who's gotten away from you, you limbless turd!" Skellan shouted. "I stole away the grimma and fed you nothing but cheap tin!"

The demon lord's gaze swept over the pinnacle like a stage light, swinging back and forth. Skellan was certain then that the collar had worked. Oesir was invisible to the demon lord. He saw only Skellan, laughing at him.

He moved with terrifying speed then, curling his long body up around the tower, crushing the walls as he climbed up. He rose with a fluid ease and arched up over Skellan. It was just as it had been in his dream—that expressionless face, adorned with scales as bright and beautiful as polished amethyst. His huge jaws gaped wide, displaying teeth like ivory scimitars and a glowing ember of fire ignited from the black chasm of his throat. The scent of camphor washed over Skellan.

Skellan closed his eyes, shutting out the sight. He concentrated on the stone in his stomach. He imagined his witchflame breaking away the mineral matrix and letting loose the thing once trapped within. Then the topaz cracked, releasing the emptiness that it had kept captive.

A chill flooded Skellan and with it came darkness like nothing Skellan had ever known. Blackness as deep and vast as the hollows between the stars opened within him.

Suddenly the demon lord and all the land below felt tiny—fleeting and insignificant. He reached out and caught the flames rolling out over him. With a breath he drew them into his emptiness and they became nothing. The demon lord swayed over him, gaping.

Skellan almost laughed. How had he been so afraid of this coil of meat before? What threat could any mortal creature pose to the infinite void within him?

Darkness poured from Skellan's outstretched hands, engulfing the demon lord, crushing and tearing through his flesh with a force too cold to mistake for hunger or hate. He took everything—writhing, lashing muscle and furious spells, all that strength, rage and terror—and rendered it down to the meager grit of creation, elements too small to even be seen. Those he dissipated across the emptiness hanging between distant stars.

And still the void remained, rising from Skellan, looming over the mortal world. Its emptiness did not hunger as the demon lord had; it did not aspire, or long for anything. It was not so complex, nor so humane. It destroyed worlds the way an ocean drowned sailors, simply by being what it was.

Skellan shuddered as the darkness flowing out of him tore apart the very elements of the air, unmaking even the wind that whirled around him. The void stretched and Skellan lurched, gagging on the pain as his whole being strained like a glove pulled too taut across a fist. His vision blurred then darkened and he knew that an infinite emptiness was eating him away, trying to tear its way out of him.

Skellan ground his teeth and focused all his will against that hollow rising up from inside him.

No. You aren't immense.

Skellan fought against the idea of that all-consuming blackness in his mind. It had been bound up once, it could be locked away again.

"You're nothing. Nothing," Skellan groaned to the void, though he knew it neither heard nor cared. But he needed to remind himself. He had to see it as it had been, constrained and crumpled down to a pebble.

You're not even so grand as a flea on my ass.

Skellan clenched his fist as if he were gripping the void and crushing it. Like acid it ate at his skin and yet he gripped all the harder. Pain was at least something, a sensation to hold up against the emptiness, a sensation to wrap around it. He made his hurt into a shell and closed it around the dark hollow.

You're so little you could fit in a stone in the palm of my hand... I could crush you into in a grain of sand, ball you up inside a pearl... a grain of sand buried in a pearl... That's what I will make you... a grain of sand...

Skellan felt the emptiness buckle and compress. He hunched himself around the void, collapsing it into its own hollow, and enclosing it deep inside himself—inside the spell of pain he built around it. It hurt him and he gripped that hurt all the harder, until he felt agony shaking through his entire body and encasing that nothingness beyond recognition.

Then at last he brought it up with a sick shudder.

The murderous void slept once more, trapped within a tiny, smooth stone beneath his tongue. A black pearl.

Blood welled up from his lungs and dribbled from his nostrils. Deep lacerations gaped across his hands and arms, and all he had to show for it was one tiny black pearl clenched between his teeth. It seemed almost funny.

He should have laughed at the absurdity of it, but instead a miserable track of tears dribbled down the side of his face. He had no idea why he was crying. For the first time in months he could see the stars of the night sky clearly. A warm verdant scent drifted on the air, assuring him that Oesir had survived.

The bells of Milmuraille rang and the silhouettes of wild forgotten things flitted through the air—all of them free at last, just as he'd promised so long ago.

There was nothing to cry about, except perhaps that the world seemed so beautiful at this moment when he knew that he was dying.

CHAPTER TWENTY-FIVE

Tower bells rang in a cacophony of alarms, wailing over animal cries and human shouts. The city seemed to be shaking itself apart, facades of buildings shattered and long tracks of streets ruptured as if blown open by cannons. Debris of pulverized stone and dirt filled the air like smoke. Strange, unnatural forms darted and writhed through the clouds of dust, as did frightened, confused and curious inhabitants of the city.

Elezar found it strange that while some people fled past him—one man nearly falling under his mount's hooves—others stood in doorways, on balconies and even atop roofs staring at the chaos around them as if watching a carnival. Elezar didn't think he'd ever seen so many illuminated windows or so many stunned faces peering out from them. Between city guards, concerned merchants and the men of the fireguard, dozens of torches and lanterns burned away at the darkness, but all their lights seemed like nothing compared to the flames and plumes of smoke that colored the western edge over the city skyline.

Thatched roofs throughout the close-packed old quarter burned like rush torches. The fires flared as they spread, lighting the thoroughfares and casting dancing, wild colors across the men and women fleeing from the conflagration. Elezar thought he recognized a few faces, but he couldn't be certain from the brief glimpses he captured. Most disappeared into alleys or doorways before the charge of the city guards. Sheriff Hirbe bellowed for the road to be cleared as he and the fireguard hauled water pumps through the main road.

Elezar urged his own mount away from the sheriff's men, to race down the nearly empty avenue that led to the sanctum. Javier and Rafale rode close behind him. Filthy and ragged as Javier looked, he still managed to call up a shining white flame, which he hurled ahead of them to light their way. It blazed before Elezar like a comet, throwing off cold sparks.

The gray stallion Elezar rode didn't like the dancing white fire, but he was a Cadeleonian warhorse and when Elezar urged him into the light he plunged ahead as if charging into battle. Ironically, the horse Javier had managed to slip away from the guards at the garrison shied back and, like Rafale's Labaran mount, sheltered behind the gray stallion's lead.

Ahead of Elezar the bells of a great tower pealed wildly and masonry high on the walls shattered, raining pebbles and dust down on the street. Elezar coughed at the mouthful of grit that rolled over him but didn't slow. Overhead, white squid-like creatures on fragile bat wings swirled above the clouds of rising dust, screeching and squealing in voices eerily like those of laughing children. An instant later they flitted away.

"Cloud imps, I think," Javier called.

"Madness!" Rafale shouted. "This is madness!"

Elezar scowled ahead. He didn't disagree with Rafale but at the same time he wasn't pleased that the playwright accompanied Javier and him in their race to the sanctum. Sheriff Hirbe had demanded Rafale join them, and Elezar hadn't been in a position to argue.

Rafale seemed to hold the sheriff's confidences, for what that was worth, and he had at least played at devotion to Count Radulf. Still, Elezar kept remembering Skellan's suspicion that Rafale had been involved in unleashing the violet flame—not a reassuring thought since they rode to aid Skellan in destroying the thing. If Skellan was right then this ruin and chaos was in some part Rafale's doing.

Elezar couldn't imagine a much worse comrade, unless it was Bois. That priest was not a man Elezar would have wanted at his back. He certainly wasn't the peaceable, loyal sacrist Bishop Palo took him for. No, neither Bois nor Rafale were to be trusted.

Elezar had already resigned himself to the fact that he might very soon have to cut one or both of them down in cold blood. He didn't expect to regret it much.

As they raced over a small stone bridge, Elezar noticed several odd female figures at the water's edge. The flesh of their naked bodies shone pale as endives and the lank masses hanging around their gape-mouthed faces were green as kelp. They crouched low on long legs. As Elezar neared they dived into the water, like toads.

"What in the name of the Old Gods were those?" Rafale cried out.

Elezar thought Rafale had a hell of a lot of gall to shout out in dismay now.

"Frogwives?" Javier responded though he sounded uncertain. "I didn't think they really existed… Not anymore."

Elezar remembered the frogwives from a frieze that decorated the wall of a cistern near the fish market. He doubted very much that he, with only a few months in Labara or even Javier who'd lived here only five years, could be more familiar with the mythic river spirits of Rafale's homeland than Rafale himself. No, the man wanted them to believe him ignorant to distance himself from knowledge of ancient creatures like the Demon Lord Zi'sai.

Certainly he understood more of the happenings all around them than Elezar did.

"How do you think Skellan has done this?" Rafale called out to Javier.

"It's not what he's done, so much as what he's undone," Javier replied.

"The sanctum wards you mean? Did he tell you which ones he—" The rest of Rafale's query was lost beneath a sudden low roar—the noise of a rock slide, but rising from below them.

The cobblestones ahead of Elezar cracked like thunder and fell aside as a huge creature hauled itself up from the ground. Elezar reined his stallion back, coming to a halt just a yard from the beast. Javier and Rafale stopped just behind him. Javier's horse whinnied in terror and Rafale's stamped in distress.

Javier's flame swirled above the creature before them, illuminating a massive eagle's head, huge dust-caked wings and a sleek, feline body. Its talons raked the cobblestones, and it cocked its head to stare at the three of them like a hunting falcon watching rabbits.

Elezar's heart hammered in his chest. He reached for his blade.

"Don't," Javier whispered and Elezar stilled, but didn't release the hilt of his sword. Javier raised his hands and his white flame curled and twisted above the big creature's head, forming an ornate Bahiim symbol.

"Your captors are gone. Your shackles broken," Javier called out. "You are free now to leave this place in peace."

Elezar fought the urge to draw his blade as the beast snapped its glossy black beak at them. But Javier appeared unperturbed by the display. In fact, he flashed the creature an arrogant smile.

"Or you could try me and see which of us ends up back in the ground," Javier called out. A halo of cold, white light lit up around him, casting terrible black hollows across Javier's handsome face and making him look, for an instant, like death itself. Elezar looked away from him, concentrating instead upon the beast before them.

It crouched low and then bounded up over the three of them, its huge wings unfurling in a blaze of gold and red flames. Scorching wind rushed over Elezar, but the creature was already aloft and rising fast. Its wings shone brighter than crescent moons. Elezar stared after it. But in a heartbeat, the beast flew too far to discern from the night stars.

Javier's halo died back to darkness and his small white flame returned to a sputtering, dancing ball.

"What was that?" Elezar asked.

"Wind-eater," Javier replied. He stared at the open chasm in the road, while Rafale still gazed up at the sky. "Forged from the sun, daughter of the moon. She who hunts lightning and devours thunder... Not an eater of mortal flesh if I remember correctly."

"It can't be," Rafale cried. "She's just a story. A Mirogoth myth."

"Yes, well, there seems to be a great deal of that sort of thing going on tonight," Javier responded, and Elezar laughed despite the shock Wind-eater had given him.

"What spell did you use to scare her away just now?" Rafale asked, and Elezar was certain that he caught a flash of avarice in the playwright's expression as he looked at Javier.

"You think I frightened her away?" Javier smirked. "No, my light simply allowed her to see that we were too stringy and small to make a decent meal for her."

Rafale opened his mouth to ask more but Elezar cut him off.

"We must be going." He urged his mount around the chasm in the street and onward to the black walls of the sanctum. Javier and Rafale followed fast behind him.

They reached the towering black walls just as the entire portcullis collapsed, sending a shudder through the ground. The horses stumbled but none fell. Black shadows winged up from the wreckage. Elezar hardly took in the ruined gates before another jolt rocked the street. But it wasn't a flock of shadowy raptors that rose up from the sanctum this time.

Instead, an immense serpentine coil arched up above the four-story-high granite walls. Purple and white scales the size of shields rippled as the body flexed, and Elezar felt the blood drain from his face when the giant snake lifted its head. It looked like it could swallow a carriage with a snap of its jaws. Its gaze raked the night like the flame of a lighthouse.

"Zi'sai..." Rafale sounded like he was choking on the word.

"The demon lord's mortal form," Javier replied in a whisper.

"Where's Skellan?" Elezar searched what little he could see of the crumbling walls and vast tower of the sanctum. The huge snake struck suddenly and the ground shook again. Coils rippled and flashed as the demon lord crashed between the sanctum walls in pursuit of something.

Skellan. It had to be Skellan the demon lord hunted. Elezar felt suddenly terrified for him and horrified at his own help-lessness. His heart raced and his muscles tensed with feverish heat and yet there was nothing he could do. He wasn't a Ba-hiim or even a witch.

"Can you help him?" Elezar asked Javier.

"I don't know what traps the witch laid. I'm as likely to get him killed as save him if I cross the threshold of the sanc-tum now," Javier responded calmly. He ran a hand along his mount's neck, soothing the animal. The demon lord struck again, and Elezar heard timbers shatter beneath the force of the impact.

God, Skellan. He had to be so scared right now and so alone. Elezar remembered the fear he'd felt when he'd laid in that barrow, bleeding beside his brother's dead body.

"Then what the hell was the point of you coming here, if you do nothing?" Elezar demanded.

"If the witch fails and the demon lord breaks out of the sanctum, then it will fall to me to end him. But it would be utter folly to rush in in the midst of their battle." Javier held his hands over his chest, and white light danced between his fingers. "We must wait."

"Fuck that." Elezar swung down from his horse. The char-ger wasn't going to do him any good when it came to climbing through the rubble of the collapsed portcullis.

"Elezar, what are you doing?" Javier demanded.

"He's alone in there with that thing." Elezar glanced back to Javier.

"How will it help him to have you die along with him?" Javier scowled at him.

"At least he won't die alone, and I won't have been the coward who left him to it!" Elezar snapped back. He didn't care if Rafale heard. Rafale, Sheriff Hirbe and even the Miro-goth grimma could all go to the hells. All that mattered to him right now was reaching Skellan.

He stumbled through the gloom to the cracked timbers and shattered stonework where the sanctum gates had stood. He groped the rough surface of a granite block. It was going to be hell climbing the wall blind. Then one of Javier's white flames flared up, a little ahead of him, lighting his way into the ruin.

Elezar let go of his earlier anger at Javier and focused himself on scaling the wrecked wall. He could see a gaping crack and the supports of a fallen walkway. He reached the height in time to witness the far wall of the sanctum collapse com-pletely. The tremor nearly threw him from his perch, and the roar of the smashing masonry and stone tore the air. Shadowy forms rolled and swayed in the billowing dust. They all looked small and pale compared to the demon lord. The snake arched up, its luminous gaze cutting through the walls of dust.

Elezar scanned the open courtyard of the sanctum for any sign of Skellan. He saw crushed trees and drifts of rubble, but nothing living. And then he heard Skellan call out from the very height of the tower rising over the grimma's palace. He taunted the demon lord, grinning and dancing as if utterly fearless. Elezar couldn't pick out any source of light at the tow-er's pinnacle and yet as Skellan raised his arms he appeared to shine, like a star against the black of the night sky. The demon lord too took note of Skellan, turning his flaming yellow eyes to the tower.

"Fucking idiot," Elezar cursed Skellan. What the hell was he doing?

Elezar half climbed, half slid down the battered walkway in his haste to reach Skellan. Exposed nails and ragged wood scraped and bit at Elezar's skin but he hardly felt any of it. He hit the ash-pale ground running, but the demon lord simply flexed his great body. His massive coils crushed the eastern wing of the palace, and in a heartbeat he wound himself up the very height where Skellan still stood.

Run, Elezar commanded him silently. For God's sake run, you idiot.

But Skellan didn't even step back. Elezar dashed across the courtyard. Javier's flame burned before him like a wild firefly. Elezar didn't know if his sword would even nick the demon lord, but he had nothing else... What he wouldn't have given for a dozen cannons right now... Or even one.

Elezar bounded over a charred mass of bones and kept sprinting. He saw the demon lord rise over Skellan—saw the gleaming white fangs and surging flames as its jaws parted— and he knew he couldn't reach Skellan in time. The knowledge that he could do nothing tore into him like a mortal wound, but he couldn't stop trying. He wouldn't.

Then the air went suddenly very still and incredibly dark. Elezar heard his own heart pounding like a drum, but nothing else. Javier's flame flickered like a lamp in the rain.

Overhead, brilliant orange fire poured from the demon lord's mouth. Skellan extended his arms as if to embrace the inferno. He raised his face into the blaze, and he seemed to blow the flames out as if he were extinguishing a candle.

Elezar stopped, transfixed by the sight. He felt certain that he read shock in Zi'sai's wide yellow eyes.

Skellan looked almost as if he were floating through deep water. He moved in a slow, weightless manner, his red hair drifting up from his face in the grip of an unseen current. As he spread his hands, Elezar realized that it wasn't the star-flecked darkness of the night sky that surrounded Skellan but a deep black halo. It poured from Skellan in smoky curls, but as it climbed over the demon lord it tore through his flesh like water dissolving ink. Gleaming scales washed away, revealing raw muscle then suspended arches of blood, tendon and bone. Finally, a column of white ribs hung above Elezar. Then that too shattered into the black.

Skellan shuddered and fell below Elezar's line of sight.

Javier's white flame flared back to life. Elezar heard the city bells ringing again and felt a cold wind rush over his face. He bolted for the grimma's palace as if released from a spell. Ash, hunks of char and bones scattered beneath his boots.

Just as he reached the crumbling entry a huge shadow loomed up over him. Compared to the demon lord the troll seemed small, but he still stood a solid four stories high. His feet and hands looked broad and gnarled as winter oaks. A carpet of moss, vines and lichen clung to the jagged mass of his thick body, while long, wild grass seemed to sprout from the root of his musky, pendulous genitals.

Elezar caught the hilt of his sword. Those loins offered a tender target but if Elezar could get behind the troll and sever the tendon between his heel and calf he'd be more likely to bring the creature down quick. The troll seemed to contemplate Elezar in return. His eyes were dark as dry wells and iron spikes jutted from his wide mouth.

Who are you? Who comes bearing my Little Thorn's signet?

Elezar didn't hear the troll's words, so much as he felt them reverberating, deep and low through the pit of his belly and hollow of his lungs. An instant later he absorbed the full meaning of the question and also recalled the ring he'd hidden away days ago in the cheat's pocket of his shirt. Hilthorn's signet.

No wonder Skellan had asked after it so persistently.

"I am Elezar. Who are you?"

I am the Holy-Green-Hill, but in this place I am named Bone-crusher.

"Skell—Hilthorn called you his friend," Elezar said.

And that I am, the troll answered. *But what are you to him, little Elezar?*

Not since he'd been an infant had anyone classified Elezar as little, though in the company of trolls he supposed he might even be mistaken for lithe and handsome. Elezar would have laughed, if he hadn't been so worried for Skellan.

"I gave him my knife and he called me his man." Saying as much aloud gave Elezar a feeling of both pride and guilt. He knew he had no business laying this claim—much less his hands—upon Skellan and yet he would do right by him, if only tonight.

The troll cocked his head, studying Elezar from somewhere deep behind the hollow pits of his eyes.

I cannot reach our Little Thorn without bringing the tower down upon him. Distress carried through Bone-crusher's low voice. His massive hands knotted together like tangled tree roots. *But you could climb the stair and find him. You will bring him back to us.*

"Not with all that rubble blocking my way," Elezar responded. "Not easily."

I will clear your way in. Bone-crusher turned and Elezar noticed the cracked spikes of iron harpoons jutting from among the saplings and shrubs that sprouted along the troll's green back. Without any obvious effort, Bone-crusher hefted fallen rubble and collapsed masonry aside. Over his mossy shoulder he added, *Little Thorn's signet will show you the way to him. But be quick, Elezar. I already taste his blood upon the stones of the pinnacle.*

"I'll bring him back, I swear it."

Elezar didn't wait until Bone-crusher had cleared the entire entry. Once there was room enough for him to crawl through he clambered into the grimma's palace. The first twenty feet were nothing but a narrow tunnel of sharp rock. Javier's little white flame fluttered around him with an air of impatient persistence. At last the scraping, tight space opened up into a large, dark chamber. At its heart a spiraling stone staircase rose up into the darkness far beyond Elezar's line of sight. The air felt still and stale. Ash blanketed the floor, and lay like snow over the fallen bodies that lay beneath the stairs. Elezar picked out the tracks left by Skellan's bare feet. He followed them to the staircase and, after taking the signet ring from his sleeve, he mounted the steps and bounded up.

Javier's flame dimmed as it rose with him. A few yards higher and it sputtered out, leaving Elezar in complete darkness.

"Fuck." Elezar caught the banister and kept moving. In his hand he felt the ring growing warmer. Or maybe it only seemed hot compared to the chill spreading through Elezar's body. The sweat beading his back and brow turned clammy and his bowels felt like ice. He forced himself to keep climbing up into the inky black. He hated the dark and despised himself for fearing it—for fearing what lay waiting in the dark.

It wasn't death that he dreaded lurking in the depth of blackness but an agony that did not end with dying—torture for the damned who defied holy law, as his eldest brother had done by taking a Haldiim wife. As he now had done in Skellan's bed. The sight of his brother's mutilated body reaching out to him played over and over through Elezar's mind as he groped blindly up the narrowing staircase. The taste of decay hanging in the stagnant air reminded him too strongly of that old barrow and of the Sorrowlands.

As Elezar climbed higher, he recognized that placeless feeling—an absence of any sense of direction—that washed over him. He'd felt the same in the Sorrowlands, and he realized that each step he took carried him further from the natural realm. He froze, gripped by utter dread. For all he knew he was only a step from damnation. His left hand shook against the banister.

Elezar cursed himself, silently. He'd forfeited faith in the Cadeleonian church when he'd risen from death and followed Javier across the Sorrowlands. It had been Bahiim magic that had resurrected him. And yet the horrors of three hells still haunted Elezar in the dark, as did the knowledge that he'd left his brother alone in the blackness twice.

Skellan's signet ring burned in his right palm.

His brother was dead, had been dead even before Elezar had managed to drag himself from that crumbling, musty barrow so long ago. No matter what he did, Elezar couldn't save him. Neither penance nor vengeance would ever bring him back.

But he could still reach Skellan.

Elezar gripped the signet ring until it burned and bit into his palm. He charged upward, taking the steps as fast as he could.

A breeze rolled over his face, but he didn't mistake it for the natural current of the night air. It felt too warm, too alive, and saturated with the scents of summer. The Sumar grimma's sanctum had smelled like this, he remembered, but much more strongly. The faintest glow of a pale green light filtered down to Elezar. Then he came around the last curve of the staircase and stepped out onto the pinnacle of the grimma's tower.

Skellan lay on the stone floor, bloody and unmoving. A handsome man with curling blond hair and bare arms cradled Skellan's head in his lap. Pale green light danced over them both. The blond man bowed his face over Skellan's as if to kiss his brow. His lips moved against Skellan's skin but his words didn't carry to Elezar.

When the blond man looked up at Elezar, gaunt sorrow showed on his face. He crossed his arms over Skellan's chest.

"Who are you to step foot upon these stones?" His voice rose as if from across miles. Elezar noticed that he could see shadows of Skellan's shoulders and chest through the man's arms and knew he spoke with not a man, but with a ghost.

"I am Elezar, and I have come here as Hilthorn's man," Elezar said, and he saw relief in the other man's face. "Who are you?"

"I am Grimma Oesir."

Elezar tried not to look directly through the man's flickering chest to the thin body that lay motionless behind him. He forced himself to meet the ghost's gaze and then he bowed.

"It is an honor to meet you, Grimma."

"You carry a stone of ancient blood in your hand, Elezar."

"I've brought it for Hilthorn." He held out the signet and Oesir smiled.

"Yes." Oesir beckoned him near. "Return his ring to him."

Elezar closed the distance in two strides and knelt at Skellan's side. He lay so still it frightened Elezar, but when Elezar laid his fingers against Skellan's throat he felt the kick of his pulse. Still, he looked like hell. Long gashes like the strokes of a razor lay open across Skellan's arms and chest, and blood caked his nose and mouth. His skin felt cool as Elezar lifted his hand and slipped the ring on the third finger of his right hand. The gold of the band seemed to tighten and the ruby suddenly flashed as if a flame had ignited within it.

Skellan's eyes flickered and then fell closed again.

"I need to take him down from here, to a physician," Elezar said.

"Wait." Oesir reached out to catch Elezar's arm but his fingers passed through, sending an icy chill over Elezar's flesh.

Neither of them moved. Then Oesir very slowly turned and looked back at the body behind him. Elezar, too, studied the badly burned arms and face spilling out from beneath the white fur cloak. One wide, dead eye stared back at him.

The ghost looked like he might weep. Nervousness sparked in Elezar; he hardly knew how to quiet a crying human being much less a ghost. He couldn't slap the dead grimma on the back and assure him that he'd be all right, could he? Nor could he tell him that he'd get over it.

"Do you feel the pain still?" The words escaped Elezar before he could stop himself. He'd been told that death offered solace to those who died suffering, but since the Sorrowlands he hadn't been able to believe it.

Oesir turned back from his study of his own dead flesh and offered Elezar a small smile.

"No, you're right. It's better like this. I'm finally free of that."

He lowered his gaze back to Skellan. "But I do not think I can remain much longer, and there is so much I need to say to him…"

"Tell me then. When he wakes I'll convey your words to him as best I can."

Oesir lifted his gaze to Elezar, and Elezar thought that he could see how this man might have charmed his way into Grimma Lundag's trust. He looked so innocent and pretty.

"I never meant for him to suffer." Oesir brushed his translucent hand over Skellan's brow. "I swore to protect him… but I feared that he would be the ruin of these lands and become the death of his father. The instant he was delivered to Hallen—Count Radulf—the count would have declared his alliance with the Sumar grimma."

Oesir glanced to Elezar.

"You Cadeleonians would not have peaceably accepted him breaking faith with you. I knew that. So I let Hilthorn remain lost… I prayed that he was safe and well, but how could I allow his father to plunge us all into war with Cadeleon and the southern counties of Labara? How long would he have lived then? And if the Sumar grimma came to our aid, what would become of Milmuraille once she brought her wilderness and beasts into our lands?"

"So you purposely left Hilthorn to fend for himself on the streets of Milmuraille?" Elezar asked. Pain flickered through Oesir's expression. But then he glowered at Elezar.

"What would your king and royal bishop have done to him when he was brought to them as a spoil of war? You burn witches in Cadeleon, don't you?"

Elezar didn't have to answer. They both knew the truth of Oesir's words.

"What will they do to him now?" Oesir began, but Elezar couldn't stand to consider that.

"It has not come to war," Elezar stated. "It will not. He is the rightful heir to Radulf County, and neither the Cadeleonian crown nor the church has reason to object to him."

"You know where his signet comes from, and you can say that?" Oesir asked.

"My prince does not want a war," Elezar answered. "Not with northern Labara, not with the Sumar grimma."

Oesir didn't argue. He simply stared into Elezar's eyes with his pale knowing gaze. Elezar glanced down to Skellan's prone body. Not even Prince Sevanyo would be happy to learn of Skellan's parentage, and the royal bishop would be furious when he discovered that the new count was not only the son of the Sumar grimma but a witch, himself. No, it would not make for an easy alliance. But Elezar had to believe that it wouldn't mean war.

Oesir sighed and his whole being seemed to dim.

"I need Hilthorn to know that I did what I did for his sake," Oesir said. When he glanced down at Skellan a little light seemed to return to his face. "Before he could be acknowledged by Count Radulf and the Sumar grimma, I realized that I would have to break the court of the Cadeleonian king. I needed the great warriors of Cadeleon in such turmoil that they would have no time to grasp after a mere northern protectorate. I needed something that would destroy the king, his lords and burn his holy men to ash…"

Elezar stared at Oesir as a sickening realization spread through him. "The demon lord? That was your doing? You meant to unleash Zi'sai against Cadeleon?"

If Oesir felt any shame, it didn't show in his countenance. His ghostly fingers stroked through Skellan's hair. "The duke of Rauma could have carried the Demon Lord Zi'sai to your king's court easily—"

"You meant that monster for Fedeles." Fury surged through Elezar and he gripped his sword hilt. Only knowing that he could do Oesir no further harm kept him from drawing his blade and driving it into the ghost's throat.

Oesir watched Elezar with a distant expression.

"I am—was—Hallen Radulf's man. My heart, my flesh, my conscience and even my vei were his to command. You may understand what that means someday." Oesir glanced back at his own dead body then looked to Elezar. "So, spare me your outrage. I have already suffered the fate I plotted for your countrymen. I've lost Hallen and roused the armies of the Mirogoth grimma against my own home. You could not despise me more than I do myself…"

Elezar wondered how it was possible to hate and pity a man all at once.

"He would have died to save me tonight." Oesir's gaze returned to Skellan. "To save us all… But I couldn't let him. Hallen would never forgive me. So, you must tell Hilthorn that he came in time and he freed my witchflame, but I couldn't accept his sacrifice. I cannot live, not even for the sake of this country, if it comes at the cost of Hilthorn's life. I've already taken too much from him."

Oesir bowed his face over Skellan's. "Everything I have I gladly give to you…"

Again Skellan's eyes fluttered. A little color seemed to return to Skellan's pallid cheeks while Oesir's faint form dimmed even further. He looked like little more than a curl of fine mist.

"Wrap him in my cloak." Oesir's voice drifted on the night wind. "And take up that pearl for him. You have named yourself his man, so let no harm befall him. Tell him I am sorry."

And then the ghost was gone, and all that remained of Oesir was his corpse.

Elezar wrapped Skellan in the thick bearskin. He noted the pearl laying in a spatter of blood near Skellan's head. He pocketed it and the tattered dog collar. Then he lifted Skellan and carried him down from the tower and out of the grimma's palace.

Shadowy birds circled overhead and the troll, Bone-crusher, followed him across the courtyard and out onto the city street.

There, Elezar expected to find Javier and perhaps Rafale—if he hadn't fled. And Javier did wait just beyond the shattered gates with both their horses. Unsurprisingly, Rafale was gone.

But what Elezar hadn't thought to expect was that half the city's population had flooded the road, filled the overlooking balconies and gathered on the roofs. Their gasps at the sight of Bone-crusher struck Elezar as almost naïve after every other monstrosity this night had revealed. But then he was exhausted past the point of feeling much of anything. Certainly not wonder.

Javier glanced up at the troll and arched a black brow and said, "Made a friend, I see."

"Bone-crusher. He's very attached to Skellan, it seems," Elezar replied.

Javier's attention shifted to the bundle of bearskin cradled against Elezar's shoulder. "Is he alive in there?"

Elezar nodded. He could feel Skellan's chest rise and fall with breath as if it were his own.

"He's alive," Elezar replied. He'd been driven so hard and by so many threats this day that the relief of just knowing that both he and Skellan had survived felt miraculous.

The façade of the Brewers' Guildhouse across from them gave a deep groan and then crashed apart. Hoots and shrieks sounded from the surrounding crowd. A dozen golden birds flew up from the clouds of rising dust. Their feathers glinted like knife blades in the light of roof fires and torches.

"It looks like the whole world is ending," Javier muttered.

It did. And yet as the verdant breath of a troll rolling over him like a mountain breeze and with the warmth of Skellan's body gripped in his arms, Elezar thought that these wild, strange creatures escaping from their prisons could as easily portend the awakening of a new world as the ending of an old one.

To be continued in Champion of the Scarlet Wolf, Book Two...

ABOUT
THE AUTHOR

Ginn Hale lives with her lovely wife and two indolent cats in the Pacific Northwest. She spends the many rainy days tinkering with devices and words. Her first novel, *Wicked Gentlemen*, won the Spectrum Award for best novel. Her most recent publications include the *Lord of the White Hell* books, The Rifter trilogy: *The Shattered Gates*, *The Holy Road* and *His Sacred Bones*, as well as the novella *Things Unseen and Deadly*, from the *Irregulars* Anthology.